MW01625190

The Two Sisters' Café

Elena Yates Eulo and Samantha Harper Macy

Illustrations by PABLO FERRO

An adult faerie tale of
two magical godmothers,
an enchanted Southern café,
and the second chance
so many of us yearn for

(P)

PORTAL
BOOKS

2010

Library of Congress Control Number: 2010921100

Eulo, Elena Yates and Macy, Samantha Harper

ISBN 978-0-9841263-0-9

1. Kentucky – Fantasy – 1952 – Fiction. 2. Sisters – Fiction. 3. Restaurant – cooking – fellowship – Fiction. 4. Magic – Apprentice – Fiction.

Published in the United States of America.

10 9 8 7 6 5 4 3 2 1

Project Management: VisioneeringOctave.com
Illustrations by Pablo Ferro
Art Direction and Design: Benjamin Cziller, ImageDriven.com

Dedicated to the citizens of Sligo, Kentucky, past and present, and especially in memory of my grandmother, Roxie Belle "Topsy" Reynolds Morgan, proprietor of the White Cottage Restaurant, and of Elizabeth "Ezzie" Fishback, who managed the Cottage. You have all inspired me with your humor, with your everlasting love, and with your skills in alchemy that were so beautifully used to turn work into pleasure.

~ Elena Yates Eulo

Dedicated to the memory of my two grandmothers, Alma LeMaster and Harriet Harper, whose lives continue to inspire happiness, wonder, and courage; to my parents, Billy and Emma; my brothers, Sterling and Peter; and all our rambunctious kin and friends from Batesville, Como, Clarksdale, Oxford, Jackson, Laurel, and Wiggins, Mississippi. Your wit, wisdom, charm, and love add to the spirit of these writings.

~ Samantha Harper Macy

"Life is a state of mind."

~ Robert C. Jones, Oscar-winning Screenwriter

"The future ain't what it used to be."

~ Yogi Berra

"O brave new world,
That has such people in't!"

~ William Shakespeare, The Tempest

PABLO FERRO

PROLOGUE

January 1952

The girl's dreams were becoming more vivid. In these dreams was a blaze of light, radiating an invitation and touching off feelings of freedom and safety for one whose days were traps of fearful darkness.

The dreams came when the sleep thinned its black coat to gray. Then a light would shine out of a knothole in a tree trunk, like candlelight from a window on a snowy night. She'd go in through the window and visit with the two who met her there. They poured tea from a glass pot and let her gaze through swirling tea leaves into other worlds, sparking memories of who she had once been, and who she would someday be again.

A sister, a sorceress of light. A worker of kindness in a world gone dark with sorrow. And then the black sleep would thicken again, swamping all memory completely.

1

People in northern Kentucky would say later that they had never seen snow fall so thick. A storm, the third of the season, had been predicted for the evening of January 28 of '52. But nothing like the one that showed up, a monster of a storm made of ice and cold and, most of all, a snow that wouldn't let up. A snow that mounded almost before it hit the ground; at least, that's the way it seemed to the people of Willow Creek.

It came on so quickly that farmers who had gone to their fields to check on their cattle got stranded and blinded, wading back to their houses half frozen. The town whore got stuck overnight in a barn with a hired hand. Cars slid off the roads or came to a halt right where they were, their drivers staggering toward the nearest houses they could find, their own or neighbors'. In most houses, the electricity was out and people couldn't watch *I Love Lucy* on TV, one of the worst things that could happen to a body on a Monday night.

Inside The Two Sisters' Café, the lights were on and the two sisters, Alma and Vannie, had long finished with the main crowd. Only two customers still lingered.

One of them, a teenage boy, sat alone in an upper dining room booth, his back to the fire, eyes fixed moodily on the front door. Such eyes—a brew pot of all that was young and old, both explosive and saddened, at once hard and vulnerable. He was a singer and a poet and a fighter and a problem at school. He had big plans tucked away inside a shabby suitcase in the seat opposite his in the booth and in the beat-up guitar case stacked on top of it. Plans long in the making. They had started practically the day, now over five years ago, that he had picked up his first old guitar and found himself plucking on the three remaining strings, tuneless and full of dust that blew in all directions under his fingers. Playing and humming, he had pictured a future that took him out of this town. The dream was close now, almost close enough to touch.

Yet, here he sat with the possibilities motionless inside him as he stared at the door. In this moment, instead of joy, he felt yearning and pain and growing anger. This, too, he kept inside, sitting rigid, buried under that unnatural silence in one so young. Only his hand moved, rubbing slowly across the gunnysack that lay beside him on the red leather seat.

Below him in the lower dining area, Burris McCarthy lingered at the counter hunkered down over his coffee, his peach cobbler scraped clean off the plate in front of him, staring out at the white wilderness that had come swirling out of nowhere.

Sister Vannie cleared the plate and asked Burris if he wanted more. He said no, meant yes, but only if it was on the house. She looked at his potbelly and didn't offer free seconds.

"Damned if I can see my house out there," Burris said, turning to squint out the farthest window.

Vannie pointed out the window and said, "It's right across the road, you dang fool cuss."

At the wave of her hand, Burris caught a glimpse of his house, a little gray bungalow with a rock and gem shop attached, standing there snug and sturdy against the storm. "Well, I still can't get there," he said, not stirring. "Damndest thing I ever heard, to see your house with your own eyes and know you can't get to it."

Vannie almost sent him packing but thought better of it. He could get to the house alright, she could see to that. But she knew he didn't want to go there. Not tonight. There were a lot of times lately he didn't want to be inside his own house. It frightened him with its ambiance since Mattie, his wife of forty-odd years, had recently died. Part of the time the place scared him with its emptiness, and part of the time it scared him with the feeling that it was haunted. Once he woke in the middle of the night and heard the sound of rocks being poured into the sorter. He went into the shop, but as he'd expected, there was no one there. Yet, a gaudy stone with more prisms than any diamond ever mined rolled gently across the counter. Not a costly stone, but the sort of huge sparkly thing that Mattie had liked to wear. He'd never been able to afford to give her anything but a small diamond cluster, not that it had bothered her. She liked the fake stuff just as well. She said in a way nothing was fake. It was all part of the world, wasn't it? That was something she'd heard the sisters say as she sat drinking coffee at the café and displaying her gems on the counter, occasionally selling something, either to the sisters or to a customer.

"Well, just sit there," Vannie said comfortingly. "Alma and I aren't going anywhere. She's cooking, and I'm doing my pies." She poured him more coffee, thinking of the adventure that was heading down LaGrange Road, coming straight toward the café. She could see it in her mind's eye; see the man at the wheel staring into the blizzard, cussing as the car swerved out of control.

Not yet, she told him in the telepathic language she spoke so well and believed to be the only true language of the world. She saw the driver blink, saw him pull the car out of the skid and keep driving. He was on his way. It was the thought of what was to come that had almost made her send Burris across the road, but she figured a good adventure would be just the thing to raise his spirits.

Voices that Burris couldn't hear suddenly rang out. Vannie smiled, looking her best tonight in a gray tailored dress covered by a hand-crocheted apron, a cameo pin at her neckline, her silver-and-brown hair piled on top of her head. Her purple eyes grew keen as she glanced through the front window. The forces were in good form tonight, bringing in dynamics of snow, ice, wind, and spectacular shades of darkness punctuated by intense flashes of light.

In the front room of The Two Sisters' Café, the two old-fashioned pinball machines and the shuffleboard were quiet and dark, and the door to the adjoining gas station was shut tight. Andy Poole had turned off the station lights, closed up, and beat the storm up the road to his brick house, where Liz waited for him with dinner, homemade cookies, and a pot of coffee. The upstairs dining room was lit in low overhead bulbs that hung down from an old wagon wheel, glowing neon from the jukebox, and a fire that crackled in the grate. The café was usually a lot brighter, but not tonight. The dimness was appropriate tonight.

Still, what needed to be seen could be seen. Light glinted on the candy counter up by the cash register, on the long slab of mahogany where Burris drooped almost sleeping over his coffee, and on the old cards and placards that were tacked up over the wooden partition that made a huge square opening between the country kitchen and the counter, through which customers and proprietors could talk. At the bottom of the partition was a wooden serving slab, empty save for an old black dial telephone.

Vannie went up the two steps that separated the lower front room from the upstairs dining room, stopping by the parrot's cage on the top step to take a cracker from her apron pocket. Banshee looked up alertly, sensing escalating excitement in the world. He accepted the cracker without swearing, a sure sign he realized something was up. His green scraggly feathers, sparse and limp with great age, were ruffled, his ancient eyes wide-open.

"He's coming," Vannie whispered so quietly that the teenager, sitting in the back booth on the right, could not hear. "It's begun." The bird blinked back at her.

She went on past his cage to the huge grate and stopped by the young boy's table. "I do wish you'd let me bring you something," she said gently. She had paid him earlier for a month of singing. For over a year he had been featured in what the sisters called "the nightclub," but what was really just a large room up back of the café with varnished wooden floors, a few dozen round Formica tables, and a small stage with a microphone. He was supposed to sing again next weekend, but instead he had apologetically explained that he might not be in town and had asked for his back pay. It was shortly after Vannie had handed it over that the blizzard hit full force, barreling in like a locomotive.

Would the nightclub ever be the same after he left? She and Alma had often wondered about that and had decided the music would remain even if the boy didn't. He had created an incandescent light in that room that would burn forever. Over and over again, he had entranced the locals, who would get lost in his magic, only to emerge from it startled when he stepped from the stage and they caught whiff of the smell of cow that never left him and remembered who he really was. There were girls, of course, who never forgot his impact up on that one-man stage. He had sung his way into the heart of one girl in particular.

The boy's eyes jolted from the door to Vannie's face as if just noticing her. "Oh, thank you, Sister. No, I'm not hungry. But is it alright if I stay awhile longer?" His voice came out in a bottom-of-the-barrel bass that startled anyone hearing it for the first time. You did not expect such low rolling thunder in so young a voice. Nor did you expect the pits of gravel that spit into some of his words. It was an oddly pleasant sound, as mesmerizing in its way as his singing voice that would become even more weathered as the years wore it down, taking on the sound of nails and broken glass. Yet that beaten-up hometown sound would make people moan with its greatness and the underlying dark poetry of the artist that could make grown men cry. Such was the possibility that lay inside this eighteen-year-old boy who had so little of anything excepting only just that: possibility.

"Stay as long as you want," Vannie murmured reassuringly. She went on to the fireplace, pausing there to add a thick log to the already roaring fire and to poke at the burning wood. Stoking the fire was one of her favorite jobs. Like stirring up dreams, it was. She stuck the bottom log with her poker and fireflies flew through the air, hissing and sputtering. She knew that language, too.

The room was ready now. Clean. Shadowy. Rife with atmosphere. It remained only to put the jukebox on. Without coins, she stood by the Wurlitzer, its neon tubes bubbling in yellow, orange, and green. Considering, she punched here and there. Soon the gaudy box was doing its stuff.

"Hey, good lookin', whatcha got cookin'?" Hank Williams wanted to know. A nice touch. It was the right music, too. The right music for the right man.

Vannie smiled as she left the young boy staring at the front door and danced down the steps past the somnambulant Burris, slipping around the counter and into the country kitchen to take her place at the huge worktable where she started mixing pie dough. "How's about cookin' somethin' up with me?" she hummed. Orange juice in the crust. It made the pastry flakier than you could imagine. People never ate Vannie's crust without talking about it. Pretty soon, she added flour to her board and started laying out her dough for the rolling.

Alma was at the stove mashing potatoes and frying chicken and okra. Vannie's cherry pie went sliding into the hot black oven alongside an apple and a rhubarb. Alma whistled softly, knowing whose name was on that cherry pie. A man who wasn't there yet, but was close. Real close.

"He'll want ice tea," Vannie said in a low voice, but Burris, clearly visible through the opening between kitchen and counter, couldn't have heard her had she screamed out the words, because the words weren't intended for him. "Even on a night like this, ice tea. Can you imagine?"

"Right there, darlin'," Alma crooned, waving her long fork at a frosty glass of tea on the table. Nights of magic were even better than days of magic. She wore a printed fringy dress, casual but somehow dressy, and an apron deep in the same high quality of hand-crocheted lace that Vannie wore. Her dark hair was done up with bone hairpins; her hazel eyes glittered with anticipation. Alma had seer's eyes, eyes reflecting elemental forces.

Vannie looked at her sister closely, knowing she was plotting ways and means. "With a crash, you think, Alma?"

"Yep-a-doodle. Let it crash like thunder in the sky. Let it shoot forth bolts of lightning till the Earth shakes."

"Don't go gettin' carried away."

Alma speared a golden-brown piece of chicken from the grease, laid it on a platter of beaten metal, and started laughing. Nobody on Earth (or anywhere else) could laugh like Alma. Sparks danced in her eyes as she held herself up on the edge of the huge butcher-block worktable that filled most of the kitchen. Behind her was the entrance of what they called the "Little Room." It was, in fact, just a little room. It contained a square table with three chairs, its fourth side snug to a window. A pot-bellied stove and a rocking chair sat beside a unit of storage shelves. A back door led to a storage room, and a front entrance overlooked a small courtyard that was enclosed by a low white brick wall where Banshee's cage sometimes sat when the sun was shining. But the Little Room was a special place in its own right. It was an intimate place, perfect for telling secrets. Not just anybody was invited into it.

Alma's head lifted alertly. Without so much as glancing out the window, she sensed, actually saw, the snow fall over three counties. Heard people shiver. Saw the same car that her sister had seen zigzagging all over the road. "Not long now," she whispered.

Vannie nodded. "He's just a few miles away. There he goes, turning onto Pendleton Road. Sliding like a goose on butter."

"Chicken's ready, okra's on the platter." Alma brimmed over with eagerness. "Should I set his place, darlin'?"

"Yes, dear, why don't you? Upstairs dining room, second booth to the grate, don't you think?"

"*Per*-fect," Alma concurred. "I'll put the mashed potatoes in a bowl family style and carry up the okra and the chicken. And the tea, of course. Oh, criminy, I almost forgot the coleslaw. For the last twelve years, the man's been dreaming of good coleslaw."

"And yours is the best. Then, of course, there's my cherry pie." Vannie smiled complacently. There was no question about what he would think of her cherry pie, served with hand-cranked vanilla ice cream.

Minutes later, it was done. All was in readiness. Sugar Curtis's place was set for him, just as he had set his own in life. And his arrival came with a crash, like a thunderbolt. There were no bolts of lightning, but the Earth did shake. It hadn't been overdone. Alma smiled, and Vannie gave an excited little laugh.

"What in Sam Hill?" Burris muttered from the counter. He was a lazy man, but he toyed with the idea of getting up to see what had happened. It sounded to him like the end of the world, but if so, he wasn't sure he really wanted to know about it. Better on the whole, he thought, just to wait it out. If it was the end of the world, he would find out about it soon enough.

Behind the counter, the two sisters touched hands and waited. Just at that moment, Sugar Curtis crawled free of his wrecked car, cast a suspicious look at the gas tank with which he had collided, wondering if it might explode, then galloped through the deep drifts alongside the white brick building and kicked his way through the front door.

"Always a flair for the dramatic." Alma's look at the man was indulgent, rather than fearful. She hardly glanced at the gun held so tightly in his rough, scarred hand.

Burris at the counter showed more respect, cowering down on his stool, both hands hovering over his coffee cup, as though, despairing of securing his own safety, he had at least decided to save his coffee. "Lord a'mighty," he moaned.

Vannie's hand descended onto his shoulder. "Don't make a big thing out of a little bit, honey."

"*Little* bit?" Burris swallowed hard and shut up. Neither he nor any other person in Willow Creek tried to make sense of the strange occurrences that often happened when the sisters were around. Added to that, they had a habit of showing up unannounced in any part of the county just when a body found himself in the most need. Seconds after he had seen Mattie dead in bed that morning, there had come a rap at the door and the sisters had let themselves in, walking directly into the bedroom where he still held his wife's body in his arms, his head buried in her gray hair.

"Everything's alright, you know, Burris," Sister Alma had said, as matter-of-fact as ever.

And the damndest thing was . . . he'd believed her, just as he now found himself believing Sister Vannie, who had just observed a lunatic toting a gun and said not to make a big thing out of a little bit.

"Okay then," he muttered, and noticed Vannie take a fresh plate of peach cobbler from the serving window and slide it next to his coffee cup. Without a word, he picked up his fork and started eating. Best stuff in the world, he thought, hardly aware that the lunatic was waving his gun everywhere.

Sugar Curtis's life had been out of control for a long time. But a gun evened things out. Made people who wouldn't look at you look. Made people who wouldn't do as you said do it. On this particular night, he'd used a guard's own gun to kill him and make his escape from the pen. The whole thing had gone wrong. He had been off-balance and scared. The guard got spooked and tried to draw his gun as Sugar jumped from the laundry cart with the prison-made knife for which he had paid four cartons of cigarettes. The guard's gun stuck in the holster and Sugar wrestled him for it. Somehow it went off, and, before he knew what happened, the bullet exploded and blood started pumping from the man's chest. He bent over him, trying to breathe air into his lungs, but it was no use. The guard's eyes were wide open, seeing nothing but his maker.

With human blood dripping from his fingers, Sugar staggered through the open door where the laundry truck waited, its driver frozen at the wheel, and ran past it, charging the wall. There was almost no hope of escape, not with the tower full of guards with loaded rifles. But just then the snow began to fall like a thick curtain around the very wall he needed to climb. Heart thudding, he heaved himself over it and ran down the deserted road. Not half a mile from the prison, he found an abandoned car someone had left running and jumped in. Putting the car in gear, he breathed steam and took off, remembering the cold freedom of his youth, freedom that had felt like a cage on those winter mornings and early evenings when he'd go milk cows on two different farms. He wouldn't have minded milking his own family's cows, if there had been any to milk, but how he'd hated running down the road to go milk his neighbors' cows. He had once been kept after school for writing a composition called "Somebody Else's Cow." The teacher found "milk squirting from the cow's teats" no way acceptable, accounting it to being uncomfortably close to speaking of a woman's unmentionables. He hadn't meant it like that and saw nothing vulgar about "Warm milk foamin' on my wrists. Dirty tail in my face. Oh, if only, if only, it was my own cow's tail." In prison, he made up other words about ownership when some grumbling fool kept raving over and over how he'd shot his wife in a jealous rage and should have got off on a passion plea. Damned faithless bitch. Wasn't even that pretty. Truth to tell, she had a face like a warthog's. Eyes the color of snot.

"I'm sick of hearing about her," Sugar had finally declared. "If she wasn't dead, I'm damned if I wouldn't kill her myself. But be fair, buddy! I already done my own murder."

The other prisoner made the mistake of trying to knock his head off first chance he got. Everybody knew you didn't come out very clean when you fooled around with Sugar Curtis. This time was no exception. Not that he particularly cared who his fellow inmate had murdered. Truth was, though he had killed someone himself, he felt more of an expert on cows than on murder. One of the preachers who regularly visited the reformatory had asked him if he hadn't bothered to look for God's true destiny for himself, and Sugar said yes, and he'd found a piece of it looking up one old cow's ass and the rest of it up another's.

Suddenly Sugar Curtis frowned. This was sure as hell no time to be raking up past memories. His stolen car had wrecked, and with it his chances of fleeing from the cops. They'd be after him right now even in this snow.

"It's a very thick snowfall, though, don't you think?" murmured the taller of the two women who faced him so calmly. She was of indeterminate age and compelling in a different way from the women in the lewd magazines smuggled into the prison. Her strong mysterious face was so oddly familiar to him that he couldn't look away, but he couldn't remember where they had met. He hoped that she, too, had forgotten. There was both shame and danger in recognition.

A wave of melancholy swept over her haunting face as she stared back at him. Then with a sudden smile, she started to speak.

"I don't want to hear nothin' from you," he told her before she could get it out. "Not from you either," he added threateningly to the smaller, silvery-brown-haired woman beside her. She, too, looked familiar, but he couldn't remember meeting her either. He heard the wind howling outside and thought absently that the café was the warmest refuge anybody could ask for.

Neither woman said anything, merely looked at him expectantly.

He glanced at the black telephone sitting in the serving window that connected the front room to the kitchen. *I'd better cut the wire,* he thought and took a step toward it.

"Don't bother," the tall woman said. "The lines are all down anyhow."

The lack of fear in either woman caused a strange reaction inside the convict's breast. Though he would never have admitted it, he had grown a little afraid of *them*. "I've killed before," he blustered. "Tonight and—"

"We'll talk about that later," the smaller woman said. "There's plenty of time. I'm Vannie, dear, and this is my sister, Alma."

"Happy to see you, darlin'," Alma said.

"What the hell are you smiling about?"

"Oh, we smile a lot. But never mind that, you're hungry. A hungry man is a grouchy man. Your dinner's on the table. Upstairs in the dining room, second booth from the fire. Come on, we'll walk you up. You like fried chicken, don't you?"

At the sound of the chicken, his fury lost its edge. He found himself walking between the two women, his gun aiming first at one, then the other. He had no idea what to do if either of them gave him any trouble. He'd never killed a woman before. Until the guard tonight, he had only killed one person, the man he tried never to think of. Now there was the guard to lay on top of his already over-burdened conscience. Still, if they gave him any trouble, he knew what he had to do. And was prepared to do it.

Neither woman appeared to notice the gun as they guided him up the steps leading to a larger dining room full of booths and tables. He frowned, noticing a boy in the next booth, who sat facing the front of the café. Though the boy stared through him toward the front door, he didn't trust him. He also didn't trust the women, no matter how nice they might seem, or even the parrot that turned on its perch to stare at him. It was an ugly old bird, probably the worst looking parrot he'd ever seen, its skin hanging on its shrunken bones. *Great God, it's all familiar. Even the parrot.* Yet he remembered nothing. Nothing.

"I'm Alma May," the taller sister told him. "And my sister is Vannie May. May isn't a middle name; it's our last name. It indicates a willingness, don't you think? While you are with us, you *may* do pretty much as you like."

"Well, thank you very much," Sugar sneered, waving his gun at her.

"You're so welcome, darlin'—"

"—Absolutely," her sister said on top of her, their voices mingling like two bell chimes swaying against each other in a mild breeze.

His gaze moved from one sister to the next. One taller and darker. One smaller and lighter. "In case you don't know it, you're both hostages." He waved his gun toward Burris down at the counter and at the boy in the last booth. "Them, too."

"That happened to a woman down the road, Dottie Boynton," Vannie said. "Lives way down one of those deserted country lanes. Isn't even screaming distance to another house. When Dottie got taken hostage, she hid razor blades on her private person, don't you know. The man was another convict; you'd be surprised how often one of y'all busts out. Anyhow, she hid the razor blades so's she could cut herself loose if the man tied her up. And of course, he did that very thing. Tied her and the kids and her husband up and left them there, so it was lucky she had the razor blades, wasn't it? Though if he'd come out shooting, those razor blades wouldn't have done doodly."

He began to sweat. A fragrant odor drifted toward him from the fireplace, reminiscent of herbs and spices and making his head swim.

"Go ahead," Alma said. "Sit. Eat."

"What?" He stopped waving his gun and concentrated with sudden fierceness on the jukebox that had begun to play. It was an old instrumental. Strange jukebox material. *You Made Me Love You,* featuring the golden trumpet of Harry James. Of all songs to be playing. Lord, he'd been a teenager when he first heard that song. It was different from the country music he usually listened to. He'd been half out of his mind in love that night with a girl from one of the few big houses in Henry County up close to the Oldham County line. Margie Roberts was her name. She was the kind of girl you knew it was dangerous to notice, because she'd only break your heart and leave you for somebody more suitable. After all, her people were educated. Her father owned property and a big general store in LaGrange. Margie would grow up to have somebody clean her house and be somebody. Probably, she'd marry a doctor or something and have a life that made some sense. Except she had eyes for him.

It was something both of them knew, that they had something big for each other, but neither of them said anything about it. How could you say anything about it when it couldn't lead to anything except getting your heart broke? So, they just looked at each other and kept their distance. Until that night. The only night in his life where the magic had happened for him instead of someone else. There he and Margie were, sitting on opposite sides of the Roberts' finished basement, since she had one of those righteous sets of parents who believed that when you had a party, you invited the whole class, regardless of who they were. And then somebody had put on an old record from the family collection.

And that sound had poured out.

Sugar had come out on top in a lot of fistfights. But never before had he been attacked by a jazz trumpet. It was more than music. Before he could remind himself that this sentimental, sappy song was not his style, the horn's warm syrup had poured into him. Too late, already drowning in feelings he could no longer push away, he realized this was the kind of sound that cried in you, shook in you, brought down your walls.

He didn't know the words, but he *felt* them. Before he knew it, he was out of his chair, standing there with a bellyful of molten gold, and Margie was on her feet, too, drifting toward him and singing the words he'd been feeling, her sweet, young voice blending in with the trumpet until you'd think it was playing just for her.

"You made me love you . . . I didn't wanna do it . . . I didn't wanna do it."

Sugar shivered like a fool, looking into her blue eyes as she went on singing to him in a voice that sounded like birdsong on top of the throbbing gold under it. He was being melted until he almost would have thought he was afraid, except he was never afraid.

"You made me want you . . ." Margie sang softly, her eyes daring him to admit it. "And all the time you knew it . . . I guess you always knew it."

He knew better than to let his defenses down like this. Most of the time he wore a sullen closed-off look that a girl in his class said drove her crazy. His brother had told him everyone thought he was going steady with a girl in LaGrange and that was why he didn't date any girls at school. He'd glowered all the more and didn't explain that he didn't even know any girls in LaGrange, except for a couple of store clerks. With your head stuck up a cow's ass, who had time for girls? And even if he did, what girl in her right mind would want to have anything to do with a Curtis?

Yet, there was Margie, standing in front of him with moist eyes, her voice trembling, but still singing along with the James trumpet: "You made me happy sometimes . . . You made me glad . . . But there were times, dear . . . You made me feel so bad."

She held out her arms to him, and before he knew what he was doing, he was holding out his wrong-side-of-the-town arms to her, too. When he felt Margie's arms wrap around him, he knew he was lost. There had never been anybody before her; he was sure there could never be anybody ever again. He was young, but he was fierce. The fierce knew how to hang onto love, just like they knew how to hang onto hate.

They danced, and Margie went on singing, but into his ear now, with half the other kids dancing and not even watching them, and the rest too struck dead with shock to say a word about it.

"You made me sigh for . . . I didn't wanna tell you . . ." He felt her warm breath on his throat. Heard the trumpet throbbing. Then in a single second, as life must leave the body at the instant of death, it all went away, the music, the girl, the room.

He was back in the café's upstairs dining room, without Margie in his arms. The jukebox had gone silent and dark. He stood between the sisters, the gun limp in his hand. And for some unknown reason, he was staring straight into the eyes of the boy in the end booth, who seemed to notice him for the first time.

"I . . . I need to go now," Sugar mumbled. Yet, he allowed himself to be seated in the booth facing the boy and the fire beyond.

"Eat now, Johnny." It was Sister Vannie. "You're very hungry. Food comes first right now, and this is the best you've tasted in a long time. Everything you like." Her eyes gleamed with the kind of light that had startled him when he had first seen it in Sister Alma's. And she had just called him Johnny. Nobody except his closest family had ever called him that, and them not since his earliest school days.

He suddenly noticed his gun was lying on the table beside his plate. He made a grab for it, but Alma said in a quick burst of energy, "For heaven's sake, just *eat*, will you? Nobody's going to run off with your old gun. Nobody wants it around here."

"Why would we want a gun?" Vannie agreed. "Go ahead and enjoy your dinner. You've been waiting a long time for it."

As both sisters headed down the stairs, Sugar's hand covered his gun once again. But with only the boy in front of him, a boy who seemed to take little or no notice of him, he relaxed and his hand fell absently away as he stared at the food. Beautiful chicken, fried to a crisp. Okra, his favorite. He popped a piece of it into his mouth. Unbelievable. His mama had made it a few times, but not much of it and not often. And it hadn't been like this. He seemed to remember food like this somewhere, but couldn't place where he had eaten it. He loaded his fork with more okra, then tore into the chicken. Then ate half a plate of coleslaw in absolute bliss. Biscuits, warm to the touch and full of melted butter, followed. Then more chicken. He lost awareness of everything else while he ate. The room faded, even as he took one last glance over his shoulder at the old man downstairs at the counter, who was eating cobbler as hungrily as he was attacking his own food. His awareness of the boy and the two sisters faded, too. There was just him and the food.

And Harry James again. A King of Swing in his day, without doubt. Startled, he looked back at the jukebox and saw that the neon tubes had lit up, sending all kinds of colors coursing through them. The familiar sound rolled over him and into him, and he could not get away. Yes, Margie and the golden trumpet had caught him with his defenses down. Then and now.

"You made me sigh for . . . I didn't wanna tell you, I didn't wanna tell you. . . I want some love, that's true, yes, I do, 'deed I do, you know I do."

His eyes filled with tears. Stupid, crazy tears. For Margie Roberts who, wherever she was, ought to be thirty years old now, several months younger than himself. He hadn't seen her since the last time in court. Hadn't said one word to her since . . .

Since he'd killed her daddy. Tears gathered in large pools and ran down his cheeks. He heard himself sobbing. If he could, he'd change everything about himself since before he'd shot Margie's daddy that night. He'd go at things differently, not from such an in-your-face attitude. That was the only way he'd ever thought he could get anything. He had learned it from his own father. But maybe, after all, there had been another way. He could still see Margie's eyes. Sad. Hurt. More hurt than angry, and that's what had surprised him that day in court when he turned and found himself staring at her and her staring right back. Her mouth had trembled like a late rose of summer left swaying in an autumn breeze. Maybe there had been a better way to get her, after all, other than that hotheaded belligerence that had set off her daddy like a lit firecracker.

He shook his head, wondering where that kind of thinking had come from. What other way had there ever been for a boy on the wrong side of town to get anything except to grab it in the roughest, toughest way? It was how the Curtis family had lived for generations untold. What was he thinking? That if he'd acted like a nice kid that sooner or later Margie's folks might have given in and invited him into their big house again as their oldest daughter's boyfriend? He must be mad to think such a thing, even all these years later.

"Take a nice big drink of ice tea, darlin'," Alma said. "It's your favorite, you know." Obligingly, he half-drained the glass. God, it was good. Lemony and icy and thirst-quenching like nothing else in the world.

She sat in his booth, facing him across the thick slab of oak wood that bore the scars of generations of carved initials and even full names. Lovers, mostly. Hearts and promises and heartache carved right into the tabletop. From the looks of things, Alma and Vannie didn't mind their customers treating their tables like wild oak trees.

Vannie came back upstairs and put a plate of cherry pie and vanilla ice cream in front of him. She sat beside Alma, and the two of them watched him take the first bite. He almost groaned with pleasure. Warm pie with the flakiest crust he had ever tasted. Hand-cranked ice cream. Wind howled down the chimney, and he looked up and frowned. What kind of restaurant cranked ice cream in the middle of a blizzard with wind whistling down the chimney?

"Something's not right here," he said, but with no real force behind the words. The room shimmered hazily. Probably from the firelight, he told himself. But there was more to it than that. He turned to look more closely. Everything seemed to have added dimensions. The upper dining room now seemed composed of many rooms, one leading into another. It seemed possible to step from one world into another one, from one time into another, or even into timelessness. He should have felt frightened. Well, perhaps he did, in a way. But part of him had simply surrendered shortly after he'd kicked in the café's front door in that high-handed way of his. He leaned over and took a good look at the door. It, too, had acquired other dimensions, becoming other kinds of openings, into all sorts of places. From that door, one might walk into another kind of existence.

"Oh, Lord," he moaned, the piecrust flaking tenderly in his mouth. Cherry juice, semi-tart and delicious, squirted onto his tongue as he chewed. "What is this damn place, anyhow?" He met Alma's eyes, positive she knew exactly what he was talking about. More than he did, for that matter.

Her eyes sparkled at him. "In the restaurant business," she began, as if she were part owner in a world-class premium establishment, "you meet lots of people. All heading different places, you know."

Vannie nodded thoughtfully. "All at different crossroads."

"Crossroads," he repeated. Saying the word sent a chill up his spine.

"We've been in business in other places," Alma said. "You'd be surprised if you knew how long we've been feeding others. And where."

"And *what,*" Vannie added in an undertone of merriment that caused her sister's mouth to quirk. Their eyes fastened intently on his face.

Sugar put down his fork. *Oh, my God, something very weird is happening here. They're going to put me in a pot and boil me for somebody's supper.* He grasped his gun firmly. Neither sister reacted. It didn't seem to bother them that it was they who were unarmed and he who had the gun. The music kept coming at him, finishing what Harry James and his instrument of pain had started: "Give me, give me, give me what I cry for . . . You know you got the brand of kisses that I'd die for . . . You know you made me love you!" The best part of him had died from his longing for those kisses, alright. Other parts of him had died, too. Tears came unbidden, rolling down his cheeks like he was a kid. Scorching tears.

"You knew I was coming here tonight," he said brokenly. He dried his tears against his sleeve. "How could you know?"

"Like we have told you," Alma said gently, "we run across many people in our business. We have acquired . . . well, I suppose you could call it a kind of extrasensory perception in a way. If that's what makes sense to you. Sense is so important to people," she added with an indiscernible pause before the last word. "Now you listen to me, Johnny Curtis . . ."

He stared at her. "How did you know my—?"

"Never mind. Let it go. It's time to let it all go. You remember Vannie mentioned crossroads. Well, Johnny, you've come to your own. You see that, don't you?"

He lowered his head. The image he'd been holding in his heart, the one of the prison guard, that look of surprise and dread a second before he fell, faded. The pain receded some, too.

"You didn't want to do it, Johnny," Vannie murmured soothingly. "You didn't want to do any of it. Life is very confusing, isn't it? It's one of the flaws of the human experience that people can rarely figure out life until it's passed them by, although that makes it all the more exciting. Challenging."

"Now eat." Alma's voice was calm with authority.

He ate silently, unable to bring himself to protest. The gun ended up on the seat beside him. Another song came on the jukebox. He froze, but this time the room was flooded with Peggy Lee singing *I Only Have Eyes For You*. He and Margie had danced to that song, too. "Are the stars out tonight? . . . I don't know if it's cloudy or bright . . . I only have eyes for you . . ." Right this minute, he could look through her blue eyes, see her deeper than anyone he had ever seen. And she was seeing him the same way.

The last of his defenses began to melt like the edge of the ice cream that touched his warm cherry pie. He had always thought losing his defenses was the worst thing that could ever happen to him. But instead of being afraid, he felt a delicious rush as the tension in his gut, a tight-fisted ball of misery and rage that had been there as long as he could remember, suddenly relaxed. He tried to remember if there had been a time it had not been there. Except that night when he'd danced the party away holding

Margie close, and their stolen moments together after that. They had promised each other they would be together forever, no matter what. But she hadn't been able to keep that promise.

"About the guard," Vannie began. "If you had it to do again, you wouldn't . . ."

Tears gushed out of his eyes, and this time he didn't try to restrain them, didn't even make an effort to dry them. "Everything got messed up," he wept. "You take what you need. I learned that from my daddy, he learned it from his daddy. My granddaddy was the meanest bastard that ever lived."

"Corman Curtis," Alma said, nodding. "He was mean alright, but he didn't hold the record. I could tell you stories . . ."

"You knew my *granddaddy*?" he almost shrieked.

"Knew of his existence, anyway. He was taken out of his reality by a fishbone lodged in his windpipe. Had a nasty few minutes of it." She shook her head as though to clear it of a vivid image.

"Who the hell *are* you?" His tear-soaked eyes darted frantically from one sister to another. In so doing, he caught sight of the man at the counter, head slumped down over his plate. He looked limp. He looked . . .

"Dead!" Sugar shouted, pointing. "He's dead, isn't he? What did you do, poison him? Is that what you do here? Am I poisoned? Am I going to die? What did you put the stuff in? The mashed potatoes? The pie?"

"Hush!" Alma said sternly. "Nobody's dead here. This is not a place for death. He's asleep, dreaming of his wife. They'd been married forty-four years when she died. He's been unhappy lately, but it's not time for him to move on just yet. Goodness, everyone needs some time away from their spouse, don't they? I doubt he'll be married at all next time. Forty-four years would do you for at least a couple of lifetimes, wouldn't you think?"

Sugar looked at her. Then suddenly the words poured out of him. He couldn't stop himself from telling the sisters. All of it. "Don't you understand?" he growled when they had listened to every word of his miserable life story without venturing a comment. "I've killed two men. What do you say about *that*?"

He looked for judgment in their eyes and couldn't find it. Instead, that same look of sadness he had first seen on Alma's face down by the counter was there again. When she spoke, there was a catch in her voice, and she put a hand to her chest, as if finding it hard to breathe.

"I will agree," she said, "that taking a life for no reason except to forward your own needs is . . . well, let's just say it can never have a good result. It brings unhappiness to all, and the most to the one who pulls the trigger. Or uses the knife or whatever other means is employed. No one gets away with a thing. Not one thing."

"That's in your opinion." He used the nastiest voice he could muster.

"I spend a lot of my life in observing," Alma said. "And over the years, I have acquired what you might call a certain perspective. But you haven't sung for us yet, Johnny."

"Sing? Me?" At her words, Sugar felt himself floating, him and Peggy Lee, words drifting around him. "Are the stars out tonight? I don't know if it's cloudy or bright. I only have eyes for you . . . dear . . ." But when he tried to sing along, the words came out of his mouth like growling bears, tearing up the atmosphere like all his music had done in the days he used to sing. Since prison, there had been no music at all. He had never sung one note since he killed Margie's father. Until now.

It was a song of prison that ground through his lips. Of hope slipping away like blood down a drain. Of violence and love gone wrong. Of a wasted life. Of regret deeper than the ocean and thicker than a quagmire. And the shame that rolled on and on, like a train roaring down an endless track to nowhere.

Vaguely, he saw the boy rise. There was a strange expression on his face, trouble boiling in his eyes. The boy's hands were fisted, as if intent on knocking him out of all time and space, and his own fury rose in response. But the sisters stepped between them.

"No," Sister Alma said clearly. "Do not touch."

Confused, Sugar felt himself stalled; the boy swimming in front of him also froze, fists raised, eyebrows pointed together over raging eyes. There was a horrible grinding as time stood still and the Earth jolted to a stop. A lot had happened to him. Terrible and shameful things; abuse and poverty. Loss of love and self-respect. But in all of his life, standing shaken and confused on a planet that had ceased to move, he knew he had never been this terrified. The boy looked frightened, too. And for just a few seconds, another feeling traveled through the misery and fear, something deeper and more profound than anything Sugar had ever felt before. *Love,* he thought numbly. *I love this boy.*

The boy wobbled, the only movement in this strangely still café.

"To stand on a motionless planet is a dizzying thing," Alma said softly. "You stand suspended in the liminal . . . in a place between this world and another. Between death and eternity. It can be very dangerous, yes, or very safe. One step, and you may fall into a precipice. I must warn you that if you take it, you won't survive."

But the pit of his stomach told Sugar he had already taken this step. That even now he was falling. It was too late to survive. *If only I'd understood. Everything would have been different.* He saw the boy's eyes screw tight together as though he could not bear to watch. Felt the Earth begin spinning again, but faster and faster, a merry-go-round out of control. He tried to steady himself, made a grab for the boy. But the force shot him backward through the dining room in a great explosion of energy, catapulting him past the parrot's cage and down the steps. Then zoomed him backward even faster past the man at the counter, who goggled at him with bulging, terrified eyes. He took one look at the three people who stood together in the upper dining room staring down at him. Then the force whipped him around, and he saw the door swing open in front of him.

For just a second or two, he tried to resist, but it was no use. He knew what he had to do. Almost gratefully, he surrendered to the unknown and agreed to whatever conditions it demanded of him. Felt the contract signed, sealed, and executed. Then he was swept out into the blistering elements.

He dimly heard the door slam shut behind him as he flew into the whiteness of the night. He couldn't feel the cold anymore, felt only the amazing grace surrounding him, comforting, and then swamping him. The blood slowed in his veins and clotted. His arms and legs grew numb. There was only one thought left in his head, and he couldn't any longer even understand what it meant.

You know you got the brand of kisses that I'd die for . . .

And then his heart stopped beating, and the interior of him grew as still as the frozen world.

The boy stirred. A coil unwound deep inside of him. He felt both pain and release. Surely, some part of him had died and something had been reborn. Yet, he could not say how either of these things had happened, only that he was sure they had. His eyes opened. Dazed, he looked up at the sisters' faces. He had thought somehow that his girl had made it through the storm, had come to meet him after all. Margie. But she hadn't come.

"Sisters? What—?"

"Shh," Alma murmured softly. "Eat, Johnny. We fixed your favorite meal, you know."

The young Sugar Curtis stirred and looked at the food in front of him. Fried chicken, okra, and mashed potatoes. Biscuits and coleslaw. Cherry pie and ice cream. Ice tea. With the sisters watching his every bite, he ate all of it. Only when he finished the last crumb of pie, the last sip of ice tea, did he remember the strange man. It must have been a dream. A bad one. It gave him pause.

"Yes," Vannie said approvingly. "That's it exactly. Pause. Think about what you are leaving."

"Margie . . ."

"What else?"

Gradually, he remembered. The fear and the poverty. His mother's strained face, the frightened looks of his younger brothers and sisters. His sister Sarah with that glow in her eyes that would surely die one day. But so far it hadn't. He had always held Sarah in his heart in a special way. Not that he loved her more than the rest, but he sensed that in some way she held the key to his family's survival. He could almost feel her watching him now.

"Sarah," he said urgently. "She's . . ."

"Very special," Alma finished for him. "And you will help her."

"How?"

"With your music and your freedom and your love. You will show her that anything is possible."

The life he was about to leave coursed through him. Old names came and went. Faces, some half-remembered. Daddy's face glowered at him. Then came Granddaddy. Choking on a fishbone. He could actually see the old man, though he had only been a baby when it happened. He was raging. Then scared. Then real scared. In the end, that was how the old tyrant went out—full of fear.

Margie Roberts came forward, her lips all shiny, her hair falling around her shoulders like gossamer. Her hands reached through the mist. Reached out and touched him. He could swear he felt her fingers on him as he sat there dreaming.

"It's time," Vannie said urgently. "The bus is almost here."

"Bus?" Even in his daze, he knew it had been snowing. But Vannie was sliding a ticket across the table. He suddenly remembered the café was a Greyhound bus stop. "Where's it to?"

She smiled. "You'll figure it out. You don't need us to tell you. Don't forget your suitcase and your guitar, boy. And don't forget to sing for your sister. She'll be listening for you. Alma and I will be listening, too! Hurry, now. Go!"

He was on his feet, his suitcase in one hand, the guitar case in the other, suddenly spotting Burris McCarthy down at the counter. Burris stirred and sat up. The parrot moved in his cage and muttered, "Bastard! Move on, stupid bastard!"

Did parrots say such things?

"Wait!" He stopped on the steps. "There was a man! There!" He pointed back toward the second booth.

"He will be just a memory fragment, nothing more," Alma murmured. "Just a flash of a dream. But if you let yourself feel that man's pain, you will feel the pain of mankind. You might decide to take it into your music and help heal the wounds of anyone who listens to you sing. Are you ready now?"

He drew in a breath, held it, and released it. "I think so, yes."

"Then bless you, Johnny Curtis," Alma said. "Now you can be on your way. Peace go with you. And remember, it will all be up to you. Make this decision count. Don't forget—it could have gone the other way. We call such a moment as this a crossing. One of those forks in the road. A second chance at rethinking a choice you had made. Ah . . . you did leave the gunnysack behind, didn't you?"

He thought of the gun up there, loaded and hidden away. He remembered his rage at Margie's father, who had surely stopped her from meeting him tonight.

The sisters studied him.

"I left it," he said firmly.

"Fine," Alma said. "We'll take care of it."

He nodded absently, and then he remembered the dinner he had eaten. The chicken. The pie and ice cream. He reached into his pocket and began to take out the money they had paid him for his singing.

"Not tonight," Vannie said. "This one is on the house."

"But . . ."

"Accepting gifts is another way of showing generosity, don't you know."

"As another kind of payment to us," Alma said playfully, "give all you have to give when you get to your destination, you hear me now?"

"How will you—?" He shut up. He knew they'd know. He couldn't figure out how exactly. But he knew they would. "I guess it's goodbye then."

"Goodbye is an awful long word." One of them said it as they each shook the hand he held out in farewell. He would never remember who. Then the green door swung open on its hinges without him touching it. Light snow swirled beyond it as he stepped into it. He took the cold breeze full face without flinching though his jacket was open, his shirt unbuttoned at the neck. The snow was nowhere close to as deep as he'd expected, but a white mist flowed between the sisters and him. Suddenly, he could hardly see them anymore, but the music followed him from the place. Not Peggy Lee. The old Swing King again.

"Give me, give me, give me, what I cry for . . . " He smiled and turned. "Margie? Are you there?" She wasn't, but he felt her urging him on. *Get on that bus—don't you dare turn back!* He saw the headlights from afar traveling down Highway 42 and crossed in front of them to the bus stop. The bus came closer and stopped. He climbed up the steps. The double doors shut behind him just as he heard the last words: "You know you got the brand of kisses that I'd die for . . . You know you made me love you!"

Behind him, the two sisters closed the café door. It was time to give Burris one last refill and close up for the night. Time to go lie down in their bedrooms across the road and listen to the snow fall and the wind swirl.

"It was a successful crossing, Alma." Vannie smiled as they went up to carry Sugar's dishes into the kitchen. "He'll keep going. I'm sure of it."

"Well, he's chosen his path, but he'll have to make a thousand other choices to stay on it, right, hon?"

"You can say that again," Vannie said, musing. "I swear that's an easy one to forget. To make supporting choices. Hey, Sister?"

"He'll get there!" Alma pinched her sister's cheeks. The melancholy that sometimes haunted her was far at bay. Joy crackled in her eyes.

As the snow drifted, the two sisters danced a bit in the lower dining room. They danced for Sugar. A man whose future was not what it used to be. Stepped off a bit of the Virginia reel for a young man who would soon understand what it meant to be . . .

Free. To do what he did best. Sing his heart out. And to make not just one girl love him, but perhaps a waiting world.

At the counter, Burris scooted his stool around and squinted through the window across the room, ignoring the fact that the two sisters were engrossed in a Virginia reel, barreling down the length of the lower dining room to the front door and back again, feet flying, hair loosening from their upswept chignons and falling freely around their shoulders. "By God, I see my house. You can see your house, you can get to it, right, Sisters? Did I fall asleep? I think I was dreaming about finding a big piece of fool's gold. That would be a nice addition to my rocks, wouldn't it? A big barrel full of fool's gold. It shines brighter than the real stuff."

The sisters moved seamlessly from their dancing into end-of-the-day chores, working, cleaning, washing, and putting away as they heard Burris shuffle toward the door, whistling the same tuneless song he whistled so often. When the door closed behind him, the front room lights went off. The Two Sisters' was closed for the night.

2

Half-past midnight. Nadine Curtis sat up cautiously in bed, hearing the house creak around her, the wind howl outside as it pushed through the cracks in windows and walls.

Shivering, she pulled an old sweater around her and inched her legs over the side of the bed. This was not a house to be traveled in the midnight hours. A moonshining husband who loved his own brew was never more dangerous than in the middle of a night when both his enterprise and his thirst had been thwarted.

Still, the gun wouldn't let her rest. She'd found it missing long about twilight, and it hadn't turned up by the time the storm forced the entire family into the house, including her husband Cleatis, his brother, and the older boys, who spent most nights hidden in the woods in one of their sheds brewing corn mash and drinking and selling it. The violence of the elements had taken out their boiler just before a batch of mash came to the necessary 173 degrees needed for vaporization, and the entire vat spoiled.

Her children had shuddered from Cleatis's anger, but it was nothing new. Neither was her own cowardly silence.

But you can't buck him. You know what happens when you try.

You had to pretend calm. The children depended on her play-acting.

Oh, God. Where is that damn gun? Calm down, girl, you know he's never used it except for shooting at a tree, or maybe a squirrel, or for scar-

ing somebody. He wouldn't fire it off in the house. He wouldn't.

But why wouldn't he? She'd felt in danger for her life before, and for the lives of her children. What if he went that extra step? One squeeze of that trigger could take them past all hope of recovery.

The baby was on her pallet on the floor. There was not a sound of anyone else moving around. But Cleatis had to be out there, maybe sitting at the kitchen table, still thinking about the ruined mash. Or hunting through the cabinets hoping to find a jar from an earlier batch and getting madder as his thirst made him crazier.

Maybe she was wrong about the gun being missing. Moving quietly, she got to her feet and felt her way across the dark room. The freezing boards under her feet shook from the storm's violence. It just wouldn't let up.

She reached out and felt for the doorframe, listening more closely. But there was no sound of anybody banging around or swearing out loud. Cleatis never gave a hoot if he woke the whole house. If he did, the children knew to stay silent.

Peering around the door, she stared into even denser blackness. Nobody was stirring, not that she could make out.

She drew a deep breath and started down the hall, stopping at the open door of the unheated room where her three older daughters slept, huddled together in the one bed under covers dragged from two empty cots across the room and piled on for warmth. Even under the noise of the storm, she heard shivering and whispers and knew the girls were too cold to sleep and were probably arguing about who should be in the middle.

Four of her boys were in the room that served as a living room during the day, hunkered down on floor pallets. Usually, Sugar would be sleeping there, too, but when she had finally gone to bed, he still hadn't come in. Maybe he was holed up someplace, waiting out the storm.

Out of the darkness, her oldest daughter's voice suddenly spoke. "Mama?" Sarah said quietly.

"Hush up, Sarah Ann . . . get back to sleep!" Nadine hissed back.

But Sarah had already left her bed. Nadine could make out the trembling child, tall for eleven, with her arms folded around herself, padding across the room.

"I said to—"

Sarah's freezing hands reached out and gripped her mother's arms. "I went out to the living room. Sugar wasn't there. Did—did you go look to see if his clothes are here? If his guitar is in the corner?"

"No, but I'm thinking he's probably caught someplace." Still, Nadine felt worry churn inside her. She tried to free herself from Sarah's clutch, wanting to go check the rack, but the child held on tight. For a long time there was silence between them, but she felt Sarah's panic. She had a hero worship of her oldest brother.

"Don't worry," Nadine whispered, wishing that Sarah would go back to bed. This hallway was no place for a child at night. "He'll be back." She tried to believe her own words.

Sarah didn't budge. "Why are you out here?"

Nadine marveled at her daughter's instincts. Somehow Sarah knew something was wrong and nothing she could say was going to talk her out of it. She looked toward the shadowy gun rack, wondering if Sugar could have taken the pistol. But that couldn't be. He was the one of her boys who hated guns. He wouldn't even hunt, much to his daddy's disgust. He was a singer, not a shooter.

No matter. She had to see if that pistol was back in the rack. Tiptoeing forward, she felt Sarah's cold fingers on her arm. This time, she didn't try to shake her off.

Reaching out, her fingers touched the rack and wandered down the barrels of Cleatis's two shotguns. Then she reached for the shelf where the pistol usually lay along with the loose ammunition.

Nothing. Then sheer desperation drove her to reach again. She froze, unable to believe her own senses. The pistol had been missing just seconds before. Yet, here it was, right under her hand.

"Mama?" Sarah whispered.

"I just wanted to see something," Nadine whispered back. "I thought one of the guns was missing, but it's there."

She heard her daughter's sigh of relief as they made their way back down the hall. Behind them, something moved. Nadine shooed Sarah back into the girls' room, saw the moving shadow as the child went toward the bed and climbed into it.

A rough hand closed on Nadine's shoulder. "What the hell are you doing?" her husband's voice demanded.

She shivered harder. "Just seeing to the children." His hand tightened.

"Get in bed. I've got some business with you." He shoved her through the open door to their room. Then to the bed.

Oh, God.

Crawling over the bed, she looked up at her husband's shadow looming over her. The night went blacker. She folded her lips together and tried not to make a sound as he fell on top of her.

She knew his grunts could be heard down the hall in every room where the children lay awake.

Be quiet, she told herself. *Don't care. Keep the peace.*

His hands grabbed and pinched.

She breathed in his stale breath and let him have his way.

3

"She's coming." Alma stopped in the middle of the kitchen floor, a stirring spoon in her hand dripping elixir from hot butter beans in the big iron pot. Behind her, the counter was crowded with jars of homemade canned goods, open and ready to add to today's menu. The sisters were nearing the last of goods "put up" during bumper crops last season and stored on shelves in the root cellar.

It was late March, the beginning of spring, and they were planning their garden. Things were already budding. Jonquils peeked out. Buttercups and hibiscus showed themselves. Wildflowers had begun to dot the fields. The windows to The Two Sisters' Café all stood open, balancing the morning sunshine with temperate gusts and sending in scents of pastures and willow ponds through the whole of the place. Breezes billowed the skirts of both sisters and played crazily with wisps of their hair.

It had been exactly two months since Sugar Curtis walked out of the café into a future quite different from the one he had witnessed from his booth in their upstairs dining room. The blizzard into which the sisters had seen him walk had looked like an ocean of snow, a swirling chaos of ebb and flow, with waves rolling into breakers and crashing onto shores in nine directions. The storm had blinded him, erasing the path that would have led him to destruction. Other dangerous paths would tempt as years unfolded, but for now, his way was straight before him. In the white blankness of the storm, a tiny drop of heart's desire fell like blood from a pricked finger onto a page of a book yet to be written and was owned.

He had music on his mind as he boarded the bus that charged out of the gaping maw of the storm to transport him from town. You couldn't see a road, but he was on it. Riding in a colored jukebox light, he passed through a portal in the cosmic sea (a porthole in the storm, Alma called it) and, for the first time, sensed the power of choice. He could choose his way to his dream. He knew it in his bones. He tipped his head back and pulled his hat over his eyes and slept inside the lyrics of a new song.

Now the sisters stood in their sun-bright kitchen amid simmering pots of cooking for today's noonday crowd. In this pause, as the spring breeze died down, hungry insects fluttered at the screens, intoxicated by smells of string beans in sugar and bacon, pork chops, skillet-fried corn, and vinegary hot pepper sauce. Cornbread steamed in iron skillets just out of the oven.

Banshee purred. A strange sound, even for him.

Silence gave way to a low hum. A sudden stir in the kitchen made Vannie gasp, but Alma smiled, seeing the fires on the stove burn brighter for the moment as though a spark of sulfur had flown into the burning flames. Then perking up her ears, she heard the shuffle of small feet stumble-walking in unlaced shoes along the dusty gravel side road to the café. The steps of a day-tripper, a dreamer for whom real life was much too hard.

"Sarah," Vannie breathed, seeking her sister's eyes as recognition hit. Sugar's sister, the oldest of four Curtis daughters, was now heading their way.

It was as though the child had heard her name on Vannie's lips. Her head came up, and she stopped, listening intently. Then she looked at the road and started walking again.

"She's intuitive, Sister," Vannie said. "But then she's been a watcher and a listener her whole life."

Alma nodded, her hazel eyes, as changeable as ever, going gray as she walked backward in time, watching snatches of scenes from the decrepit, unpainted house that had provided generations of Curtises a leaky roof over their heads, no electricity, and no indoor plumbing. Nadine had birthed ten children there. The house had witnessed her struggle to feed the nine that lived, clothe them, and somehow keep them out of the way of the man who had sired them.

"She'll be here soon enough." Vannie was back at the stove, stirring her kettles and pushing them to the cooler places on the iron surface. Peach pies were in the oven, the end of the peaches canned from last year's season. Clynese Watson's peaches had come in strong last summer, and she had sold them by the bushel to the townsfolk. There was hardly a family in Willow Creek that hadn't walked through Clynese's front gate to her orchard and bought peaches, or sat and peeled and eaten them beneath her trees. Later, she counted the pits and charged her clientele accordingly.

The seasons offered a succession of gifts. The Little Room was now lined with baskets of apples, potatoes, onions, and winter squash. Tubs for tomatoes were stacked alongside sacks of seeds and garden catalogues.

"Plenty for her to do here," Alma noted. "Lots of reasons we could use help."

"She's walking faster now, coming on a breeze," Vannie said.

"Blowin' in," said Alma. "She's blowin' in the wind." Alma loved listening to music yet to be written, plucking titles from futures that danced in her mind. Even now, she was humming Dylan's song.

Vannie allowed the humming to go on, knowing her sister's love of being chronologically out of place. Besides, she savored the music for its own sake.

Alma pulled out a bag of lemons and started cutting them for lemonade. "She'll be thirsty first. Then maybe she'd like a taste of caramel cake."

The sisters understood that sweets sometimes countered the effects of shock and provided temporary relief from pain. Their cakes and icings were made with care, and though dense to the senses, were actually lighter than air. A knock on the wood siding outside the screen door in the Little Room startled them.

Peering out, Alma saw a young girl in a hand-me-down dress three or four years too short for her with the waist rising so high it reached nearly to her armpits. "Come in, child," she said kindly. "Nothing's ever locked here."

Sarah shuffled inside, eyes down. Her hair should have been blond, but lack of care and nourishment grayed its luster. Her hands showed signs of working in the earth, but it was more from scratching in the dirt, digging up dandelions for greens and tea and helping her mama with a make-shift garden than from real farm work. She had the smell of one who had no place to bathe. She had never played in water, never known the fun of making waves or wading or splashing around. For that matter, she had known little fun of any kind. It was hard to imagine either a laugh or a smile gracing the girl's face.

"Sarah?" Vannie said gently. "How may we help you?"

The child took a deep breath and blurted: "Momma said get a job." Her face turned dark red, but she made herself stumble on. "I said I'd come try, but I don't know nothin' about a café." She studied her broken leather shoes. When she finally looked up, it was with head tilted away, ready to duck the blow that came when people sized you up and then dealt out contempt or pity.

The sisters had heard stories of Mrs. Norwick, the lower schoolteacher, switching Sarah in front of the class. Not just a swat or two, but a long, mean whipping to punish her for "not trying hard enough." How strange the human tendency to punish whose who were already in pain.

But there was not a sign of trouble on either of the sisters' faces, no hint of the worry they both felt for the child facing them, she who was by nature so shy.

"Would you care for a glass of lemonade?" Alma asked, already putting together the tall drink while Vannie beckoned the child farther into the Little Room.

"We could set a spell and discuss a possible place for you in our employ," Vannie said quietly. "Take a seat, child, and relax. You're welcome here."

Sarah edged over to the far end of the table and sat, staring out into the courtyard where Banshee was sunning himself and impertinently studying her through the glass.

"Don't mind that crazy coot," Vannie said, sitting opposite her at the table as Alma delivered Sarah's lemonade.

Sarah immediately picked out the sprig of fresh mint. "What's this here for?"

Alma took the mint and cupped it in her hand, slightly crushing the leaves. "It gives a clear head for business talks." With Sarah's permission, she dropped it back into the glass, then brought lemonade for Vannie and herself before taking the chair facing the window.

Vannie rubbed her thumb thoughtfully across the tile surface that no cloth ever graced. It was a work area where in winter, apples and potatoes were pared and in summer, peas were shelled and beans snapped by nimble fingers, as the sisters enjoyed each other's company and traversed time and space without leaving their upright chairs. Having the child here added another whole dimension. "Well, about the job," she said finally. "Do you help your mama in the kitchen?"

"Yessum, sometimes."

Silence again. The pot of butter beans and side-meat bubbled softly on the wood-burning stove. The hands of the clock on the wall clicked off the passing seconds. Sarah's eyes shot up. She stared into one pair of eyes, then into the other, as it registered on all three of them at once—a sense of having sat like this together in other times and spaces.

For an instant, her face became both younger and more ancient, her eyes more innocent and at the same time wiser. Just as quickly, the image fell away and the old Sarah blinked back at them.

The sisters exchanged a startled look. Then, sensing the girl's nervousness, they sipped from their glasses. Gracious, the child was actually trembling.

"Do you know what 'apprentice' means, Sarah?" Alma asked at last.

"No ma'am."

"An apprentice is one who learns," Vannie interjected. Best not to move too fast. "We would teach you how to run a café. And other things."

"Quite a few other things," Alma said pointedly.

Vannie raised an eyebrow but said only, "Let's enjoy our lemonade for a little while."

Sarah sank again into herself. Neither sister thought to bring out the cake. This child needed more than temporary relief from pain. Yet, she was only eleven years old, too immature to face a crossing like that of her brother's. The job they had foreseen offering her as a boon to Sugar's family after his departure had just revealed a potential beyond all expectation. To realize it, they would need to intervene in this child's life, the kind of risk they had rarely taken, if ever. Each was aware of the necessity of great care in choosing their next steps.

The child's eyes shifted to the parrot, who paced sideways on his ratty old perch and tilted his head at her as the sisters sat in contemplation, pictures of Sarah's mother, thin and worn, passing before them. Her courage touched their hearts. Nadine Curtis was ready for a change in her life, too. Both sisters felt it. As one, they nodded at each other.

Vannie looked at the child. "Can you shell peas and butter beans, Sarah?"

"Yessum."

"What would you do with the money you earn?"

"Give it to Mama."

"What about your daddy?"

"She said don't tell him."

"Bless my heart," Alma said to no one in particular.

"Tell your mama there is a job for you," Vannie said. "If she likes this deal, you can have it. We will pay your daddy one dollar a day and we'll give your mama a hamper of food for every day you work. And we'll put away a dollar for your future."

The child's eyes were stunned; she seemed speechless.

"You can have your bath and put on your uniform at our house on the mornings you work." Vannie pointed across the road to where a large white, green-shuttered house sat atop a grassy slope, looking like a bigger cousin of the café.

Alma raised her eyebrows at the word "uniform," but her face remained solemn. Even a trace of a smile would do immense damage to the proceedings.

"I'll sew your working dresses," Vannie said. "And Miss Alma will put on the trim. She decorates all our uniforms."

Hands trembling, Sarah reached for her lemonade glass and sipped. "What do I have to do?" she finally mumbled. It scared her to ask questions.

"You can help with any job we're doing," Alma said. "We will show you the easiest ways to work and offer you knowledge of many kinds, though you do not have to use what we teach you or to learn anything you do not wish to know."

"You mean . . . it's all up to me?" Sarah stirred uneasily.

"I think she's got it!" Alma said.

"By George!" Vannie shot back. "She's got it!"

Sarah looked dazed. "I . . . I gotta go tell Mama," she finally managed. She slid out of her chair and walked with her head down to the back door, then turned back to face them. "Can I asks you somethin'?"

"Go ahead," Alma said.

"My brother, Sugar. He worked here before me?"

"Yes, he did, Sarah. He's very talented. We were glad to have him."

"Yessum." The child went dark again. "See, the thing is. Sugar, he done run away. I was wonderin'. Do you know where he went to?"

Alma looked into the pained dry eyes. Perhaps the child had cried all her tears away. "We know that he's fine," she said gently. "We can assure you of that. And you'll see him again, not to worry."

The child screwed her face into a mixture of hope and disbelief. "Really?"

"Really. He won't forget you. You'll see. Soon you'll hear from him."

"How will I?"

"Why . . ." Alma hesitated only a moment. "Why through his music, of course. He'll sing to you, and you'll surely hear him."

Sarah absorbed that in silence, but finally nodded. "Yessum," she said softly and let herself out. A second later she was gone, leaving the sisters to rock back in their straight chairs and stare at each other.

"If it weren't for her almighty stubborn daddy, everything would be so much easier," Vannie said. "I swear Cleatis makes me tired."

"Only one thing to be done, Sister," Alma said.

"What's that?"

"After lunch, I think I'll make some gingerbread."

Vannie grinned slowly. "Okay, then I'll get the cat and the broomstick."

They gave vent to a chuckle. Then both sisters became lost again, this time in revelry, enjoying a future as real as any past, releasing swirling layers of wildly diverse emotion while opening to level upon level of possibilities.

The morning light bounced off the river and blinded Cleatis Curtis as he headed back to the house. It split his head into one sharp pain right down the middle, searing the backs of his eyes and inviting the rage in his bleeding gut to rise. It was always like this after a night at the still, pouring corn whiskey into jugs and quart jars and loading up the boys with their share of the deliveries. He had to watch the kids and his brothers, too. He beat the hell out of anybody he caught drinking up his profits, but he knew they still stole what they could. Worse than that, he knew the truth of where most of his "profits" went. Mostly they slid down his own thirsty throat, white-hot and stinging into his hollow belly and exploding in waves of heat lightning in his brain. Once again, he had come up empty with a sorry aching body and a rotten mood to remind him how he had spent the night.

It was the damn whiskey, he thought. The "likker" always lied. It smelled so whore-hot, promised to skyrocket him to the moon. It did that, too. It picked him up out of the nothing he felt most of the time, out of the blackness he almost didn't know was there. Flew him wild and howling only to drop him harder and lower than a mangy, dying dog, leaving him to wake in a stinking pile, sick to his soul and too proud to puke.

His legs wobbled. It had been too many days since he'd had anything decent to eat. He doubted he'd find much in his wife's pitiful kitchen. If Nadine knew what was good for her, she'd stay out of his way. And if anybody opened their mouth at him, he'd have to break their sorry head for them.

He caught sight of his oldest daughter, Sarah, scurrying toward the front porch. One look from him and she slowed and changed directions, shuffling toward the back of the house looking shifty as hell. Where had the brat got to so early this morning?

In a wave of dizziness, he stopped at the pump handle to put his head between his legs. Bile burned his throat as he rose up dripping and started walking again.

Damn. Damn them all.

In the kitchen shadows away from the window, Nadine stood trembling. She could always feel Cleatis's moods. This one was going to be bad. With the instincts of a turtle, she slid deep inside herself, forcing herself to move to the stove. She had some grits on. That might be enough for him after a night of drinking. Lucky for her, because her last hen had quit laying over a week ago. Pretty soon, she'd have to kill her and boil her up for soup. That would make him mad, but not as mad as feeding her and getting no eggs.

A thump under her made her jump, but it was only Sarah, signaling her with the handle of an old broken broom. She was in her hidey-hole under the kitchen floor. Nadine stamped back, wanting her to stay there till the sun went down and Cleatis would go with the boys to the still to sell some moonshine and drink whatever was left. Then she could pick some green tomatoes from her garden and fry them up for the little kids. She'd picked poke salad out of the pastures and boiled it up yesterday, but it was all gone now.

She almost wished that Cleatis would make Terry Joe go steal another chicken from the Miles' house over the ridge. But she didn't want no more of her babies in jail, not after what they done to Bobby Dean in there. He hardly talked to her since then, just stayed to hisself and with the men. She'd never thought she'd see such a sweet-natured boy turn mean, but he had.

Nadine pulled the grits off the stove and set the iron pot on the table while Cleatis shut himself in the outhouse. The shape he was in told her he'd stay in there for a while. That gave her time to get both herself and Sarah out of harm's way. She slipped out the back door, grabbed the fishing pole, and went down to scratch for grubs under the woodpile. If Sarah saw her heading down to the river to try and catch some dinner, maybe she'd sneak out from under the house and meet her down there. Then Nadine could find out what the sisters had said.

Probably it had amounted to nothing, she thought. It had been stupid to send her to the café, and stupid now to have any hopes about it at all.

Sarah watched the big garden spider enlarging her web on the bony skeleton of last year's squash vine just outside her hidey-hole. The garden spider had never scared her. She was big and black with yellow stripes, and she didn't chase people. She wasn't fast and mean like the fat black ones or sneaky and dangerous like the soft brown ones. Mama said the garden spider wouldn't bite and even if she did, it wouldn't hurt or make you sick. She just basked in the sun and waited for bugs to fly into her web, then grabbed them and packaged them up for later.

Sarah thought about her glass of lemonade at the sisters' café. She wished she had some more. The women had seemed nice, if maybe a little crazy. They must have been kidding her though. A dollar for her daddy, food for the family. And another dollar for her future. She had never thought about *having* a future. She blanched at the thought of working at the café right in the middle of so many people . . . could she really do it? And they'd let her help any way she wanted to and learn only the stuff she wanted to learn? Yep, they were probably crazy.

Her body felt weak after the stress of the morning, and she clasped her knees to her chest with shaky arms. Yet she couldn't stop herself from hoping.

She saw Mama passing by, heading for the pond with her pole over her shoulder. Sarah hoped she would be lucky. The last time Mama caught fish and fried them, Daddy was so happy he gave her money for groceries, and that day Mama got bacon, flour, grits, coffee, sugar, and buttermilk. Daddy and the boys ate good for a few days, and the little kids had biscuits to go with their grits for two days running.

A pot of food and a dollar for Daddy. If it really happened. What would Daddy say? He'd want the dollar. He'd try to get the dollar they were saving for her, too.

"Cleatis Curtis?"

The voice made Sarah jump. Alarm turned to amazement. That was Miss Alma's voice. Yes, it was. She'd know it anywhere.

"Cleatis Curtis?" Alma said again. "Are you home? I need to talk to you, if you can give me a minute of your time."

Sarah shrank farther back into her hidey-hole and waited.

Cleatis had finished his grits and was sitting in the kitchen ready to nod off when he heard the woman call his name.

"What the fool . . .?" He stepped out onto the broken-down porch.

"Morning, Cleatis," Alma said pleasantly.

"Yeah." His voice didn't offer much clue as to what he was thinking behind his scruffy unshaved face. It was the same voice he used for Sheriff Jimmy's visits when he came around asking questions about moonshine.

Alma's smile widened. "I've come to make you an offer. You see, my sister Vannie and I need some help at the café."

"Café," he repeated. Good God, she was one of the two crazy sisters that owned the restaurant attached to the filling station. He'd bought gas there a few times when he hadn't managed to siphon it off from somebody else's car or truck.

"Yes. We were thinking we'd like to hire your daughter, if she's available. How would you feel about that? Because, of course, we wouldn't hire her if her daddy didn't approve."

He squinted at her. "You don't mean *Sarah?*"

"Your eleven-year-old, yes."

Cleatis swayed on his feet. His head was light, his stomach still queasy. The grits had not been enough this morning. He needed some real food, but he wasn't going to get it, so he might as well try and get some real sleep. "I can't be bothered with nothin' now." Better get back inside before he said something that would get him in trouble with the law. He had whiskey to sell tonight and some to drink.

"I was afraid you might not be interested," Alma said. "But my sister and I were so eager."

Cleatis set his jaw. Turned toward the house.

"It was only a dollar a day for you and some food." He put his hand on the door. "Oh! I almost forgot. Sister and I fried up a chicken this morning, and I brought you some to try. Won't you just sit down for a bite? And I've got biscuits and pear preserves with butter, and some coffee and some of Vannie's deviled eggs. What else? Gingerbread and . . . oh, yes! The apple pie! I'll run back to the car and get the hamper."

Cleatis was dumbfounded. Yet he was so hungry his knees were weak. As Alma ran to a car parked on the dirt road and came bustling back with the basket, he wanted to order her off his property. But before he could open his mouth, she spread a cloth right on the porch and started putting out food.

"Let me make you a plate and maybe we can talk a little bit."

Still on guard, he settled down with his back to a post and let Alma pile some of everything onto his plate.

"Now, as I was saying." She poured coffee into a tin cup. "For every day that Sarah works for us, we'll pay you a dollar and send home a basket of food for the family." She passed the cup to him.

"Charity, is it, like that mealy-mouthed preacher and his bunch of do-righters that come around here with fruitcake and Bibles? I don't want none of it." He set the cup down so hard that coffee splashed over the rim.

"Not charity, Mr. Curtis. Wages earned! Sarah will be wonderful help, smart and eager to learn, we could tell that right away."

"Smart?" He sneered. "And she's going to prove it by working for you? Not in a pig's eye. No Curtis works for nobody. That ain't our way."

"Please do reconsider, Mr. Curtis." She passed him his plate, and the smell of fried chicken almost knocked him off the porch. "There's nothing to be afraid of."

"Afraid of? Me afraid?" He could not believe his ears. Or his mouth either, for that matter, as he took his first bite of chicken, then devoured a deviled egg. This was by far the best food he'd ever tasted. And it went gentle into his stomach, too, soothing and warming him inside. Nothing like that trash Nadine fed him every night. The eggs were like music in his mouth, stuffed with homemade mayonnaise and home-canned sweet relish. The butter on the biscuit was churned from milk of cows that grazed not five miles from his house. The chicken was fat and juicy and crisp and salty. It was chasing his hangover away. Pear preserves dripped through his fingers and down his chin.

"Mr. Curtis?"

He swallowed heavily, not wanting to talk, only to go on eating. He ate with such intensity that blood pounded in his temples.

The voice was hesitant. Concerned. "I don't want to intrude, but why doesn't the Curtis family work for anyone? Why don't *you* work for anybody, Cleatis?"

Something pulled at him, demanded. A suction that he fought against, even as he sensed it was no use.

"Please, Cleatis." Her voice was gentle. Lulling. In his rough life, he had heard few such gentle voices, except Nadine's in their early days. "Tell me," the sister was murmuring, "why it's so terrible to work for anyone. Why won't you?"

He clamped his lips tighter, trying to hold back. Sweat sprang to his forehead. His hands clenched. But it was no use. The words burst out of him, bits of chicken flying out along with his rage and humiliation. "You think you already know, don't you? Alright, if nothing else'll do you, I'll tell you. It's 'cause I can't *read,* alright? You happy now? And I can't *write,* neither! I can't read, and I can't write! You can't write your name, you ain't fit to work. Okay? You satisfied?" His voice broke.

Alma gazed steadily back at him.

He shivered. An unfamiliar dampness spilled from his eyes onto the rough skin of his cheeks. He couldn't believe he'd said the secret out loud. A lifetime of keeping it inside, a lifetime of being afraid everyone would find out, and he'd just told it to a woman he hardly knew. It staggered him. All these years. Carrying the fear, afraid to ask anyone for any kind of work. How could you get a job if you couldn't write out an application? How could you write things once you had the job? How could you even cash your paycheck if you couldn't write your name?

"Fear wears many disguises, Cleatis," Alma said respectfully. "It can stop us from becoming who we are, who we *really* are. So, I ask you: Are you *sure* you can't write your name? Or are you just afraid to try?"

"A man knows if he can't write his own damn name." A deviled egg slipped through his fingers onto the porch. It rolled upside down in the dirt, and he punched it with his fist. When he looked up, he was staring at a piece of paper in Alma's hand. She handed it to him, took a pencil from the bun in her hair, and held it out.

He shrank from the pencil as though she had offered him a scorpion. "I can't. Please . . ."

"It's not as if you never went to school, you know," Alma reminded him. "And think of this—a child's mind is fertile ground. Believe me, Cleatis, you retained more than you know. I assure you, you can remember what you learned as a child in school. All you have to do is give your mind permission."

"Please," he whimpered. If only she would close her eyes. He couldn't bear looking at himself in them. "I can't."

"Try, at least. As a favor to me, if you please."

He found himself wondering if anyone could refuse her anything. He, at least, could not. Face burning, he snatched the pencil from her and got ready to make his "X." His fingers shook as he dampened the lead between his lips, then touched it to the paper. He wrote and, without looking, shoved the slip of paper back at Alma. Then he clapped his hand to his head and watched his world take on new shape.

"Not bad," she said approvingly. "You've been selling yourself short, Cleatis. Amazing how many of us do."

"What?" He stared at the paper. For a moment it was all symbols. Then to his surprise, every letter that he had just written on the paper made sense: C-L-E-A-T-I-S-C-U-R-T-I-S.

"Cleatis Curtis," he said shyly. "I just wrote my name. I just read my name!" He chuckled. Laughed. Then bellowed. He pounded his fist into the porch and did not see the wariness in her face as she looked at the broken floorboard his fist had shattered.

"So. Have you decided, Mr. Curtis?"

Decided? What in hell had she been asking him? Something about letting Sarah work for her. Even now, her eyes were asking the question. *Answer, Cleatis. Say the first thing that comes into your mind.*

"I reckon that would work out alright." He was surprised at how the words poured out of him. "Yeah, I reckon that would be fine."

"Wonderful. We'll expect her at seven in the morning. Let her bring the basket with her when she comes. We'll make sure to fill it. Oh, is that your wife?"

Nadine had come walking up from the river, shading her eyes from the sun and trying to make out the visitor who had made her husband laugh. He was silent now, sitting there with his back propped against the house.

"Mr. Curtis," Alma whispered, as he stared blank-faced at Nadine. "Share the rest of the food with the family later. But please go see your wife. I've taken enough of your time." She watched him pull himself up, then stagger down the steps on his way to meet Nadine. Watched husband and wife nod to each other, then stand together for a moment in the shadow of the house.

From a distance, Alma mused, the walls they had built between them over their married years were almost invisible save for the defensive sideways slant of Nadine's body.

Only when they turned and headed toward the back door did Alma lean over and stick her head into the hidey-hole. "Sarah? Is everything right with you now?"

The child's face looked out at her, showing a mixture of amazement and apprehension. "Yes ma'am, but . . . I'm . . ."

"What is it, child?"

Sarah nervously opened her mouth, then shut it. Then opened it again. "Are you sure you really want me, Miss Alma?" she whispered shyly. "I . . . I don't know nothin' much. I might just go on over there and—and mess everythin' up on you."

"Sweetheart." Very gently, Alma reached out and touched Sarah's tangled and dull hair. "Please don't worry about that. You'll do just fine. Believe me."

"How do you *know?*" Sarah whispered, still in an agony of doubt. "What if you got me by mistake?"

"Sister and I aren't making a mistake, child. And neither are you. You can do this. Will you dare to try?"

Sarah's eyes darted to Alma's and held there, but she lowered them before she answered on a long breath: "Yessum, I will."

Alma was almost overcome by the love she felt for this neglected scrap of humanity with so much sweetness still intact. It seemed almost impossible that the child had managed to retain so much of her true nature. But then she was no ordinary child. She and Vannie had come to that realization hours ago.

"Come on up and have a chicken leg, darlin'," she murmured. "Give your worries a rest. Tomorrow, you'll come to us at the café."

"Thank you, ma'am."

Riding back in the car, Vannie mused, "He responded well to you, Sister. Of course, we knew he'd be less afraid of one than two. It doesn't sound like much, but two-to-one are terrible odds to a fearful man."

"He surely loved those deviled eggs," Alma murmured. "And Sarah's coming to us." Her smile gave way to a slight frown. "I still don't like leaving her in that house. Through the ages in all our traditions, that has never been the way! Learning magical arts is challenging enough as it is."

"She is needed where she is."

"You can be stubborn as a mule, Vanessa."

"Who else could melt Cleatis's tough old heart? Who else can make her mama smile? Right or wrong, Sister, I just can't see it any other way. Please bear with me on this one."

Alma looked at the tilt of Vannie's chin. Saw her knuckles white from her grip on the steering wheel. "Alright, have it your way. I know better than to go against you when your blood is up."

That was true. And it worked both ways. Whenever the sisters disagreed, passion often settled things. The one with the strongest feelings on a matter prevailed. The two would fight it out, make a decision, and take action as one. If the decision brought trouble, they'd meet it together.

"But it galls me," Alma said, not quite ready to let it go.

"Well, we owe something to Cleatis after intervening as we did. We can't take such a step with a soul so unripe and just walk away and forget him."

Alma snorted. "Who could forget Cleatis? He's going to be a handful."

"Ah, well. May as well get out all our old books of magic and dust off our crib notes. There'll be doin's we haven't had to bother with for centuries just to help him along on this trip we've pushed him into. Worth it though. Worth it all for her. He'll be no more trouble than a thorn in your toe."

"Or a snake in your ear," Alma shot back despite herself.

"Or an itch in your privates!" Vannie shook her head. "We'll have to watch him like a hawk. No telling what he's liable to do."

They rode on through the farmland, bumping from the dirt road to the main road back to Willow Creek and to The Two Sisters' Café. Their hearts were quickening with excitement. The time had finally come. After all the waiting for her, the two sisters were getting their first apprentice.

The child was wounded, that was true, and visions of how she might heal herself while helping them with magic for others danced in the heads of both sisters.

"What goes around comes around," Alma said knowingly.

It was too much joy to contain. Vannie's fingers found the beat to it, tapping it out on the dashboard. The feeling grew until Alma piped in with an open-throated warble that pulled them both into a full-tilt yodel, Vannie on high trill, Alma on the lower note. Pretty soon both windows were down, and the sound went ricocheting off trees and echoing through the meadows. New flowering weeds trembled in response as they picked up the vibration and spread it one to another. The very grass rippled in answer to the unabashed warbling in two-part harmony that went on and on, building in resonance as the sisters gave themselves to the sound of it, putting their heads out their car windows and letting the sound bounce like a ball. Bounce off the sky and onto the country road as they made their way home.

4

No fewer than five tornadoes were spotted in the black and rainy Willow Creek skies on the morning of March 31, the selfsame morning when Elmer Bailey came by the café with his Plan. Wouldn't it be so, the sisters would say in years to come. It was, after all, no ordinary day, not with the Plan to change every other day that was to follow thereafter.

"And isn't it lucky," Alma whispered to Vannie, "that Sarah's school is cancelled for the day so she can be here for it?" She glanced toward the upper dining room where Sarah was all but on top of the jukebox, listening intently. When Alma looked back at Vannie, she found her sister's fists on both hips, her eyebrows on the rise.

"The only question I have for you Miss Alma . . ." Vannie began.

"Yes, Sister?" All innocence.

"Was Sarah's school cancelled because of the tornadoes, or were other hands at work here? There *are* after-school hours, wouldn't you agree?" The thin line of accusation in Vannie's voice went ignored by her sister. But then that had always been Alma—unrepentant.

"Sorry is as sorry does," she would say, knowing full well that it made no sense.

As impatient as Vanessa could get with her older sister, she wished Sarah had a little of that same spunk. In the ten days that the child had been working for them, she had reacted with shame about everything from spilling a drop of milk to tripping over a crack in the floor. And now, here was Elmer who felt neither shame nor remorse about anything. The man was as pumped up over his own worth for as little reason as anyone could figure. As Carolyn Houseman once said, "That man goes through life as his own disciple."

This morning he had come by for fifteen-cent all-you-could-drink coffee. He never ordered more than that, but he was always crafty enough to look long and hard at the fresh pastries and finger his pocket, knowing he could make the sisters come across with two big jelly-filled donuts on the house. They always had, always would, Elmer thought complacently. He knew how to make the world work.

Today, he didn't even have to go into his routine. The donuts were already on the plate, his coffee poured and waiting when he walked in the front door, the wind slamming it heavily behind him. It was as though they had been expecting him. Even nicer was the deference the sisters accorded him. They always gave him their full attention, but not like on this particular morning, bent forward across the Coca-Cola case, eyes riveted on his face, and hanging on his every word. Everything in their manner said they considered him much more interesting than five mere tornados.

"What kind of music is the child playing?" he asked, glancing toward the little girl who was glowing in lights from the jukebox.

He could not see that the song she played was not coming from the big machine. Instead, it spun on a small record player beside her that was painted to match the neon colors of the jukebox. The record was a gift from the sisters, a small circular disk with a label marked "Dream Records" at the top. Around the bottom edge, tiny letters spelled out "Future Hits."

The child (an odd, backward child, as Elmer judged her) was mesmerized by a song sung in a gravelly voice so deep that it might have dropped from the cellar of the man's soul: *"It must be hard to be the only one . . . who dares to dream of happiness to come . . . But it's dreams that fire the very sun . . . Come bring your light . . . I'll be your knight."*

"Irresponsible dreaming is no good," Elmer observed. "Gives the young the impression that life is frivolous. Easy."

"Maybe some feel that way," Alma said with a glint of steel in her eyes. "But there's been little in Sarah's life to make her so inclined."

"It's just a song in any case," Vannie said swiftly.

"Who is that man singing anyhow? Sounds like he's about to choke to death on his own words." Elmer enjoyed it when both sisters laughed. The pleasure of having his humor appreciated almost made him forget the weather. He leisurely unfolded his paper napkin, tucked it carefully under the collar of his shirt, and rearranged the donuts on his plate to please his critical eye. He would not, he told himself, let the weather upset his equilibrium. He would put his own power up against a tornado's any day. Adjusting his coffee cup to his left so that he could drink left-handed, he smiled at the sisters. "I suppose you wonder why I always drink from my left when I'm right-handed?"

"Oh, no," Vannie said. "We understand totally." She noted that Sarah had eased away from the jukebox and was now sitting on the top step of the dining room beside Banshee's cage, her eyes fastened on Elmer. "It's because there are so few left-handed, as compared to right-handed, people in the world. Therefore, since you're in a public restaurant, you choose to drink from the side of the cup that fewer people have used."

"Perfectly understandable," Alma concurred. "One must do what one can to control one's environment."

Elmer was surprised. He had never before heard anyone come up with the same theory as his own. He studied each sister's face for signs of levity, but found only serious agreement there. "Do you do the same, Sisters?"

"Well, actually no," Alma murmured. "We go out of our way to experience life in the way a normal person experiences it."

"We'd probably drink from the right even if we were both left-handed," Vannie said with a quick wink.

"Hmm. Sounds peculiar." Generally, he respected only his own opinions, feeling that other people's theories on life were inferior to his own.

He knew himself to be an interesting and intelligent man, one of a kind. Introspective. Full of unique talents. If he had any regrets at all, it was that he was not well educated. Because of this, doing lawn work and odd jobs far beneath him had become his fate in the town. Could he re-live his life, he would become a scholar and go to the university. Possibly get a degree in psychology. Then he would write books in which he would instruct the world on how to lead more enlightened lives, hang up his shingle, and begin solving people's problems, while at the same time making a handsome bundle for himself.

"How is Edith?" Vannie asked, watching as Elmer cut a slice of donut rich with strawberry jam filling.

Elmer commented that Edith was just fine. But then, he wondered, how could any wife of his be anything else? She was a superior woman, suited to his taste, or he wouldn't have chosen her. She was full of goodwill, perhaps more than he would have preferred. But then everyone had their faults, he thought regretfully, and Edith was better than most. True, she was not the housekeeper for which he would have wished. She had no real liking for dusting and still less for vacuuming. Her organizing skills were even more of a disaster. But she followed orders very well and allowed him to teach her how to dust, wash, clean the dishes, and keep her pantry arranged to best advantage. He was not pleased with the amount she spent on groceries, but then like most people, she lacked the understanding of how to get good value for her dollar. No matter how often he went over it with her, she could not get down the principle of how well two people could eat on four dollars a week, which he thought was a generous allotment simply for food, cleaning supplies, and things like cough syrup and toothpaste.

"I heard you and Edith flew to Texas last week," Vannie went on.

"My nephew got married in Dallas." Elmer smirked. "He's a big oil company executive down there. He's building his bride a mansion, of course, heck of a place. I went over the blueprints and made a few suggestions."

Alma cleared her throat. "How was the flight?"

Elmer's face grew eager. "I'll tell you, Sisters, flying was the experience of my life. The only thing that could have made it better was me piloting the plane. But I sat right by the window and imagined myself at the controls. I had such lofty thoughts as I cannot adequately express to another mortal. All my theories about life floated in the air all around me as fully realized as though they'd been published in the Divine Book. I could almost hear God's voice whispering in my ear, saying, 'Elmer Bailey, I have heard you . . . and the way you live is so . . . *right*!' Truly, Sisters, it was one of the most poignant moments of my life." A tear sprang to one of his eyes, and he dabbed it efficiently with a tip of his napkin.

"I thought Edith wanted to sit by the window," Alma said.

"And do *what*?" Elmer said with a flare of impatience. "I just took her and hauled her out of that seat and tried to explain to her how much more it would mean to me than to her. Not everyone is born for the window seat, Sisters. And when you couple that with the enlightenment I've just mentioned . . . ah, well." He relaxed back, chewing strawberry donut appreciatively, his eyes growing dreamy. Though the windows rattled and a sound like an approaching freight train shook the air, he was oblivious.

The sisters peered through the windows at the gray-black sky, took note of the rain that lashed at the windows with the erratic staccato of a snapping whip and the fast-approaching tornadoes beyond, then regarded Elmer closely. He smiled back vaguely, still lost in another world.

It was one that the child seemed to share as she leaned on her knees on the step, eyes half-closed, but following every word.

"You should have seen the sunset on the flight home," Elmer went on after a while. "It glowed, radiated the consciousness, stroked the soul with its eloquence. I described every last nuance to Edith, every beam of light, every color, every dazzling insight that such a spectacle should inspire within the human soul."

"Edith couldn't see the sunset?" Vannie queried.

"There's seeing, and there's seeing, Sister. It was my *description* of what she was seeing, not the sight itself, that finally brought her to tears."

"Quite so," Alma said dryly. "By the way, how is Edith's health? Sister and I have been concerned that she doesn't take adequate care of herself. She really is not well, you know."

He frowned. "Not at all. Actually, she's in the pink of condition. That woman glows with health. Though the pity is that she refuses to acknowledge it. She's got a doctor for every last body part she owns. Everyday something new aches, something twinges, something goes kaput. She worries about every new bump, every bruise. Well, why wouldn't she bruise the way she lets herself fall all over the place? Even worse, she's got a pill for every occasion. I used to have an agreement with Charley at the drugstore for free pills. But now that's over, so something's got to give. That's why I've come up with my Plan." He set his jaw determinedly, his eggplant-colored eyes gleaming, then dimming as he noticed the sisters' keen interest. He found himself wishing for a diversion.

"Incidentally, Sisters," he said, "you could improve your serving window with an organization unit. A kind of inset where you could set condiments and order slips and so forth, perhaps in the lower right-hand corner. If you're interested, I could give you a price on building you one."

"Thanks for thinking of it," Alma said. "Though actually we prefer the wide open view from kitchen to counter. Uncluttered, you know. And it makes us feel more connected to the rest of the café this way."

"About your agreement with Charley, Elmer. What exactly was it?" Vannie inquired.

"Oh, well. I'm not sure I should . . ." He glanced swiftly at the child, motionless on the steps and apparently drinking him in.

"You can trust us, Elmer," Alma assured him.

He turned back and found her persuasive eyes pouring into his. Though he'd had no intention of ever telling that particular agreement to a living soul, it was hard to refuse Miss Alma anything when she fixed those eyes on you. "Uh, well, you see," he began, "Charley's wife . . . has a little problem . . ."

"You mean her sad addiction to alcohol."

Elmer frowned at the last piece of donut remaining on his plate. "Charley asked if I might look in on her while he was busy at the drugstore and make certain that she was safe. In exchange, he wouldn't charge me for Edith's pills. It seemed a fair exchange," he added a bit guiltily, as though the sisters had reminded him that Charley's house was only two doors down from his own and service to a neighbor should be free. The town already whispered that Charley paid him too much for lawn care. Yet to Elmer, the extra drug allowance seemed more than fair. Still, his ears turned fiery, the red crawling over his plump cheeks and down his neck. He couldn't imagine why he had told the sisters such a private piece of business, especially with that odd child listening.

"So," Alma continued, "why isn't Charley giving you the pills anymore?"

"He's hired a damn fool housekeeper to look after his wife. You imagine that? Said he won't have to trouble me anymore. Sounded like he was talking to a hired hand, not a friend. I hauled off and told him he didn't need a housekeeper, he needed to take the reins of his marriage into his own hands. He wouldn't hear it. The way he talked to me, I doubt I'll even mow his lawn anymore unless he gives me a pay increase."

As he spoke the words, he thought he heard a humming. Then he realized it was just more wind. Something other than the freight train noise that still reverberated in the distance, but not so faraway as he'd thought. The humming seemed closer yet, as though it was inside the café. He knew it was wind though, because it brushed his forehead, drifted down his neck until he drew his jacket closer and looked around apprehensively.

"Do you know what to do in a tornado, Sisters? Aren't you supposed to open a window or something?" Or hadn't they already opened one? Everything appeared locked up tight, but if there wasn't a window open, then where was the draft coming from?

"You're safe here," Alma murmured. "But do tell us. What is this Plan of yours, Elmer? About the pills?"

His face cleared, and he smiled proudly. "I've decided to wean Edith from them."

"Wean her?" Vannie repeated, her lips twitching.

"You got it! Sisters, the woman controls me with her damn hypochondria, the doctors lay down the rules with their cockeyed medications, and I sit here and pay the bills. But all that's about to change, *one prescription at a time*! You hear me? Here's how it works. She's got thirteen kinds of asinine pills. My Plan is to eliminate one prescription every month. By God, in just thirteen months she'll be totally weaned, and I'll be back in charge! When I finish with her, she'll be a new woman."

"She will indeed," Vannie said. "But are you sure that's wise, Elmer? Are you really quite certain that you know what you're doing?"

He drew himself up stiffly on his stool. Affront at being questioned bit into his mood. It also bothered him that the child had left her step and was now sitting at the counter just two stools down from him.

Eavesdropping on me, he thought angrily. *Well, let her listen. She might learn something*. He might be only a handyman and a landscaper, as he liked to call himself, but he was also a man of innate wisdom. And he wanted to be recognized for it. If his parents had done their job and his teachers had done theirs, he'd be in an important profession by now and own the world. Nobody had ever listened to him back then, that was the problem. His jaw tightened. All they talked about was his bad grades, though they never did a thing about it. Of course, his parents weren't highly educated. How could he have come to be born to such people? That was the real question. In his heart, he believed it possible that his true parents had left the hospital with the wrong baby, and he had been left to grow up in a family of fools.

"I know exactly what I'm doing, Sisters," he snapped. "Edith is my wife, and I always do what is best for her. Tomorrow, the first day of April, I will begin by eliminating one prescription. Thereafter, on the first day of every month, I will eliminate one more. Exactly thirteen months from today, my wife will be free of her addiction to those damned pills, and you can quote me on that."

"Oh, yes?" Alma quirked her eyebrows.

"Absolutely. Tell anybody you like. Spread the word. It'll be one of those life lessons that will benefit the whole town. Hypochondriacs everywhere. Half the people I know live at the doctor's front door. If they need advice, tell 'em to come to me." He grabbed his knitted cap from the counter and pulled it precisely over his neatly trimmed gray hair, then donned his gloves with the same care.

"By the way," Vannie said, when he was at the front door, peering through the window alongside it searching for any more tornados that might be forming in the sky. "Does extreme weather scare you, Elmer?"

He whirled and faced them. Never before had he felt so angry at the two sisters. In fact, he had never before felt angry with them at all. It was hard to understand, in fact, how he had come to be so furious. He was even angry at the child. Remembering belatedly that he hadn't paid the fifteen cents for his coffee, he reached into his pants pocket, awkward in his thick glove. "Damn the weather, anyhow," he mumbled, groping for change. "Unpredictable stuff." He yanked off his glove, dug again, and produced a nickel and a dime. The two coins slid across each other as he rubbed them between thumb and forefinger. He'd intended to slap them down on the counter and get the heck on out to his truck, but a sudden flurry of movement behind the counter froze him. It all happened so fast and was over so quickly that Elmer thought his eyes must be playing tricks on him. Yet there had most definitely been a small puff of white smoke and a crackle of tiny sparks in the space between the sisters.

The child gasped. Now Miss Alma was holding something behind her back like she was hiding it from him. Why would she think he cared what she was hiding, for Pete's sake? Stranger and stranger. Added to which, there was Miss Vannie pulling a paper napkin from the holder and shaking it out in a fancy kind of move that made him think of a magician's assistant holding a cape or some sort of magical cloth.

"Ta-dah!" With a flick of a wrist, Alma hurled what she had been hiding into the air and set it spinning.

It hung suspended in front of Elmer's face, turning in perfect circles just beyond his reach. Its donut shape invited. Called. Set him to yearning. So familiar that shape. Like the tire tube from a pickup truck that had been the only life raft Elmer had known as a child. He flashed on a memory of holding onto it in the swift currents after unexpected summer rains had swelled the creek, threatening to sweep him away. The memory dissolved as Vannie reached out with her napkin, plucked the spinning object out of the air, and waved it in his face. What the Sam Hill? A donut! Just a glazed donut. He must be coming down with something. The thing looked plain ordinary, now that he could see it clearly. He vaguely perceived that the child had clapped her hands to the sides of her face in wonder. Her dropped jaw gradually widened to a smile.

"You may be wanting this later," Vannie said, popping the donut and napkin into a small paper bag.

"And put your money back in your pocket," Alma added. "Today, everything's on the house."

"Well," he said, relaxing a bit. After all, that was very nice of them. Most kind. "The donuts were delicious, Sisters. Thank you very much."

"We're glad you've enjoyed them, Elmer," Vannie said. "And do come back soon. We'll be so interested to hear how Edith comes along."

He managed to open the door against the wind, stuffing the paper bag into his pocket as the wind slammed the door behind him. The sound of the freight train thundered even louder now, so loud it hurt his ears, but he saw no new funnels in the sky. The wind picked him up and literally swept him toward his pickup truck which was parked as usual, pulled in headfirst just off the road, facing the café. His torso tipped forward at a frightening angle; his feet had to run to catch up, barely saving him from a disastrous fall. He could never remember having felt so out of control. It was a frightening feeling, made worse when he slammed into the side of his truck so hard it knocked the breath from his lungs. He hung onto the door handle, trembling and shivering. Why on Earth had he ever come out on such a morning? What had possessed him? He had found himself longing for a donut from the café, and nothing else had penetrated his mind except the need to get there. Not even the fear of the five tornadoes that he had spotted in the sky.

Holding on as best he could and leaning his body against the truck, he inched along until he worked himself to the driver's side and climbed in. Safely inside, he found himself panting as he looked toward the café and saw the two sisters standing with the child by a window. The three of them stared back at him. He blinked and they were gone.

"What the hell's happening?" He found himself halfway expecting an answer, but there was none. Nothing at all, save for the roar of the freight train, so deafening that it seemed to envelope him. Then in a mind-popping WHOOSH, the wind roared through his ears, nose, and mouth. It shook him so ferociously that it occurred to him that he might have swallowed the tornado. His ears rang from the sound; his body gyrated. Then in another clean WHOOSH, the wind left him. For a second, he lay back in his seat, weak and shaking. Now there was no sound at all. The quiet was eerie.

Elmer said aloud in the weak prattling voice of a scared child, "I'm in the eye of the damned thing. I'm right in the cold black evil eye of it."

Panic, hard and cold, overtook him. Hand shaking, he managed to fit his key into the ignition and start the motor. In most uncharacteristic fashion, he hit the gas pedal too hard, screeched backward onto the road, lurched to a stop, then reversed gears and took off for home like a man on the run. All the while, he imagined the sisters watching him with the child beside them, her eyes huge and alarmed. He went faster yet, but they were still there, planted solidly in a pinprick of light that he now realized was a dot inside his own brain. *Never mind,* he counseled himself, trying to still the pounding of his heart. *Nobody gets the best of Elmer Bailey. And tomorrow, I start the Plan.*

5

It happened on the night of April 1. April Fool's Night, as the townspeople kept telling each other after Edith died. Windy night, too, folks said, though no new tornadoes had been spotted. Still everything was swirling, from clothes twisting on the lines to dust flying through the air. Dirt penetrated the cracks under the doors and badly insulated windows and blew down the chimneys, causing a terrible mess. Not to speak of the sound, somewhere between a shrieking and a horrible moaning noise as ominous as a thousand spooks screaming hellfire and damnation. The wind blew all that night and continued through the second day of April, some saying it was an orchestration in honor of Edith's death.

If so, it was a long one. The skies still blustered on the afternoon of April 3 when the sisters and Sarah left the café to make their way from Willow Creek to the Patterson Mortuary in LaGrange where many Willow Creek people chose to lay out their loved ones. The mortuary was a handsome, light-brick building with a circular driveway and mature oaks and elms located in a residential neighborhood not far from the elementary school. The elegance of the place was said to soothe; and besides, nobody on Earth could lay out a corpse better than Roger and Irma Patterson. Or, for that matter, coordinate the entire affair, everything from mood lighting to funeral parades. ("Soup to nuts," Belle Taylor always said.) One way or the other, in the Pattersons' hands the rawness of grief attained a semblance of dignity. One forgot the rumors of how the Pattersons' teenage daughter would invite friends over for sleepovers and how they would tell ghost stories and sneak down and take turns putting their fingers on the corpses at midnight.

Today though, serenity eluded even "Patterson's," as it was called familiarly. Tree branches whipped and groaned, colliding and scraping together in disharmony. The short grass blew flat as a misshapen crew cut. Clouds of dust and debris swept through the air and invaded eyes, noses, and throats of mourners who fought their way from the parking lot and up the bricked pathway to the front entrance. Yet few were deterred from making an appearance. Virtually, the entire town of Willow Creek had showed up to honor Edith's passing.

"An impressive showing, " Vannie murmured, parking their ancient black Buick behind the mortuary in one of the last remaining spaces.

"Very nice," Alma agreed approvingly. "Sarah, tie that scarf in a good knot, or this wind will have it for a kite."

The sisters moved down the pathway, Sarah between them, all of them bent double against the strong wind that whipped at their coats, chilled their skin, and stung tears from their eyes. Though they found themselves almost pushed backward as they continued toward the front entrance, the sisters lifted their chins and welcomed the air against their faces.

"Acknowledge the elements, Sarah," Vannie called out to her. "Feel their wonder, power, and beauty, and they will begin to know yours."

"I can feel the wind talking to me," Sarah called back. The wind seemed to have blown her usual tongue-tied bashfulness away. Impulsively, she pulled her hands out of the sisters' grasp and opened her arms wide. She would have been whipped away from them and back toward the parking lot had Vannie not grabbed her coattail.

"Whoops," Alma said, arching an eyebrow at Vannie and dragging all of them forward. "Best save that lesson for a quieter day, wouldn't you say, dear?" She smiled, delighted that this time it was Vannie who had jumped the gun as far as Sarah's lessons were concerned. They made the door as the first splashes of rain hit them.

Vannie shook her head, reminding herself to take care with the child. Her spirit was awakening quicker than they had expected beneath that quiet exterior, and she could not be predicted. Without proper respect, the forces could be deadly, no matter how great one's affinity.

"Crazy day, isn't it?" Irma Patterson asked from the front entrance. Twenty-two years of dealing with the dead, and she was still on her game.

The sisters ushered Sarah inside, shaking the rain from their coats. Irma, pen in hand, directed them to the guest book, unruffled as ever, even when the door blew open again and she and Alma had to wrestle it shut, heaving their bodies as one.

"A lot of dirt in the air," Irma observed.

"Not so much anymore," Vannie said, signing the registry. "I swallowed more than my share."

Alma, behind her, turned from scrutinizing the nearby showing area where Elmer stood solemn-faced, bewildered, and alone at the head of a white casket. She bent over the guest book in turn. "It would appear," she said, glancing once again toward the open casket, "that Edith never looked better in life."

Sarah looked cautiously at Edith's still face in the casket, her head resting on a flat white pillow. After a quick shiver, she decided that the dead woman was not so frightening as she had expected. "She does look nice," she said shyly.

"For one thing," Irma said, directing a venomous glance at Elmer, "she's got a decent hairstyle on her for once." Her frown deepened as she continued to stare at the new widower, who looked more lost every moment.

"What were you saying about hairstyle?" Alma murmured, diverting Irma's gaze.

"What? Oh, I called Ruby Morgan and asked her to do Edith. Being from Willow Creek, I figured it only fair to give her the business. Besides, she's the best there is, though she's always hated working on corpses, says it makes her wake up screaming. Still, as I told her, she simply had to make an exception in Edith's case. Her fool of a husband wasn't going to fix her hair, not after murdering her in cold blood. You know, Sisters, that idiot over there has cut his wife's hair every month since they've been married. Thirty-two years of looking like a shorn sheep, can you imagine? I said to her many times, 'Edith, if that man had a hoop handy, you'd jump through it twirling a baton.' If *I* was married to Elmer, I'd have slipped a bad mushroom into his soup a week after the ceremony."

"He looks very alone today," Vannie murmured, noticing his ravaged countenance.

"After what he did with those pills, he deserves what he's getting. You should hear Charley Muggins talk about it. He tried to warn him, but of course the fool wouldn't listen. It's his own fault he's alone."

"Murderers belong alone," Carolyn Houseman said, coming up alongside the sisters. "When I came in, I just looked at him with my hands on these big hips and said, 'Satisfied with yourself now, Elmer Bailey? Now that you've put your wife into her grave? At least, she won't have to listen to you ordering her around inside the pearly gates, because that's one place you won't never go to and that's a fact. You can mark that down in your book on life.' You think that was clear enough?"

"Well," Vannie said, "you could have put the handcuffs on him. Otherwise, I'd say you went about as far as you could go."

"He hasn't budged," Alma said in a low tone. "He doesn't know what in creation's happening to him."

Belle Taylor came up, gave each sister a hug, and smiled distractedly at Sarah. "Poor Edith. I can't help feeling that we're all guilty, Sisters, and that's a fact."

"But what could we have done?" Carolyn put in, frowning at the moaning from outside, a creation of wind against earth and mortuary that caused Sarah to clutch at Alma's sleeve.

"Tied and gagged him every once and awhile," Martha Burden said, drying her tears on the black shawl she'd worn to every funeral and viewing for the last ten years, "just to give Edith some time off." As poor as she was, newly widowed and mortgaged to the hilt from her husband's medical bills, she still found it in her to enjoy a funeral. But this one afforded her no pleasure.

"Once I went to return a pie plate from the church bake sale," Martha went on, "and I saw her through the window before I rang, all alone and staring at the wall with the most peculiar look on her face. When she opened the door, I could see she was upset, but she didn't explain and I . . . well, I couldn't just nose in, could I? Of course, it was his doing. Poor thing, her house was a prison. Oh, hell's bells, I'm so mad I could spit. Know-it-alls like that should have their tongues surgically removed."

"Don't need no surgeon," Donnie Marble put in, shoving himself away from the wall by the door, where he was lounging and chewing a discreet wad of tobacco. He was in his church suit, his hands almost clean of mechanic's grease. "All we'd need is a good pair of pliers." There was a silence as the truth registered that it was too late for any measures, no matter how drastic.

Into this hush came Nadine Curtis. As Nadine stopped at the door, uncertain whether or not to sign the registry, Sarah ran to her with a little cry. Of course, Nadine's hesitation was understandable to every person in the mortuary. She wouldn't feel significant enough to put her name in the book. Yet, when Sarah gently inserted the pen into her mama's hand, Nadine bent and signed, her other hand clutching the collar of her threadbare, black coat, holding it close to her throat. It was another gesture understood by all. Nadine didn't want anyone to see whatever mismatched rags were under that coat. Laying down the pen, she put her arm around Sarah. She lived for her children. For them, she could smile. Everything else about Nadine was as skittish as a colt, nervous as a wallflower at a school dance.

"Is there any sympathy at all for Elmer?" Alma said into the frigid atmosphere that belied the over-pouring of wreaths and floral arrangements that filled the showing area. Willow Creek residents had been generous to Edith in death, wishing they had paid more attention to her in life. In truth, they had avoided her, for she was almost always on the arm of her husband. And to hang around Elmer was so depressing, with him instructing you on how to do everything from paying your taxes to laying your kitchen floor linoleum, that one tended to stay away.

Nadine braved a fleeting glance at Edith from across the room, hugged Sarah, whispered something in her ear, then slipped furtively back toward the door. To try to blend with the town as though she were one of them was asking too much. No one tried to stop her as she ducked her head into the wind and disappeared, fighting the door closed behind her.

"Lovely that she came," Alma said, knitting her brow and looking to Vannie for confirmation. Yes, she could tell her sister felt it, too. Cleatis was at it again. In such a short time. But with the crestfallen child walking toward them, chin tucked down, they had to let it go for another time. Later, they would take a better look at what was coming down the pike with Cleatis. It was already brewing, building steam, finding its direction.

"Well," Alma said, slipping her arm into Vannie's and taking Sarah by the hand, "let's go pay our respects. Come along, Sarah, we must let Edith know we're thinking of her."

Elmer was still frozen to the spot. One hand was on the casket, not far from Edith's head, the other was in mid-air as if getting ready to assert a point. But today, there was no point to assert. For once, Elmer Bailey was speechless.

The sisters smiled at him. Theirs were probably the first pleasant expressions he'd seen since Edith woke up suddenly two nights ago, touched his shoulder with a smile, and said, "Darling, did you say something? No? I was sure I heard a voice . . ."

"You must learn not to imagine things, Edith. It shows a weak mind to dream things so vividly they become real."

Minutes later, she was dead. No, surely, all that had been a dream. A dream that had begun with the wind. A tornado. A figment of horrible imagination. It couldn't be real, any of it. He was sure it had all happened inside his head. It was impossible that it could be anything else except a nightmare. It was impossible; yet, here he stood beside his wife's casket, jaw agape.

Vannie touched his hand, the one that was suspended in mid-air. "Elmer?"

He blinked. His lips moved. "Wouldn't you know," he said hoarsely, his eyes darting from one sister to the other, even casting a quick look at the child, "that the first damned pill I eliminated would have been her epileptic medicine?"

"Such a pity," Alma murmured.

"Isn't it?" Vannie patted Elmer's arm.

Sarah began to weep, tears slipping down her face, her sorrow blending into Elmer's in perfect harmony. Together, they were performing a duet of sadness.

"Sisters," Elmer said, sounding bewildered, "Edith went to heaven without me. She's never gone anywhere without me before. Not even to Louisville."

"All the way to heaven," Alma said, keeping her eyes downcast.

"You won't be there to describe it for her or explain it to her," Vannie said. "Every light beam. Every flutter of an angel's wing. Every profound thought that the vision of heaven inspires."

"It's a fact, Elmer," Alma said, seeing that Sarah had emerged from her introspection and was listening. "Edith will have to see it all with her own eyes."

Elmer's gaze went dreamy. "I wonder if she'll be able to appreciate it. Well, I shall reach her in meditation, Sisters. I shall do my best."

"Oh, I think not," Vannie said. "Poor Elmer, I expect you'll be distracted. You'll have problems now, you know."

"It will be difficult for me," he admitted mournfully. "I never thought of how life would be without Edith. She never said much; still, she was great company, somehow. I've felt the most crushing sadness since she left me, Sisters. This loss is the most terrible weight my soul has ever felt. I have no idea how I can bear it."

"Poor Mr. Bailey," Sarah whispered.

"It will be even worse in prison," Alma said.

His mouth fell open. "What? *Prison?*"

Vannie leaned closer. "That's what they're saying."

"What . . . *who's* saying?" His Adam's apple bobbled painfully above his white collar. "Prison? Why?" Fear laced with grief.

"Murder," Alma said confidentially. "They're saying you wanted Edith's insurance money."

He gawked at them, beyond replying.

"Look at them all staring at you." Vannie nodded discreetly around the room. There wasn't an ounce of good fellowship to be found in the entire mortuary. "They're determined to get you, Elmer. Look over there at Donnie Marble."

Elmer glanced in the direction she indicated and saw the mechanic's face glowering back at him. Standing next to him was the druggist, Charley Muggins, looking even more hostile.

"Nobody is angrier than Charley," Alma murmured. "He's the one who's leading the whole movement."

"What's his problem?" Elmer wondered. "Probably upset over losing all those pill orders. When I think about it, I've been keeping the damned man in business for years."

Neither sister offered an opposing opinion, and the child simply stood there, tears still in her eyes. For some reason, her tears went straight to his heart. At last his eyes fell. Absently, he patted the white casket and muttered, "What am I going to do? I've lost Edith and everybody else along with her, I guess. You know something? I never realized until now that I needed a soul. Isn't that strange? I used to think that if the whole world were empty, I wouldn't mind much. I'd have that much more time to sit and think my own thoughts. Now my mind . . . it seems blank. All I can feel is this terrible weight of sadness, Sisters. I don't know how I can bear it."

Elmer Bailey lowered his head. An instant later, he felt compelled to raise it and to meet the sisters' eyes. Their eyes. He shuddered as he looked into each pair of them in turn, first the golden amber mist in Alma's gaze and then the shimmering violet glow in Vannie's. In them he saw Edith's face, the smile fallen from her lips and her head thrown back as she went into the seizure. Caught in the overwhelming memory of the way she had thrown her body about, helpless to control herself, the sounds she'd made, then the knowledge that she had swallowed her tongue, Elmer shut his eyes and buried his face in his hands. "Oh, God, I'm not asking to understand this, just grant me the strength to bear it."

"It's the other way around, Elmer," Alma said. "You won't find your strength without understanding. The question is: Are you *willing* to understand?"

Fear descended on Elmer's soul. He who had considered himself enlightened had never expected to be afraid of knowledge. Yet, he knew in this instance that to understand meant to face his own imperfection.

"Elmer?"

"Yes," he wept. "Yes. I'm willing."

Hands touched his face. A finger pressed gently at first, then harder. It bored into the area above and between his eyes, the area he had always heard referred to as "the third eye." He didn't believe in it. Never had. Yet suddenly, Elmer Bailey's third eye opened. With mouth agape, horror written in deep lines across his face, Elmer saw himself for the first time as others had seen him for so long. The expert. The one in charge. The one above all others. The braggart. He realized by Sarah's gasp that she, too, had seen the picture inside his head. Seen him for the colossal idiot that he was. That he had always been.

A clown, Elmer thought, blinded by the light that flooded his interior. *The know-it-all. The gardener who charged too much. The son of a laborer. A fool. I've been a fool.*

The finger released its pressure and withdrew. All was so silent that Elmer could hear his heart thud like that of a trapped rabbit's. Such darkness descended on his soul that he could not rouse himself for what seemed hours, but could only have been moments. Still, when at last he raised his eyes, the sisters and the child with them were gone from the mortuary, along with the rest of the townspeople. Only Roger Patterson stood by the open door, looking distinguished in his dark suit, his affable expression aimed at a late departing guest.

And so, Elmer Bailey had finally reached his one-time aspiration. He felt completely alone on Earth. Except for the sisters.

Thinking of them, he found himself absently reaching into the pocket of his suit coat, and as he did, his fingers touched something strangely unfamiliar. Something he did not recognize at all. It felt like . . . what? Pulling it from his pocket, he saw it was the paper bag the sisters had given him at the café. The donut bag. What would that be doing in the pocket of his good suit? And where was the donut that had been inside? The bag was flat now, and a circular greasy spot marred its surface.

Elmer was appalled at having this filthy piece of garbage in his hands. On this of all days, he'd wanted everything clean, neat, and in order. He was here at the mortuary for the viewing of his wife, for criminy's sake. He tried to stuff the bag back into his pocket, but the smell of grease and sugar overwhelmed him. He heard the paper crackling and saw a puff of pale white smoke rising out of it as soft as a will-o'-the-wisp that twisted before his eyes. In the smoke were those two sets of the sisters' eyes. Inviting him. But where? To the café? Surely not tonight. Above him an image of the sisters hovered. He could almost make out the thoughts in their heads. Something about work to be done.

Well, I've been through enough for one day. I won't see them, he assured himself. *I've got to get my thoughts together. Try to figure out what I can do. The funeral's tomorrow. Oh, Lord, I'm going to bury Edith.* Looking at her pretty face lying on the white cushion of the casket, his eyes flooded with new tears. It was such a sweet face. So loving. So patient. *Poor Edith. All I've put her through.*

Why had he done it? How had he come up with these grandiose opinions of himself? And Edith had simply accepted. He saw now, quite clearly, that she had been undeceived. She had known the true Elmer Bailey, had accepted the worst of him. How could she? For all those years? How could she stay with him, listen to him, and never give up on him? He thought hard, but couldn't give himself any explanations why Edith had stayed with him.

In fact, for the first time, Elmer Bailey found he could not explain much of anything. Nor did he feel the need to be inspired by his thoughts of the world or by the smell of the lilacs and the roses. And the gardenias. Good God, the gardenias. He had never before realized how sickening a roomful of gardenias could be. Nothing at all inspired him. Even confronting death face-to-face had given him no new theories on life. It had only exposed him as a fool. He felt stupid. Empty. Afraid.

He tried again to push the bag into his pocket, but it would not go. He remembered the sight of Edith staring back at him through the eyes of the sisters and trembled, while he grew steadily sicker on the scent of gardenias and of stale grease and sugar.

Even Roger had stepped from the room now, leaving him totally alone. Yet, Elmer stood his ground, stiff as a statue, feeling that to move might be to shatter his heart that was cracked to the core.

Again, he fumbled with the greasy bag. Again, it resisted his efforts to push it down into his pocket.

Frustrated, he grabbed it with both hands and with a surge of white-hot anger rising from his feet, he used the force of his rage to rip it wide open and tear it to shreds. The ripping felt good. It felt wonderful to destroy something. He shredded it again, his fingers getting sticky with sugar and his heart pounding. With all of his being, he fought to vent his anguish.

He was so busy ripping and wrestling with the bag that he hardly noticed the streaming white vapors spilling from it as it tore. Twills of white mists, translucent as the glaze on Vannie's pastries, sheer as the white heat of Elmer's rage, poured out, more with every shredding tear. He was but dimly aware of what was taking place in the face of his frantic efforts. Only from a corner of his mind did he notice the pearly haze collecting in the room all around him.

It was the sound that made him stop and look up at the spectacle overtaking the mortuary. All the colors of the rainbow glittered in the sparkling white of the shimmering mists. A roar went through the room as the mist began to move, transforming into a river of light, a sparkling flow of rainbows both bright and pale. The river squealed and flashed, rounding to take the shape of an electric eel. Glistening, twining. Alive! It slithered through the rows of chairs and up to the ceiling and down around Edith's coffin to a spot in front of Elmer, where it suddenly turned on itself and coiled to bite its own tail. There came a screaming moan as the primordial vortex began to spin, as if switched on by an unseen hydraulic mechanism.

"Holy Toledo." Elmer stood absolutely still, his voice almost calm. Somehow he knew that this donut shape before him stood for more than a breakfast treat or even a life preserver. Something in the oldest part of his brain sat up and blinked. "Uh oh."

He felt his feet slipping out from under him as the vortex picked up speed. He was being pulled, sucked, toward that gaping hole of fragmented light. He tried to hold onto Edith's casket as his feet slid toward the opening in the spinning hole. Flower petals and stems, whole wreaths and arrangements were going in now. His fingernails dug into the wood of the casket but could not hold on.

A last thought passed through Elmer's mind before he was sucked into white and then into blackness. He didn't have to worry about the storm anymore. The eye of the tornado had come for him. He gladly went into it and into the vapors beyond, thinking he was following in Edith's shoes.

"Breathe deeply," a voice said.

Sister Alma's voice, he thought. *I'm dreaming of Sister Alma.*

"Oh, but dreams are every bit as real as what you've always considered reality, Elmer. Relax now and let yourself dream a new life."

Weeping, he said, "I don't want a new life. I want my old life with Edith."

"Oh, well, there's no sense in going backward, is there? How about a step forward? Are you willing to give up teaching the entire human race? Before you answer, here's how you sound to your friends and neighbors. It's how you sounded to Edith, too."

He heard it now. Humming, like when the tornadoes were outside the café while he sat there eating jelly donuts. It grew louder. And louder.

It was like all the bees in the world were flying into his ears.

Stop, he thought wildly. *It must stop. I can't bear it. The sound . . . I'll go mad. I can't stand it, I tell you!!!*

"Are you willing to give that up?" Alma asked. "Are you?"

As the humming grew still louder, until there was no other sound but the droning of the bees, he started screaming, "I'm willing! Anything! Just make it stop!"

Silence. Blessed silence.

Blinking, he saw that a film of white now swirled around him, quiet as it was new and virginal. It reminded him of the clouds outside the airplane window.

"Wait." He was aware that something was about to happen. "First tell me one thing. Why did Edith stay with me all those years? Why didn't she just give up on me?"

"Because," Alma said, "she saw the real you. The wonderful real you that you didn't trust enough to see for yourself. She saw it for you."

Then he was falling.

"Elmer, in the bag," Alma said. "They're there."

"What's there?"

"What you need. It's April 1, Elmer. April Fool's Day, remember? Don't forget to look in the bag."

Still falling, he was stunned to feel himself land on something soft and cushy. For a moment, he had no idea where he was. Then he realized he was lying in his own bed and that the donut bag was lying on his chest. He put a shaking hand on it, and smelled the sugary, oily aroma that wafted up at him. His head swam as he stared at the bag, then he pulled himself to a sitting position against the headboard. He must look inside.

PABLO
FERRO

Fumbling in the bag, his fingers closed over a small vial. He gripped it, not understanding, then drew it out and examined it. A bottle of pills? He looked closer. Edith's pills. The ones he didn't buy the other morning.

No, wait. *This* morning. Sister Alma had said it was April 1. *April 1.* And the time . . . His hand shook as he fumbled for the bedside clock. Ten o'clock. More than an hour before Edith had died.

Edith . . .

He looked to his left and saw her lying beside him. His heart jumped, and then settled in his chest. *Wait,* he thought. *Don't do anything yet. It has to be right. I have to be a new man.*

Finally, almost timidly, he reached out and touched his wife's shoulder.

She sat up quickly, as she always did when he beckoned her. Even when she was sleeping soundly. And she smiled the same smile. So gentle, so full of love. "Yes, darling?"

"Edith, dear," he said, trying not to weep for joy. "I forgot to give you one of your pills. May I get you a glass of water?"

The sisters drifted through their house in their long robes, their feet bare on the smooth boards. They were too happy to sleep, wanting time to absorb Elmer's joy. Edith's, too. They wished Sarah were with them, but knew that she had dreamed of Elmer and Edith's happiness from her own bed.

"Lovely," Alma murmured. "Just lovely." She opened the front door and stared at the sky as Vannie came to join her and enjoy the clear night air. A breeze moved through their budding trees, whispered through the grass and the shrubs.

These sisters had traveled together for a long time, and even outside of it. But there was no time so good as the present.

"Right now," Vannie said in deep contentment, still thinking of Elmer, "I'd say this one might be my favorite."

"Mine, too," Alma said. "But you know how it is. Nearest to hand, nearest to heart. Though there's room in the heart for all."

"Isn't that the truth!"

They turned silent, staring up at the sky. The stars shone brightly.

The amber light in Alma's eyes clouded, turning them to the color of dark smoke. She was remembering the look on Nadine's face at the funeral parlor. "After all, Sister, none of this was Cleatis's idea . . ." she began.

"Yes," Vannie admitted. "We did intervene, and with a very immature soul, to boot."

"No doubt we're in for it, Sister. Every action provokes an equal and opposite reaction, don't you know?"

"Quite so. And we injected a lot of light into that man. We're gonna get a full-on negative blowback."

No use denying what they both feared. In those prepared for a step forward, resistance to change could be handled. But deeply negative personalities could be insulted by sudden light. Initial feelings of relief and hope were often replaced by shame and rage, overwhelming the one who, for a moment, had tasted freedom and sensed the dream.

The full force of his hatred would fall on whoever had shone the light. Vannie and Alma were not worried for themselves. But if the volcano in Cleatis were to erupt, Sarah would be squarely in its wake.

6

The white house sat quietly on the hill across from the café, its windows finally dark. Stars as hard as diamonds shone cold against a black sky. Creamy light that had only moments before filtered through the lacy curtains and spilled across the wooden floors in the house was gone now that the moon had set.

Inside, the two sisters slept, riding their dreams into canyons deeper than memory.

Vannie, happy and in no mood to dream of anything troublesome, made pies in her sleep—cherry, apple, blueberry, chocolate, peach, and rhubarb. They bubbled in ovens and covered countertops and piled up on bakers' racks, their sweetness finally lulling her into a dreamless rest.

For Alma, it was a different story. Her first dreams had been light, a continuation of the celebration for Elmer and Edith. Vannie and she, nightgowns on, were dancing in the moonlight. But in no time, things turned strange. The light grayed around them and exploded in a gust of wind that blew their nightgowns off over their heads.

Alma found Vannie and herself dressed up again and back in the Buick with Sarah, the three of them arriving at Patterson's for Edith's visitation.

Once again, they got out of the car, helped Sarah tie her scarf in a double knot, and held her hands as they fought the wind up the pathway.

Vannie's mouth was moving, and a deep voice could be heard saying:

"Acknowledge the elements, Sarah."

And then it happened. The worst of nightmares.

The child again pulled her hands away from theirs and began to be whooshed away by the tornado winds. They reached wildly for her coattail like before. Surely, they'd catch her.

But this time they didn't.

The end of her coat slipped through Alma's fingers, leaving her holding a tiny thread that she clutched between thumb and forefinger. One thread. Alma fought to hang on as the coat unraveled, the child blowing away from them down the path and then skyward.

"Pull the string, Alma! Don't let it slack!" Vannie grabbed onto the length of thread beyond Alma's grasp, clucking her tongue all the time like a series of corks popping out of bottles. "Honestly, Sister. You'd think you'd never flown a kite!"

With that, Alma grabbed back at the string and the two sisters wrestled back and forth with shouts of *"give it to me!"* and *"you let go!"* and *"I've got it, move back!"* and *"get away!"*

They were starting to feel it in their arms and legs when Vannie's eyes rolled skyward. *"Look! Look!"*

Sarah had caught the top winds and was in full flight now, coat spread wide, arms and legs stretched open. The wind had flattened her like a pancake.

"Keep that string tight!" Vannie yelled, grabbing for it again. *"We've got to reel her in!"*

This time, Alma let her help. Together, they began expertly wrapping the string around Alma's elbow as if it were a spool.

Sarah danced on the string in response to their tugs. She dived and recovered, bobbed in rhythm to Vanessa's windings.

"She does make a fine kite," Alma sighed. But then, she noticed that the more they yanked on the string, the harder the gale blew against them. It screamed and moaned in ferocious blasts.

"Help me, Miss Alma! Help! Miss Vannie! What should I do? What

should I do?"

Sarah's cries streamed through Alma's ears, twisting through her body in a whirlwind. In them, she could feel every blow Cleatis had ever struck Nadine or Sarah or any of the other children.

What should I do?

Something whispered to her: *This is not a dream.* "Hold on child! We've got you!"

But they didn't. The string slipped off Alma's elbow, and she couldn't catch it with her other hand. Vannie leapt forward and caught the last of it just as it soared skyward. For a moment, it looked as if there were a chance. Then the worst that could have happened did.

Lightning. Bolts of it crashed loudly around Sarah, one electrical crack after another. The third one was a direct hit, a jagged light that went off like a giant firecracker, blasting the darling child out of the heavens. Bits of cloth from Sarah's coat fell in burning rags. Alma watched the string fall limply from the sky. Despair took her to the ground. Lying there, she stared at the sky and saw that the wind was dying. Most of the flaming cloth had turned to ash. It drifted down in scattered showers of black dust. Of the remaining flames, two did not fall, but stayed fixed, two fiery eyes, holding their own in the sky with singular determination.

In spite of her pain, Alma could not look away from those eyes. Something about them, so familiar. *Oh no! No.* She wept again. Then dived into unconsciousness, hoping to end the dream.

To drown it in oblivion.

7

Notes from the quarterly meeting of the Willow Creek Town Council, held on Tuesday night at 7:15 p.m., at The Two Sisters' Café, Mayor Will Winburn presiding. Secretary: Carolyn Houseman

Well, I've told everybody they chose the wrong secretary for the Town Council as I don't know shorthand and my typing is bad to worse. Me being a secretary is as funny as me trying to get a job modeling bathing suits. Well, not quite. When I was a girl, I did learn to hunt and peck on my daddy's old Sholes & Glidden machine, a pretty thing with clusters of bright blue and red flowers painted over it. In those days my fingers were skinny enough not to get stuck between the keys and didn't have the arthritis.

But no man would take the job, and most of the women said they had to cook for their families before meetings. With my children grown and Ben agreeable to heating up his own supper, I said I'd take it on. Alma and Vannie told me not to worry, just to jot down what seemed important. I said, "In this town, one wart on your bottom could be the most important thing that happened to you all week."

"Carolyn," Vannie said, "will you leave your anatomy out of this?"

Yes ma'am. Don't get your pee to boiling. Here we go.

First off, I want to report that since last quarter the sisters have taken on a new helper at the café, little Sarah Curtis, daughter of the moonshiner, that no-good piece of rubbish, Cleatis. I guess I shouldn't have put that part in. But I feel like spitting into that man's eye every time I think about that poor hungry brood of his, and Nadine too proud to take charity. Anyway, the child is so shy she hardly says a word, but then that's a good thing in a waitress, I've always thought.

"You sit at the table with me so I can see you're marking things down right," the Mayor said.

"I'll sit at the second table with Ben," I said. "Having you looking over my shoulder would drive me batty. I'll type you up a copy, and you can put it in the record."

"Well, just . . . er . . . try to keep it appropriate," he said.

The Mayor and his wife Mildred have a table up front with the Reverend and Grace Harmon and Abner and Louise Algar. Once, Abner decided to be a professional boxer and the whole town showed up to watch his first match. He'd mail-ordered his boxer pants at two hundred pounds, trained down to one-eighty, and had to sew in the waist to make his pants stay up. One clean jab to his waistband, and Abner had to punch with one hand and hold his pants up with the other. He's back to raising tobacco now.

Off the bat came Trip Robinson and Leon Malone, neighbors for ten years and yelling about crabgrass that one or the other of them dug up in the pasture and used to fill in patchy spots in his lawn. Now the stuff is all over the place, and each of them blaming the other.

"What we need," Trip said, glaring at Leon, "is a fence between our properties, for good and all, to keep this idiot's mistakes in his own yard."

"And it better be a damn tall one," Leon added. "This fool is liable to haul in poison oak for his next landscaping idea."

"So build one," Mr. Mayor said. "What's the problem?"

"We had the county surveyor out. If we was to build a fence, here's what it would look like."

Up they came to the front, each one battling to control the orange stick at the bottom of a placard showing their property line. That line could make a body seasick. Here's what it looked like:

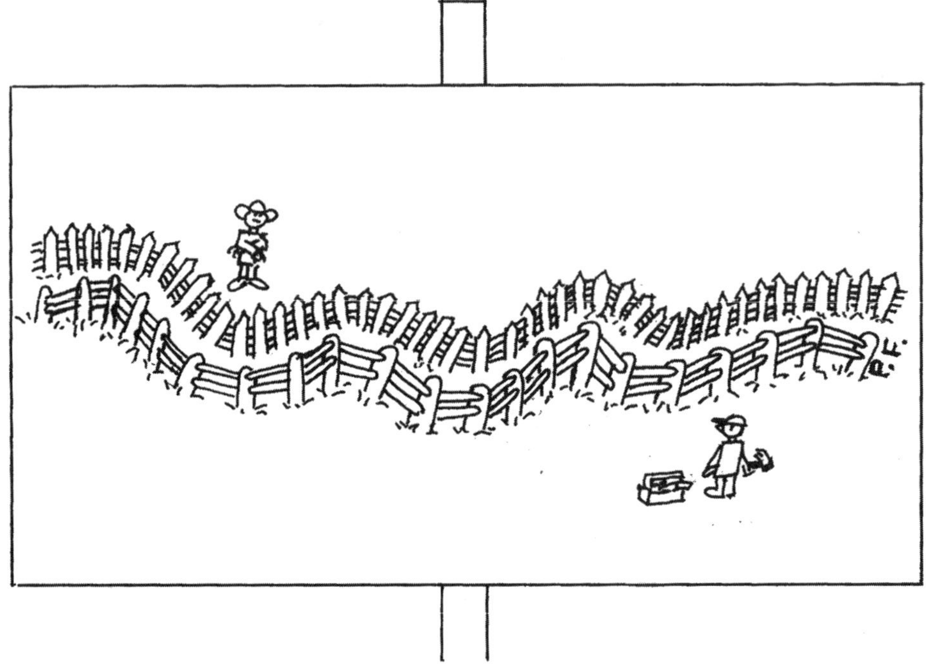

“So. what are you aiming to do about it?” Trip growled to the Mayor.

“I’m gonna fire the county surveyor, you dang fool, for wasting council time!” Mayor Winburn said. “No wonder he didn’t show his damn face tonight. He’s home laughing his butt off thinking about you two jackasses standing here holding that board he drew. Figure it out yourselves. Next!”

Helen Blackerby, owner of the auction house at the south end of town by the drive-in movie, stood up. She didn’t get paid again. I have yet to go to a town meeting where Helen didn’t get up and say somebody didn’t pay her for something or the other. Half the time, it’s the same person that didn’t pay her last time. It was all Ben could do to hold me in my seat and stop me from yelling, “How come you keep dealing with the same deadbeats?” Speaking of deadbeats. About the only thing Helen pays regular is auction house consignment money because if she didn’t pay that, she’d go to jail. Helen in jail would be funnier than onions in

Jello, her with her airs. She can't sit in any car except her old Cadillac because nothing else is soft enough for that behind of hers, much less any chair or bed to be found in a jail. Story goes that the last time she took her list to the bill collector, he handed her back a stack of bills thicker than a horse's neck. "Here," he said, "you just saved me a trip."

"Can you believe it?" she grouched. "Somebody even took two Cokes out of my cooler and didn't pay me for them."

The Mayor dug in his pocket and handed over two dimes. "I can't do a thing about what anybody else owes you, but I'm the deadbeat who took the Cokes." He banged his gavel. "Next!"

Andy Poole hurried in from the gas station, banging the screen door between the station and the café and galloping up the steps to the upper dining room. He had a bone to pick with the whole town. It was a matter of moral *lassitude,* he said, with not a blameless one among us.

"Good God," the Mayor said. "Moral lassitude, is it?"

Since Andy became a deacon and started spending time with the Reverend, all kinds of strange things come out of his mouth. What he meant was, he wanted everybody to stop going to Donnie Marble's mechanics shop. "I opened up first," he declared, "and if it wasn't for me, you'd all go without gas. But the minute somebody needs a carburetor adjusted, off they run to Donnie. Can somebody explain that?"

Trip Robinson jumped up, still mad about his property line fiasco, and said, "Because you wouldn't know a carburetor from a horse's ass! Besides, Donnie lets his customers come to his dove shoots. And he can tell a hell of a joke. You couldn't remember a punch line if somebody painted it on your station wall!"

"You're trying to say I can't tell a joke?" Andy screeched. "Those stupid dove shoots are the joke! All you sharpshooters with your shotguns standing out there on a baited field, peppering at a flock so thick you can't see the sun shine through it! He's luring you same as he lured those birds. It's moral lassitude, I tell you, and it ought to be illegal!"

The Mayor banged his gavel. "Take a seat, Andy! If a man can gas up where he wants, he can choose whoever he likes to fiddle with his carburetor. Next!"

Burris McCarthy stood up and wanted something done about the disturbances in the Baptist cemetery. "Maybe if we had a deputy on duty a man could have a peaceful visit with his wife."

"Exactly what kind of disturbances are we talking about?" Sheriff Jimmy asked. As usual he was in the back booth. That man loves the fire.

"You know good and well what I mean! There's ghosts and the like all over the place the minute the sun goes down! Nobody stays put in their rightful resting places. If this keeps up, even Mattie's liable to get stirred up and come shooting out of the ground."

"You wouldn't be afraid of your own wife, would you, Burris?" my Ben wanted to know, grinning at me like he'd let me spook him anytime, if I should go into the grave before him.

"I wouldn't like her jumping out at me!" Burris snapped with a red face amid all the guffaws. "Y'all can snicker all you want—I tell you strange happenings are going on out there!"

"Put up one of them 'Wanted, Dead or Alive' posters with Mattie's picture on it, Sheriff!" Leon hollered. "She'll be glad to hear it was her husband who sicced the law on her."

"Oh, to hell with all of you," Burris bellowed. "Just forget the whole thing."

Next up was Naylene Ashburn, the Reverend's oldest daughter, who runs a florist shop out the back of her house. She wanted to supply the flowers for the Oldham County Fair over in LaGrange. "It just isn't fair," she whined. "The same two LaGrange florists supply every bloom year after year. Why, the Miss Oldham County Pageant alone uses more flowers than ten funerals, what with the bouquets and the escorts' carnations and the decorations on the award platform and along the parade walk. Why shouldn't they buy some of those from me?"

"Uh, Naylene, honey," the Mayor hesitated. "We don't live in Oldham County, remember? We're in Henry County."

"We spend just as much money at that fair as anybody in LaGrange!"

"That may be, but—"

"I want to sell my flowers!"

"Come on, Naylene," the Mayor groaned. "Would you think it was fair if the LaGrange flower shops decorated for a Miss Henry County contest?"

"We don't *have* a Miss Henry County contest!" Naylene wailed.

"Well, honey, if we ever get one, you can decorate for it."

Naylene will have to find another use for those three-day-old blooms she buys half-wilted in Louisville.

We waded on. The Mayor tabled road repairs and a handrail over the railroad bridge. Then Donnie Marble passed around a hat to collect funds to save Martha Burden's house after she mortgaged it to save Ed's life. Of course, he died the minute the last penny was spent. The hospitals have it rigged that way, just like if you sue somebody, the amount just barely covers your lawyers' fees. We raised a whopping seven dollars. Maybe Martha can keep her front door.

All this time the Sisters and Sarah had been coming up and down the steps, filling a big table with pies, cobblers, cakes, tarts, and cookies of all description, all proceeds to go to Martha. Maybe she'll also be able to keep a window or two.

The Mayor had his eye on hot apple pie and raised his gavel all ready to slam it down when the Reverend stood up, Bible in hand. "Er . . . Reverend . . . I suppose you want to . . . that is, will you consent to leading us in the closing blessing?" the Mayor finished reluctantly, knowing the customary lengths of our religious leader's prayers. That man is full of wisdom and light, but bless his heart there are times he can bore the ears off a sugar bowl.

The Reverend beamed. "Well, thank you, Mr. Mayor, I'd be honored! But first, I have a matter to put before the Council."

Sitting across the table between Ben and Will Yeager, Donnie Marble groaned. "Lord, I humbly pray that you will stricken our preacher with what we creatures here on Earth refer to as 'the laryngitis.' Amen."

"Amen," everybody in our area repeated except for Vonnie Yeager who sat on my other side. "Don't you start up, Donnie Marble," she said nervously, remembering the Sunday Donnie got her so tickled that she accidentally dropped a quarter in the communion cup.

The Reverend removed papers from his Bible. "Dearly beloved," he began importantly, then stopped, red crawling up his neck as it occurred to him that nobody at the Council meeting was getting married. He took a closer look at the top paper in his hand, then stuck the sheets back in the Bible and took out more, rifling through the new pages in a satisfied way.

"He's got at least forty-five minutes worth there," Donnie hissed. He claims to have won over three hundred dollars predicting the length of the Rev's sermons, and another two hundred predicting how many of the already-saved would line up at the Baptismal font on a given Sunday looking for a little extra added insurance.

" . . . not the occasional good deed or mission contribution that will be remembered," the Rev was saying. "No, it's our everyday lives that will be judged in the end. Those precious moments we've squandered when we should have used them for God's work, the little sins that mound up like Mt. Jehoshaphat."

"*Valley* of Jehoshaphat," Donnie quietly said, making a little mark on his napkin. He always keeps track of the Rev's mistakes. "It's the Valley of Jehoshaphat leading to *Mt.* Olive. I'm guessing twelve slip-ups before his backside hits the chair. Anybody want to bet a dollar on less or more?"

Ben edged his bill out with his thumb up, meaning he was betting on more, then passed it over to Donnie. Will passed over a dollar, too, but he didn't have a thumb, having lost it to his bush hog, so he leaned over and whispered, "Less. Surely to heaven he won't talk long enough to mess up twelve times."

Trip Robinson, from the table behind, punched me in the back and passed over a dollar, hissing, "Less," and Claire Baker, who likes to bet so well that talk says she married a man she didn't like, all because she lost a wager with his sister on how many double yolks she could get out of her best laying hen in one week, passed over a dollar from Trip's table, too, hoping the preacher could hold his flubs to under twelve. Pretty soon, Donnie was collecting from all sides, most guessing the Rev would wind it down before he got to twelve screw-ups.

I was ready to make Ben put his money back in his pocket, but we can always use an extra dollar, and when our preacher gets on his feet he's been known to go on so long the organist has more than once resorted to jumping the gun on the Doxology. Even the Reverend can't prevail over two hundred voices all belting, "Praise God from whom all blessings flow" (and praise Esther Malone for her heavy foot on the pump).

"I get a point under and over for a tie," Donnie whispered, putting a saltshaker on the piled-up dollars. The heads all nodded.

" . . . think we will agree, one and all, that The Two Sisters' Café, here, is the heart of our town," the Rev was saying.

I noticed that the sisters had quit carrying trays up and down and were lounging on the steps with young Sarah. They all seemed real interested.

"Therefore, like any gathering place," the Rev droned, "this café needs rules of access."

My Ben leaned forward and pointed at the napkin. "He meant accord," he whispered, pleased to see that Donnie was already making the mark.

"That is . . . er . . . ordinances, you know," the Rev continued frowning, feeling a bit unsure of his own words. When he gets this rattled, he's been known to spill a cup of grape juice on one of the faithful.

"Yes, very good," the Mayor said, with another longing look at the big apple pie that seemed to be dividing itself into slices if my eyes were serving me right.

Wondering if I was the only one seeing things, I looked at the sisters who were concentrating on the Reverend. Sarah, between them, looked excited. Only the parrot, sitting grumpily on his perch, had a bad attitude. A croak was rattling around in his throat, as if the old bird was cussing to himself.

"First off, we must all be concerned about the amount of imbibing going on in the shadowy nicks and crannies of these very premises," the Rev continued.

"Nooks!" Trip hissed.

"Right-o." Donnie marked it down.

"Specifically, I am referring to brown bags."

"Amen," said a loud chorus of voices from the strictest Bible thumpers. Most of the hard-line Baptists, their richest and most prominent members being John and Emma Prewitt, of Prewitt's Feed and Fertilizer, were sitting in booths down the left side of the room, forming a core of theology experts bent on abolishing alcohol, cursing, gambling, and every other form of entertainment that mankind has found to amuse itself with. That bunch wants hair in buns, skirts mid-calf, and blouses buttoned up past the point of fantasy. There isn't one of the lot who drinks a drop, at least not out where anybody can catch them at it.

"I want an ordinance passed," the Rev said proudly. "I suggest a fine of five dollars for every violation!"

The Prewitts led their contingency in a round of enthusiastic clapping as Sister Alma gravely made the note in her writing tablet.

"Very good, Reverend," she murmured. "Sister and I will see to it."

"And, naturally, the money goes to the missionary fund," he added, lest through some misunderstanding the fines might end up in the sisters' cash register.

"Of course."

"Thank you."

"Hear, hear!" Ozzie Miller thundered from the second left-hand booth. His fellow theologians chuckled at their most flamboyant member's loud second of the motion. He's their proof that they're as witty and daring as anybody else, and they love it when he gets a little outrageous, once going so far as to suggest we should play "Praise the Lord and Pass the Ammunition" during collection for our overseas missions, a joke that made Emma Prewitt laugh so hard she choked and had to be slapped on the back.

Donnie went pale at the idea of fining brown bags. "I love our Rev, but the man's gonna bankrupt me," he whispered, having the keenest taste for moonshine in town.

Our preacher looked pleased at his success thus far, giving a little bow to scattered applause by several other supporters. "Thank you. Thank you. Now . . . hum . . . where was I? Ordination Number Two, correct?"

"Ordinance," Claire moaned. "Oh, shoot, I knew I should have bet over."

Donnie marked it down.

"Ah yes . . . the pinball machines," the Reverend said, warming to his point as loud dings and thuds sounded from below where younger folk were clustered around three different machines, two of them with flippers and silver balls and a third one with sawdust, a circular disc, and a miniature bowling alley. Cheers went up as somebody made a strike. "And that would include shuffleboard, as well. It's all gambling, pure and simple, playing to win free games. Somethin' for nothin'. It's addictatory!!! And it must be stopped!"

Donnie growled and marked down "addictatory."

"The machines are fine to look at. Nice decorum. Look, but don't touch, is always a good motto." The Rev looked up, hoping for a chuckle at his slightly naughty joke, but it sailed right over the Bible thumpers' heads. "After this," he continued, "there will be a one dollar fine for the use of any pinball machine. All proceeds . . ."

"To the missionary fund!" Alma briskly made a note. "Got it."

Tongue in cheek, Donnie marked down "decorum" and put a question mark by it in case a dictionary challenge was needed when the points were added up.

The Prewitt bunch was joined by at least a dozen others in a loud AMEN in support of the pinball ordinance. More than a few have problems with those noisy machines, especially since everybody's sons, daughters, and grandchildren keep begging for money to play them. There were a few sour faces, though, and a low rumble backlash. More than one adult likes to come in during lunch hour and beat the flippers. I'm one of them. And there are worst things for kids to do after school, or so it seemed to many parents who looked to be getting restless in their chairs.

The Reverend's beaming face suddenly frowned as a blast of Hank Williams singing *Jambalaya* boomed out. One of the younger set must have snuck up and turned on the jukebox. So much neon poured through its musical veins that the box looked to be belching fire.

> "GOODBYE JOE, ME GOTTA GO, ME OH, MY OH
> ME GOTTA GO POLE THE PIROGUE DOWN THE BAYOU
> MY YVONNE, THE SWEETEST ONE, ME OH, MY OH
> SON OF A GUN, WE'LL HAVE BIG FUN ON THE BAYOU!"

Through a flashing red, green, and purple haze, I saw kids dancing on the bottom level, skirts twirling, jumping, kicking off their shoes. For two cents, I'd've drug Ben down there and showed that young set a few moves.

> "JAMBALAYA AND A-CRAWFISH PIE AND A-FILLET GUMBO
> 'CAUSE TONIGHT I'M GONNA SEE MACHEZ AMIO
> PICK GUITAR, FILL FRUIT JAR AND BE GAY-OH
> SON OF A GUN, WE'LL HAVE BIG FUN ON THE BAYOU!"

The Reverend's mouth opened, but before he could get the words out the jukebox stopped playing, the kids stopped dancing, and the café stood still.

"That . . . that's a form of cussing," the Reverend said faintly into the silence.

"I'm sorry?" Sister Vannie said with concern.

"That son of a gun stuff . . . " He looked shaky. "You and I both know it's usually son of a something else. They're just cutting around the edges." Sweat dripped down his forehead. He mopped it off with his pocket handkerchief, his eyes riveted to the bottom level of the café, where just seconds before Lettie Radcliffe had twirled so hard her skirt had come within an inch of showing her unmentionables. "There will be no more dancing, no more of that kind of music, no more jukebox *period.* If you don't think I'm right on this, consult the scriptures. There are both old and new testicular prohibitions of dirty dancing, and I say we do away with it at the café!"

"Oh, God," Donnie groaned, slashing a mark onto the napkin, and disappearing under the table where he could laugh in peace.

"All public dancing will be fined at the rate of five dollars a dance! Do you have that marked, Sisters?"

Sister Vannie looked up from where she sat poring over her sister's notes. "Got it! Fines for everybody on the dance floor. Perhaps Sister and I should be deputized," she added, "just to keep it legal."

"And chain the jukebox! Violators pay a dollar a song!"

"Bullshit!" the parrot said, clear as a bell.

Shrieks of muffled laughter rang out, with people pressing knuckles into their mouths. Donnie was still under the table that had begun to shake after "testicular" and didn't show any signs of stopping.

The Rev's face turned into a rotten tomato as he flung his sweat-drenched handkerchief on top of his Bible and glared at the sisters. "About that parrot," he said furiously. "That bird is on my list! It must be muzzled."

Alma looked up inquiringly, as the bird suggested shrilly where the Reverend might put his muzzle.

"If somebody doesn't make him stop, I'm gonna bust a gasket," Donnie moaned from underneath the table.

"Ah, what kind of muzzle did you . . .?" Alma murmured.

"Some kind of rag or something tied round the bird's beak," the preacher said dourly. "A . . . a kind of . . . of small mouth diaper, you know."

"Mouth diaper?" Alma repeated solemnly.

"Yes, you know, so that when dirty things come out of its mouth, then the mouth diaper would collect them all."

"Ah, good idea."

Donnie's hand came up, wavered for a few seconds over the napkin, and then retreated back under the table. Mouth diaper went officially unchallenged.

"Ten dollars," the Reverend said firmly, "for every stinky word out of that feathered foul mouth!"

Trip Robinson and Leon Malone leaned onto each other's shoulders and hooted, their quarrel forgotten. More tittering came from all sides. Fingers pointed at the napkin, but Leon called time and waved them off. He looked up with leaky eyes and asked weakly, "Pardon, Rev . . . would you be meaning F-O-U-L or F-O-W-L?"

The Rev knitted his brow, not knowing if he liked the laughing or not. It seemed to have occurred to him that more of us might be getting his jokes than usual, though it was clear he didn't know what he'd said to be funny. Then he surprised everybody by saying in a loud voice. "What's the difference? Either one will do!"

Donnie started to put down a mark on the napkin, but the less-than-twelve betters pushed his hands away. Score one for the Rev.

"He's a foul fowl!" the Rev said, warming to his own humor.

"Ten dollars it is," Alma said serenely.

"More than fair," Vannie agreed.

Sarah was giggling into her hands, exchanging crafty glances with the bird over the tops of her fingers.

The parrot, strange to say, seems to have quite a liking for the child, though generally he's an unfriendly cuss, bite your finger off soon as look at you.

"Well," the Mayor said hopefully, "am I to consider that we've finished with these crazy . . . er . . . these ordinances?"

"Not quite," the Rev said firmly.

Both the laughter and the vigorous approvals for the Reverend's fines died away, with more than a few, I was sure, wondering the same thing I was: What under the canopy was he going to come up with next?

He frowned. "We have one more important item to consider. It's about the amount of time and the *quality* of the time that people invest in coming to the café."

Everyone waited warily to hear what he had in mind. Nobody in Willow Creek takes our café for granted. Take our money, take our liquor and our music, put a mouth diaper on our parrot, but don't even talk to us about taking away our café.

"It is my job to interpretate the scriptures and direct their appliance and daily activation," the preacher said with disdain, "and it has become clear to me that the idle chatter and . . . and . . . what do you call the . . . oh, yes, the gabble and . . . and all the *conjoining* that goes on in this place is tantamount to false witness."

Donnie crept back up into his chair, made several slashes on the napkin, and then used the napkin to mop his eyes. "When does all this conjoining go on?" he whispered in a rather interested way. "I must be coming here at the wrong hours."

Almost every mouth in the place had fallen open. Except for Donnie and a few gutter rumblings coming from the parrot's cage, no one said a word. Though the Reverend's eyes confidently swept the booths of his most ardent admirers, not even the dearest of his flock smiled back. Even Emma Prewitt was glaring at him. She and her lady friends enjoy breakfast at the counter or share a table in the downstairs dining room almost every morning, along with a little harmless information about their neighbors over their biscuits, eggs, and endless cups of coffee.

"One dollar fine for every piece of gossip," the preacher decreed. "And while I'm about it, I have taken the liberty of setting limits for time spent on these premises. Where is that list? Oh, yes, here we go. Breakfast . . . twenty minutes if you must, no more. Eat and run, that's my motto, and get to work! If you've put in a good morning's work, then once a week you may take thirty minutes for lunch in the café. And fifteen minutes on any weekday for snacks, if you haven't been in for breakfast or lunch on that day. It's either/or. No cheating and having, say, both breakfast and a late snack. That won't do at all. Though we could set three-quarters of an hour for dinner, perhaps, but that includes dessert and paying the bill." He grabbed his handkerchief and mopped his perspiring face and neck.

"I seem to be feeling faint," he said apologetically. "Perhaps it's hunger. It's such a responsibility feeding the flocks that I need to be fed myself once in a while. Now let's see here." Feverishly, he studied his list. "I think I've covered everything. Oh, excepting on Sundays! I was thinking, Sisters, that since you are so nice about providing dinner for the preacher and his family on Sunday, that we could allow longer for that meal. After all, it's a time for congregational rest and visitation by the fire in harmony, so we might linger as long as an hour even . . ."

He looked like a blimp running out of hot air. Or better put, like a locomotive running out of steam, sweat gushing down his face and neck, soaking his shirtfront and collar. His eyes mistily drifted to the dessert table, where there was shuffling among the plates of cookies, cakes, and pies as though mice were loose in the goodies. There was also a rumble coming from the walls of the room as antique farm equipment hanging there unhinged itself from the walls and floated alongside at least a dozen cookies and several pies that had just risen from the table. I looked at the sisters to see if this was some kind of trick they had pulled, like puppeteers pulling strings, but they were both engrossed in Alma's notes.

Above us, the lit wagon wheel took to spinning, sending light flashing in all directions. The Reverend goggled; sweat poured off him like river water. By now the dessert table was in full motion, I kid you not, napkins flapping, tablecloth swaying. Everything not nailed down was in transit.

"I'm so hungry," Reverend Harmon complained, holding his stomach. As everyone knew, not only was his wife a good cook, but his parishioners faithfully filled the parson's house with baked goods and casseroles. Yet, there he stood staring at the desserts with famished eyes starting to sink into his face. His body was changing, too, caving in upon itself until he looked more and more like the mission pictures of starving children as he raised his fists and bellowed till the rafters shook: "LET ME BE FED!"

WHACK! The first pie caught him square in the face, dripping goop onto his wobbling Adam's apple. The gaping crowd froze, wondering what devil would dare throw a pie at the preacher. It was full of thick berry filling that oozed over his lips and down onto his shirt.

"I swear if it doesn't look like somebody sure enough fed the man," Ben muttered.

"You hush," I told him. "I think our preacher's lost his mind for good and for all."

He pulled the pie plate away and dug his fingers into gobs of blackberry filling. Then, to everyone's shock, he leaned over and took a lick. Then another. He was gobbling away when an entire jam cake came flying and hit him on the back of the head.

"What the hell?" Ben yelped, unable to believe that our preacher had just grabbed a big handful of jam cake off his head and shoved it into his mouth along with the pie.

WHOMP! SPLUSH! SPLAT! Pies, cakes, and cobblers came flying so fast it looked like the café had come to life and was hurling desserts. Amid the flying sweets, the Rev stood blissfully eating gooey handfuls of pie and cake and frosting, not bothered a whit that a whole peach cobbler had just up-ended itself on his head. Peaceful as a child, covered with whipped cream and cherry pie, pumpkin filling dribbling down his nose, jam cake sliding down his neck, rhubarb down his front, and cookies stuck everywhere, he was a living work of pastry art. Whoever threw those pies—surely, the walls hadn't really hurled them—had outdone himself. There wasn't an inch of the Rev left. He was all sugar and spice and everything nice.

Into the dead silence with everyone's eyes stuck on our preacher, mouths all hanging open, came a strange humming. All eyes turned to the jukebox. Even the kids at the pinball machines were staring up at their sweet-covered minister. The tubes were flashing again, the colors inside them simmering. What in hell could happen next?

> "GOODBYE JOE, ME GOTTA GO, ME OH, MY OH
> ME GOTTA GO POLE THE PIROGUE DOWN THE BAYOU
> MY YVONNE, THE SWEETEST ONE, ME OH, MY OH
> SON OF A GUN, WE'LL HAVE BIG FUN ON THE BAYOU!"

The jukebox had switched itself back on, its neon lights surging through its tubes in flashing purples, blues, reds, greens, yellows, and oranges glowing honky-tonk hot as the box bawled out a rip-roaring invitation:

> "JAMBALAYA, AND A-CRAWFISH PIE AND A-FILLET GUMBO
> 'CAUSE TONIGHT I'M GONNA SEE MY MACHEZ AMIO
> PICK GUITAR, FILL FRUIT JAR AND BE GAY-OH
> SON OF A GUN, WE'LL HAVE BIG FUN ON THE BAYOU."

The Reverend jerkily moved from the table where he'd been standing tight against the back of his chair. His bloated stomach, like that of a starving child, grew flat, his chest full. His eyes rose from their sunken stare.

"He's twitching," Ben said suddenly. "The preacher's having a seizure."

At least, the lower half of his body was. His legs had begun to gyrate. His arms flapped in wild playful swoops. Then his head took to bobbing. Pretty soon, his entire body was shimmying like a wild thing.

"Good Lord," Donnie said. "Look at him go."

Our Rev had just broken into a full-out jig, blasting out an open-throated duet with Hank Williams:

> "THIBODEAUX TO FOUNTAINBLEAU, THE PLACE IS BUZZIN'
> KINFOLK COME TO SEE YVONNE BY THE DOZEN
> DRESS IN STYLE, AND GO HOG WILD ME OH, MY OH
> SON OF A GUN, WE'LL HAVE BIG FUN ON THE BAYOU!"

He pranced down the length of the dining room with Mrs. Rev looking after him with her mouth hanging open, while a few of his flock, led by Donnie and Trip, started in clapping and stomping their feet to the music.

"Come on, Sister," the Rev yelled, yanking up Sister Vannie, "let's show 'em what we've got!"

> "JAMBALAYA, AND A-CRAWFISH PIE AND A-FILLET GUMBO
> 'CAUSE TONIGHT I'M GONNA SEE MY MACHEZ AMIO
> PICK GUITAR, FILL FRUIT JAR AND BE GAY-OH
> SON OF A GUN, WE'LL HAVE BIG FUN ON THE BAYOU!"

Both singing at the tops of their lungs, he and Sister Vannie jigged back down the floor with Sister Alma and Sarah in hot pursuit, extending invitations on all sides for everyone to join in.

Pretty soon, there we were all jigging and singing, young and old, most dancing by the dessert table to grab handfuls of an endless supply of sweets. Flying down the floor with Ben, I caught a glimpse of the parrot stomping to the music on his bar, screeching along with the rest. Skirts went a-flyin'; hair popped out of buns and ponytails. Donnie was in his sock feet, dancing with Emma Prewitt, and she was giggling like a girl. Ben and I ended up in a circle with the sisters, Sarah in the middle, and I caught an eyeful of the Reverend scooting by with his wife, who was blushing and batting her eyelashes at her husband as he twirled her here and there, then promenaded with her down the center of the floor.

Every soul in the place, eating and dancing either alone or in twos or threes or in large groups, joined in to roar so loud that the roof rumbled over our heads:

> "JAMBALAYA AND A-CRAWFISH PIE AND A-FILLET GUMBO
> 'CAUSE TONIGHT I'M GONNA SEE MACHEZ AMIO
> PICK GUITAR, FILL FRUIT JAR AND BE GAY-OH
> SON OF A GUN, WE'LL HAVE BIG FUN ON THE BAYOU!"

Just like that, the music stopped as suddenly as it had begun. Dizzy as a goose, I looked around expecting to see my circle. Instead, I was back at my table with Ben and Donnie and Will and Vonnie. The jukebox was silent and dark as a plague, and all the folks were back sitting at their tables like they were before all the jigging and bellowing started. Not a soul among us was sweaty or even breathing hard. The Rev stood at the Mayor's table without a speck of food on his face or shirt, and the sisters and Sarah sat on the step. Downstairs, the kids pinged away on the machines.

"Weren't we all just dancing?" I whispered to Ben. "Wasn't the Reverend just covered in a hundred pounds of pie? Or have I just gone nuts?"

Ben looked back at me, white as a sheet, not quite remembering what had just happened. Even Donnie looked off-balance, squinting down at his feet and trying to figure out why he wasn't wearing his shoes.

Chills played jump rope on my spine as I realized I was the only one in the place who remembered all of it. I turned toward the sisters and saw Alma smile and put a finger to her lips.

"B-but Sister . . ."

Somehow she heard me, though I'd only just whispered. And I swear if I couldn't hear her, too, clear as a bell. "We need a witness, Carolyn," she said. "One witness, to let it be real. Will you agree to hold this memory of the Reverend's inner child for our community?"

"Uh . . . I don't think . . . that is . . ." I might have been loony, I might still have been imagining things, even Alma's voice, but I felt somehow . . . oh, I don't know how to say it . . . honored, I guess. Me, a witness, when they could have chosen anybody.

"Do you agree, Carolyn?"

I felt myself grinning. "Yes, Sister. I agree."

"With your permission then," Alma whispered, "it's real."

My spine was one big tingle. The Rev didn't look all that steady either. The Mayor frowned. "About that last ordinance . . ."

"Ordinance?" The Rev blinked. "Who needs ordinances?"

The Mayor stared at him. "You were *joking* about fining the brown bags? And the music and the parrot and the time schedules?"

"Well, you surely didn't think I was *serious*!" The Reverend rocked back on his heels and laughed so hard and with such goodwill that the entire café smiled and laughed with him. "LET'S EAT!" he hollered.

Everyone did something then that had never been done before in my memory. We all burst into applause for our Reverend. Donnie got on his chair and cheered; a good many other folks followed suit. In fact, you couldn't hear yourself think for all the cheering and applauding. I saw Donnie crumpling the napkin. When somebody has been that successful, you don't count his bloopers. Everyone took their money back, and in groups of smiling friends and neighbors, we all crowded around that wonderful dessert table and filled the basket with money for Martha Burden's house.

I tell you, there were tears in my eyes. Oh, it was such a wonderful Town Council meeting!

Respectfully submitted,

~Carolyn Houseman, Secretary

Letter to Mayor Will Winburn:

Dear Mr. Mayor:

I am enclosing a copy of the Minutes of our meeting and hope that you will add your suggestions so I can make copies and hand them out at the next meeting. Wasn't the sisters' chocolate pie delicious?

Yours truly,

~ Carolyn Houseman, Secretary

Letter to Carolyn Houseman:

Dear Carolyn:

Enclosed please find your redacted Minutes. Please copy them and distribute them at the next meeting. Looking forward to seeing you at the church benefit for Martha Burden.

Sincerely yours,

~-Mayor Will Winburn

Redacted Minutes:

Trip Robinson and Leon Malone resolved their dispute about their property line. Helen Blackerby submitted bills for three dollars and forty cents, most of it disputed and thus tabled for the time being. Other issues were dismissed. A delicious dessert table was prepared by the sisters and enjoyed by one and all.

Respectfully submitted,

~Carolyn Houseman, Secretary

8

The smell of warm cobbler left over from the Council meeting sweetened the ride as the Buick rolled over the dark hills toward the Curtis house. No one in the car spoke. Not Sarah in the backseat or the sisters up front.

Vannie was at the wheel as usual. Ordinarily, she zoomed along in a test of engine, tires, road, and the patience of any peace officer that happened to see her fly by. Tonight she drove erratically, slowing around turns or beneath the crests of hills on the dark road. Then stomping her foot on the pedal to zoom again, but with an uncharacteristic grimness. The speedometer moved from its customary mark of around 70 mph, drifted down to 50, then shot up, pushing toward 80.

Like she's chasing something she doesn't want to catch, Alma thought. Sister obviously felt the same foreboding as she herself. Alma waved her hand as if shooing a fly, pushing the thought down. There was nothing to be done about it. It had been decided. Sarah would live at home, and that was that.

For the hundredth time, Alma regretted letting Sarah live under the same roof with Cleatis. Then again, Vannie had been right. It wasn't theirs to "let" the child leave or to "let" her stay. Especially with Nadine.

Years later, when Alma tried to remember what happened next, she could never be sure what came first—the thought of Nadine, or the screech of the tires skidding on pavement, making sparks fly and stinking up the air with the smell of burning rubber. They sat panting, two sisters in front and a child bracing herself against their seats, all three as motionless as the doe who stood mere inches from the front fender, her black eyes reflecting the glare of the Buick's headlights.

Sarah had been curled next to the hamper, tired but unable to sleep, hoping that the leftover dessert, a loaf of homemade bread, and a small ham and all the trimmings, would somehow make things right at home. Now she and the sisters sat transfixed by the doe frozen in front of them. The look on the animal's face was familiar to Sarah. It was like the one on her mother's face when Daddy would explode.

Like last week when he'd caught Mama and the little kids out in the garden. Sarah hadn't been there and did not want to know what caused her mother's bruises. But the scene unfolded now, coming through the windshield like a show at a drive-in movie. There was Nadine, blindsided. Lately she'd thought he was getting better and had let down her guard. Maybe he had done it because of that, because it was so easy. Or perhaps he'd sensed a growing strength in her, the way she had begun dressing herself with a little more care. Next she'd be wanting to go to town. Talk to the women in the stores. Show off as the mother of the little girl who prissed around working at the café. Or maybe it was for a reason no one could ever understand that he walked up to Nadine on that sunny morning and, without warning, slapped her to the ground. She fell without a sound. Lay there like the dead. Only when he took off his belt and started in on the kids did she struggle up, pulling at his arms and screaming "*Why?*" over and over again.

He hit harder, snapping the belt buckle at Nadine's back, arms, and legs, not even hearing the words out of his own mouth: " . . . show you who's boss . . . maybe now you'll stay where you belong . . . something to remind you, missy . . . *And leave those children alone. I haven't finished with them yet.*"

But she wouldn't leave them alone, she kept pulling them away, putting herself between them and him. Then finally, she'd had too much and collapsed sobbing.

"That's better." He stood taller, prouder. Surveyed the line of red tear-streaked faces, then turned to go. At the muffled sound of wailing, he spun back on his heel. *"Shut your mouths, every damn one of you."* He nudged Nadine with the toe of his shoe, worrying at her until she looked up at him. "I don't want to have to do this again. But I will if it needs doing. Understood?" He waited for Nadine's tear-soaked nod—the prize for the win. After he got it, he swaggered on, buckling his belt.

The scene was so vivid they might well have been there. Vannie grimly switched the lights off, and the doe bolted off the road and into the brush.

"Sister?" Alma nudged Vannie.

Vannie nodded, turned the lights on again, and put the car in gear, rolling slowly forward. Alma shifted in her seat. She wanted to plead with her sister to keep Sarah in their home where she would be safe from all they had just witnessed, but the argument must not take place in the child's hearing. Sarah's face told them she was focused on only one thing. She wanted to go home. Wanted her mama.

Understanding, Alma began to hum and then to sing quietly. It was an unfinished song, midway in the writing. She saw the boy sitting there on his bed, plucking at his guitar, the words rumbling from his lips so quietly they might have been distant heartbeats. Hair falling over his forehead, Sugar stopped to write the new lyrics down, and then went back to strumming.

He thought of his mother and his sisters. He thought of his brothers, and that image of their father that had held itself in front of them all like a dark beacon, guiding them to a future as hard to resist as any siren song that lured lost sailors to the rocks. Hadn't he been pulled hard toward those rocks? Hadn't he almost had his own shipwreck?

Swallowing the lump in his throat, he went back to singing in that same almost silent way, the words coming easily. The song was writing itself. The familiar process brought a touch of calm. Maybe it would reach through the night and touch his mother. It was written for her:

"Don't let him darken your sky, Lady,
Don't let the stars grow dim.
If he cannot cling to the honor you bring,
Then Lady, shame on him."

Vannie startled Alma and Sarah by bursting out with a second verse of the song:

"Don't let him drive the moon from your eyes
With his rage or by his whim.
If he will not know all the love you bestow
Then Lady, shame on him."

Sarah leaned forward, pushing her face between the sisters' seats and grabbing them by their shoulders as if to say: "Stop! It's my turn!" Then in a clear voice, she started a third verse alone:

"Don't lay your dreams at his feet, Lady,
Don't let your tomorrow turn grim.
Has he made you ashamed to ca . . . to carry . . ."

The child stopped, stricken.

Vannie slowed the car, looked back and caught Sarah in her steady gaze, and then finished the line for her:

"Has he made you ashamed to carry his name?
Oh, Lady, shame on him."

Sarah gave a little cry, but she did not flinch.

Vannie pushed on the gas pedal, bouncing the car over ruts in the road.

They were close to the house now, but she and Alma didn't want to stop singing. Maybe Sarah could take Sugar's song home with her. They found the last verse, all three singing it together, just as Vannie pulled the car onto the rutted lane that passed for the Curtis driveway:

"You've no need to doubt what you're all about
It's time now to dry all your tears . . ."

"Hush!" Alma hissed.

Vannie pressed her lips together, and Sarah covered her mouth with her hands. Up ahead, the house sat dark and quiet; not a soul stirred. Yet, someone waited in the shadows of the porch. A ghostly presence, there one moment, gone the next.

Hitting the button on the dashboard to kill the headlights, Vannie cut the engine and let the car roll forward. The figure stepped soundlessly off the porch and into the starlight. Nadine in her housecoat ran on tiptoe to the car and motioned Sarah to open her door quietly. "It's alright," she whispered through Alma's open window. "He's asleep. Come on, Sarah, hurry up!"

Sarah grabbed the hamper and slid it out of the car, bumping it a little against the door.

"Honey, be quiet!" Nadine's alarm carried through her croaked whisper. "Let's go!" She smiled at the sisters, her lips moving in a soundless "thank you." Then mother and daughter ran like rabbits, joined by their hands on the handles of the hamper, disappearing around the side of the house and dissolving into the shadows.

Alma and Vannie sat for a moment, trying to catch their breath. Then Alma pointed toward the dark yard and Vannie nodded, understanding her intent and slipping the gear into neutral. Moving quietly, they left the car and leaned their weight against the frame, one on each side, rolling it backwards out onto the gravel road and far enough from the house to be safe to start the engine. Vannie drove to the main road before switching on the headlights. They rode in silence, hearts racing like those of frightened teenagers.

Alma switched on the radio. It surprised neither of them that Sugar's song, written or not, was playing. An acoustic guitar before the last verse spoke in a language all its own as it would next year on the Hit Parade. Then Sugar's voice came in with the finish of his song:

"You've no need to doubt what you're all about
It's time now to dry your tears.
Though Eve always thought it was all her own fault,
It seldom ever is."

9

A wave of moonshine hit the town during the next weeks. Everybody and his uncle seemed to need a jar of the homebrew. The Curtis stills cranked overtime to deliver merchandise because, through the greatest of luck, they were the only stills that hadn't been axed down during a series of zealous raids inspired by the church councils of all three counties in the Willow Creek surrounds.

"That wasn't luck," Donnie Marble declared. "That there was just good ole still hiding, passed down from Cleatis's pappy and granpappy. His only luck was having those other stills hacked down. It made everybody thirsty, me included!"

A hectic calm hit the Curtis house as Cleatis went around counting his money, even handing out change to the children, something unique in Sarah's experience. He caught her looking at him on a Saturday morning as he doled out a nickel to Lillie and gave his eldest daughter a strained smile. "Just remember this, missy," he said. "The man of the house has more clout than a couple of old ladies with a pan full of fried chicken." He held out a dime to her. "Here," he said. When she stood motionless, he held it out farther. "Take it."

"I don't need it, Daddy." She eyed the coin with a shiver. "Give it to somebody else." But seeing the shadow that crawled across his face, she held out her hand. "I guess I could use one of those pocketbooks I saw at the dime store." She tried not to flinch as he dropped the dime into her palm. "Thank you, Daddy."

"That's alright then." He relaxed and walked on out the door. Sarah noticed his swagger, the walk of a man with money in his pockets.

Lillie was still examining her coin. At eight years old, she had never before had a whole nickel to herself. She looked up at Sarah. "It's so shiny and pretty! Is Daddy rich, now?"

Sarah studied the dime that still rested on her palm. "I don't know." Was "rich" the right word for someone who pumped out homemade whiskey that left men drunk on roadsides or asleep in fields while worried wives and kids searched for them? Or for someone who took money from poor folks who were stuck on hooch?

Later at the café, she couldn't get the image of her father out of her mind as she sat behind the cash register and made change without seeing the customers who held out their hands and made small talk. She hardly even saw the sisters, who plied her with fresh chicken salad, deviled eggs, and peach cobbler with vanilla ice cream. She swallowed the food without tasting it.

"Is everything alright at home, Sarah?" Vannie asked.

Sarah said too brightly, "Daddy's being good, Sister Vannie. Really good. I doubt he'll ever go back to being that other way now that he's making so much money." She hadn't asked a question, yet she searched the sister's eyes, looking for confirmation.

Vannie took the child's trembling fingers in a warm grasp. "Here's a riddle for you."

"Tell me." Sarah got that intent look that meant she had just transformed her mind into a steel trap.

Vannie spoke slowly: "No matter how long it gets, it keeps going around in a circle. It acts like one thing but is always something else. It flies in your face but hides in the dark. It claims to educate but always brings ignorance."

As the last word was spoken, Sarah was already muttering to herself, occasionally asking Vannie to go over the lines again. "I can't," she said at last, red spots of vexation on her cheeks.

"Open your mind, Sarah."

"I *am* opening my mind!"

"Think. It claims to educate . . . but always brings ignorance."

Sarah's head snapped toward her. "Wait. I know what it is. It's a lie!" She laughed triumphantly. "I got it right, didn't I? It's a *lie*. It keeps growing because the liar keeps making up stuff, but it keeps circling back . . ." Her forehead wrinkled.

"Maybe because only truth has any point to it? It acts like the truth, but it's really just fooling you."

"Right," Sarah breathed.

"It flies in your face, don't you see, because the liar keeps talking and talking at you, but it hides in the dark, concealing the truth. It pretends to teach you, but it deceives, and thus keeps you in ignorance." Vannie sought to temper her next words. "This is why I can't lie to you."

Sarah's smile froze. "You mean about Daddy getting better."

"That's up to him, of course."

"But you don't think . . .?"

"Anything that's based on a temporary condition, such as having the only . . . ah, business of its kind in town, seldom lasts. What can last is a positive state of mind, Sarah, independent of external circumstances. And not just for your sake. For the sakes of your mother and your sisters and brothers, even the whole wide world. You have that kind of impact."

Sarah's eyes grew wide. "I do?"

Vannie tugged playfully at a lock of the child's hair. "Don't let it go to your head, kiddo. Everyone does."

Just then the door to the café opened, and Nadine and Lillie walked in heading for the candy case. Lillie's hand was knuckled around her newly acquired loot.

"Something chocolate," she said, her usual shyness gone as she gazed into the case.

Nadine was silent, but the sisters saw on her face a deep foreboding. From this time forward, they must not let their guards down about Cleatis Curtis.

10

The next night the joint was jumping, and the jukebox was at full blast. Saturday nights were wild of late. Alma, clearing a table of empty plates to make room for dessert, caught Vannie's eye at the next table, from where she was serving a round of Coca-Cola along with glasses of ice. She nodded at a certain paper bag she had just laid on the tray alongside the plates prior to setting down several dishes of cobbler. Vannie raised an eyebrow. It was plain to see that a new brand of illegal brown paper bag, adorned by a pair of intertwined "C's," was circulating under The Two Sisters' tables.

"C's indeed," Alma chuckled, holding up the confiscated bag as Vannie and she met by the jukebox. She pointed to the smudges of ink from the pen Cleatis had used to add class to his business. "That Cleatis since he remembered how to write. Well, come on, Sister, you'd better build a row of pimento cheese sandwiches, and two more of ham and chicken salad. I'll get some fresh coffee going and put burgers and onions on the grill. Beat 'cha round the turn, Sister!"

Challenge no sooner hurled than accepted. Vannie tore past her with Alma in hot pursuit.

"Crazy bitches," Banshee grumbled as they almost knocked his cage off the top step, each trying to elbow the other out of contention as they scuffled past him. Vannie flew down the steps and around the counter and managed to get her toe past the kitchen archway a second before Alma's foot landed squarely on top of it, her squawking "Foul! Foul!" as Vannie jerked her foot free and pushed her way into the kitchen.

"You cheated," Alma snapped. "That bird got in the way."

As the night wore on, the town drinkers became still more rambunctious. While the sisters dealt with food, drink, and dishes, a group of young men sneaked out to where Vannie had banished Banchee's cage to the courtyard. The rowdy group of four slipped liquor into the parrot's tin cup and got the old bird drunk; then full of what they had done, they took him to LaGrange just before midnight and left him at Fourth and Main to direct traffic. The bird had a fine time cussing everyone who happened by on wheels or foot at that late hour, and wore out every vile word he knew on the preacher's son, who was the one to bring him back to the café at 2:00 a.m. where the joint was still jumping.

Moments after Banshee's return it happened. Nobody but the sisters heard the sudden sound like the *CREAAKKK* of a rusty gate opening. Vannie and Alma paused on their way to the dining room, each casual under the weight of several loaded trays they carried overlapping up and down their arms. It was a feat of balance that would have been more admired if the two hadn't executed it with such ease.

The *CREEE-AAAKKK* grew louder. No one noticed the sisters as they exchanged glances, each realizing that a door had just opened in a mind almost thirty miles away in an apartment in Louisville, as a reporter by the name of Loretta Smith tossed fitfully in her sleep.

"Who woulda' thunk it?" Vannie whispered to Alma. "All because of a parrot getting drunk and using a little salty language."

"One ripple on a stream," Alma returned, "changes the whole state of the world, don't 'cha know?" The sisters continued to listen as a murmur came to them, carried on the wings of telepathy. They sent back their own message in response, then Alma nodded. "It's done."

"Yes, Sister. She accepted our invitation."

"I guess we need her as much as she needs us. We must make sure to have Sarah here when she comes. Hmmm. I do believe there's a holiday scheduled on Monday. Administration business between teachers and the school board, isn't that so?"

"Now that you mention it."

The sisters solemnly continued on their way.

Banshee slept most all day Sunday, and by late Monday morning when Loretta Smith had left Louisville behind her and was nearing the café, he was still in one of his moods.

"Look at him," Alma said, lounging on the last stool at the counter only a foot or so from the two steps leading to the dining room. The birdcage was on the top step, settled among a mess of soggy seeds and spilled Coca-Cola from one of Banchee's two tin cups that he had upended.

"He's being the worst possible slob today," Vannie observed, leaning against the end of the counter by her sister and sipping from a bottle of frosty root beer.

"I never seen him so droopy before," Sarah said. She sat beside the cage on the top step holding a canister of sunflower seeds on her lap and patiently poked fresh seeds into Banchee's cup, even as he made grumpy sounds in his throat. The bird's monster hangover had left him at his surly worst.

"Limp as mashed squash." Vannie put down her root beer and began to wipe down the counter, shining up the shakers and the sugar canisters as she went. "The old coot won't put out the energy to get better. He takes his stubbornness after you, Sister."

"Oh, ho, look who's talking," Alma snorted. "You have been hardheaded since you were a girl . . ."

"Oh, come now, Missy. You've always been the know-it-all."

"How can you tell? You never let me get a word in edgewise."

"What a convenient point of view, Sister . . ."

They paused as a white Plymouth pulled off the narrow country road and inched toward the café to park facing the window. An unsmiling woman in her late twenties emerged from the driver's side. Every inch of her boxy figure was a stop sign to humanity.

"This won't be easy," Vannie said as the woman marched toward the front door with briefcase in hand, a camera case swinging from her shoulder.

"I like challenges." Alma leaned over the cage and poked a sunflower seed from Sarah's canister at the parrot. "And to think, Banshee, you helped bring her to us."

Banshee looked at the sisters, who gazed back lovingly, and uttered a hoarse expletive, followed by "Get out of here, old bitches."

At a look from Alma, Sarah covered her ears, though she'd heard far worse in her own home. "How did Banshee help?" She broke off when the front door swung open on a fresh blast of expletives from the bird, causing her to cover her ears again.

Loretta Smith, coming through the door, cast a matter-of-fact glance at the degenerate bird. He had never looked worse. His color was dull, his beak stained, and his feathers hung on him like an old man's skin. "So, it's true," she said. "He does cuss like a sailor."

The sisters chuckled appreciatively.

"Frankly," Vannie confided, "you haven't heard anything yet."

The sisters came forward to shake hands with the woman with short dark hair and eyes that were whiskey-colored and contrary as a wayward wind. Every inch of her was disciplined arrogance, save only for her fingernails, painted with clear polish and buffed, but bitten to the quick.

"I'm Loretta Smith," the out-of-towner said briskly. "From *The Courier-Journal.*"

"Ah, the big paper," Alma said. "Sister, we're being visited by a real professional."

"It seems your bird piqued my editor's interest. He got a call from a local resident about the traffic light incident. I suppose it's true? Yes, I can believe it now that I see him." Eyeing the bird, she set the briefcase on the counter and removed a camera. "I wouldn't usually be assigned something like this . . ."

"You're probably used to working on far more important stories," Vannie suggested.

"Yes, but apparently the paper has grown desperate."

"Probably not enough murders and mutilations lately," Alma said.

"You don't mind if I take a few pictures? The light isn't very good, but that's where he usually sits, I guess?" Loretta aimed her camera, and the bird spit an expletive at her as a flashbulb exploded in his eyes. "If you don't mind my saying so, that bird should be confiscated by the Board of Health." She snapped another picture.

"I doubt the Board of Health would have him," Alma said. She opened the drink cooler and began moving the cold bottles of soda to the front, in preparation for replenishing the case. The child rose from the step and moved to the open cooler, bending over to help arrange the bottles.

"Your names, please?"

"Alma and Vannie May," Alma said obligingly. "And this is Sarah Curtis, our apprentice."

The reporter's eyebrows rose at the word "apprentice," but she didn't bother a comment. Instead, she wrote in a small notebook she had removed from her briefcase. "A-L-M-A and V-A-N-N-I-E, not Vanessa?"

Vannie shrugged. "I answer to either. But then you have a nickname, too, don't you? Lorrie, isn't it?"

The out-of-towner's gaze shifted to her. "How did you know that? I haven't been called Lorrie for years."

"Isn't it a common name, dear?"

"I don't think so, not really." With a brief flicker of an eyelash, Loretta terminated her interest and moved about the room taking notes as to where and when the incident had happened, who had been involved, the café, the bird, and the small town atmosphere. Out of the corner of her eye, she saw the apprentice and Vannie hauling full cases of soda pop to the cooler, while Alma loaded the new bottles behind the cold ones. "Tell me," Loretta said. "Just as a matter of curiosity, how do you stand it out here? There are no conveniences, for God's sake. No drugstore, no movie houses . . ."

"We're an official Greyhound bus stop," Vannie said with a touch of pride. "Right across the road in front of the rock and gem shop you can climb on a bus that will take you clear to Cincinnati, if it's excitement you're after. But Willow Creek, of course, is just a little byway. Some of us choose to make our homes here, but others are just passing through. If you look to the left of the rock shop, you may notice Sister's and my little motel. Nothing fancy, but we offer ironed sheets, good towels, and ceiling fans. More than once we've had visitors who've decided to stay."

"Overnight, you mean?" Loretta Smith said.

"Or forever. There have been those who actually moved here."

"To do . . . *what*?"

"Oh, nothing much," Alma said. "Just live. But people looking to fill up their lives with activities don't stick around long. They find the concept of time too big in the country. The silence too deep. The stars too bright. Anyone uneasy with the idea of living on a planet that is revolving around the sun is somewhat bothered by starlight."

"And moonlight," Vannie put in. "And the streaming nurseries of stars, portending the birth of all possibilities. Can you imagine such a thing? You would if you lived in Willow Creek. We have the brightest night skies you ever saw."

Loretta said nothing. A few beads of perspiration popped up on her forehead, and she swayed slightly on her sensible low heels. Both Vannie and Alma stood beside the open cooler, their task seemingly forgotten, while beside them the child sat on a high stool with her chin propped on one small fist.

Alma looked at the reporter who began to bite at a thumbnail. "I take it that you, yourself, would never want to live in a little place like this? A place that is also a nursery of stars, at least to Sister and me. That doesn't appeal to you?"

Loretta jerked her hand from her mouth. "God, no. But this isn't about me. This is about a small town bird that directs traffic and curses a blue streak. How do you spell his name?"

"B-A-N-S-H-E-E." Alma shut the lid to the cooler. "Please sit down, Miss Smith. Have a cup of coffee. Perhaps a country ham sandwich. We cure our own ham. Or a piece of pie on the house?"

"Just black coffee, thank you. And I'll pay for it." Loretta was surprised to feel her hands tremble around the thick white cup when it came. She sipped cautiously, gazing over the lip at the smaller sister, who had the only purple eyes she had ever seen. It occurred to her to make a note of it, and she put down her coffee and reached for her notebook.

"Please don't," Vannie said, not without humor. "It's not good to note *everything*, you know."

Loretta opened her mouth and then shut it, lost for words.

"What is truly amazing," Alma interjected, "is how *much* you don't like small towns. One might almost think you came from one yourself."

"Well, I . . ." With effort, Loretta Smith restrained herself from admitting that she had indeed come from a small coal-mining town, Cainsville. Tears came into her eyes, blurring the words as she stared into her notebook, at the memory of the two-room tarpaper cabin, her daddy's soot-covered face, the other half-starved children, and how she had craved to get out of that existence. "I've made a good life for myself," she muttered.

"Yes, very." Alma sounded suitably impressed. "You managed to get your education. Got a job in journalism for *The Courier-Journal.*"

The child slid off the stool and looked up admiringly. "I never knew anyone before who wrote in the paper," she said shyly, moving back toward the parrot. "Wait till I tell Mama."

"I suppose it's unusual enough in a place like this," the reporter said condescendingly.

"Quite," Alma agreed. She smiled at the reporter who ran her finger under her collar as if it were too tight. "Yes, it's easy to see that your life is in the city now. Small towns have little to do with you anymore."

"That's true." Loretta turned to a new page in her pad, noting that the bird had shoved his head against the cage bars in order to enjoy the head scratches that the child was administering dreamily. *Scraggly old bird and beautiful fresh young child,* she thought. *What a pair.*

"Now as I hear it," she went on, "the parrot was brought home at 2:00 a.m. by the pastor's son. Is that correct?"

"Wonderful man, the Reverend," Vannie said, nodding. "A great friend of ours. Fine son, too. Just feeling his oats a little, you know."

"I see." Loretta jotted it all down and walked to the door, peering toward the rock and gem shop and the row of small houses behind it. "Is this all there is to Willow Creek?"

"Oh, my, no," Alma said. "We've got a unique crowd of interesting and funny people. Beautiful, fertile farmland. A creek with real personality. All the complexities of life, just seen through a tiny lens. The miniscule world is just as vast as what's beyond the stars, don't you know? It's just how you choose to look at it. And if you went to one of our dances, you'd hear some of the best music in the world, all from local musicians."

"I'm sure." Loretta returned to her stool and restively stirred her coffee.

"If you're after local color," Vannie said, "there's an old graveyard beside the church that bears investigating. When you die in a small town, you don't go very far, you know. Generally speaking, you're right where you always were . . . among friends and neighbors, never far from memory. Every tombstone holds a drama. I'm sure you'd find characters there that would interest you."

Alma nodded. "Like old man Beery. The poor man rocked himself off his front porch and died of a heart attack. And Mrs. Jessie Woodcock. She believed she had a cancer of the intestines and hung herself in the cellar. Wasn't anything but too much black beans and cabbage. And poor Martin MacKensie, bless his heart. He mangled himself in his bush hog. Shoo."

"Left everything he owned to his dog," Vannie remembered. "And his dog's will left it all to the hired man, who killed the mutt within a week. It doesn't do to make a dog rich, especially when he's got a human heir."

"If you don't mind, I'd like to concentrate on the story I was assigned to write." Loretta preferred not to think of graveyards. Her father and brother were buried in one. She had never gone to pay her respects. In life, she'd left them to face poverty and hardship, never looking back after she'd made her escape. Now from death, they dared her to face them every night the moment that sleep finally took her. She frowned at the parrot.

"I could tell you a story about another bird," Vannie offered. "Although my story is more about the hobo who came through Willow Creek, wouldn't you say, Sister?"

"Absolutely."

Loretta tried to stop her before she could begin her no doubt long and dreary tale, but to her amazement, she could not utter a word, nor could she budge from the stool as Sister Vannie gave a grave curtsy, as though she were a keynote speaker taking the podium at a black-tie event.

"Well, you see, the man who came through our town a while back was indeed a hobo," she began. "He knocked on people's doors and some gave to him and some didn't. But by and large Willow Creek is a generous town. He did as well as a hobo who was compelled to live on the kindness of others could do."

Try as she did not to listen, Loretta felt drawn to hang on to the storyteller's every word.

"When the hobo had filled himself on the town's kindness," Vannie went on, "he found he still had room for one more chicken."

"Exactly one," Alma added.

The reporter blurted out, "You can't fill up on *charity*! That kind of food just makes you hungrier. Or . . . or at least, it would me."

The sisters nodded. Yes, it would be that way for Loretta.

In a small voice, Sarah said, "Nobody likes charity. Sometimes from the church they bring . . ." She broke off, her eyes going cloudy.

"Now on this particular night, when the hobo passed through our town," Vannie continued swiftly, "the sky was black. Dark as pitch, hardly any moon, no stars at all. As I've told you, this is highly unusual for us. We are known for our bright skies. So, you will appreciate how odd it was that on that one night, Willow Creek just happened to have black empty skies, a perfect setting for a hobo who came passing through on the sly."

Loretta shivered.

"Every wanderer has his own reasons for roaming the Earth," Alma murmured. "But in the end, the quest is usually quite similar. Most people want to go home."

"Not me," Loretta Smith said. "I don't want—"

"Shh," Alma whispered. "This story isn't about you. You're a successful reporter, not a hobo. You pay your own way."

With words, Loretta thought. *Meaningless words.*

"In any case," Vannie continued, "on that particular night, that very dark and misty night when the hobo had been fed well by the town, he still had that gawl darn hunger for just one more chicken. For something the town had not supplied him. For something he could take for himself in the black of night when no one was looking. That way, you see, he could eat without shame."

Loretta nodded, remembering a time when the mine where her father and brothers worked had closed down. They had been out of work for months, and the family was forced to live on food supplied by neighbors whose men had jobs in other mines. It was hard to take food from people who couldn't afford to give it, but it was eat it or starve. As shame deepened, Loretta began to hate the food that was delivered to their house. The hunger began then, a kind of hunger that could never be filled by charity. After all this time, she remembered once taking a pie off the window ledge of a kindly neighbor woman. The ill-gotten cherry pie had gone down like nectar. Only after the entire pie was devoured, had she become aware of the sickening sweet aftertaste left on her tongue. Like the taste in her mouth when she coaxed people's tragedies out of them. *If it bleeds it reads* was the cry of the newsroom. She nervously licked her lips, noting that the sisters' apprentice was watching her.

"Since it was so nice and dark out," Vannie went on, her voice taking on the tones of a storyteller at a campfire, "the hobo decided to do what he did best."

"Take for himself what he thought he needed," Loretta Smith said bleakly.

"Exactly. So he set off up the road, and pretty soon he found a likely farmhouse with all the lights off."

"Folks in this town go to bed so early you might not believe it," Alma said.

The out-of-towner believed it. In Cainsville, it had been a point of honor to be fast asleep before nine and up by five. It seemed hard to believe that she had once tumbled into bed that early and slept like a baby. These days, she usually read until she dropped off, leaving the bedside light on until the alarm rang in the morning. Not that she slept straight through. No, countless times during the endless nights, she woke and found her place in her book, dozed off, and woke again to find the book still open on the bedcover.

Loretta pictured herself with her brothers and sisters frolicking with the robust energy of their youth in valleys surrounded by mountains. And inside the small house, with Daddy playing the fiddle and her mother's smile flashing as she strummed a washboard and Brother Boy hopped around the floor dancing with a mop. She jumped when she heard Vannie's voice again.

" . . . and he screamed. And screamed. Screamed for all he was worth. Because he'd stepped square into a trap. There are traps all over the place in the country. Not just hunters' traps. Farmers set them, too, for foxes and the like."

"Ummm." The reporter found her voice with difficulty.

"Well, pretty soon, the hobo was lying there, still screaming, still pleading for the mercy of God to save him from his pain, when a man he'd never met bent over him and said, 'You don't know me, sir, but you can trust me.' That's the kind of friendliness you can find in a place like Willow Creek."

The out-of-towner set her jaw. "I've never been much for friendliness. Usually when someone is being friendly, they want something from you." Like herself, when she was trying to wheedle people for details of their worst moments.

"It's funny you should say that," Alma said. "That's how the hobo felt."

"That's right," Vannie agreed. "In fact, he cussed the friendly farmer even while the farmer was springing him from the trap. Then when he helped the hobo inside his house, bandaged his wounds, and offered him food and drink, the hobo refused to take anything. The only kind of food he was in the mood for was something he could get on his own. There are times when stealing feels like gainful employment."

Loretta curtly nodded. "Go on."

"So," Vannie resumed, "when the farmer invited the hobo to sleep over for the night, he said no. He cussed out the farmer again and limped out of the house, refusing to be driven anywhere. For that matter, he didn't have any place to be driven to. He'd abandoned his makeshift lean-to out in the woods the night before. He wasn't even sure he could find it again. All this time, the man's mood was growing worse. He wanted . . ." She paused, looking at the out-of-towner as though expecting her to supply the word.

" . . . something?" Loretta Smith ventured. "Maybe he didn't know exactly what."

"Ah." Vannie raised her eyebrows. "Yes. He wanted 'something' fierce. He started looking around, stumbling over rocks and the like, trying to find that something when all at once he saw it right in front of him. An apparition! Gleaming in the night. A snow-white hen. Strutting around, reminding him that some people had hens and big fancy houses, and he had none. At the sight of that hen, the hobo felt black bile rise up inside him. And wouldn't you know, right at his feet there was an old empty burlap bag. Remarkable how such a thing came to be right where he needed it, when he needed it. Quick as you could spit, he had that chicken in the bag and the bag slung over his shoulder as he high-tailed it back into the woods and somehow found the pitiful little pile of sticks he had stacked up the night before and the ripped piece of tarpaulin he'd called a roof. There was nothing to wringing that bird's neck and roasting her over the fire.

"*Wait a minute,* he thought, *I made that fire last night. How could it still be burning?* But his hunger was more pressing than such minor details. When the hen was done to a turn, he cut her up with his pocket knife . . ."

"How do you know all this?" the out-of-towner asked suspiciously, pulling herself from her dreamlike state. "You weren't there, were you? You didn't actually see him stick that bird in the bag, did you?" Because if she could see that, couldn't she also see a reporter knocking on the door of a woman who had just lost her family and pressing for the horrible details? Loretta was terribly afraid this was indeed possible.

"I think the stolen hen was common knowledge," Alma offered.

Loretta blotted sweat from her forehead with her napkin. "What about the rest of the story? The way he cooked the bird and cut it up?"

"Did I have that bird on the fire yet?" Vannie asked. "Oh, yes. Well, the man about swallowed the bird whole, bones and all. That was the kind of hunger that had built up inside of him. As keepers of a café, we understand hunger."

Loretta had no doubt that these women in this God-forsaken town understood hunger on a level that no one else in the world did. "Where did you come from?" she asked weakly.

"From many places," Alma said. "At different times."

"You weren't born here?" The real question was whether or not they had been born on the planet.

"Yes!" Vannie said at once, understanding perfectly.

"No!" Alma answered at the same time, also understanding perfectly.

Neither was lying. Vannie did lay claim to an earthly birth in this lifetime, whereas Alma stubbornly clung to her story of popping into the world at the age of three shortly after Vannie's birth, rewriting the memories of all concerned. Save for Vanessa's, of course, as she'd often been reminded.

Loretta's stare was becoming more and more fixed.

"As my sister was saying, we know hunger very well," Alma said with a smile. "Hunger, young woman, is the lack of anything you need to keep you warm, fed, sheltered, loved . . . on other planes, we could add fluid, opalescent, elevated . . . oh, yes, there are many types of hunger. Do you understand the hobo's hunger that night, dear?"

Loretta nodded slowly. "Perhaps."

"I understand, too," Sarah said, thinking of her embarrassment when the church people showed up with their baskets.

Vannie continued, "No sooner had the hobo devoured the entire bird than it hit him—a taste worse than anything he'd ever known in his life. You see, the chicken had something wrong with it. Leon Malone, that was the farmer's name, said it had gout. You know what gout is? When a chicken gets it, she goes rotten from the inside out. That's why Leon never bothered to fence in that particular chicken. He doesn't like killing, has a hard time slaughtering his hogs. In the case of this chicken, he wasn't going to eat it, which made killing it out of the question. The hen roamed free until she met up with Mr. Hobo." Vannie chuckled. "When that tramp went running out of town, early rising farm folks who saw him swore he had to stop every five minutes to heave. More coffee?" she asked, noticing that Loretta's cup was nearly empty.

"Oh, my God." Loretta recoiled from the cup. "Gout. Rotten from the inside out."

"If he'd waited for the light before he ate the bird," Alma murmured, "he'd have seen something was wrong with it."

The reporter felt sick. "Why did you tell me a story like that?"

Vannie shrugged. "I thought you might be interested, you being from out of town, too, like the hobo. And the way you spoke about small towns, I just thought . . . I suppose there's no chance that you might move back to one, after all?"

Loretta ignored the question. "Why do you think that chicken and the burlap bag fell into the hobo's path that night?"

"In some way he was ready to face inner questions," Alma explained. "I'm sure his future was altered from what it would have been had he not eaten that particular chicken on that particular night."

"You mean . . . the hobo . . . put the chicken in the bag for a particular reason? Other than just hunger?"

"I believe so, yes. Though maybe he didn't realize it at the time."

Loretta pondered that in a dark study. The two sisters kept out of her way as they worked steadily behind the counter, finishing with the Coke cooler while Sarah dragged the empty cases to the door for the truck to pick up later. All this time there was never another customer, not unusual for after breakfast on a Monday morning. The weekend, full of customers and talk, was over, and a new week had begun.

Finished with stocking drinks, the child wandered up the steps to a small record player set up beside the jukebox and put on a song, swaying back and forth in front of it and humming along with the gravelly-voiced singer. Watching her, the reporter thought she looked otherworldly.

A peevish squawk sent Sarah wheeling, even as Loretta slopped coffee into her saucer and shifted her gaze to the parrot. Banshee lifted his head and stared back at her, coffee streaming from his crooked beak, then leaned over to take a mouthful of seeds. The old bird crunched through them, then spit out a beakful of dripping shells to test his range. As usual, he was fully capable of spitting ten feet in any direction.

"That bird is the most repulsive thing I've ever seen," the reporter said, reaching for her camera. She snapped more pictures, some of the bird alone, others with Sarah sitting beside him, and several shots of the sisters standing behind the counter.

"On your way back out of town you might stop to take a look at that restored farmhouse up the road," Vannie said as Loretta fitted her camera back into its case. "The pretty yellow one with the white lattice work around the windows and the wraparound porch. It's for sale now, but it used to be owned by a ring of burglars."

Loretta looked at her. "You're kidding."

"Oh, no. A whole outlaw gang lived there, a more modern day version of Butch Cassidy and the Hole-in-the-Wall Gang you couldn't find. They had a black-market warehouse, sold stuff out of the barn and the attic."

"They had one of those special rooms," Alma added. She turned to the child, who was listening with rapt eyes. "It was a secret space nobody but them knew about, in case the cops came around to make an arrest or something."

"Neat," Sarah breathed.

"Or it could have been used if some other gang came gunning after them," Vannie speculated. She refilled Loretta's coffee cup. "So the boredom of a small town would get to you if you stuck around longer?"

"Not exactly," Loretta said. "But well, you can't go home again, can you?"

"Why not?" Alma murmured.

"Because you can't. Everyone knows that."

"What about the prodigal son, darlin'? As I recall, he blew everything his family had provided for him. Threw it all away like it grew on trees. I guess if he could go home, just about anybody could."

"Not . . . just . . . anybody." Tears filled the reporter's eyes, and she could say no more. In that moment, she knew the truth about herself. *I'll never have a home.*

"You're ready for a change, aren't you, child?" Alma leaned forward and drummed her fingernails three times in rapid succession on the back of Loretta's stool.

"Have courage, dear," Vannie said gently.

For Loretta Smith, ace reporter from *The Courier-Journal*, those were the last words in a vanishing world.

The next instant Loretta found herself spinning helplessly on her stool, slowly at first, then faster and faster. Feeling sicker with every rotation, she stopped trying to hold things in place. I'm out of control, she thought. But then she was tired of being in control, exhausted with it. It felt good to give in to the increasing velocity of the spin, not only around and around on the stool, but now somehow tumbling end-over-end, forward, down and around, somersaulting, her head falling forward and her knees and feet sailing back over her head, and still spinning round and round on the stool, the competing spins pulling her in two directions. She was being pulled apart.

She had known something like this could happen, had felt it when she drove into Willow Creek and found herself smack in the center of the most profound quiet she had ever heard. Now the rigidity inside her groaned against the stress of being caught in gyroscopic forces, splintered like wood, as fissures shot through her tightly held world. Everything was a flying blur, a syrupy mix of the sisters' faces and Sarah's, as the child hung on to Sister Vannie's apron. The shell at Loretta's core protracted, bulged outward as her molecular structure strained, then broke into atoms that were hurled toward the edges of the universe. As the last of her unraveled, the lump in her center gave way, shattered into subatomic particles. She was everywhere at once. And nowhere at all.

An instant later, Loretta Smith entered the most primordial blackness she had ever encountered.

"Country people," Alma said from the dark, "trust what's inside them. Out here in farm country, you can hear yourself think. People shouldn't live in crowded places until they know how to live in a small town, and until they have learned to carry that small town with them. Once you've got the small town inside you, then you can go anywhere, and you'll never be away from home again."

"I don't understand anything you're saying," Loretta said, "I'm afraid . . ."

"Careful, Loretta. In this space, whatever you imagine will instantly become your reality. We wouldn't want you to start thinking of things that go bump in the night."

Loretta moaned, trying to turn her mind from the specter rising inside her. But it was like trying not to think of a white bear after someone whispers in your ear, "Whatever you do, don't think about a white bear!"

"Where am I?" she blurted.

"Look around," Alma whispered. "You're in familiar surroundings."

Loretta found herself in a windy and dark night, no matter how much her reporter's insistence on facts told her that it was actually mid-morning at the counter of an old country café. Hesitantly tilting her face toward what she knew to be a white ceiling, she perceived a moon high in a dark sky. A strong wet wind whipped at her suit jacket and blew full on her face. She was suddenly freezing.

"Oh, God," she shuddered, knowing where she was. With branches of a scraggly oak lashing at her hair, Loretta Smith closed her jacket against a raw wind and gazed out over the dark expanse of the Cainsville graveyard. Dread swam in her head as she saw a black swirl of flapping, shrieking night that flew at her on unearthly wings. She cried out, cowering and covering her ears, arms over her head.

"This is the dream you've been afraid of facing," Vannie said. "This is what keeps you awake with the lights on. Look, Loretta. See what lies in the dark of your mind."

The reporter who had walked brazenly amid other people's grief, asking questions for which there were no answers, clung to the sisters like a frightened child and begged to escape.

"You didn't come to this place to hide, Loretta," Alma said. "You came to face your worst fears and have done with them. Until you do, you will never rest."

Sweat ran from Loretta in rivers; her ankles wobbled and her body shook. Yet, she nodded in almost imperceptible agreement, even as she saw the graves ahead of her—the two graves she imagined when she thought of Daddy and Brother Boy. She tried to pull back, but was dragged forward. Then almost vomited as she saw . . .

"They're open, Sisters," she moaned. "The graves are open."

"What are you afraid of, Loretta?" Vannie asked. "That your father and brother are dead and lost forever? Or that they are here and angry with you and want to punish you?"

Before she could answer, a shadowy figure swooped from underground and fastened itself to her ankle. "Ah, God," she cried, fighting to free herself. But how did you fight with ice-cold, clammy death that gripped you as a vice? "Billy? Is that you?"

The force field that touched her trembled and clung harder. "You've finally come to us, Lorrie. We knew you would."

With the words, a coiling force unleashed itself from under the second grave and came at her in a smothering hug of putrefying death, wrapping around her chest and throat. She gagged, smelling the decay that had tormented her in dreams, saw her father's face in front of her, rotting strands of skin over his skull. Bony fingers moved in her hair. Skeletal jaws snapped as they opened and closed.

Like in all bad dreams, she found herself unable to scream and rooted to the spot. "Help me!" she gasped, squeezing her eyes shut. Her arms flailed. "Help, Sisters! *Pleeeease!*"

"The only help you will find is in looking fear in the face," Vannie said as the reporter struggled. "Open your eyes and see what you are hiding from yourself."

"Do it here," Alma urged, "in the presence of allies."

Loretta fought to open her eyes, then fought to peer into the empty sockets in the missing face of the father she had left so long ago, the father who had worked a dangerous job down a dark hole while she climbed toward comfort and success. She'd realized that she was doing it for him, too, and for Mama and her brothers and sisters, only after hearing he had died a lonely death within a mine, more than a year after her last letter home. *Too late, too late.*

Loretta steeled herself to face him.

"Go ahead," she whispered. "Say it." She wanted him to open those hard-snapping jaws and to condemn her once and for all, to have done with it. She felt open and weak to her core, a condition for which she had no name. In fact, Loretta Smith had done something very unusual for her. The tough star reporter had disarmed herself and stood here in this spook yard, as vulnerable as though she had been carved from butter. If need be, she would die here and be laid to rest beside her father and brother.

"Go ahead, Daddy," she murmured into the wind. "I'm ready now."

Very slowly, the specter stretched out his fingers. She shuddered and then sighed at the gentle touch on her cheek. As the fear slid away, she felt calmness roll over her, reminding her how she had felt in the old days. Back home. Nighttime. Her father would walk in from the darkness and fill their drafty house with his warmth.

The skeleton receded slowly, transforming before her eyes. In its place, Loretta saw her father's hewn features, head tipped toward her, and his patient gaze as he looked into her tear-filled eyes.

How could I have forgotten his eyes?

"Guilt numbs and blinds, Loretta." Alma emerged from the darkness, a hurricane lantern held high in one hand, its light streaming into Loretta's mind. "It's time to remember, now. Do you dare?"

No sooner asked than it all came flooding back. The family gathering around Daddy as he came home from work and scooped her up against him, the smell of coal dust wafting from his shirt. Brother Boy, so beaten from his labor, yet longing to get his hands on his fiddle.

"Stop! I don't . . . I don't want to!"

"Feel it, Loretta," Vannie urged. "Feel your way home."

She broke then. "Oh, Daddy!" she wept, remembering. The good times were as hard to bear as the bad ones. She missed them all. Her mother and siblings and the music they played together on Saturday night, the jokes from tired men that tickled the kids and made them laugh at the boogeyman. Her father's hand stroking her hair. Pictures that had haunted her nightmares and lingered in the back of her daily wakefulness flashed: her brother crushed and dead at once (or so some other news-hungry reporter had written); her father trapped, his legs pinned by falling rock and forced to face his death alone in a dark coal-choked pocket in the Earth. Loretta turned in her daddy's arms. "Oh, Daddy," she whispered into his throat. "I'm so sorry. So sorry I was gone so long."

Alma touched her lantern and the light blazed as of a sun encapsulated within a glass shell and shone upon specter shapes of carrion birds around father and daughter, folding their dark wings as they lost substance and faded away.

"Look to your brother, quickly now, while there is still time." Alma swung her lantern to where he waited in the shadows. Her light shone on his face, not skeletal at all or angry. Just Brother Boy flashing his smile and holding out his hands asking her for something.

"He is asking you to release what separates you from him," Alma explained.

"But I don't know . . . I can't . . ."

"Let him help you, Loretta. Trust."

Her brother's cupped hands reached out again. What could he possibly want? Yet she felt something move deep inside her this time, the lump of misery that had been lodged in her gut for so long that she could hardly remember not having it. It lived in her like an ulcer, a blockage that was much more substantial than a mere sore made of pus and mucous. Alone in the dark, she had sensed pride and shame and judgment boiling inside it, and even more "stuff," so much of it that there was no getting to the end of it. She didn't even want to understand all that mess, it was too exhausting, much too big to untangle, too messy and murky, but, oh, she wanted rid of it. It was suffocating her. She could hardly breathe anymore.

But if you can't understand it, you can't get rid of it, she thought hopelessly.

And why not, dearie? It was Alma again. *Does everything have to be processed through your mind, young lady?*

Loretta, startled at such a question, had no answer, but the sister's voice was so light, so playful, that she found herself on the verge of yet another uncharacteristic decision. *Why not?*

Her brother must have been waiting for that. No sooner had permission been given than she felt his shadowy fingers passing through her flesh, then gripping hard on the mass.

Tightly bound to her innards, it twisted against a hard knot. A jerk from her brother's hands, and it burst free, the relief leaving her faint. Her brother had the ugly mass now; she saw him flash his smile one last time before he disappeared with it.

Her father placed a finger on his heart, then pointed it to her and followed after his boy. Yet, she could feel them in a place she hadn't been able to feel them for years—inside her own heart.

"It is done," Alma said gently. "You'll see them again someday, but now we must go, child. First, however, claim something to take back. It can be anything you want so long as it does harm to none."

"Be careful what you ask for," Vannie cautioned. "You will surely get it."

Loretta's mind circled, then zeroed in on an idea that made her heart beat faster. But could she ever? She frowned, unsure of herself as she stepped one foot and then the other into the shining light and stood there, the light growing brighter, searing her with its heat.

"It's your choice, Loretta," Alma intoned. "You can remain a city reporter, living alone in your apartment, sleeping with your light on, without family or friends. Or if you want to, you can come home. But you must decide quickly."

In that moment, Loretta sensed herself being drawn back across vast distances. Again, she felt the sensation of twirling around on her stool, spinning, somehow, in two directions at once. "I want to go home," she whispered, and at once felt foolish at expressing such childlike sentiment.

"No, not foolish at all," Vannie reproved. "Not when you remember that in a small hometown there is room for every individual. Everyone is important. There is a chance to be anything and everything you ever wanted to be. Many well-known writers come from small towns, you know."

"Wish for it," Alma directed. "Breathe it in and claim it."

"I do," Loretta said. An instant later, the light faded.

"Relax, dear," Alma said. "Just sit here quietly and tell us your plans."

"What plans?" Loretta blinked and found herself sitting at the sisters' counter. From the step, Banshee sat ruffling his feathers and making a gravelly sound like a cat's purr. Beside him, Sarah beamed up at her.

"About moving here to Willow Creek," Vannie said, joining the apprentice on the step. "And that particular house is the most beautiful place ever built in these parts. Plenty of room for your mother, if you wanted to bring her to live with you. Take a sip of coffee, that's it. A little more. Goodness only knows what living in a place like that might inspire you to write. Crooks and adventures and who knows what."

"You mean . . . the yellow house?" She saw it in her mind. The yellow house with the wraparound porch, once home to an outlaw gang. What a perfect home, the one she had been looking for her whole life. Suddenly, she was in a hurry. She had some money saved; she hoped it would be enough.

"Exactly enough," Alma said reassuringly. "Don't try to bargain with them, it's a fair price. If you pay less than the house is worth, it won't mean as much to you. It won't be a home, it will be a bargain. And by the way, I was wondering if the Rodney Smith family up the way might be some relation. They live up by the drive-in movie between Smithfield and Willow Creek. The theater put speakers in their backyard so the kids could come out nights and enjoy free movies."

"Rodney?" she repeated incredulously.

"And there's his sister, if I'm not mistaken, that lives not too far from him. Melissa Houston? I remember she said her maiden name was Smith. She's married with three small children. She has a face that reminds me of yours."

"My sister? My sister is in Willow Creek?"

"You did make the decision, didn't you?" Vannie looked at her meaningfully. "To come home?"

Loretta took a last shaky sip of coffee and rose, putting her cup on the counter and fumbling for money inside her briefcase. "I'll be back soon. I need to see the realtor as soon as possible."

"If it's your home, it won't be sold," Vannie assured her. "And that coffee is free. Our way of making you into a regular customer."

She, who never liked to accept a thing from anyone unless she had fairly earned it, smiled. Her hand fell away from her change purse, and she closed the briefcase. "Thank you, so much. Thank you for everything."

"You might take a minute before you leave, young lady, and thank the parrot, too. He played a great part in bringing you to where you've been longing to come for so long."

Loretta laughed and accepted the huge orange seed that Alma pressed into her hand. She offered the bird her thanks, and presented him with the seed before dashing out the front door. Moments later, her car backed smoothly out, then turned and headed up Pendleton Road toward the LaGrange real estate office.

"And you," Alma told the parrot as he spit the seed halfway across the lower dining room, "were on your best behavior. You didn't spit out the lady's offering until she was well out of range!"

The sisters had to have a laugh about that and pretty soon Sarah began laughing, too, the three of them sitting together on the steps with the parrot watching them closely, their images upside down in his metallic eyes. Then with a raucous shriek, the old bird joined in.

11

He found a job strumming and singing in a little shabby bar and restaurant called The Iron Dipper. Hearing the rattle and clanking over by the two pool tables and the patrons' talk and laughter, he figured his singing was just more background noise. But the listening was up to them. His part was the tune and the melody. And the feelings.

You could use music so many ways. Once, when he was at The Two Sisters', he'd been sporting a black eye and a bad attitude. After he finished singing, he found Sister Alma at his table. She said nothing about his performance, didn't even mention the new number he'd composed in black fury after his pa had left him bleeding on the floor of the still, his face cut and his hair full of moonshine where Cleatis had upended his cup over his head.

"What did you think about Black Heart?" he finally asked her, interrupting her mutterings about a tone-deaf monk who could sing complex harmonies, but only while on his knees offering thanks to God. ("He had to feel the gratitude," she'd been saying, "before he could get the blessing, you see! My, you should have heard the sour notes that came out of that man when he was of plain old ordinary mind. But moved by grace, he became a regular choirboy!")

"Black Heart," he repeated firmly, knowing full well she'd heard him, but was avoiding answering the question.

"Oh, yes. It simmered with hate and violence, didn't it? Made quite the impression."

"On everybody?" He was pleased.

"No, dear, on you. That's who it was for, wasn't it? A chance to rage at whoever gave you that black eye?"

"What's wrong with raging at a damn bully?" he growled.

"I thought we were talking about performing," she said, seeming rather confused.

"Uh . . . what do you mean?"

"Well, a musician performs for others, doesn't he? One of the things that makes you so special onstage is that you love the people listening and they feel it. Tonight all you loved was your black eye."

Now he looked over the noisy Nashville crowd and felt both the gratitude that had turned a tone-deaf monk into a choirboy, and the love that had fashioned the no-account son of a moonshiner into a poet and given him a ticket onto the bus that had brought him to the capital of country music.

A few people looked up from their beer mugs and shot glasses and glanced at the roughhewn singer sitting in a circle of light on the small stage. He looked both impenetrable and remote.

A man sitting alone and out of the action had been about to rise, but he sat back down, noting that the busy room had drawn quiet around him. Most eyes were fastened on the stage, where the singer was growling out something about white lightnin' making for a "good night and a bad morning."

Good God, from the sound of that deep voice, the boy might as well be singing from inside a gravel pit. The man took out a pen and jotted down the name tacked to a signboard at the side of the stage. Sugar Curtis. He was as rough and raw as they came. And nobody who heard him sing was going to forget him.

12

Sarah's sleep was deeper and blacker than usual as she lay on her cot in the too-silent Curtis house. Her brothers and sisters had also sunk like stones into unconsciousness, seeking its depths as places to hide. A chill blew in the air outside the house, but the cold inside stemmed not from weather but from fear. The children and even Nadine had tried to escape tonight by dying to the world, lying motionless, barely breathing.

Nights had been like this of late, after days of mounting tension. The coil inside of Cleatis was winding tighter; soon he would blow. His pleasure in making money had passed quicker than anyone could have expected.

Now with his famous Double C's flying in the face of the law and earning a gleam of respect in the eyes of the drinking public, it had dawned on Cleatis that even illegal work was still work. He was as bored and tired of his good fortune as he was dreading the day, not far off, when it would peter out. Soon the pussy-footers, as he called them, would have their fill of hangovers and guilty mornings and decide to go straight. Many of them had only been buying booze to irk the teetotalers who'd busted up his competition. Now that they had established they could drink if they wanted to, they wouldn't want to. Only the brain-fried geezers and the occasional town idiot who didn't know the party was over would be around.

The kids recognized the hardness in their father's eyes and the steel pumping into his arms and fists. He was turning mean again. The children drifted deeper into black sleep, escaping nightmares.

Deep in such sleep, Sarah heard the sound of her own name. *"Sarah! Sar . . . rah!"* She came slowly awake, not into the everyday world, but into a world inside slumber. Though her mental eyes opened, her physical eyes stayed closed and her body as motionless as a fallen tree. *Dead to the world.* This was the thought that crossed her mind as she rose over her sleeping body.

"Sar . . . rah! This way, child!" She knew the voice, but could not quite place it. In this world where she had risen, it was enough to know that the voice was friendly and that following it was the right thing to do.

"Sarah! Come along, sweetheart!" a second voice chimed on top of the first.

The walls of her room opened, revealing a deep forest, black in a moonless night. She took a step into the woods, and then another, walking in the forest as if its daughter, brushing past trees, through ferns and saplings, using her fingers to find her way, following the sound of her own name.

"Sarah!" It was a chant now. She hurried forward, broad leaves brushing against her cheeks and hair, the forest floor crunching under her feet as she pushed through the brush, avoiding the large roots that sprang up along her way.

"Sarah! Here! Here we are, darlin'!"

She jogged forward, feeling her way past a large stump and stumbling up an incline. And there was her special tree, standing alone in a clearing, barely visible in the night. She moved to it and wrapped her arms around its huge trunk, hugging it.

"Say your words, child." The voice came from inside the tree; there could be no question of that.

Sarah wrinkled her brow. Why couldn't she remember her magic words? Maybe it was because she was still so fast asleep back there in her bed.

She shook her head to clear it, breathed in the sharp night air, and whispered: "If I were a tree . . . If I were a tree . . . you . . . would be . . . me." Even as she said the words, she knew they were not quite right. Sure enough, nothing happened. "Um . . . If I were a tree, who would be me?" *No, that's not right!* She strained to hear inside the tree, but the voices had gone silent. Clearly she needed her magic words to gain entrance.

Looking up, she saw a single star flickering down on her through leaves and branches. Her star! She said with more confidence: "If I were a tree, what tree would I be?" The answer immediately swelled inside of her, and she imagined herself as *this* tree, growing in the dim forest. Gazing upward, she saw her star again, and then another star and another, as if a lamplighter were traveling across the sky, igniting thousands of stars over where she stood.

The tree warmed to her touch. Stepping back, she saw that a knothole in front of her had begun to glow, becoming brighter, as if from a lit window inside the tree trunk. The light shone into her center, making her long to ride it into the heart of the tree.

Nothing for it but to try.

With a sigh, she fell forward into the light, and immediately was slurped into the unknown. Losing her nerve, she yelped, "Help! Help!" But it was too late for that. Zipping forward, she landed in the world within the tree, a familiar place as it turned out. A familiar place indeed.

"Have a sip of tea, Sarah," Vannie said, pouring for her. Alma was also in the room. The tree had been their place for mutual dreaming for some time now.

Alma pulled gingerbread from her apron pocket, placed it on an oaken slab, and sliced three small pieces. "A taste, child, then there is business that cannot wait another night."

Sarah watched the color of Alma's eyes shift, turning from gray-green to deepening amber. "Daddy!" she whispered, understanding. The sweetness of the gingerbread cloyed her tongue as she remembered her mama's new bruises, deep purplish-blue, this time caused not from a belt, but a fist.

She'd seen them tonight, the skin broken over the worst marks. Gazing into Alma's eyes, she saw what tomorrow might bring, heard the crack of a broken bone and her mama's screams.

"No!" she gasped. "We can't let him!"

"Then we must act now," Alma said. "Your father has just dreamed the last of this night's dreams, and his unconscious mind is open, but not for long."

"But . . . how? I don't know h-how!" Sarah stammered.

"Together is how," Vannie said. "Sister Alma and I are here to assist, but it is you, as his daughter, who has access to him. It's not just your common blood. It's about love."

"Love?" Sarah looked down at the gnarled wood curling beneath her feet.

"Even love that has been tainted with violence is a power. The ghost of love between the two of you over the years, what was there and what *should* have been there, is a psychic link to your father."

Sarah gulped but did not turn away, even when she heard another of Nadine's cries from a future that she must not allow to happen.

"Show me," she said. "Show me, now!"

The Earth moved as it can only do in dreams, smearing their surrounds into streaks of night browns, misty grays, soft yellows, and woodland greens. Sarah saw that they were no longer inside the tree, but in a circle clearing in the forest.

Strange chants spilled from her lips, joining those of the sisters', building, building, all of them swaying together, till the Earth responded in low rumbling quakes.

"Call your father, Sarah," Alma said. "Demand that he meet us here in the depth of his sleep. Hurry. Time is short."

She was afraid to call him. Still her voice surged out of her like a tidal wave. "DADDY! DADDY, COME TO THE CIRCLE!"

"Once more," Vannie murmured. "Three is the charm."

Sarah took a deep breath, remembered her mother's screams, and shouted: *"DADDY! COME HERE! COME NOW!"*

For a moment the circle and the woods beyond stood silent. Then at the center of the circle shone a ghostly light. Within it, an oval-shaped doorway was revealed, through which a bewildered Cleatis straggled, pulling his suspenders over his shoulders and struggling to fasten his pants. "What the fool—?"

"Fool is right!" Vannie's glare stopped him head-on. Alma positioned herself behind him, her hazel eyes boring through the back of his skull. He stood trapped, a frog gigged from two directions.

"Daddy!" Sarah crept toward the rim of the circle, which was visibly etched into the earth, enclosing her father within it.

"Stay away from him," Alma commanded. "Don't go even an inch inside the circle."

Sarah edged her toe back safely behind the line. She saw that her daddy could not free himself from Vannie's magnetic purple gaze. As afraid of him as she was, she hated to see him trapped. Surely this wasn't right, to defy her own father in such a terrible way. Even now he was willing her to free him. She inched toward him once more, despite her efforts to stop.

Swack! Swack! Swack! Cleatis thrashed about, flipping and flopping like a big game fish being pulled onto a boat, the sisters struggling to hold him. Twisting and rolling and flexing his anvil-hard muscles, he wrestled with their line, trying to snap it, only to have it tangle thickly around him.

They had the feel of it now, two ancient fisherwomen battling the catch of a lifetime. Struggling to free himself, he lost his footing and crashed to the ground, still bent on escape, clawing his way forward on hands and elbows, only to be dragged backwards time and again. He would not relent. Yet, the more he struggled, the tighter the line drew around him, all the easier for the sisters to jerk him back to the center of the circle, holding fast against his grappling. Worn-out, drenched in sweat—or was it seawater from which the fisherwomen had lugged their human fish?—he collapsed. A last bellow roared from his throat; his red face scowled at them. He made for a terrifying spectacle.

Swallowing hard, Sarah eased her foot well back of the circle's edge.

"Cleatis Curtis!" Vannie's voice rang throughout the clearing. "It is irregular for us to restrict any living soul from the execution of his own freewill. But these are unique circumstances. Your daughter is here to witness what we do. She is part of us, and we are part of her. You do not like this, but it is so. Because of this, you have become more of a danger to your family than before. In this we have responsibility, thus a right to power.

"We have placed Sarah on your left, your receiving side, to give her access to participate, should she choose to do so. Regardless of her choice, you are in our power now, and we bring the full force of it to you."

Sarah watched her father squirm, his fury undiminished.

"These will be your restrictions," Vannie continued, but though her lips continued to move, no more sound issued forth. Instead, a funnel cloud appeared in air, the larger end near her mouth gathering her words, the smaller end moving toward the struggling Cleatis. It swept over his head and pierced the base of his skull, her words spiraling through the funnel and pouring into the root of his brain. All the while Alma sang in a lilting undertone, the words barely discernable, about some changes to be made, then finishing on a crescendo:

"THERE'LL BE SOME CHANGES MADE TODAY! THERE'LL BE SOME CHANGES MADE!"

Sarah realized it must be a magic spell as Vannie kept speaking into the funnel, no doubt binding Daddy to her will.

THWACK! THWACK! Sarah jumped, thinking he was fighting again. But no, it wasn't that. It was bundles of briars and brambles falling from the sky. *THWACK! THWACK!* They tumbled into place, forming a barricade around him; thorns flew out of the air nailing the structure together. *THWACK! THWACK!* The cage rose from the ground, her father raging inside it.

The sisters fell quiet, listening to Cleatis thrashing around inside his prison and waiting to see if the fortress would hold. It seemed to grow stronger and tougher each time he battered against it, sending him howling from the thorns that bored into his flesh, only to try again. Over and over, he hurled himself against the bramble fortress, causing its walls to rattle and more bellows of pain to issue forth. Sarah tried not to imagine her daddy inside the barricade, bleeding and sweating, his clothes ripped, his body torn as he continued to rage, choking on his own bile. Finally, he stopped.

Silence fell over the clearing. The spell was done. The sisters opened their arms upward and outward in thanks, then went to their trembling apprentice.

"That should hold him for a while," Vannie said, dabbing tears from Sarah's cheeks and smoothing a lock of her hair. "Don't worry, he'll be fine in there."

Cleatis stirred again, rattling around inside the brambles, yelping every time he bumped into one, as though surprised by each new thorn prick.

Vannie kept her fingers on the lock of Sarah's hair, smiling as she twirled it round and round. Her soothing touch made the child sleepy. Her body in her bed called her to join it, though she tried to hold back, wavering between two worlds.

"Let go, child. Let yourself go back."

"But how will he get out?" A new wave of sleepiness overtook her. No effort could prevent the rise of her dream body and its flight over the forest to her house, then through its walls. She hovered over her sleeping form, resisting the slide into warm flesh, holding out for an answer. No matter what he had done, she hated to think of her daddy locked inside a prison of any kind, much less one made of thorns and brambles. Yet Vannie had said he'd be fine.

"It's just part of him that's stuck there," Alma whispered into her ear as the child settled into her body, her eyelids flickering. "And the biggest problem is not how he will free himself."

"What is the biggest?" Sarah could barely stay conscious long enough to hear the answer.

"The larger concern is *when* he will get out, for he surely will. That's what we'll have to watch for."

"Okay, we'll watch." Sarah dug her head deeper into her pillow.

In the dark of the Curtis house, only one set of ears heard her voice. Alma touched a palm to the sleeping child's forehead, closing her third eye. "Goodnight, sweetheart."

13

Sarah started across the road from the sisters' house, heading toward the café with an armload of fresh tea towels and a sack of apples from the front porch. Her dark blond hair was tied back with a rose-colored ribbon matching her simple work dress under a white lace-trimmed apron. The sisters always incorporated rose into the fabric of her clothes. Sarah had heard Alma say that by wearing that particular shade she was reclaiming the sweetness of her childhood. Lately, that sweetness bubbled up like sugar in a simmer of raspberry jam, despite an unease stemming from the behavior of her father, which had been so different from his usual self as to be downright peculiar. He hadn't raised his voice or a hand to anyone in almost two weeks. What was more, he was eerily polite from sunup to his unaccustomed early bedtime just after sundown each night.

"He's like a bee on a string," Sarah had overheard Vannie whispering to Alma several mornings ago. "Buzzing around in circles."

Sarah had no memory of the spell that she and the sisters had cast over her father, and the sisters chose not to tell her about it. They had worked magic for the common good. If the child did not remember, it was better so; yet both sisters kept an eye out for signs that she might need telling. It was a time for delicate balance. Cleatis had them seriously on edge. They had known the outcome of their spell would be temporary and unpredictable, but had expected some grit of resistance. They needed it, in fact, to help them gauge when his dark side would resurface. Instead, he was becoming more hidden from them every day.

"Something's not right," Vannie said when the Reverend mentioned that Cleatis had dropped by the church asking for help in finding a job and that Silas Ellis at the hardware store was considering taking him on as a delivery man.

Alma remembered Cleatis fighting them, a fish being hauled toward a boat on the high seas. Now the vision changed. She and Vannie were on a boat, alright, a big fish on their line. Sarah was with them, hanging onto the rail. Only now their fish wasn't fighting any more. The line was slack, lying limp on the water.

"What the hell is he up to?" Vannie breathed.

Both sisters hoped he hadn't turned on them somewhere in the deep like Moby Dick in a sea of revenge, swimming at them even now, gaining speed to smash their boat to smithereens.

The important thing was to keep Sarah as peaceful as possible. She was growing in grace, becoming easier in both the company of adults and of her own peers who had once mocked her for being poor and unwashed. Her days of being whipped by the cruel hand of Mrs. Norwick were distant memories now. Sarah was finding new hope.

Today, however, she chewed her lower lip and looked distinctly guilty as she entered the side door to the Little Room, passing Banshee along the way, whose cage had been placed on the patio so he might enjoy the sunshine. An outraged squawk from the bird that favored Sarah's company above any others' went ignored as she set down the towels and began unloading apples into a bowl on the table.

Vannie saw the blush crawling up the child's throat. "Sit down, hon." She took her own seat by the wood-burning stove that even on this warm day was stoked and boiling up a pot of ham hocks. The aroma was delectable, but Sarah, who thought there was nothing any finer than ham hocks and a bowl of bean soup to go along, didn't even glance toward the stove. She reluctantly took the chair closest to the door and avoided Vannie's eyes.

"Every day holds its own lesson," Vannie commented, unfolding newspapers and laying them across the table. She pushed a knife at the child and began using her own to pare apples. Sarah followed suit, her nimble fingers adept at doing almost any kitchen task. For a while, there were only the soft squawks from the parrot, the offended bird ruffling his feathers until he had almost puffed himself into the size of a beachball.

"Nobody's watching you, you crazy old bird," Vannie said under her breath with a smile twitching her lips.

Sarah looked up. "Have you ever seen a grape the size of a walnut?"

"No, but I've seen a tomato the size of a watermelon."

The child's face flushed again. "There were some grapes on the vine beside the little white house next to yours," she said miserably. "Big purple grapes."

"Concord grapes," Vannie said. "Thelma Blaney grows the best Concords in the county. I swear they taste like wine. Pop one of those things between your teeth and feel that delicious squishing on your tongue . . . ummm! For a nickel, I'd run over there right now and grab me a handful. If she wasn't looking, that is."

"You mean . . . swipe 'em?"

"That's one way to put it, I guess. But the vines are so close to the house, running right against our garage, and we've suffered through enough snake problems, thanks to those grapes, for me to feel a part ownership in that vineyard, copperheads and all. I'm of the opinion that every snake in a hundred miles comes calling in grape season. There was one there last summer that had to be six feet long."

Sarah's face showed horror. "I hate snakes."

Alma appeared suddenly. She had been selling candy at the counter and now came strolling through the kitchen and into the Little Room as though she had heard the whole conversation. "If you hate snakes, you should have seen the one I saw the other day wrapped around Mrs. Blaney's chimney. Made that six-footer look like a fishing worm."

"On her chimney?" Sarah gaped at her.

"Yep. Head stuck right down the hole." She nibbled some ham hocks. "These are good! Any more tender, they shouldn't be. I'll start dishing them up. We're taking a hamper to Thelma Blaney."

Sarah squirmed. "I'll stay here and watch the counter."

Alma began ladling ham hocks into a large bowl. "Why not come with us, darling girl? We didn't scare you talking about those snakes, did we?"

"Well, maybe a little," the child said wretchedly. "But there's something else. I saw those big purple grapes this morning, and before I knew what I was doing, I . . . I grabbed a handful and put 'em in my mouth. *I stole Mean Old Mrs. Blaney's grapes!*"

Vannie put down her paring knife. "Ah, well, they probably won't put you in jail for that. Fact is, there aren't many who wouldn't pick an apple off somebody else's tree or a strawberry out of a patch and not feel free to eat it, if a body was alone and unobserved. That said," she added, "don't take any more grapes from Mrs. Blaney unless she says it's alright."

"Yes ma'am," Sarah said nervously.

Vannie got up to cover the ham hock bowl, and Alma removed a hamper from the kitchen worktable and carried it to the Little Room. Peeping inside, Sarah saw a rhubarb pie, a jam cake, a closed container of bean soup, a crock of home-churned butter, and a slab of napkin-wrapped cornbread.

"Oops! Hold on a minute," Alma said, heading back to the front of the café.

"Why do you care about Mean Old . . . I mean, Mrs. Blaney?" Sarah asked curiously. "The other day Tommy Burgis tried to sell her a jar of his mama's preserves, and she done chased him clear across the lawn with a rake."

"She can be ornery," Vannie admitted. "But you see she had a dream she was going to die last night. She needs bean soup and cornbread, rhubarb pie, and a big slice of jam cake with vanilla ice cream to get her perk back."

Alma came in carrying the container of ice cream and handed it to

Sarah. "Here, darlin'. You carry this."

Sarah shuddered at the thought of walking up the sloping green lawn and knocking at the mean old woman's front door. There must be a horrible smell to the place, and probably the old woman would scream at them and maybe throw something. Or get the rake again. She'd screamed at Tommy that next time she'd take a butcher knife to him. And the two sisters wanted her to go with them to such a place? "How did you know she had a dream last night?" she wheezed, clutching the cold container of ice cream. "Did-did s-someone tell you th-that s-she . . .?"

Alma fixed her gaze on the child's face. "Sarah, you know better than to ask questions when you already have answers. Don't you, now?"

Sarah hesitated, then nodded. "Yes ma'am."

"You know how Vannie and I know these things."

"I guess so. I think I do. You go into people's dreams. Like you do mine sometimes."

"That's one way," Alma agreed.

"Come on." Vannie picked up the bowl of ham hocks, while Alma hoisted the hamper. "We're on our way to grandmother's house. You did know she was a grandmother, didn't you?"

"No ma'am." Sarah felt sorry for any grandchild that belonged to the mean old woman. She hesitated as the sisters whisked past her into the courtyard. "Shouldn't we lock up the café before we leave?"

"Whatever for?" Alma asked. "Let's go!"

14

Alma knocked only once before the door snapped open and a gaunt old body exploded through the opening. For a horrible moment it seemed to Sarah as though the woman's beady eyes might pop right out of her wrinkled brown face. It was a tough face, melted down, but in the way cement dries, in solid rivulets. Lines ran down, mouth looped down, eyes swooped down. But there wasn't a sag to any of it; it was all hard as rock. Even her neck was sinewy and tough.

She belongs on a broom, Sarah thought in horror. *Or maybe on the block on chicken-killing day. She looks as tough as an old rooster.*

"What are you bothering me for?" the mean old woman snapped. She waved both bony arms at them like a scarecrow come to life in a bird-infested field. "I ain't sick. Nobody told you I was sick, did they?"

Vannie pointed to the hamper. "We've got bean soup in there, Thelma. Two hundred and thirty-nine beans."

The old woman paused in her flurry. "How come two hundred and thirty-nine?" she asked suspiciously.

"I'll tell you if you let us inside," Vannie offered.

Alma held out the hamper. "We also have ham hocks, cornbread, rhubarb pie, jam cake—"

"How the hell do you know what I like? What are you, GD snoops? Sneaking around asking what kind of food I like. Food's as personal as perfume. I hate people that give you perfume, too. What business is it of anybody's what I want to smell like and what I want to eat?"

"Hush your mouth, and take a good look in there, Thelma. Jam cake with thick caramel icing. And guess what Sarah has for you?"

Trembling, Sarah held out the cold container. "There's vanilla ice cream in here, ma'am. Home-churned."

The old woman grudgingly stepped aside. "Nobody ever brings me any food, they're all hoping I'll starve to death. I don't have family anymore, just heirs. That's the way I think of the whole greedy bunch of them. You know that great-niece of mine, the one they named after me, trying to butter me up? She calls herself 'Thel'—did you ever hear such nonsense? Thel this and Thel that. Sounds ridiculous. My nephew says, 'Thel really likes your ring, Aunt Thelma. You 'spect it'll maybe belong to her one of these days?' I say back, 'That there ring is the only diamond I ever owned, and it'll be buried with me unless you cut my finger off with a butcher knife, that's how tight I'm going to curl up my hands right before I die. Just bunch up the fingers, until the rigor mortis sets in, then nobody'll ever slip that diamond off my finger less they break the danged bone with a hammer.' I've caught them going through my silverware and my antique hand-painted plates. I've half a mind to have the whole kit and caboodle buried with me. I'd get a king-sized coffin and tell Mr. Patterson to stick in the silver, the dishes, and my sewing machine if I wasn't afraid they'd dig me up to get at everything. How come there are exactly two hundred and thirty-nine beans in that soup, Sister?"

Vannie twinkled. "Well, Thelma, you know very well that one more bean would make it two-farty."

The mean old woman thought that over for a moment and gave a crusty smile. "Since you've bothered me, you'd just as soon serve me the food. I'll pay you for it. There's a dollar in the sugar bowl."

"Just can't bear to be beholdin', can you, Thelma?" Alma noticed her hobbling toward her favorite chair and gave her a hard shove in that direction.

The mean old woman half-fell into the easy chair. "What the hell are you trying to do to me now, Sister? Kill me? I didn't leave you anything in my will."

"That's the way you like things, isn't it?" Alma asked. "You don't trust a gift; you think you have to pay for it. You'd rather have a hard push than a helping hand any day. Settle down, Thelma. Put your bony old feet up on that ottoman, and I'll set up a tray for you."

While they served, Vannie assigned Sarah to the worst duty, making polite conversation with the mean old woman.

"Nice day, isn't it, ma'am?" Sarah said miserably, watching her butter her cornbread. She had remarkably dexterous fingers, even if they did look like claws.

"You got something real to say, say it," the woman snapped. "But spare me that polite dribble. Lord Almighty, every time anybody comes to the door, we get around to the weather. Search your mind and say the first real thing that comes to you, little snippet, I don't care what it is."

Sarah sighed and tried to think of something. Everything in the room seemed to be waiting for her response, even the loud-ticking grandfather's clock that sat in the corner. All in all, the house was nicer than she had expected. It was much cleaner, for one thing, with not a speck of dust to be found, and lacked the horrors she had imagined (like a pile of dead chickens in the corner, perhaps, or a mangy yellow cat that slinked around with terrified eyes, waiting for the next poke from the old lady's rake handle).

But the parlor in which she found herself was nonetheless grim. For one thing, it was very dim, almost all the light blocked with tightly drawn gray curtains. For another, there was little decoration except for a few singularly ugly goose-necked lamps and some aged and faded pictures on the walls of long-buried people in old-fashioned poses. The furniture was plain and drab, especially an old dining table that stood dwarfed beneath a grotesque, antique chandelier in a corner near the kitchen. The woven scatter rugs were of dull colors and unimaginative design, mainly plain ovals caught in a pattern of boring repetition.

Under the slurping of bean soup and the loud ticking, Sarah could swear she heard a little girl crying. Startled, she looked around the room, almost expecting to see a cage with children being fattened for the oven.

"You come up with anything yet?" the mean old woman asked, her mouth full of soup.

Sarah shrank back into her chair, trying to block out the crying. Maybe it was a cat or a mockingbird outside the window. No, wait. Now it seemed to be coming from a closet across the room. A wailing, like from a very young child.

"Can't think of anything, right?" The woman waved a dismissive hand lined with creepy blue veins. "Just another head full of lint."

"No, wait, I thought of something."

"It had better not be the weather again."

"No ma'am. It's snakes. They're on your roof and in your yard. They come to eat your grapes."

"So that's what you think, stupid girl?" The old lady speared a ham hock. "Snakes don't eat grapes. They eat mice and the rest of the vermin that rob my vines. Like little girls who have a taste for grapes that don't belong to them, hmmm?" She stuck the ham into her nearly toothless mouth and gummed it. "There's one of them snakes now, right behind you. A big slivering devil. *Boo!*"

Sarah screamed and jumped from her chair, only to find the old woman laughing so hard she was almost choking on her ham hock. Even worse, something was happening to her skin. It looked like wet cement that was fast baking under the sun. In only seconds, it was dry, hard, and so hot it was smoking. Thelma Blaney was solid stone. There was nothing human about her now, nothing soft or yielding to the touch. Nothing alive.

Sarah staggered back, sending her chair smashing against the floor. "She's dead! She looks like . . . like a statue!"

"Yep, she's hard as a rock," Alma said. "You hear me in there, Thelma?"

A deep growl came from the stone woman's throat.

"Don't growl at me, you're the one who decided to be all mean and ornery. You've been hardening for years. All we did was add a little soup for heat and hydration."

"That and a little cornmeal to cement the mix," Vannie said, reaching out to thump a stiffened jowl. "A little over-cured, but you'll do."

Sarah was well aware that you didn't make cement out of bean soup and cornbread; still, with the sisters, you never knew. Anyhow, that was the least of her worries. She was hearing that same wailing sound. Somewhere close, a child was in trouble. She peeked around the edge of Thelma's chair, almost expecting to see a little girl crouching there, but there was no sign of her. Maybe she was in the back. She crept closer and looked between the chair and the small fireplace. Nothing.

Yet. The sound. Was louder. Was the child already in the oven in the old lady's kitchen? She inched closer to the stone woman's chair. The wailing grew louder yet. She was beginning to get a terrible hunch. *Surely not.* She leaned forward cautiously and inclined her ear toward the woman's stomach, almost expecting to hear a cry for help from within. Instead, a low rumbling vibrated the soles of her feet and shook the floor beneath Mrs. Blaney's chair.

But under the sound was the weeping again, and not far away.

"Sisters?" Sarah whispered, glancing up at them.

But they paid no attention, being too busy arguing across the top of Thelma's half-bald rock head as to protocol for moving freshly hardened cement.

"The last thing we need is to break her," Vannie said. "Let's just let her sit."

"It wouldn't hurt to straighten her out so we could at least lay her on the couch."

"In case you didn't notice, Sister, she's congealed. Nothing's going to straighten her out."

The sisters didn't seem to hear the crying at all, but to Sarah it was growing louder all the time.

Not in the woodbin, she thought, peeking in. *Not in the bottom of the grandfather's clock. Not under any table or chair.* She opened the door of the closet. *Nope, not there either.*

Reluctantly, she eased back toward the stone woman and heard it again. A child sobbing.

The sisters were still busy squabbling. Gathering her nerve, Sarah made a fist and tapped gently just below the woman's breastbone.

The crying ceased.

"Knock-knock," Sarah whispered. "Who's there?"

There was no answer, but a tiny circle of dim yellow light appeared around the spot where she had knocked. In its center was a small golden disk, which began pulsing, emitting wave after wave from its perimeter, a new wave with every pulse. Before Sarah's eyes, a mesmerizing push-pull of magnetic force was taking place. The inner waves expanded as they moved out, and the outer waves contracted as they were dragged back toward the golden orb, which was receding into the stony edifice that only moments before had been the flesh-and-blood body of Mrs. Thelma Blaney. A vortex was slowly opening into her third chakra at her solar plexus.

Whoever was in there gave a loud shriek, and Sarah tried to pull away, only to be sucked forward. She dug in her heels, but it was no use. Inch by inch, she was being dragged into the portal. Then she was inside, plunging end-over-end, not into a stone canyon as she had half-expected, but rather into a swirling energy that was neither air nor water, though the sensation was like spiraling down a drain.

From the energy chamber in which she spun, she glimpsed a stony outline of a fast-receding other world composed of frozen veins and a thread-like filigree of other vessels and squiggly lines, some of them hung with tiny pea-pod shapes, all forming the spidery network of Thelma Blaney's hardened interior.

As the physical world faded, Sarah continued to spiral into the depths of Thelma's etheric energy, a regular soup of fear, anxiety, anger, sadness, rage, frustration, loneliness, and despair. Sarah screamed and moaned. She might have perished on the spot had these feelings not been intermingled with glimmers of deep pleasure, excitement, and a strange peace that she had hardly felt in her life.

But these lovely sensations were no sooner experienced than they were drowned by the sobbing of the child that she still could not find, but who pulled at her, dragging her deeper and deeper into the whirlpool.

The farther she descended, the thicker the emotions, especially the terrible ones. Sorrow drenched her. Rage scalded her. She convulsed with fear and wailed like a lost nightbird with loneliness and despair, only to hear her own cries echoed by those of the other child.

The crying abruptly stopped, and Sarah found herself looking at a very pretty little dark-haired girl about four years old. She looked happy to see Sarah, but pouty at the same time.

The little girl wiped away tears and sniffed. "I guess you won't like me. Nobody ever does."

"Well, of course, I like . . ." Sarah gulped and stared harder at the picture slowly forming in front of her. The little girl wasn't alone. She wasn't even free. She was snugly wrapped in the coils of the longest, ugliest snake that Sarah had ever seen. The creature was dark gray with splotches of brown, each large splotch eerily outlined in white, and had a forked tongue that flicked out of its mouth, tasting the air in the way that hungry snakes do when in search of prey.

"Whatever you do, don't make any noise," the little girl warned, "or he'll come get you. But he'll probably smell you anyway."

Sure enough, the pitted triangular head shot toward Sarah.

The scream that ripped out of her was bigger than she was. In fact, it was the loudest sound she had ever heard in her life. Louder than her daddy's yelling. Louder than his shotgun. Louder than her own heartbeat when she lay in the dark listening to his stumbling footsteps heading down the hall.

The snake's elliptical pupils glowed yellow and hypnotic as its lower jaw dropped open like a trapdoor, revealing dozens of upper teeth slashed backward toward its cavernous throat. Sarah imagined what it would be like struggling to free herself from that mouth, the sharp barbs piercing into her, pulling her farther inside and forcing her down the endless throat.

DOWN. DOWN. DOWN.

The little girl was no longer crying, though muddy yellow tears lay frozen on her cheeks. "You know me," she said uncertainly, shivering a bit as the serpent turned its attention back to her. "Don't you?"

"No." Sarah edged backward, wanting to leave this place, to forget this little girl wrapped in the snake's coils. Fresh adrenaline shot through her body as the snake cocked its head in her direction. Its face snapped to alert. The creature was interested in her fright; there could no doubt about that. It slowly loosened its grip on the child and inched in Sarah's direction.

Parasite, Sarah thought, trying to quiet her fast-beating heart. It reminded her of the time her brother got worms. She shivered. But those worms had been small, not like this monster. What did the thing live on, anyway? How many little girls came to visit the world inside Mrs. Blaney, for Pete's sake? He must have been eating something else; otherwise, he wouldn't be so big and fat.

Though she had thought the question and had not asked it aloud, the little girl answered: "It squeezes you and drinks your tears, or if you get a new puppy, it eats that."

"Oh, it couldn't!" Sarah gasped. The snake slithered closer, flicking its forked tongue toward her jittery belly. "Not a puppy!"

"No, but Papa drowned it. That's when the snake came. It grabbed me and started squeezing and hurting me real bad." The blue eyes brimmed with tears.

Familiar eyes, but Sarah was not concerned about where she and the child might have met before. Not with the snake raising its head and weaving back and forth, its gleaming yellow pupils eagerly examining her face. "Does . . . does he also eat little girls?" she managed through clenched teeth.

But even before the dark-haired child shook her head, Sarah knew that wasn't it. Not exactly, anyway.

"I think he saves little girls for last. First he eats how you feel when your mama doesn't love you. He eats how you feel when you fall down and scuff up the new shoes your daddy paid good money for and everybody says you're spoilt and selfish and good for nothin'. He eats how you feel when the children in school are mean to you. *You* know."

Sobbing overtook the child, and the snake's head immediately flipped around, the better to study her. Then quietly, with purpose, the monster began to slither back toward the weeping girl.

So that's it! It likes pain. As relieved for herself as she was, Sarah felt a wave of pity for the little blue-eyed child, who had been pursued by this serpent for heaven only knew how long, and which was now nudging her again with its long snout.

Sarah's eyes welled with tears, and her throat constricted with stifled sobs. She moaned in spite of herself, and at that moment, the snake froze, its head turning once again toward her, its yellow eyes like pockets of rotting autumn leaves. It seemed torn between the two anguished children, unsure of which to claim first.

Sarah desperately searched her mind for a way out, but could only stand frozen to the spot.

Apprentice! Alma's voice spoke inside her. *If you are to escape with the child, it must be now. Come out, Sarah, and bring the young one with you.*

"But how can I?"

Enter the silence.

Sarah immediately clapped both hands over her mouth.

The inside-your-head kind of silence, the voice said with humor. *There is no pain below thought, nothing there in that quietness to feed the serpent. Shhhh. Hush your mind, child, so it can't sniff you out. Act now. Hurry.*

Just as Sarah was sure it was impossible to find a hush in her racing mind, she found it. There it was, below the cries of the child and under the thunder of her own blood pumping through arteries and veins—a blissful hush. In the calm, she looked cautiously around and saw more clearly the rippling walls of the whirling chamber that surrounded her. Above her a light shone, like from the mouth of a cave opening into the outside world. The round walls consisted of rings of energy, woven together and stacked, yet moving and dynamic in their dance of expansion and contraction. Would they hold the weight of two little girls?

The young one had stopped crying. The two children stared across at each other, the great snake dormant between them.

The command came out of the silence: *GO!*

"But—" Sarah gulped.

GO!

Sarah went. Clearing the snake in a running leap, she snatched the little girl's hand, and dragged her toward the ringed perimeter of the vortex. Yanking the child behind her, she gingerly stepped onto the first ring, the soles of her feet buzzing on the whirring circuit. The ring dipped sharply under their weight, then snapped back to orbit with renewed strength.

Whew!

But there was no time to waste. With the child clinging tightly to her skirt, Sarah bounded upward to the next ring, struggling to block the onslaught of thoughts pounding at the edges of her mind.

I mustn't think . . . mustn't think . . . She panted, seeking quiet on the in-and-out of her breath.

The child beside her lost her balance and screamed.

"Shhhh!" Sarah warned, pulling her up. Too late. The snake reared its head behind them, gathering its coils and licking the air for their scent. To make matters worse, there was a rumbling deep inside this crazy world and a rattling, as if Thelma's core was coming unhinged. The loop under their feet wavered, slicing down and bucking upward in arcing waves.

Sarah looked over her shoulder and saw the snake slithering after them, energized and electric, whipping "S" shapes up the side of the chamber.

Frozen, the children clung together and screamed: *"HELLLLP!"*

As if on command, a hidden panel slid open alongside them revealing bookcases that housed an extensive library of thick ancient tomes. The cases curved up the walls of the vortex, stretching all the way up to the spinning portal that opened to the outside world. As the rumbling continued, books came flying.

Stumbling upward, using the cases for support, Sarah caught glimpses of titles. *THE HIDDEN DANGERS OF LAUGHTER* was teetering on the shelf above her head. She dodged as it fell, shielding the child, but was nailed right in the noggin by *HOW TO ENJOY YOUR OWN MISERY.*

The child shrieked. "Look out! It's right behind us!"

Sarah looked back to see the rectangular head, mouth agape and reaching for the little girl's ankle. "Come on, we're almost there!"

Sure enough, the opening was just a few feet ahead, spinning faster now. But the rumbling and the shaking were more violent, and the last of the journey was the hardest, with more heavy books cascading down on them and the rings shaking violently under their feet. Any minute, the whole place would give way. Holding the child's hand firmly in hers, Sarah vaulted onto the last ring, just missing being clobbered simultaneously by two Blaney favorites: *HOW TO KILL JOY IN YOURSELF AND OTHERS* and *MY LOVE AFFAIR WITH PAIN.*

There was a swimmy sensation inside the children's stomachs as they hurdled toward the opening. Then they were grabbed and whirled, turned up and down and all around. The next second, they landed in a *splat* on Thelma Blaney's hardwood floor.

Sarah lay there in a puddle of her own perspiration. She looked for the child and saw her scrambling onto the sofa, seeking safety there. It had been too much for such a little one. She settled in, eyes closing, and began sucking her thumb. Almost at once, she was sound asleep.

Sarah looked back to the vortex and shuddered violently at what she saw: a dark, triangular head poking through the spinning opening—*and Alma heading right for it.*

Sarah screamed, but the sister paid her no heed. Instead, she calmly plunged her hand into the hole and grabbed the creature around the neck. It writhed, whipping its tail, trying to wrap its coils around her arm.

"That'll be enough of that, thank you very much!" she chided, shaking the snake hard three times, almost as if shaking out a dusty rug.

Was it Sarah's imagination, or did the serpent get smaller with each snap of Alma's wrist? Surely that couldn't be so, any more than it could be true that Alma was now actually indulging the creature, permitting it to wind itself up and down her arm from shoulder to wrist.

Sarah's dizziness, intensified by the bucking of the rumbling floor, turned into a nauseous blackness that spread through her mind, not unlike the smoke that was beginning to rise from the top of Mrs. Blaney's skull. Frightened, the apprentice struggled to her feet, but took only a few steps before the bucking floor hurled her across the room and into the rocking chair. She curled into it, clung to the wooden arms, and watched everything fade as she rocked back and forth.

The last things she saw before closing her eyes were Alma with the snake still wrapped around her arm and Mrs. Blaney rising like Vesuvius in the middle of the living room. Deep rumbles sounded from her interior.

She's gonna blow, Sarah thought. *And I'm gonna miss it. It's gonna be a real lollapalooza, too.*

But she didn't miss it, not entirely. The memory would lie in the shadow of her mind, feeding the roots of her understanding until the time came when she could fully process it.

Thelma Blaney blew. It was as Sarah had predicted—a real lollapalooza.

Tectonic lateral thrusts shook her, starting from her feet of stone. Then blasted through her legs and into her pelvis, the raging force breaking new fissures as it traveled up beneath her towering rock surface. Her growling belly contracted, emitting a roaring crescendo of violence that burst into the stone chest and heaving bosom, then thundered on up through the bulging old throat. Thelma's eyes glowed yellow fire. Her mouth popped open, yet no sound escaped the gaping hole. Pressure rippled her temples.

CRACK! The top of the old woman's head blew off, leaving a bubbling crater of liquid fire. A second blast shook the walls and the ceiling; plumes of steam and ash spewed upward in towering columns of poisonous looking fumes. Blackness smothered the light. Deafening blasts roared through the room sending the floor whipping up and down like an untamed bronco crashing through a corral gate.

The whole house swayed on its flimsy foundation, rocking the two unconscious children and bringing down the monstrous old dusty chandelier that smashed onto the table.

"No loss there," Alma shouted above the din, surfing the waves of energy with her charmed snake hanging on fast and enjoying the ride.

The pyrotechnics were by no means over. Fragments of pumice rained down from a super-heated broiling cloud into rivers of molten lava that streamed across the floor. Amid the fire, boulders crashed; smaller rocks peppered the ceiling and walls, sending pictures sliding. Plates, bowls, and serving platters flew from the china cabinet. Mirrors, lamps, tables, chairs, everything that wasn't nailed down, crashed to the floor.

In the midst of the chaos and against all odds, the grandfather's clock maintained its stately upright position in the left-hand corner of the living room near the front door.

"Relentless," Alma muttered, staring through the glass door of the clock, where its inner works moved in synchronicity as they had for all of Thelma Blaney's life. "If I ever saw a Blaney clock, you're it. Just determined to hold on to the way things were, aren't you?"

The clock's weights dropped. Its pendulum swung faster.

"Don't sass me, you're just a big show-off. Never a break in your stupid rhythm. Always afraid that Thelma might accidentally slip between your tick and your tock." The snake's head was on her shoulder; it seemed to agree.

The room began to quiet. First, the floorboards settled, then the air currents slowed, releasing strings of dust and soot—the residue of all that had once clogged Thelma Blaney's interior. Finally, there came a deep liquid silence that flowed across the room. There was not a sound, except for the loud ticking of the unyielding old clock.

In fact, it had never ticked so loud. Or so fast.

Behind the glass doors, the chains rose higher and the weights lowered.

The pendulum swung wildly. There was no doubt about it. Alma's goading had thrown the clock into a state of intense stress. Its metal hands moved faster, trembling as they struggled to keep up with the accelerating pace. But the end was near. The cabinet was rattling, vibrating on its short feet.

Tick-tock, tick-tock, tick-tick-tick . . .

The chain *brrrupted* upward. The three weights clanged down to the clock floor. The pendulum halted mid-swing.

There came one last tick. Then silence.

Alma's eyes gleamed. Few could have navigated the space between the tick and the tock, but she managed it with ease, striding calmly across the room in no time. Living in the present moment was one of her specialties.

A snake crawled through Sarah's dream. She fidgeted in the rocker. Cried out as she spotted a little dark-haired girl sleeping on the sofa across from her. Was she a dream, too, like the snake?

And was the mean old woman's house really full of rocks? And the furniture all smashed? Was everything filthy, the walls about to fall in? She remembered how clean the woman's house had been and felt sorry that it was all spoiled.

But the sisters were there in her dream, and they didn't seem worried or sorry at all.

What a terrible nightmare. Sarah moaned, seeing Sister Alma stroke the head of the snake that was wrapped around her arm. There was nothing Sarah hated more than a snake. She thrashed about, trying to wake up.

Not yet, Sarah. Keep sleeping, dear. It was Sister Vannie's voice. *Calm yourself, be still, and you will feel it.*

Sarah shivered. *Feel what? Will I see it?*

No. It's not to be seen.

Will I hear it?

No, it has no sound.

Will I smell it?

It has no smell either.

Why not?

How can you see, hear, or smell nothingness?

Sarah wasn't crazy about "nothingness." It spoke to her of death and ceasing to be. Of evaporating, of turning off like a wind-up doll when the string retracts into its back, of falling into a deep, dreamless sleep from which you never emerged.

Yet Vannie's voice had lulled her, and she surrendered.

And then she did, indeed, feel it. Peace. She wondered if the others in the room felt it, too—the young girl sleeping on the sofa. The sisters. Oh, and the mean old woman was there, too . . . what a sight she was! For a moment Sarah had mistaken her for a misshapen, scorched old mountain, but the burnt-out figure was Thelma Blaney alright.

She couldn't worry about her though, couldn't worry about a thing, because she felt that *nothing* kind of feeling that Sister Vannie had been telling her about, and Vannie was right—she couldn't see it, or hear it, or smell it. But oh, it felt good. All the tension whooshed out of her.

Tension about what, dear one?

Well, this morning, Daddy . . .

Oh, I see. But that was then. This isn't "then" anymore. This is Now. Breathe it in, child. Feel how still and wonderful the Now feels? This is the peace come of living in the moment at hand.

Sarah entered it deeply. When guided, children go there easier than adults, and this child easier and more completely than most. Which was one reason among many that she had been chosen as the sisters' apprentice.

The NOW spread over the entire room, a vibrant nothingness, that was neither large nor small, thick nor thin, airless nor ventilated, dark nor light, dry nor wet. Nor, in fact, was it anything that could be experienced through the ordinary senses. It was dimensionless, yet full of everything that existed. It was eternal, yet lacking yesterday and tomorrow. It was nothing, yet within its nothingness lay the potential for all that Thelma Blaney had ever needed or ever would need.

Still planted in the middle of the room, Thelma stared uncomprehendingly through the dust and gloom at the wreck that used to be her pristine little home. Her polished tables and chairs were splintered, her mother's whatnots smashed. Her ceiling was dinted. Her family heirloom chandelier, a cracked and broken relic of the past, had crashed through her dining room table. Her usually immaculate flower-papered walls looked as though a wrecking ball had had at them. Boulders lined the floor; rocks were scattered across the room and heaped along the walls. Clouds of dust rose in veils of filth, shrouding the ruins. And still Thelma Blaney stared blankly, breathing in the NOW.

"Hello, sweetheart," a voice said. It belonged to Sister Alma. She was standing in front of Thelma, a dark snake twirled around her arm, elbow-to-wrist, like it was the most natural thing in the world. "You really cut loose, didn't you? Bean soup can do that to you." She smiled at Thelma. "But are you sure it all came out? Come on, darlin', get it all up."

Thelma's mouth opened obediently. A great belch issued forth, threatening another eruption. But all that came out of her this time was a mouthful of pebbles and a puff of black, foul-smelling smoke.

"That's the last of it," Sister Vannie said decisively from where she was keeping watch over Sarah, asleep in the easy chair. "Better rest your feet for a few minutes, Thelma."

Attempting a ponderous move toward the sofa, Thelma looked like an extinct and ancient creature that might have been a prehistoric relative to a hawk preserved in a tar pit and brought to exhibition in all its grime. A thin stream of gray smoke still spiraled from her open skull, and she appeared dazed and confounded and in search of something, she knew not what. But something.

"You might look over there," Alma suggested, stroking the python that was growing cozier every minute, its snout now nuzzled into her throat. She pointed toward the sofa where the small dark-haired child slept.

Thelma looked, and her heart beat faster. She knew this little one from old pictures. "Sister, this child is . . ."

"Yes?"

"She's *me*. I mean, I'm her. Or whichever. Both."

"Hmmm. Well said."

Thelma didn't care how well she had or hadn't expressed herself. She didn't care about anything at the moment except the child. How pretty she was! A pretty little Thelma, imagine that. She giggled at the thought.

But before she could reach for the child, Alma lifted a cautionary hand. "Wait! Not yet. Remember, we're still between the tick and the tock, in the NOW, where new choices can change a life forever. So?"

"So what?" Thelma asked nervously.

"So, are you ready to choose?" Alma held up her arm, and the snake languidly began untwining itself, its eyes fixed on the old woman and no longer looking so tame.

"Keep that thing away!" Thelma said, hobbling back to put her body between the snake and the child on the sofa.

"But you'll *need* it, darlin'. That is, if you want to keep everything the way it was."

"The way it was?" Thelma blankly echoed.

"Yes, you know. Acting crazy as a loon. Using your tortured inner child as an excuse to chase boys with rakes and cut off your whole family . . . that sort of thing."

Thelma stared at her, mouth working silently. "And I suppose it's alright for people to call me the snake woman?"

"Oh, well, that's because they sense your venom," Alma explained. "All that poison in you that puts the 'feel good' in making others feel bad."

"I never do no such thing. I'm just showing 'em they can't put one over on me."

PABLO
FERRO

"Put . . . one what?"

"Anything!" Thelma snapped with a dose of her old vinegar. "Everything! Oh, hell's bells, Sister, you can't go all soft. People will eat you alive if you let 'em. Did I ever tell you what my own daddy did to my poor little puppy?"

"No dear, but I'm sure it was sad and pathetic. No doubt it could inspire a library full of pain books."

The woman looked at her, whiskery eyebrows raised. "You mean like *WHEN I'M SAD, I GET GLAD KICKING YOU*?" A wry smile spread across her lips.

"Exactly. Lovely example. Well, you'd better choose before that clock tocks on you. You can have everything back, just the way it was. Your child locked in a dungeon beneath a library of pain, your wicked serpent eating both of you alive, and a pristine house that nobody wants to visit. Or, it can all be different. It's just a choice away. *Your* choice." Alma's eyes were twice their usual size; she was using her powerful gift of persuasion. Every drop in her arsenal.

But Thelma didn't answer. Nor did she even glance at the sister. Instead, she silently stared from snake to child. And back again.

Inside of her dream, Sarah listened and watched as Mrs. Blaney deliberated, still standing amidst the rubble, between the child and Sister Alma, who was holding out the wriggling snake.

"You can't have them both," Alma said, not budging.

Thelma hesitated. There might have been a pout on her lips. Or was it a smile, turned inside out, so unused was she to showing her softer side? Or was that just another trick of this smoky room, yet another illusion created by the sisters?

Even as she had the thought, a breeze found its way through a cracked windowpane, and Sarah saw the smoke rise on it, as if a flock of gray geese had found the wind under its wings. The formation flapped toward the unlit hearth and made its orderly exit, swooping down toward the grate and then upward into the chimney, disappearing with such a faint rustling in the stack that Sarah might have imagined it.

Just as she might have imagined the dark-haired child on the couch. The little girl was hardly there anymore. There was a bit of a smudge where her hair might be; the rest of her was a blur of shimmer and shine moving toward the old woman, as to a refuge. There was a fluttering, not unlike the sound the birds had made disappearing through the chimney as Thelma opened her arms to the child, then closed them. Was she really embracing the little girl or merely folding her arms across her own breast? Maybe the latter, because now Sarah could see no child at all. Only a woman with softening features and a new innocence in her eyes.

Even Alma was a shadow now, tall and stately, standing at the door holding what looked to be a very small garter snake. In the fading room, Sarah could barely discern the sister reaching into her apron pocket, pulling out a plump grape, and popping it into the snake's mouth.

But I thought snakes didn't eat grapes.

Ah, well, child, you can't believe everything people say. Or was that just a whisper of wind? Anyway, it was gone.

Out of the silence came a single sound: TOCK.

Sarah's eyes snapped open. She was horrified that she had apparently fallen asleep in the middle of the mean old woman's meal. Her cornbread and bean soup were half-eaten, and Thelma Blaney was still hard at it. What an appetite for an old woman, Sarah thought. Then paused inside her head. Was she crazy, or did Mrs. Blaney look at least twenty years younger all of a sudden?

"I was thinking, Thelma," Vannie said, "that you really ought to bake one of your famous oatmeal cakes for the church benefit. It would be sure to bring in three dollars toward that new stained-glass window."

Thelma looked up and twinkled. "Well, I could be persuaded. That is, if you'll part with your renowned recipe for piecrust."

"What a horse trader. Deal!"

Thelma cackled and winked at Sarah. "Share a piece of my cornbread, young lady?"

Sarah blinked back at her, unable to believe the pleasant look on Thelma's face or the hints of humor around her lips. "No, thank you, I—"

"Say yes," Vannie whispered. "Never refuse to let other people give."

Sarah took the cornbread and smiled timidly at the woman. "Thank you very much!"

Thelma slurped up a spoonful of bean soup and said, "Wonderful child. Pretty little thing, plus, she's smart. You can always recognize a quick child. Reminds me of my great niece. She was named for me, you know. One of these days, Thel—that's what she calls herself—will get this ring on this old hand. In fact, I think I'll give her the damn thing tomorrow. I'm probably going to see a hundred, and why should she wait? Ain't nothin' like seeing a ring you want on somebody's hand to make you wish they was dead."

"We wouldn't want that," Alma concurred.

"Not my sweet baby. I want her to keep on loving me forever." Thelma looked at the other three in surprise. "Good gracious, why am I eating alone? Cut us all a big chunk of that jam cake and let's dig in."

"Thank you, Thelma," Alma said. "We love our own cooking. Sister, will you do the honors?"

"Love to," Vannie said, cutting four thick, gooey portions and plopping them onto cake plates. "You first, Thelma."

"I've still got three teeth left," the woman said, snatching the cake. "Only thing about living past a hundred is I probably won't have one tooth in my head."

"Isn't that the lump in the gravy," Vannie commented.

"One thing about soup and cornbread, ice cream and cake, you can gum it real well."

The two sisters laughed. Since there wasn't anything they did better than laugh, Sarah joined in. Thelma laughed, too. Alma scooped the ice cream into little dishes and Sarah proudly served them. The sisters said that any fool could see it was time for a celebration.

15

The café settled into a down gear, as it usually did between lively lunch and rowdy dinner crowds. The quiet afternoon mirrored a shift in the sisters' apprentice that had occurred over the last weeks since Cleatis had become a model citizen. Sarah was going silent on them. They knew it, even if less attentive people might have missed the change in her. It was all the more worrisome to the sisters because it was so subtle.

"Subtle and *deadly*," Vannie had privately opined to Alma.

"So true, Sister."

As the last of today's dawdlers left, Sarah kept her silence and continued wiping down the kitchen table. Then she swept the floor and scoured pots and pans. Once when she bumped into a pantry shelf, she winced and held her arm. Her brooding look made her older. She was all earth tones today, deep-washed brown and rusty gold, with tinges of burnt orange.

At 6:00 p.m., while Sarah went to change from her apron and work dress back into her school clothes prior to going home, Vannie unearthed a taped package from a deep cupboard under the worktable. When the apprentice came back across the road, schoolbooks under her arm, she saw the package lying on the table. She shrieked and ran toward it.

Too late. With one slice of a sharp knife, Vannie opened it, while Alma stood looking on in an interested manner, drying her hands with a tea towel.

"Oh, my." Alma surveyed the mangled clump of dried clay that Vannie unearthed, squinting as though uncertain which end was up and which down.

Sarah sprinted to the table, snatched up the object, wrappings and all, and hugged it to her chest as though trying to hide it.

"Sarah?" Alma's voice was indulgent.

"It's terrible," Sarah screeched, tightening her grip. "She's dawg ugly, awful-looking. I don't want nobody to see her. She looks like a . . . a long disgusting worm or something. I hate her. I just hate her!" She followed her words with a stamping of both feet.

"Rather a little temper tantrum, missy?" Vannie murmured.

"Come on now," Alma said, holding out a hand. "Let's have it."

Caught between shame and an inability to say no to the sisters, Sarah laid the object in Alma's hand and burst into tears. In the silence, there was a slight crash as if something small and fragile had broken.

"Once broke, twice mended," Alma reminded Vannie, who looked on the verge of cowardly retreat. Intractable as ever, Alma spread out the strangely assembled object, pulling patiently here and there until long, stringy ropes of legs and arms revealed themselves.

Vannie pointed to a small shrunken, blackened object on top, looking like nothing so much as a malignant mushroom. "The head, isn't it?"

"Right, you are, Sister," Alma said. Mirth threatened until she took another look at the sobbing child.

Sarah held out her hands. "That's my doll," she said rudely. "Give her to me. Give her to me *now*!" Stamp, stamp.

Alma and Vannie hardly looked at her, so absorbed were they in peering at the lumpish object on the kitchen table. Vannie dubiously felt the raggedy bit of paper that clung to the doll's stomach. "Goodness, this isn't a dress, is it?"

"Of course, it's a dress!" Sarah snapped. "And it's just as ugly as the rest of her. Everything about her is ugly, ugly, ugly. That's why I took her from arts and crafts and hid her. I didn't want nobody to see her on festival night."

"Anybody," Alma corrected absently. The sisters had enrolled Sarah in an arts and crafts class that met Thursday afternoons at the old General Store. "Didn't want *any*body to see her. I can certainly see why. Something's a little off, isn't it?"

"Got arms like potato peelings," Vannie said.

"Hum. Feet stuck on like cloves in ham," Alma added.

Sarah flailed out at the doll and was neatly prevented from tearing her limb from limb by a deft hand on each side of her. In what seemed effortless persuasion, the sisters nudged her from the kitchen and soon had her out front by the candy case, chomping off some of her agitation on a wad of chewing gum.

"Atta girl." Vannie produced a pretty barrette from her apron pocket.

Sarah's eyes lit on the sparkly decoration. "Is that for—?"

"For her, isn't it?" Alma murmured, taking the doll from the counter.

"She could use some hair." Vannie snipped several of Sarah's soft locks. "Perfect, you'll see." She laid the hair on the counter.

"On that little head?" Sarah asked in disgust, still chewing. "You should've seen everybody laugh their faces off when they saw it. I made the worst-looking doll in the whole class. And," she added in an inspiration of over-statement, "I bet I made the worst-looking doll's *head* in the universe."

"I think I could glue this barrette right in back here," Vannie said.

"Wait, Sister. First, let's get some paint from the storage room. The ivory trim we used for the curly-Q's on the ladies' room sign, I think."

"Like that's gonna do something," Sarah said, but with less hostility. She watched with a smattering of interest as Alma brought the paint from out back and Vannie used a small brush to dab at the blackened blob of a face.

"Well, of course, there's the shape of it to consider," Vannie said, changing dark smudges into ivory. "Something's got to be done about—"

"I know!" Alma cut in. "Little side locks of hair like Sarah's. With those pretty curls." Before Sarah could move, Alma reached out with the scissors and clipped several of the curliest locks on Sarah's head and laid them beside the other hair strands.

Sarah stared mesmerized as Alma continued arranging hairpieces and Vannie turned her attention to the doll's stringy arms.

"Nice thin arms, aren't they?" Alma said. "Lots of women would love to have nice long, thin arms like those, wouldn't they? 'Specially if we rub 'em with a little flour paste and even 'em out some, then let 'em set. It'll give 'em a little form, you know. I'll get some flour and water from the kitchen."

"How smart you were, Sarah," Vannie said, beaming at the child who sat on the tall swivel stool, "to develop a frame for your doll first. So many would have mashed her right together, and that would have been that! No further room for growth."

"We like works in progress here," Alma said. She went into the kitchen and came back several minutes later with a bowl of flour paste. Using a short, thick butter knife, she started applying it to the doll's arms and legs, stopping occasionally to mold here, smooth there. For a while, there was no conversation, and no one appeared at the door, though it was a prime gathering hour for early dinner. The sisters and their apprentice could have been alone on Earth.

Sarah's frown had given way to a bemused smile. She actually clapped her hands as Vannie sewed hair to the barrette and carefully glued the mass of curls to the ivory-white head. The doll's small face was now framed by a curly hairstyle that was not unlike Sarah's own.

While paint and paste dried under a fan that Alma had set up by the cash register, out came a box of doll clothes.

"These old things used to belong to *my* doll," Vannie said, sorting through the box.

"Look!" Sarah said shyly, pointing out an apron and pinafore.

"Oh, for heaven's sake, your work dress, Sarah. I must have remembered this old doll outfit and designed your work getup around it. Imagine that!" Like a conjurer, she produced an old-fashioned child's paint box with a palate of many colors and a slender pointed brush.

Sarah's eyes lit up. "Oh, gee, Sister. Do you think I could—?"

Vannie smilingly laid the brush in her hand and set the paints at her elbow. The child was soon immersed in creating blue eyes, a pink mouth, and flushed cheeks. The doll's eyes grew lashes and brows on top. Her lips bowed, became fuller. As Sarah painted, she drifted, imagining herself walking down a row of trees. It all seemed so real somehow, like the trees had taken root down the center of the café. But no, there was a green field, wildflowers, and a breeze that blew the leaves and rippled the grass . . . and another small girl approaching. The girl stopped only a few feet away.

She was a shabby little girl, barefoot and ill-dressed. Her face needed scrubbing; her hair straggled down her neck. Her short dress could have used a washing.

And there was a bruise on her upper arm that looked like a man's thumb.

"Poor little girl. She never thought he'd do that again." Sarah stroked the doll's hair gently. "He was so glad to have all that money . . . and he said he wouldn't . . . his little girl thought he'd never . . . b-but then he . . ." Her lips trembled. Tears leaked from her eyes, and her hand went to the painful spot on her arm. "Maybe he won't ever get healed."

"His healing is up to him," Alma said, taking Sarah's hand. "The most you can do for him, sweetheart, is to hold the belief that your daddy can be a better man. Wish this for him with all your strength and might and with all the love you can muster. Then, dear child, you must let go. Surrender your father's fate to him. Only he can decide how much change he will allow. In the meantime, you must protect yourself."

"But how—?"

"Look, Sarah, look again!"

Wonderingly, Sarah saw yet another little girl duck from behind a tree. This child was pale and clean and dressed in a pinafore and apron, her curls in a barrette. Her blue eyes glowed, her cheeks flushed, her bowed lips smiled. Sarah's eyes cut away from her toward the shabby child.

"Which one am I?" she whispered.

"Both," Alma told her. "You're a work in progress. Close your eyes tight, child."

Obediently, Sarah scrunched her eyes closed.

"Good. Now feel the presence of someone who walks just beyond the tree line. You can't see her yet, she's just a shadow in your mind, but, in truth, she is with you."

"But I do see her!" Sarah gasped. "She's in a long purple dress with glitters all over it. Some of them are falling on me!"

"How wonderful," Alma whispered, slipping her arm around the child's shoulder. "Now, Sarah, listen to me. If you are ever someplace where you feel frightened or out of control and neither I nor Sister Vannie is with you, you can feel free to call on that lady. She will help you know what to do."

"Is she an angel?" Sarah asked.

"Some would call her that. Actually, she's a part of the light within you, but she shows herself to you this way, so you can perceive her more easily. Ready for a surprise? Open your eyes and see what you see!"

Sarah's eyes flew open, and she gasped. In front of her lay a beautiful doll with milk-white skin, pink cheeks and lips, and blue eyes. Her soft curly hair was pulled into a barrette. Her pretty legs had tiny feet in tiny shoes. And, of course, she wore a pinafore and an apron. Her arms reached out to Sarah.

Sarah put out a hand to touch her and suddenly shrank back as she saw it: a wicked-looking bruise on the doll's upper left arm, in that same perfect outline of a man's thumb.

She whimpered, and then felt the sisters' presence on both sides, enfolding her, weaving a grid of protection that stood firmly between her and the threatening evil. "He still scares me," she whispered, trying not to look at the spot on the doll's arm.

"Fear is not always a bad thing, child," Vannie said gently. "When you face it, things can change."

"We are all works in progress," Alma added. "Remember that, okay?"

"Okay," Sarah whispered.

"Now look, dear one. Look!"

The apprentice's eyes slowly turned back to the doll, and she stared wonderingly as a handful of sparkles scattered over the new curly hair, spilling onto the fresh-painted face and down onto the doll's dress.

At Alma's urging, she opened her hand and saw what was inside. Her palm lay gilded, sparkled with glitter, purple and gold.

After Sarah left them, the sisters were quiet. Making the child aware of her inner resources had been the only move available to them at this moment, yet it did not seem like enough. Though they retired to the house, bathed, and donned nightgowns, neither slept. They lay in their separate bedrooms, gazing out their separate windows into the bright night sky, each calling allies from earthly realms and distant stars. One request went out to all: *Protect our beloved apprentice.*

16

It wasn't five minutes after Jim Morgan limped out of The Two Sisters' Café before the talk started. Of course, Jim was the best-looking man in Willow Creek, so heads always turned when he was around, just as tongues wagged as soon as he was out of earshot. He appeared to be happily married, with a sweet wife, a six-year-old daughter, and baby twin sons. But when a man was only twenty-seven and had a face like a movie star with that long, lean, muscular body to match, who could keep from wondering?

"About that bad leg of his," Julie Spillman said, dropping into a hushed tone. "He says he gimped himself by stepping in a snake hole."

"Which, I must say, is highly unlikely," Liz Watson noted, knitting her brow and choosing her words carefully. "He's a big man with great big feet that probably wouldn't even fit into a snake hole, especially given the boots he wears. Not to call him a liar. Maybe it was a gopher hole, but it was no snake hole *I've* ever seen." She cleared her throat. "And how come him to be out duck hunting, like he claims? Yesterday was Friday, wasn't it? Didn't he have to work?"

The two women sitting together at the counter exchanged glances. The disparity in their ages (Julie was only twenty-two while Liz was over forty) did nothing to dispel the electricity that charged their conversation.

Alma came in from the kitchen with a pimento cheese sandwich for

Liz and a hamburger for Julie, complete with sweet pickles on top of each sandwich and a side order of fried onions for the hamburger. She set the plates in front of the women and then fetched a cup of coffee for Liz and an Orange Crush from the cooler for Julie.

"Did you notice, Sister," Julie asked, flushing in spite of her effort to contain herself, "that Jim Morgan's got a bad ankle? We don't know exactly how he got it, but he skipped out of work yesterday and nobody knows why." That the "nobody" consisted of only herself and Liz didn't seem important enough to mention.

Alma rested her chin on one hand. "Interesting," she said, as Vannie came in with dishes of coleslaw and potato salad for the sandwiches. Liz and Julie talked over the top of each other, filling Vannie in on the news while she served the food.

"Now if we put this together right," Liz said, "we should be able to figure out what's going on."

The sisters and Julie waited.

"Beginning with the age-old truth that men carry their brains between their legs," Liz said conspiratorially, "this must have something to do with Vivian Taylor. Lord, I've been worried about that woman for a while now."

"And what, might I ask, brings you to Vivian?" Alma popped the top off a bottle of root beer and took a swig.

"All kinds of terrible things happen when you don't do right," Liz said darkly. "I haven't wanted to say anything, but Vivian's been flirting with Jim something scandalous for months. Never mind that he's married with three kids."

Julie gasped. "Wait a minute! O-ma-god, I just realized something."

Liz's eyes snapped. "What? Tell us!"

"He said he went duck shooting yesterday. And *you-know-who* lives out that way." Her eyes slid past Alma and Vannie's neutral gazes to Liz, who almost choked on pimento cheese.

"You're right! Bill and Vivian Taylor live right out that way!" Her face suddenly fell. "But we can't go getting ahead of ourselves. After all, Vivian goes to work the same time her husband does. Bill drops her off every morning. She keeps the books for the vet, you know."

"*Who* keeps Henry Miller's books?" asked a new voice. Marilyn Harback had come in just in time to hear Liz's last words.

"Vivian Taylor, of course," Julie Spillman said, scraping the entire saucer of onions onto her burger.

"Oh, she doesn't work in Henry's office anymore," Marilyn said with a trace of importance that went with being the wife of Willow Creek's only lawyer. Further, she ran her husband's office and was privy to the town's affairs, from the details of Willow Creek wills (which she kept scrupulously within the family) to the occasional wife who dared buck public censure by filing for divorce. In Willow Creek, it was more acceptable to fool around a little than to break up a household. You lived with your sorrow as with your joy. "I'll take a bag of chips and a Dr. Pepper off your hands, Sister Vannie."

Liz and Julie stared at Marilyn with mouths agape as Vannie laid the chips on the counter and went to fetch the Dr. Pepper.

"You mean Vivian quit work?" Liz asked.

"Oh my, yes." Marilyn opened her bag of chips carefully along the seams. "She gave a month's notice and helped train a new girl before she left last week."

"Last week!" Julie repeated. "And she didn't take another job?"

"Not so far as I know. Strange she left, isn't it, seeing how well she and Henry got along and the wages so good. Plus, she's crazy about critters. Remember that litter of skunks she found under her house? Claimed they were de-scented? But Lord, the smell of those things."

"That's a myth about skunks losing their smell when you take out their scent veins," Liz said, eating pimento cheese. "They don't squirt anymore, but they stink forever. Cute little creatures though, and they say they're real affectionate. Though you have to pin your nose to pet 'em."

"So," Julie said, wanting to get back on topic, "Vivian left her job . . ."

" . . . for some mysterious reason nobody can figure out," Liz finished.

The sisters listened from behind the counter, neither participating nor offering objection.

Marilyn looked from Liz to Julie. "Somebody tell me what's going on."

"Jim Morgan claims he caught his foot in a snake hole yesterday," Julie blurted, beating Liz to the punch. "But we can't help but feel something's off. You know that foot of his—"

"—that great big foot—" Liz put in.

"—wouldn't fit in any snake hole," Julie finished. "And Jim claimed he stepped in the snake hole while he was out duck shooting and, well . . ." She paused, blushing.

"You know where he hunts," Liz said meaningfully, her voice dropping to a church whisper, "and it just so happens that Vivian Taylor and her husband live out that way!"

"Vivian Taylor," Marilyn breathed.

"And you know she smiles from ear-to-ear at the very sight of Jim!"

"What woman doesn't?" An appreciative grin lurked on Marilyn's lips. "I have to admit I love a gorgeous man."

"Gorgeous or ugly, he was hunting more than ducks yesterday afternoon," Liz said slyly.

"But we thought we must be wrong," Julie put in, "because Vivian would've been at work yesterday, but here you are saying she quit her job for some strange reason that nobody knows." She stopped, out of breath.

"Oh, my Lord," Marilyn said. "You really think—?" She looked up as the front door opened again and Ruth Jessup came in.

Ruth found time to keep irons in every community fire, despite raising three children alone on an insurance policy that her husband had left her at his death at age thirty-two, supplemented by her part-time job in the LaGrange City Hall. Luckily, the insurance policy had been a large one, but then it was said that George had always been a pessimist, and wouldn't you know he'd bet everything on his own death? The lucky bastard won when he dropped dead on the ninth hole of the golf course. He'd seemed so healthy, too, but then George would have felt cheated if he hadn't cashed in on that policy.

"So, what's goin' on?" Ruth asked, having an excellent nose for community news.

"You mustn't tell a soul, but Vivian Taylor's having an affair with Jim Morgan!" Julie stated with great moral regret. "She quit her job so she'd be alone in the house weekdays, and Jim cut work yesterday and took a gun and pretended to go duck shooting, and then something happened while he was at Vivian's house, because he's limping like an old hound who cornered a mean raccoon!"

"Oh, gracious," Ruth said with relish, settling down at Marilyn's left elbow. "Vannie, give me a dish of vanilla ice cream and a Hershey bar to crumble on top. And just a squirt of chocolate syrup, if you please." She gave a satisfied sigh and considered the facts. "Now isn't *this* a mell of a hess, as old Clyde Mack would say, poor addled cuss."

"I just wonder," Liz said, puzzling it out, "if Vivian's husband came home too early and caught them together!"

"But wouldn't Bill have shot Jim somewhere else besides his foot?" Marilyn wondered.

"He obviously missed," Liz retorted. "Wait a minute, what if he was climbing out the window headfirst. Just think about it! He might have just *dove* out that window, half-dressed. His feet would have been the last thing out." She cocked her finger. "*Ker-pow!*"

Ruth gave a strangled laugh. "Lord help us."

"That man," Marilyn said in awe, "is walking around right now with a *bullet* in him and doesn't dare tell a soul, even Doc. Because you know he'd have to report it, wouldn't he, if a patient showed up with a bullet in his ankle?"

"If you ask me, I think he'd take his chances telling Doc," Liz said briskly. "Being as Jim is a friend and a neighbor, and, of course, Doc being just another man, I think he'd just dig that bullet out, tape Jim up, and send him home!"

"That's exactly what happened" Julie exclaimed. "You could see his ankle was taped. I bet you dollars to donuts Doc did it!"

The door opened again, and Tillie Whittaker and Bess Hunter came in, waved at the women, and took a table near the back wall.

"Damn," Liz hissed. "You know that Tillie, she can't keep a thing to herself. *Hi Tillie! Oh, I love your blouse, Bess!*" Under her breath she said, "We need a little music in here, and the louder, the better."

Julie scurried up the steps to the jukebox, dropped in a coin, and punched buttons till Frankie Laine's *Mule Train* blared out, then hurried back to the counter.

"Ah, that's better. So, ladies, here's what happened," Ruth summed up, under the strains of *Mule Train*. "Jim Morgan took his gun and pretended to go duck hunting. But instead, he sneaked over to see Vivian Taylor, who quit her job with the vet to get time alone with Jim. While they were together Bill came home unexpectedly, caught them, and shot Jim in the ankle while he was diving out the window."

From across the room, Tillie Whittaker rose from her table and yelled, *"What's that?"*

"What's what?" Liz asked.

"All that about Jim and Vivian," Tillie said breathlessly as she arrived at the counter with Bess trailing behind her.

"How in jiggedy did you hear all that with Frankie Laine driving his mules at the top of his lungs? Oh, well, I guess you were going to know sooner or later. Jim and Vivian were messing around together, and Bill caught them and shot Jim in the ankle. Doc bandaged him up on the sly. The only thing we haven't figured out is why Bill came home early."

Tillie pursed her lips, a little offended that they hadn't meant to include her, being as she was a pillar in the church and chairman of both the membership and fund-raising committees. If anyone had a finger on the community pulse, it would be she, and sure enough she had the answer. "Bill had to run a church errand yesterday, as a matter of fact. He left work early to drive out to the nursery to pick up the perennials that Ned Tucker donated for the churchyard."

Everyone gasped.

"You're kidding," Liz said, trying to look horrified.

Tillie let them hang in suspense a few seconds longer before she graciously continued. "Bill dropped them off at about three-fifteen. I'm guessing he thought it was too late to go back to work by then, so he headed home."

The five ladies gaped at each other in stunned awe.

"I blame *her*," Tillie said. "Men can't help themselves."

Julie whispered, "Is . . . committing adultery against the law?"

"If it was," Liz said dryly, "there wouldn't be ten married men in Willow Creek without a prison record."

"What about shooting a man who's sleeping with your wife," Julie said darkly. "Isn't that a crime?"

Tillie snorted. "I don't think there's a judge in Henry County that would convict a man for shooting another man in the foot, if that man was after the first man's wife."

"Ah," Ruth said, "but remember Bill wasn't trying to shoot Jim in the foot! He was trying to shoot him somewhere that would count," she added suggestively. "That's an important distinction."

"And as a lawyer's wife," Marilyn said, drawing herself up, "I can tell you that shooting anybody anywhere is against the law. Good Lord. I do believe Bill will be tried for attempted murder!"

All this time, Bess Hunter had stood by the counter, silenced by the momentum of the conversation. That wasn't unusual. She had always been quiet and retiring, the type that never liked to interrupt or step on other people's toes.

The sisters, also silent, were looking at her now, beckoning her to join them farther down the counter as the rest of the women went on whispering.

"I think this is your time to speak, darlin'," Alma said encouragingly.

"Oh, no, not me. I'm not a talker, Sister," Bess murmured.

"But sometimes it's necessary, don't you know?"

"You mean . . . *bust in*?" Bess gasped. "*Why?*"

"Just because you're not a talker, as you put it. And because people know when you use your words, it's always to speak the truth."

"I doubt people know this." Bess flushed.

"Believe me," Alma said, "they do know. People who speak the truth are always recognized."

Bess started to object, then found herself staring from one smiling face to the other, almost blankly. *Why, of course, she's right; I may not talk a lot, but I do speak the truth. That's exactly me.* She slowly turned to look at the excited women lined up at the counter.

"If you say so. I'll try, Sisters."

Obligingly, she headed back toward what suddenly seemed to her to be nothing more than a bunch of geese squawking away at each other, each wanting to be the one heard. *Goodness, you can't understand a word. How strange.*

It was almost as if they had begun to speak another language, one totally unknown on the planet.

Bess looked back at the sisters, saw them motioning encouragingly, and heaved a deep breath. Now or never.

"Ladies," Bess said, her heart in her throat. Every startled face turned to hers. She resolutely continued. "You know I've run old Doc's office for twenty years."

Silence, as every eye studied her warily. There wasn't a woman present who didn't have a built-in meter for a party pooper.

Liz Watson said reluctantly: "You're not about to tell us that Jim Morgan *didn't* get shot in the ankle?"

Bess cleared her throat, feeling nervous again. She wasn't used to being the center of attention.

"If you know something about Jim's ankle," Julie whined, "you'd just as soon tell us."

"Well . . . maybe we could work backward?" She was surprised to find herself suddenly calm. "Let's start with why Bill left work early yesterday. Maybe he did pick up perennials, but the main reason he took off was to bring his wife to the doctor's office."

"Did *she* get shot?" Ruth brightened marginally.

"Goodness, no! She's expecting, and she and Bill are thrilled, especially since Doc thinks it's twins. She'll need a lot of bedrest, so she had to quit her job!"

This usually exciting news went over like a deflated balloon as the ladies stared at her.

"If she's expecting, why has she been twinkling at Jim Morgan?" Liz snapped.

"Was she twinkling? I guess that would be because they have something in common, what with Jim and Brenda having twins. Seems to me those two couples have been spending a lot of time together lately. Bob and I ran into them at the movies last weekend."

Marilyn drooped on her stool. "What about Jim's ankle?"

"He got his toe caught in a snake hole while he was out duck shooting. You know those big awkward feet of his . . . the man trips over sidewalk cracks. Well, his little pointy boot toe stuck in that hole and down he went. I know because Doc bandaged his ankle."

"What was he doing duck shooting on a Friday?" Tillie asked, desperate to salvage a crumb.

"That's easy enough when your boss is with you," Bess giggled. It was uncharacteristic of her, but she just felt like laughing for some reason. "He'd been after Jim to take him duck shooting for months and finally gave him the day off to get there. Then Jim had to ruin it. Judging from his boss's face, I doubt Jim is going to get that raise he's after. Poor boy, because *his* wife is . . ." She broke off as every eye turned her way.

Before any questions could be asked, Alma leaned forward over the counter and said, "Here's your cherry Coke, Bess."

Bess stopped talking and reached for the glass of Coke that was brimming over with cherries. She rejoined the sisters at the end of the counter and sipped peacefully.

"If there's one thing I hate, Sisters," she murmured, popping a cherry, "it's gossip. That's why Doc has kept me so long, you know. A nurse in a doctor's office *must not* gossip, or the whole community would be affected! Oh, what I know . . . but it must all go untold, Sisters, and I believe it's for the best."

The ladies began to stir. Liz and Julie paid their bills and left their stools. At the door, Liz looked back. "Weren't you saying something about Jim's wife, Bess?"

Bess grinned and put her finger to her lips.

"Well, I guess we'll hear about it in time," Liz said distractedly.

Behind the counter, the sisters took more orders as the Saturday lunch crowd arrived. The hum of voices was pleasant to their ears, as neighbor visited neighbor and got filled in on the week's news and the doings planned for the weekend.

"Twins," Vannie said in the kitchen, building a row of ham sandwiches at lightning speed. "I do love twins, Sister. So many times, they have such perfect communication."

"In a way, you and I are twins, you know, Vanessa. After all, I was constructed from building blocks I plucked from your hair."

"Don't start with that, you crazy fool," Vannie shot back. "That makes about twenty-seven hundred versions you've told me of that tale so far." She laughed in spite of herself, then bit her lip considering. "Seriously, Sister, how long did it take us to learn that words hold the power of creation?"

"Too long," Alma said. "It's a bit easier in other worlds, especially outer space. I came here straight from the Pleiades star cluster, you know, though I did stop to chat with an old faerie friend on my way in. Time is so tricky in that realm that I almost missed your birth . . ."

Vannie snapped a tea towel and scored a yelp as Alma rubbed her behind.

The sisters worked on, basking in the shifting resonance in the café, the integrity of Bess's words still rolling like waves over tables and chairs and on into the service station where the men sat gabbing with Andy Poole. Then back again to lap at the countertop and to roll on into the kitchen and the Little Room where so many came to talk.

Vannie looked at her sister. "Alma, do you remember what Mama used to say about that woman who lived across from our house—*in this lifetime*," she added before Alma could say anything. "The one whose slip showed all the time?"

Alma stuck her tongue in the side of her cheek. "I believe she said she had a pretty petticoat."

"Oh yeah," Vannie said. "That was it. But you know . . ."

"What?"

"Well . . . it was the way she said it, wasn't it?"

Alma grinned. "It certainly was, Sister."

Vannie's eyes clouded. "Let's hope what happened today will stop a few tongues from wagging for a while. Sarah has enough on her mind without feeling like the whole town is talking behind her back about her daddy."

Lost in thought, they returned to their work, no longer smiling.

17

It was a black night with volleys of hail that pelted the old black Buick, an assault that spoke to the sisters' anxiety. They hadn't seen Sarah after the elementary school play that night, hadn't expected to. Sitting in the audience with their eyes on a small princess, a trembling tinsel crown on her head, they had smelled Nadine's fear as she sat beside them, head continually turning toward the auditorium door.

Cleatis hadn't shown up, of course. To Sarah, his absence had hit hard. She had expected him. With a child's high hope, and being apprentice to Vannie and Alma, she had let herself believe he would come. After all, she had seen the sisters work magic on strangers from afar and neighbors as close as next-door. Surely, their magic would heal her father. He had retreated in the wake of last week's outburst, seemingly contrite after squeezing her arm that night so hard that it had turned blue. He had gone to the last PTA meeting, had been sober for over two weeks. He would be at the play; she knew it. But he hadn't come.

To Nadine his absence meant trouble. She knew Cleatis's moods, as did no one else. Knew his restlessness. Could feel when his rage started to build. When things came to a head, she tried to stay one step ahead of him and chalked desperate strategies: If I have dinner ready early . . . if I let him do the talking . . . if I keep the kids quiet. It was hopeless, but she kept trying. There was no other choice.

Tonight, she hurried backstage and snatched Sarah away before the curtain call. The assembled company of children, all waving and smiling at the whistling, applauding audience, was missing a princess in a tinsel crown.

The sisters, white-faced in their anxiety, had edged into the aisle and were gone from the auditorium before the lights came on. Even so, there was no sign of Nadine's old, battered Ford in the school parking lot. Worse, they had tuned up their antennae and were acutely aware that Cleatis had fallen off the wagon tonight. Drunk, he was winding his way home from the still, blown by the freak storm, stinking with mash, and roaring with fury that steeled his fists into danger. And now he was on a collision course with Nadine and Sarah. His oldest daughter confused him these days. Made him think less of himself, with her hopeful eyes and the way she ducked her head and ran past him out the door to find "the purple lady."

"Who the hell is the purple lady?" he had asked Nadine.

"Someone she made up," Nadine said.

That reassured him. He didn't want some crazy purple lady on the property.

"He's outside the house," Vannie said in a low voice, almost drowned out by a barrage of hail on the roof of the car. "Even in this storm, he's out there waiting for them to get home." She gunned the engine. "I can see him, Sister. He's never been so furious. He may be strong enough to break the circle. I can hardly bear it."

"Calm yourself, Vanessa May. We'll be there in five minutes." Alma kept up her tranquil screen, but she was shaken in her interior. Vannie had always insisted that Sarah's place was with her family, but Alma had come to that conclusion more slowly. And it had been her decision, the concession she had insisted upon, to meet with Cleatis in the inner planes, there to set boundaries. Sarah would remain at home as long as Cleatis stayed within them. She, Vannie, and the child had invoked his soul and drawn a line in the sand, a circle of protection, actually, to keep him from their young apprentice. In that space beyond time, they had let him know in no uncertain terms that he was never to cross it with intent to harm his daughter. He was already challenging the perimeter.

"It's happening right now," Alma said, her voice shaking. "They're getting out of the truck." A new barrage of hail pelted down. "And he's passing through the circle this minute." She pointed out the bumpy path leading off the main road. On black stormy nights, finding cow paths was harder than finding pearls in pig slop.

"Hang on." Vannie swerved onto the frozen dirt road, sending Alma hard against the door.

All the while, Cleatis blundered on, stumbling over rocks, and crashing through the first boundaries of the circle he had vowed to respect. Dimly, at a distance, he heard cries, perhaps belonging to his wife and children. Perhaps they belonged to the spirit world—to those he had met there in that nightmare. He had spoken to someone, made a bad bargain that he hadn't meant to keep. But some fear in him, fiercer than his anger, had made him delay breaking it. Until now.

The circle was more complex to cross than he'd figured. Surely, it was just a marking in the sand, yet it sprang up like a city or a briar patch. He went thrashing, blundering, knocking down thorny branches that he couldn't see. Sharp thistles bit into his flesh as he strode forward, his head down like a charging bull's.

Ahead of him, just beyond the perimeter, he discerned Sarah's small dim form, the hail falling on her, her white face blazing in the night as she stared at him through dilated pupils.

Those eyes of hers.

"You make me like this," he whispered, knowing she heard him like no other, heard him with her love, her fear, and her pity, that heated his rage into loathing. She flinched and stood her ground, her slender white form shining in the black night. He would have his hands around her throat in less than a heartbeat.

"Now, Sister!" Alma's ringing tones were those of a warrior. *"Put the car in the last gear!"*

Vannie's foot pushed the accelerator into a new dimension; flames shot out and around them. She was no longer bothering to steer; the car had taken over. Something screeched, dug into their ears like icepicks, yet they continued. Only when they exploded onto the next level could they take their hands from their ears.

"Our rules now," Alma said, her face as fierce as ever her sister had seen it.

As Cleatis's hands slid around Sarah's throat, the sisters slammed into his front yard, horn honking, lights blinding, and a high-pitched warrior's cry tearing from Alma's throat, louder than the screeching brakes or the skidding tires across the scruffy barren clay.

Cleatis stood blinded, frozen in headlights that stopped only inches from him with his small daughter, her mouth working frantically, still held in his grip. He stared at the figure of Alma flying at him through the storm. She bore no resemblance to the woman who had served him so kindly and then sweet-talked him into letting Sarah work at the café. Now she was a giant, an Amazon in full gear, hair flying, armored, girded in steel with cuffs of hard metal. In her right hand above her head, she brandished a hand-beaten sword. Cleatis was stunned by the vicious glint of its blade, so sharp he already knew how it would feel slicing his throat.

Alma felt the heft of the weapon in her hands, the hail bouncing off its steel. An ancient bloodlust pounded through her veins, hardening her muscles and her heart. She swooped in on him fast. Seeing him at last within range, his huge hands around Sarah's throat, swept away all thoughts of mercy.

She was all cold rage now. Both hands on the hilt, she whipped the sword back, only vaguely hearing her sister's howls, snatches of words streaming from her lips—the words separating magicians from mere pretenders. She hesitated, her mind filling with images of shattered limbs and pooling blood, of eyelids peeled back so this man could watch his own death, his drawn and quartered body split open, spilling his bowels onto the ground in front of him.

The words! They rose from the very depths of her soul in answer to

Vanessa's insistent calls.

"In the name of all that's good and true, Alma!" she cried. "For the sake of all we've worked for! *SAY THE WORDS!*"

"Eiiiiiieeeeeeeeiii . . ." Part of Alma resisted, lusting for vengeance.

"ALMAAAAAA!" Vannie's voice rose over the sound of the hail. She would not relent.

Alma knew what was required, but she loathed it. Yet, sweating, reaching deep into her truth, she found the most important words of her life and bellowed them as she hurled the sword end-over-end on its flight:

"HARM TO NONE!"

The words clashed together, an affirmation of both victory and surrender. A sorrow, too, as the sword missed Cleatis by the split of a whisker and stuck into the wooden support post of the Curtises' front porch.

Alma stood panting and drenched in sweat, feeling the defeat of her shadow self and realizing how difficult her victory of character had been, how close to failure she had come. Her rage was still jumping like electrical juice around the sword's surface and passing down through the post into the earth—lightning pulled through a rod into stone, drawing the whole of the storm with it, funneling its full force into the earth like water down a drain.

Alma eyed Cleatis through the sudden calm, curled into a ball where he had slithered beside the porch step, arms wrapped around his knees. He was entering alcoholic shock and delirium. Whimpering from this dreamlike state: "Don't hurt me. Please don't hurt me. Just take her and leave me alone."

Sarah stood behind Nadine, pulling at her skirts, as both of them stared down at a man they hardly recognized.

"Daddy's crying," the child said wonderingly.

Nadine stroked Sarah's head and said what she always said during the bad times. "It'll be alright, baby. Don't worry."

In the car on the way now back to the café, a shaky child between them, the sisters thought of how Cleatis had let Nadine lead him into the house, how he had continued to cry like a baby even after they assumed their familiar forms, just Alma and Vannie May come by to tell the family how much they loved Sarah in the play. And to take her with them. Nadine had nodded assent as they gathered the girl's few things into a pillowcase, then gently said goodnight to the family.

"Don't fear for your mother," Vannie tried to reassure Sarah in the car. "She'll be safe for a good long time. He always needs her when he's sick, and he'll be very weak for a while after this."

The child said nothing.

"Wipe up those tears, sweetheart," Alma said. "Trust me, we aren't through here yet."

Sarah remained closed into herself as the drive continued, the short journey seeming as endless as the rolling darkness beyond the Buick's headlights. Vannie finally passed by the café and made a right-hand turn into the graveled parking lot of the general store. Above them and to the right stood the sisters' white, green-shuttered house, crowning a long grassy slope. To their left, on the lower sidewalk level, was the old store, another popular gathering place for locals and the school bus pickup spot for many of Willow Creek's children.

"We're here, Sarah," Alma said softly.

The child did not answer, only stared through the windshield as Vannie turned the car up the drive and into the open garage between their house and Thelma Blaney's vineyard.

Sarah looked tired and pale as she followed Alma out through the passenger side of the front seat and trudged toward the porch at the side entrance of the house, head down. The sisters wished they could carry her like a baby, tuck her into the safety of innocent childhood, and protect her from the world of problems and pain, but that was impossible.

"We are all princes and princesses, sons and daughters under the heavens," Alma said, opening the screen door. "Sometimes a princess's life plays out easy in sunlight and under the moon. Sometimes she sits at a knee to learn. There are times she can expand imagination and become a fairy in the school play. But sometimes, dear, even a princess comes on hard times."

"I KNOW!" Sarah interrupted. Then more calmly, and with the wisdom that sometimes pours from children who have seen hardship: "Sometimes even a princess has to go to war."

"Yes," Alma said thoughtfully. "Sometimes, that is the way of it."

For a moment Sarah stood still, her eyes staring through the night, down the hill and across the road to where the café loomed in white relief, as though a light had been left glowing. Then she turned and went inside the house.

18

Article from Henry County's new local newspaper, The Hole In The Wall, September 9, 1952:
BATTLE LINES FORMING IN WILLOW CREEK MYSTERY
By Loretta Smith
Editor-In-Chief

WILLOW CREEK – In the wake of "unearthly" lights, accompanied by strange shrieking noises last evening, Sheriff Jimmy Dorn is keeping his eye on human suspects here in Willow Creek and rules out, at least for now, invasions from outer space.

Proponents of UFOs are mustering their forces to prepare for what they believe will be an imminent invasion of our town, even while our own sheriff looks for more traditional reasons to explain last night's unsettling events. Early this morning, at the sheriff's station believers in outer space invasion shot questions at Sheriff Dorn which he fielded with his usual down-home common sense. He urged residents to stay calm.

"The outer-space theory might come off alright in California," the sheriff opined. He spoke wearily, having destroyed two local stills last night, only to find himself confronted with reports of UFO attacks on the tail of an unpredicted hailstorm. The sheriff added, "But for our kind of folks, this alien stuff won't wash. Why would people from out there," he gestured toward the sky, "bother themselves about Willow Creek?"

Dorn stated that the inhuman screams and sustained bursts of intense hovering lights were first reported by neighbors of Cleatis Curtis, and may be connected to an altercation during illegal activities. He pointed out that stills are traditionally accident-prone, both in distilling liquor and in irresponsible gun handling by inebriated patrons during confrontations with the law. Noting that last evening's freak hailstorm carried little moisture and afforded no relief during these dangerous drought times, he stated that fire hazards presented by illegal whiskey stills can no longer be tolerated.

"We don't need these kinds of shenanigans anytime," Dorn stated, "but we especially don't need them when the fields are dry as kindling wood. Unless we get weather relief soon, an explosion of a still could set the whole county on fire."

The sheriff is asking local residents to keep an eye out for hazardous activities, including unauthorized bonfires, fireworks, and illegal production of drinking alcohol. In addition, he vows to deputize a dozen citizens to forward this same cause, hoping to put the plan into effect by Monday.

But the UFO contingency will not go quietly. At this morning's meeting, they enlisted dozens of unpaid volunteers to search for lawbreakers of an outer space variety.

"We can't be too careful," local farmer Ed Houseman said after signing up, adding that he had never heard anything like the shrieking that echoed through woods and fields around nine o'clock last evening. "Almost like some alien woman's voice. Not that I believe in space ships, but if one did come down, who'd want to miss seeing it?"

A peevish Sheriff Dorn rejected the idea of an official UFO watch. He said he had his hands full with humans, especially the likes of Cleatis Curtis, who could not immediately be reached for comment. Mr. Curtis's wife, Nadine, told *The Hole In The Wall* that her husband is in bed with the flu and too weak to be interviewed. His brother, Harley Curtis, who was visiting the Curtis home, did speak to us, complaining that one of the Curtis tool sheds had been wrongly called a still and blown off the map. He vowed that when his brother was up and around again, they would sue the county for lost money in work tools and building replacement.

Sheriff Dorn assured the *Wall* that not only had over a hundred bottles of mash been recovered from the demolished "tool shed," but that this was not the first such incident on Curtis property. He also insisted that the words "blown off the map" were excessive. He stated that no explosives were employed, and, in fact, that a few well-placed hammer blows had been more than sufficient to bring the old shed down. He nevertheless agreed that Cleatis Curtis is entitled to his day in court and that he will support any decision reached by local jurisdiction.

Perhaps the popularity of the UFO theory shot up a few points among those who had hoped this would be a confrontation between Earth citizens and UFO space creatures, not a confrontation between friends and neighbors. To Willow Creek residents, alien invasion seems to be the less threatening of the two. Add to that, more than a few are in sympathy with certain members of the Curtis family.

The Hole In The Wall finds itself in agreement.

19

Sarah was just waking up in the big house when Sheriff Jimmy shooed the last of the UFO contingency from his office.

From the center of the ornate bed that the sisters had ordered from a Boston furniture store, she pushed the covers from her head, where she had lain in a cocoon of her own making most of the night, and woke back to life slowly. An uneasy sensation of something wrong swam in her, followed quickly by unwelcome memories.

Now here she lay, her stomach contracted into a hard knot as she gazed around at the beautiful room. Unfamiliar sensations flooded her, and she shivered, not sure if it was from dread or a chill from the breeze that swept through the partially opened window.

What am I doing here? Why aren't I home making Mama some tea, maybe combing her hair, she loves that, and saying, "Hush, Mama, don't you cry!" Mama would look at her with love in her sad eyes, and suddenly everything would be better.

Knuckling away tears, Sarah sat up in bed against the blue-leather headboard and swallowed hard. A voice inside her whispered, "Let it go, Sarah-girl. Let it all go." But she disobeyed the voice and pressed her lips together, determined not to cry. It wouldn't do for the sisters to find her crying. They might make her cocoa and hold her in their arms where she'd always felt so safe. Yet, she didn't want that now. A dreadful thought surfaced. After last evening, she wasn't even sure she knew who the sisters were anymore. Her last night's feeling that their actions had been necessary faded. And now she sat frozen, conflicting emotions bouncing this way and that, the breeze rifling her curls like a cool hand tousling them.

The sisters. She missed being able to turn to them, hated this new fear when she remembered what they had done last night. She wondered if they knew how she felt and believed they somehow did. They always seemed to know everything. They had given her a rose-colored nightgown and put her in this white room with its light-wood floor spread with velvety area rugs, one of rose brocade and the other holding every color in the rainbow.

Her eyes traveled from the ornate walnut furniture with blue-leather insets, a dressing table of blue beveled glass that held a hand-painted powder box, a silver-backed brush, comb, and mirror set, and atomizers of every description and size. A tall wardrobe stood opposite the bed beside a bureau whose any one drawer would hold more clothes than she had ever owned. Near the window was a desk with secret drawers, lots of cubbyholes, and stationery with her name embossed on it. Vannie had mentioned that the furniture had won an award at a furniture design show in Boston and that nobody had ever used it before. "This is yours now!" she'd whispered last night.

How long had they known she'd be coming to live here? Her gaze found the far reach of the room, where a recessed reading nook was furnished with a small, curved loveseat and built-in bookshelves crowded with books. There was a gooseneck lamp by the loveseat and a crocheted shawl to cover herself while reading.

In the brightness of morning, Sarah thought about this room. It was so lovely, she wondered if it had been created in a "poof!" by the sisters' magic. The thought drew a frown to her face. After last night she was no longer sure she liked magic. Hadn't it taken away her mama and her daddy? Her mama who would be sad without her. Her father who . . . no, surely he hadn't really tried to . . .

Sarah's hands slid up her nightgown and trembled as they found her throat, closing timidly, experimentally around its thin column. Daddy's hands had squeezed just so, only much tighter until she fought to breathe.

Then the sisters roared up in front of the house and . . . and . . .

Shivering, she remembered what the two had looked like, the energy that had exploded from them. Their wild hair, loud screams, muscles of iron, and painted war-like faces. Alma had seemed a giant, Vannie a whirling, screaming animal of sorts. They flew and swooped, terrifying her, even as Daddy released her and cringed from the shrieking women. She pictured him cowering by the porch steps, pleading for his life. She had never heard him beg before, had never thought of him begging anyone for anything, much less mercy. Other people begged *him* for mercy, not the other way round.

Shame for her father's brutality entered Sarah. Shame for his cowardice in front of the sisters. Shame for herself, her own—she hesitated—her own . . . *being*? Could she be ashamed for even being alive? But why? She had no idea. She didn't know anything except she dreaded seeing the sisters this morning. Last night, the two of them had seemed like monsters. Yes, in a way, it had been like they weren't even human beings anymore.

Through her partly opened bedroom door, she heard noises past the stairwell just outside her room. They must be down in the kitchen making breakfast. She heard them talking; then they fell silent. They must be aware of the war raging inside her. Why weren't they talking into her head like they so often did? Maybe they knew she was afraid of them now.

Padding barefoot to the door, she pulled it until she heard a click, then scurried back to bury herself in bed, pulling the covers over her ashen face.

Downstairs, the sisters worked in their kitchen, careful to be quiet for Sarah's sake. The child had been through so much. "Best let her sleep," they said to one another, neither adding what each had sensed since daybreak, that Sarah was awake and frightened in her room and wanted them to stay away.

"Are you sure we shouldn't—?" Alma ventured, squeezing orange juice she wasn't sure anyone would drink.

"Positive." Vannie put a pot on the stove for poached eggs. Of course, they could use telepathy to reach her, could overwhelm her with their love and use their magic to ensure she came around to them. But they had vowed from the moment they accepted Sarah as apprentice to never force her in any way.

"Of course, you're right, Sister. The choice must be hers."

Vannie turned on the burner under the kettle, listening to the silence flowing down from the upstairs bedroom. If Sarah didn't come down soon, they would quietly go upstairs, leave her a tray at the foot of her bed, and hang clean work clothes on her wardrobe door. Then they would go about their business, leaving her to herself, each taking a shift at the café so that one of them would always be in the house—a presence, but not an interference. After all, this child had used solitude to keep herself sane all her life.

It wouldn't do to move too fast. Not at all. And so, they listened and waited.

Vannie closed the café and joined Alma at the house as ten o'clock came and went. Alma had seen the child only once all day when Sarah was summoned down briefly to meet with her ten-year-old brother, Kelly Lee. He had come to return an unopened basket of food meant for the Curtis family, saying that his daddy had ordered him to put the basket in his sister's own hands. Sarah had turned pale, set it down on the floor, and then run back upstairs without a word.

Now the sisters sat by their kitchen hearth, each involved in handcraft, working by firelight and candles instead of the electricity that was only a light switch away. Without stirring, each heard the tentative bare feet padding slowly down the stairway and knew she was coming to them at last.

It seemed to Sarah that she was entering another time as she passed through the open kitchen door—a time that was gone from her memory, yet familiar. She gazed at Alma's crocheting that lay atop her sewing box on the table, studied the thin hook and fine silk thread and the chain of single and double crochets in the intricate lace pattern.

Vannie sat stitching a garment that looked like a dress for Sarah. Not a work dress, but a delicate, white garment with pale blue ribbons.

Still, what the girl found most impressive in the room was the wooden spinning wheel with its large spindle and smaller distaff set up in front of the open hearth and Alma's mastery as she sat there spinning. Sarah's heart skipped, remembering having seen the antique before, stuck in a back corner of the downstairs storage room that contained old furniture and musty smelling trunks with strange markings. She'd pulled out a velvet cloak lined with iridescent hues from the one trunk Sister Vannie had let her open and slipped it on over her work clothes. Vannie let her traipse about in it for a while, then whooshed it back into the trunk saying, "Time for more of this another day!"

Sarah also remembered a harp-like musical instrument and an ancient black flute that had sat propped up against it. Now the huge wheel responded to Alma's will, spinning rapidly. Watching it, Sarah was swept from resistance into the thrill of synchronic motion, seeing the rough fiber being drawn out from the distaff and twisted into one continuous thread onto Alma's spindle, the wheel twirling in response to her foot on the treadle.

A spark exploded inside Sarah's head, and for an instant she saw a progression of women spinning, from ancient societies to modern, some so primitive as to live in times before reading and writing, yet expertly intuiting the use of handheld spindle and distaff, twirling wisps of fiber into thread to bind families and kingdoms together.

"Would you like a cup of tea?" Alma asked amiably, bringing the wheel to a smooth stop.

Sarah nodded, looking older than her years as she dropped into a chair beside Vannie's. "Thank you," she mumbled, not meeting their eyes.

Alma went to the counter and put three spoonfuls of English black tea into the pot. Then she carried the pot to the stove and poured boiled water from the kettle over it to brew three cups of plain tea, one for each of them.

It wasn't right to treat Sarah as a little girl now. She didn't need sugar to improve her mood and no herb concoction to soothe her, either. Tonight, they three would have the most important conversation they'd ever had. No consciousness-altering substance had a place in it.

Sarah's hands trembled as she cupped them around her warm teacup. Noticing a few stray leaves that had sunk to the bottom, she took a teaspoon and stirred the brew, gazing as the leaves swirled into a pattern, the whirl so like the spin of Alma's wheel, so like . . . Sarah blanched at the memory of the spinning warrior. The sound of the screeching banshee now beside her. Yet, being close to the sisters in their own kitchen seemed so good, so right. She longed to feel safe with them again.

"How did you do that?" she asked, her eyes still downcast.

"Do what?" Vannie knew perfectly well that the child meant their exhibition of shape-shifting the night before. "Oh, *that*." Her fingers flew, basting a hem in the short sleeve of the garment she was sewing. "That was nothing much. A mere glamour, the kind of illusion any second-year apprentice worth her salt can do with a little practice. Not complicated."

"Not complicated at all," Alma put in, "compared to the work of real magic."

Real magic. Sarah sipped the hot liquid. "What is magic, anyway?" She lifted her head to meet Alma's gaze. "My teacher says it's just make-believe."

Alma used a gloved hand to add hot water from the kettle to the teapot. "For now let's just say that magic is not what most people think it is, not by a long shot." She added a little of the weaker brew to Sarah's teacup. "And it's not what *you* think it is, either. Even though you have already seen more than most will ever know." She returned to her wheel. "Magic is not a way of pitting your own will against that of others, Sarah." She rewound the distaff a fraction to make her thread taut, then put her foot to the treadle. "No matter how it seemed last night." The wheel spun faster, fracturing the firelight.

"It's not even about controlling events," Vannie put in. Seeing the girl's raised eyebrows, she added, "Magic is much bigger than that!"

Alma continued to spin, looking over to find the child's eyes on her. "Magic is a circle," she began. "It spirals within an ever-spinning wheel. It is not a straight line with a beginning, middle and end. The problem with learning magic is that you must jump in the middle and work your way from hub to rim and back again. Each turn of the wheel is in a new location, don't you see? Magic spirals forever onward."

Vannie smiled at the apprentice. "You have seen magic at some of its highest levels, have jumped in to assist us, bringing your innocence to partner our expertise. You have done this with only the barest consciousness of the underlying principles. We knew of no better way to start you on your journey than to first show you the future of your craft, the excitement, and the possibilities. Now you must learn the basics before you go flying off the wheel and be lost to us."

"We will never force anything on you, Sarah," Alma said over the whir of her spinning. "It will be up to you whether or not to start your studies in earnest. Are you willing to begin?"

Sarah knitted her brow. She had heard stories about witches who fooled young girls, then cooked them up in an oven along with the gingerbread. What if the sisters were not what they seemed? They had showed her another side last night. Which side was the real one? Still, they had not hurt her father, even as angry at him as they had seemed. She had never heard of them hurting anyone. She studied the half-sewn dress Vannie had left on the table, smelled the tea in the fine china cup, glanced at Alma's face, soft in the firelight, and felt their love for her.

"I'll try," she said hopefully.

20

"The whole of magic is quite large," Alma said. She had ceased her spinning and come to join the other two at the table. She might invite Sarah to gaze into the wheel and be transported to other realms on another night. For now, it was enough that the wheel had opened her perspective. "Yes, the whole is bigger than we could ever grasp," she continued. "Magic circles the globe and shows up in endless forms. It is part of the inner life of all people, though most wouldn't call it by that name."

"Even though everyone uses it to create their lives," Vannie added.

Sarah frowned. "If everyone creates their own lives, does that mean we're all magicians?"

"In a way, the answer to your question is yes, child. One could make a case for calling all human beings magicians, but most don't understand the nature of their power and so don't always use it to their highest good. It takes consciousness and skill to be a true magician."

"There are magicians of all shapes and sizes and from every culture on Earth and beyond," Alma said.

"Oh, absolutely," Vannie agreed. "The Earth's sun never sets on magicians at work. Medicine men or priests, lone witches or wizards, politicians, servants, poets or saints, anyone, anywhere, from any walk of life, may be one. Or they may not."

"How can you tell if someone is one?" Sarah asked impatiently.

"By the actions they take and how they approach life." Vannie paused to choose her next words. "Magicians are aware that they are creating their own realities, Sarah, and take responsibility for the process. By delving into deeper and deeper levels of the workings, they are able to make more conscious choices than others can."

Sarah looked at her closely. "Did you and Miss Alma choose to do . . . what you did last night?"

"Yes, honey. We chose to protect you from your father's rage. With harm to none." There, it had been said out loud. She reached for her sewing and plucked her needle from the fine cotton of the dress, then held it up to watch it gleam in the firelight before plunging it back into the fabric.

Sarah had felt a ping of alarm at the words, yet almost immediately she felt the bubble of panic deflate, as though Vannie's needle had punctured it. At home, the source of the danger went unnamed; it was a shadow in every room of the house, a boogeyman. It was felt in the strained silence, in seeing Mama's bruises, or in the sudden slash of a hand or belt. "With harm to none," the apprentice repeated timidly. "That's what you said last night. I remember."

Vannie withdrew her needle and held it in front of the girl's eyes. "Yes, dear. Even when a magician has to battle, she never deliberately hurts any other person, body or soul."

Sarah took a long sip from her cup as she thought it over, surprised at how good it felt to be talking about magic with the sisters again. Her chin snapped toward Alma. "But you had a *sword*!"

"I did. And there might have been a time when I would have used it to draw blood," Alma admitted.

"But fortunately, Sister and I have learned to create realities where there is no need for . . ." Vannie stopped mid-sentence, thinking of Cleatis and possible future dangers for this child. She clucked her tongue, faced with the dilemma of a man so bent on destruction now being a part of their lives. Cleatis was giving them a run for their money.

"Sister," Alma said, "we cannot say we could never do deliberate harm. We could. We live with that possibility, as do all beings. The fact that we could do harm and yet don't is a secret to our power, a secret we must share with Sarah now."

Sarah frowned, not liking the word "power."

"So you don't like that word," Alma said, nodding. "Well, it's no wonder, since it's been so misunderstood. What if we use the word 'ability' instead? The ability to change things by choice."

"I don't know." Sarah nervously kicked at the legs of her chair and watched Vannie who was again sewing. There was a soft click as the thimble pushed the needle through each stitch, making for a relaxing rhythm as she worked.

Vannie twinkled at her. "I wonder if one so opposed to power would care to see a magic wand?"

Sarah tried not to look excited, but failed miserably. *A magic wand!* In spite of her reservations, the thought of it brought chills.

"Let me see, where did I put it? Oh, there you are!" Vannie said. She pulled her needle from the dress she was working on and held it up for Sarah to see. "Ta-dah!"

Disappointed, Sarah squinted skeptically at the tiny needle.

"Not what you expected? Don't go judging by appearances. It's only one of many wands you will come to know and use, young lady. It may seem small and ordinary, but it can be a fine teacher of magical art." She tied off the short thread and cut it near her perfect knot.

Sarah wondered if it was her imagination that made the needle give off rainbow beams in the firelight.

"As I was saying," Vannie continued, adeptly pushing new white thread through the needle's eye, "this is just an everyday wand. But let's observe how to use it, perhaps to demonstrate how a magician exercises her abilities. Just how does she create the various aspects of the world around her? Why, the same way that every other person in the world does it. She generates it in her dreams, tries it out in her imagination, takes action that is appropriate, then releases the outcome so that her dream can come true, often in surprising ways. It sometimes comes easily; it fails sometimes for reasons we'll discuss another time. Regardless, this is the how of all human creation, no matter the degree of consciousness used."

She held the needle up to her eye, admiring its sharp point. "A wand is for focusing one's intent. And what does intent carry with it?" She stretched out the thread before Sarah's eyes. "Just what is this thread that the needle directs?" She put thimble to thumb and fell back to work on the dress.

Sarah moved closer to observe. It was always a thrill to see Vannie's fingers fly in a precise and nimble dance that somehow changed bits of cloth into elegant garments.

Once the girl became lost in watching, Vannie spoke again in a changed voice. When she engaged in her special storytelling magic, her tones and words mesmerized. "This thread is directed by the wand to bind, pleat, and tuck, and also to gather, hold, and shape. Where does it come from?" She pointed at the raw fiber in the basket where Alma had seated herself again at the spinning wheel, drawing the fiber onto the distaff, and spinning it into new thread.

The child sat mute and spellbound.

"Why, it comes from her dreams, of course!" Vannie went on. "The fiber in the basket is like the raw stuff of dreams. Out of dreams come tufts of desire, strands of imagination, and streamers of expectations." She pointed at twirling fibers being twisted together on their way to the spindle. "Desire, imagination, and expectation merge to make a magical thread with which to fashion a magician's world."

As usual, Alma marveled at the flexibility of her sister's mind. Vannie claimed that the Muses intervened when she told her stories, be they truth or fiction, guiding them in ways she could never have planned. Characters in her tales sometimes miraculously sprang to life, circumventing the birth process altogether. Truthful metaphors spun themselves, bringing an otherworldly mystery and power to her words.

This was a talent rare even among the immortals, Alma marveled, swelling with admiration for her sister. Under Vannie's spell, she now spun a dream for Sarah—that tonight the door of vision would crack open for her. Smiling, she noted that Sarah's face now out-glowed the candles in their holders on the mantel and tabletop.

Vannie tapped her needle against her thimble, drawing the child's attention back to the dress she held in her lap as she pushed her needle through the cloth. "A magician puts her magical thread through the eye of her needle, her wand. Then she reaches into her interior and captures a bit of belief in herself and in what is possible." She was making gathers of the fabric with her needle. "The magician then plucks together attitudes to support her beliefs." She continued to gather the fabric, arranging the gathers to the proportions of Sarah's waist, measuring only with her eye, then took a moment to pin the gathers to the waistband, already sewn to the bodice. She pushed the pins through the several layers with ease, then began to baste.

"She builds on those beliefs, those attitudes," she continued, "with thoughts and feelings about what she is creating, the more precise and intense, the better. Detail and passion are important." Her fingers flew in an even-looping stitch to the end of the band. Finished, she tied her knot, cut the thread, and held the needle up to catch the firelight as she slid in new thread. "Most importantly, she empowers her wand with her *choice* to let the magic happen and allow her dream to come true. Then and only then can the wand wield all its magic."

At that, Vannie stretched the waistband, now basted to the skirt, over her forefinger and stitched in earnest, her needle sliding through the layers of fabric in quick, tiny strokes, strong and neat and as accurate as any machine could make. In the glint of the flying needle, Sarah felt a warm rush inside and suddenly knew what it must be like to create something you wanted mightily, using a wand of focused intention and a thread from a dream.

Once again, Alma left her seat at the wheel, moving closer so that she and Sarah could watch together. Before their eyes, the sewing was turning into a finished garment. Much more than just pieces of cloth sewn together, it was now becoming a dress with its own particular form and grace.

"And that is the magic of this wand!" Vannie held up the soft garment for them to see. "A rudimentary look, of course, but a peek at a magic that knows no bounds." She put the garment down to look Sarah in the eye. "That's how all people create their worlds, child. Only most don't understand the process. Some are confused; some have conflicting desires. Others hold rigid and narrow beliefs. Most importantly, often their choices are not conscious to them. They may think they are choosing one thing, when in actuality, they are choosing another."

Vannie hung the dress in the hall closet. The hem would come later, along with Alma's lace for the neckline and sleeves. The child was tired now. Still, there was one piece of business that should not be put off.

Alma spoke into the sputtering fire. "Getting back to last night. The sword . . ."

Sarah's body jolted as adrenaline surged through her. Yet, she said nothing as Alma reached into her skirt pocket and pulled out a miniature sword, six inches long, in a light-colored suede scabbard. Its hilt was encrusted with semi-precious stones: amber, turquoise, aquamarine, and citrine. Sarah saw at once that this sword was exactly like the one she had seen fly through the air and stick in the post on her front porch the night before, only smaller. *Much* smaller.

Alma slid the blade from its holster and held it to the candlelight. "The sword is one of four gifts given to a magician at her initiation. It represents her power and her responsibility to be sharp of mind, to cut through mental confusion in search of truth when dealing with her own ego. She'll need to cut through ego's shallow desire to always be right, to get even, to punish, and to seek revenge, in order to find a deeper truth. Only then, can she work her magic with harm to none. You will someday be given a sword and be taught to wield it."

Sarah watched Alma cut the air with the blade. Though small, it was perfectly proportioned. Slivers of her own reflection danced in and out of

PABLO
FERRO

it as it moved in the candlelight. In the reflected glow, she remembered Alma's fury of the night before, her up-raised sword.

"Last night," Vannie said, "you saw my sister's character tested. She was called upon to discern the difference between her ego's voice and that of her true self. She had to rely on her character that she had built from her ideals and on the rules she has made for herself over time. Those rules are called principles. Living by them shapes a person's character."

"Character," Alma repeated quietly. "Adherence to principles. When you understand these things, you will no longer fear personal power, Sarah. Actually, you have begun to learn the foundations for strong character already. Can you think how?"

"My mama shows me how to try to do right," Sarah whispered. "And you show me, too."

"And then there is your own instinct toward right action. Eventually, you'll sort out your principles and have the strength to live by them. Not perfectly, but well enough. You will make your own rules, the ones that ring true in your soul, and you will be able to handle power without fearing that you will abuse it.

"*Our* first rule is harm to none." Alma carefully slid the sword back into its sheath as Vannie swept snippets of thread from the table and closed her sewing box.

"That will be mine, too," Sarah said eagerly.

"Wonderful! But enough for tonight. It's bedtime for the three of us."

"But shall we leave Sarah with a riddle?" Vannie suggested, putting dishes in the sink. "One that may help her on her quest for ideals and the principles that can support them?"

"Yep-a-do," Alma breathed, gathering her thoughts. Then she came to take Sarah's hands in her own and intoned:

> "How can a warrior make war
> Without harming a hair on a head
> Without bruising a heart
> Or breaking a bone?"

"We'll give you a clue," Vannie said, steering Sarah toward the stairs. "And it's in the form of this question: *Who is the enemy?*" She said it in a way that made Sarah think it might be a trick question.

Alma stepped over to the counter and reached for the cookie jar. She pulled out a large oatmeal cookie, placed it on a cloth napkin, and handed it to Sarah. "That should be enough to chew on for one night!"

Vannie covered the glowing coals in the fireplace with ashes and turned off the light. Sarah wrapped up her cookie, vaguely realizing she had hardly touched food all day.

"Last night, you had your first brush with the magician's sword," Alma said to her as they headed upstairs. "Tonight came your first look at a wand. You will eventually find a shield and also a chalice."

On her way upstairs, Sarah realized she was starving. She felt grateful for the cookie wrapped in the napkin in her hand, but before she reached the landing, it felt like lead. Her mother's thin face and tiny frame flashed into her mind. Was Mama hungry tonight? Were the other kids? Alma and Vannie had sent them a hamper of food, but Daddy had sent it back. Kelly Lee had brought the hamper up to the big house, still smelling of fried chicken, butter beans, cornbread, and blackberry pie. It had torn Sarah up to see her younger brother tugging back on the handles, reluctant to let go, eyes darting from the basket to the truck where Cleatis sat waiting in the graveled parking lot below, weak and sickly looking, but still managing a couple of blasts on the horn.

Now, at midnight, as Sarah entered her beautiful room, sorrow overtook her. How could she enjoy having so much, when others she loved had so little? What good was learning about a magic that couldn't help the ones she cared most about? Her father had resisted healing, which meant that all connected to him would keep on suffering, day after day, *forever*, as they waited for him to change. Because he never, ever would; she knew it.

No way out! She wondered if it might be easier to give up now, sneak downstairs and out the door, and go sleep in the drafty room she shared with her sisters and sometimes her mother and the baby. The feel of her father's hands around her throat washed over her, the sound of his belt whipping through the air.

Swallowing the bitter tears in her throat, she flung the cookie into the wastebasket and threw herself onto her billowing featherbed. She would stay here for a while. She just didn't know how long.

21

The drought of late summer wore on into the hottest and driest September in Willow Creek's recorded history. Livestock thirsted; crops withered in the fields, parched now beyond hope of harvest. Stray dogs and cats were found dead in ditches and alongside the road. Cisterns dried up; lawns burned to straw. Every day the sun grew hotter.

It was Donnie Marble who found a name for all the heat and thirst. He called it "the Beetle Drought," because he said he had never in his life seen so many beetles as those that appeared that summer.

"Like damn vampires," Donnie said, holding court in his mechanic's shop. The regulars were there: Burris McCarthy, Leon Malone, and Ben Houseman. "The damn things are sucking the water out of every leaf on my trees. Just look here!" He showed them a can of gasoline and said he must have drowned two hundred beetles in that can this day alone. He'd gotten them out of his "fork trees" as he called his two beechnut trees that grew across each other at a strange angle. Almost like an "X," he said often, where you might expect to dig for treasure. Donnie had built his shop alongside those trees just to stare at the spectacle. He often contemplated doing a little digging to see if the treasure was there, but in his heart he knew he never would. This way, he could always believe it might be.

"Listen here," Donnie announced that noon in mid-September. "I want to spread the word for folks to meet at The Two Sisters' tonight about this damn drought."

"And do *what*?" Ben said on his way to his car that had just acquired a tune-up and a new set of plugs. "How the hell do you intend to fight an almighty drought?"

"I'll think of something," Donnie promised, ripping off another handful of beetles from a tree. He crushed the bugs angrily, then dropped them into his gas can. "Just tell everybody you see to be at the café by seven. And tell Carolyn to make phone calls."

Since Ben was agreeable to an evening at The Two Sisters' Café and since his car purred like a mother cat, he said, "Alright, Carolyn and I'll do our part."

All that afternoon the word spread, and, as if to spur everyone on, lightning flashed high in the northwestern sky for over an hour, then disappeared up north to give Indiana and Illinois a good soaking rain. People stood outside their houses and watched the clouds disappear, pushed by winds that continued to blow hot and dry over the town.

By seven that night the citizens of Willow Creek were gathered at the café, feeling robbed of their rainfall and tasting the dust in the air. Even the children played in a restrained fashion, Sarah among them. Vannie and Alma noted her mingling with her schoolmates with relief. In spite of her progress on the night of the needle and the spinning wheel, Sarah often still seemed remote. The sisters sensed how deeply she missed her mother, sisters, and brothers. They knew she missed Cleatis, too, though the thought of him sent butterflies through the girl's stomach that they could feel in their own.

With all this she was making headway in her studies of magic, traveling easily into other dimensions and expanding her consciousness in diverse ways. At those times she rose out of herself to live up to her considerable talents, but afterward her mood crashed again. One thing was for certain, Sarah wanted no mention of the riddle they had put to her. On the single occasion when Vannie had brought it up, she was met with a look that was both stony and pained.

Now Sarah moved quietly from one group of children to another. She helped choose songs on the jukebox that was turned to a lower volume this evening, then left to observe the group downstairs at the pinball machines, turning to watch silently when several boys teased the parrot on the steps.

"Ugly children!" Banshee squawked, then screeched it in a more raucous style as the children laughed. Which made the old bird garble something in his throat that sounded for all the world like "Children soup! Children soup!"

Through it all Sarah barely smiled. The sisters hoped the event heading toward them at this very moment would give her something to hold onto in the face of the nightmarish threat that came ever more intensely from Cleatis. Vannie and Alma held the anticipation of it with every new person who entered the café and found a place at the crowded tables and booths.

"I don't mind telling you, I'm nervous," Belle Taylor said to the room at large. "My Aunt Lucy always said that if our creek bed was ever to run dry, we'd all come to a terrible end. She said our town was founded on that creek, that it was the source of our power, and that we'd be doomed if Willow Creek ever dried up. I was out there today, and the damn thing's nothing but a trickle. I'm worried sick."

Belle's Aunt Lucy had carried a lot of weight in the community in life and perhaps even more in death. Legend was she had "known things" and had predicted an unsettling amount of occurrences that had come true. Her penchant for "hexes" had also been feared, and the story was still remembered of the day after a quarrel with her husband, the Judge, when she had pointed her finger at his tires and yelled, "Four flats today!" just as the Judge pulled from their driveway. Four flats it had been, three during the day and a fourth as his car limped back into his garage that night. And now here was Aunt Lucy's pronouncement from the grave about the town coming to a "terrible end."

Trip Robinson put down his Coke and asked as nonchalantly as possible, "Ah, did your aunt say exactly what kind of end we could expect?

Famine? Fire? I guess under the circumstances flooding is out."

"Oh, shut up," Helen Blackerby said. "I don't take any truck in this superstitious nonsense, but this drought's bad for the auction business. Nobody feels like cleaning out attics in this heat, much less lugging furniture down to the auction house. I'd be willing to pay ten dollars to anybody who could put a stop to it."

"Ten dollars!" Trip whistled. "Now *that's* enough to get the best minds on the problem. Though the only way would be to seed clouds, and the clouds blew past us already."

"Let's think about seeding," Donnie Marble said, feeling pleased that a mechanical solution might save the day. "We ought to be prepared. If we'd been thinking, we'd of had a plane on alert so when those rain clouds blew in, the plane could have gone right up and in. It's too late now, but next time . . ."

While the talking continued, the sisters moved through the dining room refilling coffee cups and clearing dishes from the desserts that most of the townsfolk had enjoyed. They kept their excitement inside, though their dresses were rather festive, each wearing a white lacy blouse trimmed in dark green, tucked into a green skirt with a handmade apron embroidered in green and yellow in Alma's favorite diamond stitch.

When the lights suddenly went out just after eight o'clock, they appeared with lanterns and candles. Sarah left the other children and helped distribute them, moving around the dim room quietly and efficiently. A good sign, Vannie noted. The girl was conscientious, a strength that could see her through.

"Fuses, I reckon?" grunted Andy Poole, getting up to check the fuse box. He went down the steps and through the screened door connecting the station to the café.

Earl Taylor, who was considered something of a poet, always scribbling things about the voice of the fields, the truth in a strawberry and the like, raised his head alertly. "Something's happening," he muttered.

"What do you mean?" Julie Spillman asked nervously.

Earl's eyes were dreamy in the lantern light. "Something's headed toward us. You know I have an ear for atmosphere. Always did have. Last night I heard one of my trees say . . ." His voice died away in the wake of Andy Poole's hoarse whoop from outside. It came near to being a scream, and was echoed in a blood-curdling fashion by the parrot.

"Oh my God," Belle said, "it's already on us!"

In a fevered hush, the townsfolk rose as one and hurried downstairs, some filing through the gas station and out the door leading to the pumps, and the rest pouring through the front door. The *oohs* and *ahs* of those already outside made the ones behind quicken their pace. Pretty soon they all stood together, gaping into the starry night sky, the younger children and some of the older ones clinging to their parents in fear.

"Bless my heart," Belle murmured, "I've never seen such a sight in my life."

"You mean you've never seen shooting stars before?" Trip asked. Even as the words left his lips, he knew they were dumb. His brain froze as he observed the blazing wash of light above him. Aunt Lucy's dire prediction of the town's end suddenly took on new weight.

"That's no shooting star!" Carolyn Houseman snapped. "It's a comet."

There wasn't a doubt in anybody's mind that she was right. Though it was true that stars seemed to be falling from the dotted black of the night canopy, there was a far more striking sight in their midst. A blazing cone of fire, not shooting at all, inched along on an arcing journey across heaven.

"Look at the tail on that thing!" Belle whispered.

"Why in the world didn't we know to expect this?" Earl wondered. "They always warn people in advance when such a thing is coming." Everyone agreed it was odd. Imagine a comet appearing and not one prediction in any newspaper or a single mention of it on their radios or TVs. One of the smaller children started to cry, then others followed suit. Hot as it was, people found themselves shivering.

With his wife tending to the twins, Jim Morgan took his daughter into his arms and pointed out the comet's beauty to his weeping child, its dazzling wide tail and the purity of its brightness that shifted constantly in intensity, showing strands of bright color one moment, then in the next softening to silver or golden white.

"It's a sure sign of something," Earl declared, putting his arm around Belle. "Remember Granny Rollins? How she used to tell all those stories of happenings that came with comets? Could be that . . . I tell you I can feel it! We're in for it, sure enough! Somethin' . . ." He felt his wife's back tense and bit back his words, not wanting to say out loud what he'd always heard, that comets were thought to be precursors of evil events.

As Earl finished speaking, they saw the man. He came walking down the center of the road, not the old highway, but the country road that led down from Smithfield and the new highway intersection. Under the light of the comet, he looked to be a god come down from the sky with light sparking off the considerable amount of silver and rhinestones that he wore, so much so that even his skin took on a blazing iridescence.

"My Lord, it's Judgment Day," the Reverend said, falling to his knees. He was not scared; somehow his fear of meeting his maker had evaporated completely in the past months. Still, it couldn't hurt to pay due respect. A good many confused folks followed his example and knelt just in case, keeping their eyes on the luminous stranger who was still walking down the middle of the road, head raised to the heavens.

"He don't look a bit like Jesus, he looks more like John Wayne," little Robbie Jessup said in a loud voice, only to be hushed immediately by his mother, Ruth. Just in case it was the Lord Himself coming, she didn't want her son to incur displeasure. Though surely, Ruth told herself, even the Lord on High wouldn't mind being compared to John Wayne.

The stranger kept coming, his gaze shifting from the sky to the mob of people outside the café. The closer he got, the handsomer and the taller he got, and the more he took on the brilliance of the comet, until it seemed in some way that he and the comet had become one.

More than one townsperson felt that perhaps the comet could be just as Earl Taylor had said, a sign of something coming to them, possibly something important. And maybe . . . this luminous stranger was *it*!

Sure enough, just as he arrived in their midst, the comet pulsed brighter and abruptly dimmed, as if a veil had drifted across its piece of sky. The canopy darkened, and the odd light show came to an end. Still nobody said a word, but every eye was trained expectantly on the stranger.

"Virgil Hunter, at your service," he said into the silence, his teeth flashing. The electricity of his presence told every man, woman, and child that he was quite capable of having manufactured the comet just as an introduction for himself. His eyes moved around the frozen circle of people, until he found the two sisters standing to one side with Sarah.

"Alma May and my sister Vannie, proprietors of The Two Sisters' Café, at your service," Alma said calmly. "And this is Sarah Curtis, our apprentice."

The stranger touched Sarah on the head, acknowledging her as something more than just a young presence. He was thinking: *Never leave a stone unturned.* Caution was the name of his game. "Perhaps we could go inside?" he suggested, extending his hand.

Alma shook it. "After you, sir."

With another dazzling smile, he stepped through the front door. A moment later a loud hum sounded through the café's wiring, and all the lights suddenly bumped back on. The jukebox whined and struggled back up to speed, resuming its blue country sound. The overhead fans began to turn as customers flocked silently inside, following Virgil Hunter and the sisters into the upper dining room.

"I tell you it's a sign," Boomer Hawkins, a stout man who lived alone in a trailer not far from the graveyard, kept muttering. He had forgotten that Earl Taylor was the first to come up with that idea and had taken it as his own. Years later, he would tell the story of how he had known that the comet was a sign of the stranger's coming.

"Well," Vannie said, "lights in the sky do speak of miracles, don't they, Sister?"

"Light itself is a miracle," Alma said. "And it's curious how it has a way of showing up in the darkest times."

The sisters and Sarah moved about the dining room, blowing out and collecting the lanterns and candles from the tables and storing them back in the cupboard. No one took any notice of them. Every eye was riveted to the stranger with the square jaw and blazing eyes, who did indeed hold an amazing resemblance to John Wayne, cowboy hat and all. The hat was studded with rhinestones, and his collar and shirtfront were liberally sprinkled with silver and more rhinestones, with his collar tipped in silver.

"I wouldn't mind having a hat like that," Andy Poole said wistfully, but no one even looked at him. The atmosphere was too tense for anyone to so much as chuckle at the image of Andy's entire head being swallowed by a hat like the stranger's.

"I can well imagine how you all must be feeling, folks," Virgil Hunter said in a hypnotic voice. "I suppose you've been talking about the drought!"

This brought a surprised squeal from Julie Spillman, but she was quickly hushed by at least a half-dozen people. No one stopped to think that in a farming community at least a fair amount of the conversation would have been about the drought.

"Of course, you have," Virgil Hunter said softly. "Everything so hot. So still. The ground hard and unproductive; the animals thirsty. The energy wrung right out of you. If only . . . if only . . . it would rain." The word *rain* fell from his lips like nectar, a promise of comfort and hope. "Rain," he repeated. "Our show of mercy from God. As Shakespeare wrote, mercy 'droppeth as the gentle rain from heaven.' When we go for long periods of time without rain we feel almost desperate. Are there any farmers in this room?"

He nodded sympathetically as dozens of hands went up. "Even worse for you. But something else is going on here. Don't deny it. I can feel it!" His eyes picked out Belle Taylor, who sat wringing her hands. "Tell me," he said, his eyes holding hers. "Tell me the problem."

Flushing, Belle stammered out the story about the dry creek bed and the foreboding that lay over the town. "We're threatened by disaster," she ended. "Something horrible. Only nobody knows exactly what."

Virgil Hunter's eyes flashed. "Then *that's* why I've been sent to you!"

He removed his hat with one hand and swept it over his breast with a theatrical gesture that made every woman in the room gasp. The hat had concealed thick, golden-bronze hair and a noble and unlined forehead.

"You mustn't let a drought take the heart out of you," he remonstrated. "The courage. The soul. Clearly, you're in hard times. And what are hard times? Only times that must be gone through gallantly. Tests, if you will. Yes, that's it! This drought is your test. Now will one of you ask what is *my* test?" He chuckled. "For the price of a cup of coffee, I'll be glad to tell you."

Alma gestured to Sarah, who hesitated for only a second before dashing down the steps and back again on a dead run, arriving like quicksilver, coffee sloshing down the sides of the cup onto the saucer in her hand, to a room full of mesmerized people.

Another good sign, as far as the sisters were concerned. Sarah knew something was up, and her spirits had been lifted, at least for this moment.

Virgil Hunter accepted the coffee, pleased that the girl had spilled it. That told him he was in his power mode. You could always tell by the way children reacted to you. He sipped slowly, then set his cup on the nearest table.

Donnie Marble stirred. "Exactly what are you . . . er . . .?"

"Aha. Your instinct is to ask not who, but *what*!" Virgil Hunter's voice rose proudly. "I am the man you've been waiting for. Not a figment of your wishful imagination, not a vagabond or a jack-of-all-trades. In fact, I have but one trade. Yet in that trade, I am not only a master, but *the* master. Whether you are a farmer or simply a homeowner whose lawn has died, I am the answer to your prayers. If you have cattle thirsting in a dry field, I can help. If you are worried about the creek bed going dry, I am the solution."

Not an eye moved from his handsome face that held a sheen of moisture. Sweat, the unromantic might have called it. Elixir, the poet might have said.

"Ladies and gentlemen," Virgil Hunter said, "I am a dowser."

He watched the impact of the word work through the room. The awe on every face was more intense than if he'd pulled a nickel out of a handy ear. Dowsing magic, as he well knew, was better than any other act going, especially when there was a drought in town.

"You understand what dowsing is, yes?" In the blink of an eye and from seemingly nowhere, he produced a forked implement, holding it in practiced hands. No common tool, this. Most local dowsers used hazel-wood sticks, nothing like this one of finely carved bone. It glinted white in Hunter's upturned palms, each holding a branch of the fork. The look of him standing there, the polished bone shining in his hands, would have raised the hackles of a bulldog. He seemed as much mad as sane, as satanic as holy, and full of the promises they wanted so badly to believe.

At the murmur that filled the room, the dowser felt like laughing. Lord, he had known even before he walked into the café this sweltering night that he was walking into a goldmine. Like everyone else in Willow Creek, he could taste the dust in the air. But the dowser could taste the money even more.

To think that a prophecy of doom lay over the town, and that a comet had virtually announced his arrival! Never had he ever had an opportunity to equal this one. He thought quickly of the dry creek bed and the method he could employ to exploit it. In an instant, he had it. It would make him a mint.

Money, he thought, his empty heart's caverns opening its jaws to the possibilities. *Money, money, money.*

Such was his sense of his audience that the dowser felt a sudden pull to glance toward the sisters. He always knew when special care was needed to draw in a certain person. There usually was at least one in the crowd. Tonight, there were two. Maybe three, if you counted the little girl. She was standing between the sisters now, her face as inscrutable as theirs. What a strange child.

"Whalebone, I think," Alma said.

"Beg your pardon?" He had lost his concentration. A bead of perspiration rolled slowly from his right temple towards his chin, and a chill trembled through his arms, making the whalebone dip in his hands.

Leon Malone roused himself. "Point's going down," he observed. "Seems we might strike water right through your dining room floor, Sisters. Okay if we start digging?"

Trip Robinson's hearty laugh rang out followed by several chuckles.

The dowser was annoyed. It was unlike him to lose his focus. Without a doubt, his magnitude had diminished. "Yes, whalebone," he said, regaining his balance. "The finest whalebone fork ever made for a dowser, passed down through three generations. Such talent as mine, you know, runs in families."

"Personally, though," Burris McCarthy said, "I've never gone in for dowsing. I don't believe in this nonsense that a fool stick points out water in the ground. I've known folks to try it, and it never amounted to a damn thing."

The dowser stood speechless, though he knew he should interrupt. He tried to assert himself but could only stand there, rubbing his jaw that had locked into place. His anger grew as he listened to them laugh, knowing that sixty seconds ago he'd owned them. Now they dared to speak with derision.

"I only heard of it working once," Donnie Marble said. "This man from Bedford pulled out a hickory stick and—"

"Hickory wood's all wrong," Leon Malone interrupted. "It's got to be hazelwood. Hazelwood is what pulls toward the water."

The dowser didn't let himself frown, although he couldn't remember a time when he had lost a room so completely. His voice usually dominated, ruled the hour. But tonight of all nights, in this perfect situation, he had somehow lost his command.

"The power," he said, straightening his spine and showing his dowser's fork to advantage, "is not in the stick, or the pendulum, or the L-shaped angle rod. It lies in the dowser. The power moves *through* the implement. That's why this lovely whalebone is so perfect. Just see how attuned it is to me. Why, it moved downward before your eyes, *not to predict that the water is under this floor . . . no, that wasn't it*! It was to tell you that there are untold quantities of water buried in this town. I can feel it. My bones ache with water. The dowser's tool answered me." He felt more sweat coming, but it was alright. This sweat was from power. There was heat in this sweat, not chill.

"What I wouldn't give to have water in my field," Earl Taylor said quietly. "My cattle would bring tears to your eyes, mister."

The dowser doubted it, but he nodded and said as he always did: "Does anyone know who the first recorded dowser was? None other than Moses himself. You do remember?" He made a dramatic striking motion with his hand and pointed toward his feet as though indicating a miracle. "He brought forth water by striking a rock with a rod. I remind you of this to do away with anyone's belief that dowsing has any of the satanic implications that people would have you believe. No, friends, dowsing is of Biblical verification, and you can feel justified in faith to be the first to sign your name to the list!"

Paper and pen appeared in his hands with all the suddenness as had the dowsing tool. "Only a hundred dollars a field, twenty dollars retainer, payable in cash this very night. And, folks, your money is guaranteed! No water, no payment. Your twenty-dollar retainer fee is absolutely 100 percent refundable. I stake my whalebone on it! Now are there any questions?"

"What about the creek bed?" Belle Taylor asked timidly. "How can finding water help a dry creek?"

Virgil Hunter smiled into her eyes and watched her face flush. "Dear lady, perhaps you didn't know that where there's water, there's generally *more* water. Upon commission, I will find that water source, and if I can get some able bodied men to bring spades tomorrow at dawn, we will begin with that very project. It will most likely be found in one of the fields nearest the creek bed, so it's only good sense to look there first. Once we find the water, we will dredge into the creek bed, and, with our intervention and a little luck, that creek will never go dry!"

He laid the paper in front of Belle. "You strike me as a lady of sensitivity and intelligence. I'd like for your name to head this list."

Belle's forehead crinkled. "But twenty dollars?" Her fingers flexed around her pocketbook on the table in front of her. The Taylors lived close to the bone.

"That's right, just a twenty-dollar retainer fee. I said it, and I'll stick to it. Sign right there on the top line. And don't forget—no water, and I'll refund every penny. The money is a faith payment."

Earl reached over and squeezed Belle's hand. "Pay him, Belle. And twenty more for our field. Here, I've got my wallet."

There was a hubbub of voices as hands reached for wallets all over the room. Some gave money to help with the creek bed; still more poured money into the dowser's hand to find water on their property. Homeowners wanted wells. The twenty-dollar bills kept coming, and people kept signing the dowser's contract.

He carefully folded the money into his clip. My God, he must have over three hundred dollars. Most nights he'd be glad to get sixty. He smiled and snatched up another twenty. The bounty was making him sweat. He reached for a napkin on the nearest table and dabbed at his forehead. In fifteen minutes, he'd be out the door and heading for his car that he'd hidden up the road beside the bridge. Too bad he couldn't get paid in full, but two pocketfuls of twenty-dollar commissions were plenty. He only worked in summer and earned more than enough to support himself for the entire year. It was simple. Mesmerize the people with his good looks and his way with words, then hit the road. Come tomorrow morning, he'd be a hundred miles away, thinking about all those suckers gathered at the creek bed waiting for him to find water. Feeling someone staring at him, he glanced over his shoulder and saw the sisters watching him. *Their eyes . . .*

He felt a sudden sickness in his head. The room slowly tilted and swam. The twenty that someone had just put into his hand blurred before him. Where on Earth was he? He wasn't sure. This morning he had been in northern Ohio having breakfast in a diner. All of a sudden he'd gotten a feeling he was needed elsewhere. And before he'd known what he was doing, without any clear idea of where he was going, he was in his car, accelerator pressed to the floorboard.

Going where? Here? He hadn't even known Willow Creek existed.

"Sit down, Mr. Hunter." Vannie was beside him, her sister on his other side, as together they helped him carefully into a chair, while the little girl handed him a glass . . .

" . . . of water," he said aloud. "Water." Sweat streamed down his face.

"Drink, Mr. Hunter," Alma said. "Refresh yourself on the nectar of life."

"Have I made all my collections?" he babbled.

"Oh, yes, it's all done," Vannie said softly.

He saw the townspeople filing past him, as silent as though he had dreamed them into existence and had finished with them.

And then the dowser, worn out by his own game, saw himself poised on the brink of a fall. Arms outstretched, he drew one last deep breath and then took a graceful dive into the vast abyss. He couldn't see bottom. He just fell.

22

"Mr. Hunter? Are you awake now?"

He blinked up into a night made black by inky webs of clouds that blew across the sky, painting the full moon and blocking out the light.

"Mr. Hunter?" the voice persisted.

A face lowered itself over his, and he saw the piquant smile of the smaller of the two sisters—Vannie, he remembered her name was. The taller sister loomed over her shoulder, and the little girl squatted beside him wearing a white scarf over her long thick hair.

"A full moon," he said in a weak voice. "It pulls the tides, you know. Pulls water from its source. You can *feel* the water on a night like this."

"That's why we chose it," Alma said with a sudden laugh that made him shudder. Her sister and the little girl joined in. The laughter rang out over what he perceived to be a large field. Beyond her, he could see listless cattle in the scant light of the veiled moon, silhouetted as they stood at the edge of a parched white creek bed. When the laughter died away, the sudden silence was the deepest he had ever known.

"This is your field," Vannie told him. "For the time being it belongs to you even more than it belongs to Pig Blackerby. Because, Mr. Hunter, this is the field where you are going to find water tomorrow morning. The field closest to the creek, just as you said."

His blood ran cold at the thought. "Water," he whispered weakly. "I'm . . . I don't think I can . . ."

"Oh yes you can," Alma said firmly.

"Oh yes you can," the little girl repeated.

He was terrified at the power he felt flowing through them.

"Ah, but that's the very way people feel about *you*," Vannie said, as though she had read his thoughts. "The power that flows through you awes them. They are frightened, but they put themselves in your hands. They even pay you, Mr. Hunter. For the possibilities you offer."

"Do you dare put yourself into our hands?" Alma smiled. "We won't charge you a penny, though our services are quite real."

The child leaned forward. "Why don't you hold on to me?" she suggested. "I'm smaller, and I won't scare you."

"Sarah," Alma said, faintly remonstrating.

"Not that the sisters would either," the child said. "But anyway," she added soberly, "I'm just an apprentice and a little girl. You're safe with me."

He found himself smiling at her as she tugged gently at his hands until he was on his feet. Turning to look at the barren landscape all around him, he felt better, almost recovered. He could almost remember who he was. A reassuring flash of himself driving away in his car made his muscles relax. There was plenty of time yet. "I must have had some kind of sinking spell. How kind of you to cover for me, Sisters," he said cordially.

Then hand-in-hand with the child, he followed the women as they encircled an area that they had seemingly mapped out. They kept nodding to each other, indicating perimeters with their hands. Pointing here. Pointing there. Circling again. Feeling safer, he let go of the little girl's hand. She walked just ahead of him then, following the sisters, dotting the ground with seeds that she took from her apron pockets and tapping them in with her toe.

"What are you planting?" he asked to be polite. *As though,* he thought, *anything could grow in a September drought.*

"Hope," she said. "Excitement. Trust. Gratitude. Aliveness. Joy. And . . ." She looked to the sisters for help, but then suddenly remembered, " . . . Oh, yes! En*thu*siasm!" She let go a handful of seeds for emphasis.

The dowser's eyebrows crawled toward his hairline, and he almost laughed in the dark. "And you believe, do you, that these seeds can grow without water?"

Vannie turned from her careful circling path to regard him solemnly. "Oh, but they're going to have water, Mr. Hunter. You're going to find it."

His morale pitched low again. All he wanted to do was go find his car and get back to upstate Ohio. To the diner. He was hungry. He hadn't had a bite of anything from the café. He hadn't even drunk his coffee. Only a sip of water.

Alma stopped and pointed. "Right there, Mr. Hunter. Sit."

"But, Sister—"

"Sit!"

His knees gave way, and he sank to the ground. It was dry, stony, and smelled of the intolerable arid dust that always lined the inside of his nose, regardless of the season. It was sometimes enough to madden him.

"You're exactly in the center of our circle, Mr. Hunter," Alma said with satisfaction. "It's been sown with hope, excitement, trust, gratitude, aliveness, joy, and enthusiasm. Now you're ready to hear a story about change."

He groaned. "If you don't mind, I'm not exactly up to a story tonight, Sister. I'm tired. My head hurts. And I'm *starving*."

The little girl reached into yet another pocket of her apron, pulled out a hard bun and put it into his hand, her eyes shining at him in the dark.

"Eat it," Vannie told him gently. "It's made of all those ingredients my sister just mentioned. Everything that this circle is sown full of. And it's served to you with all the purity that only a child can bring."

"Sisters," he said, dismayed to find himself weeping. "I can't find water. I'm a fraud . . . a . . ."

"Shhhhhh." The sound came from all three of them, a curiously lovely sound that sounded like waves rolling onto a shore, caressing, healing and forgiving.

"Everyone get comfortable now," Alma said. "Sister will tell you a story about possibilities, Mr. Hunter, and transformation and love. Do you like such stories?"

"No."

"Lend yourself." She shook her head as though he amused her greatly. "Go ahead, Sister."

"Thank you," Vannie said happily. "Alright now, just listen and relax. Once upon a time . . ."

He groaned.

"But so many stories begin like that, Mr. Hunter. Bear with me. Once upon a time there was a great snowfall. People in Kentucky would say they never saw the snow fall so thick. And as it would happen, on this particular night there was a prison break in LaGrange. Do you know of the reformatory there?"

"I don't see what—"

"I wasn't really looking for a comment, you know. It was more of a rhetorical question. Anyhow, there my sister and I were alone in the café just before time to close up, when there sounded such a crash as you've never heard, and then along came this gentleman with a gun bashing in our door. It seemed he had killed a guard. Now, in one sort of story that could serve as the end, you see. The guard was dead. But my sister and I chose to believe that possibly the guard *wasn't* as yet dead. That perhaps there was no prison break on that particular night. At least yet. We're so liberal in such matters that we could even entertain the notion that there was no snowstorm!"

"No night!" Alma added, sparkling at him. "But we chose to let the snow and the night stand."

Both the sisters dissolved into hilarity at this idea, and the little girl laughed too, though when tears sprang to her eyes, he sensed her mirth was tempered from a sadness so deep that it probably never left her.

"I always love to hear this story," Alma said.

He looked at her warily. She was a hard one to read.

There was silence.

"Well?" He turned from one face to the next.

"Well, what?" Alma asked, seemingly at a loss.

"What happened?" he asked impatiently.

"Oh, you're engaged in my story, after all," Vannie said, pleased. "Well, for right now, you've heard the end of it."

"*What—?*"

"Since you liked that one so much, let me tell you another one. We went to see an old woman who had made a terrible mess of her life, lost every friend she ever had, and alienated her entire family. Isn't that interesting? We thought it was."

"Go on."

"That's the end."

"If your stories don't have any continuation," he said with frustration, "it's rather pointless to tell them, isn't it?"

"It was the people inside them," Alma said, "who got to determine the continuation. Just as you, yourself, will determine your own from this moment on. Here you are in one of the most important moments of your life and surrounded by witnesses to see what you choose." She made a gesture that included her sister, the child, and herself.

He had the eerie feeling that the field, the cattle, the full moon that ducked in and out of the scattering clouds, and even an intensely bright star shining directly over his head were listening and watching as well.

"You are surrounded by witnesses, Mr. Hunter," Alma murmured. "My sister, Sarah, and I are the most visible among them, but you are sensitive enough to know that there are others all around you as well. The breeze that moves against your skin brings inspiration. The earth underneath you is an anchor and a support. Then there are the stars in the heavens, sources of wisdom and power, and many more invisible observers. In fact, there is an army of allies and counselors, angels and guardians, all around you and beside you. Not one of them has come to see you take a step backward. Please receive that knowledge, Mr. Hunter. Please do it now."

He felt a sudden jolt of hope for himself and raised his face to the sky. The clouds had disappeared, and in the shimmering silence he sensed the friendliness of the moon now standing so clear in the heavens. Yet even as he marveled at her unearthly light, his face fell. For no fathomable reason, he found himself thinking of the comet he had seen in the skies on his way into town. An odd churning in his stomach accompanied the thought. He knew that famine and pestilence often followed in a comet's wake. Visions of his own doom popped into his head. Perhaps a jail cell waited for him at daybreak. Or worse.

"That comet was quite a sight, wasn't it?" Vannie murmured appreciatively. "Did you realize you were staring at your own reflection sprawled across heaven? Yes, Mr. Hunter, it was your light, the light inside you that has gone ignored for a long time now. Your light's essence is pure, unequaled beauty, yet for many who have trusted you, it has been associated with grief and loss and the worst kind of pain. Is that what you want for your destiny?"

"You mean . . . the comet is *not* bad luck?" He watched her closely.

"Still the self-centered response, eh, Mr. Hunter?" But she smiled agreeably. "Well, the luck of it remains to be seen. Everyone who saw it last night will be impacted, no doubt. You, however, are in a unique position, as you are central to the current situation. What you do will influence what the people of Willow Creek create for themselves out of all this, though they do hold personal power."

"Quite a turn of mind, isn't it?" Alma put in. "Two truths opposite from each other, if grasped and held at one time, expand the mind and open new perceptions. Can you sense that even though the responsibility for personal outcome lies with each of those farmers who gave you their money tonight, you here at the center of their circle have tremendous sway in the matter? Once we recognize the weight of our impact on others, our responsibility for it is seared into our hearts forever. Tonight you face that responsibility and the opportunity that flows out of it. Tonight you will choose for yourself what kind of omen your streaking tail of fire shall be."

He found himself once again standing, this time with his whalebone dowser's tool in his hand, shivering as the sisters rubbed the dust from the earth into his wrists and hands, into his face and his neck. The little girl massaged it into his ankles, working it down into his socks and onto his legs. To his astonishment the dust felt moister every moment, as if rain were falling from the stars, mixing water with dirt.

He felt it dripping down his neck and rolling off his face and reveled in it. He got down and rolled on the ground that had suddenly become mud and kept rolling until he had rolled himself into a mudpack. The thick wet feel of the mud comforted and nurtured him. He relaxed then, his whalebone nestled under his chin, and stared up at the sisters and their apprentice.

"Now sleep," Alma told him. "Tonight, you will be visited by your shadow. It holds a gift for you. In the morning, you will know what to do. Whether to run. Or whether to find water."

"Will I be able to find the water?"

"Only The Shadow Knows," Alma said spookily, causing Vannie to shake her head in disgust, then to chuckle in spite of herself.

The little girl leaned over him with a last handful of seeds. "Oh, Mr. Hunter? I'm sowing all these good things in you now. They'll be with you when you need them."

He felt the seeds raining down on him in a fine spray of pellets, then the women and the child left him in a mound in the middle of the magic circle. Almost instantly he slept and dreamed of starving, thirsty animals and gray people struggling in a dusty world and felt a despair that burned his tongue, the insides of his cheeks, the roof of his mouth—all of it turning into what felt like the dusty lining of a vacuum cleaner bag. His dry heart cracked; thirst ripped the throat right out of him.

Then he saw a star with a tail like a peacock suspended over him in mid-sky, its unearthly white radiance pouring directly into his skull. A moment later cool water trickled onto his lips, and he looked up into the eyes of the child. She smiled and poured more wetness into his open mouth, then vanished into the night.

The moonlight grew so bright then that it cast his shadow, long and black, a giant inky specter sprawled across the field. The dowser saw his shadow sit up, peeling itself from the ground. Thin as a piece of paper, the dark shape stood and walked to him, reached down and touched his forehead with a weightless hand. At once his brain flooded with painful buried remembrances. He saw himself as a child with his grandfather's whalebone, making his own first strike, finding the water all by himself, his grandfather so proud, the clear, pure water gushing forth.

Then the word got out. Instead of accolades, he got jeers. Was shunned at school. "Mr. Black Magic" became his taunting nickname. There were those afraid of "the devil's magic," and others who envied him and called him a fake, saying he hadn't really found water, had just been lucky. But even those who mocked him were scared of the very powers they scoffed.

He had returned to that field where he found his first water. Lying there in the wetness, he cried to the heaven to take the power away. But even after that, he had stumbled upon other hidden springs in the company of witnesses who broadcast the news far and wide; water seemed to follow him like a nightmare. In the end he managed to destroy his talents, shoveling over a well he had discovered unobserved and swearing never again to use his power, never even to remember he had once had it. He threw his shovel into a bush and strode into an existence that was no different from the lives of his friends.

From that day on he was just like everybody else. When his dowser grandfather tried to change his mind, he shunned the old man. As with all who walk from their human grace, his joy had dried up like a town in drought season, yet this he blamed on others and vowed to make the world pay for his pain. He had extracted that payment in the guise of one scam after the other, but there had been no triumph. Nothing but emptiness had filled his heart every time he robbed another stranger of his or her money.

All through the dreamy night he felt the mud working on him, the packed thickness of it drawing the hurt from his tissues. He sensed the hatred, the fear, and the lust for revenge being filtered from his blood, siphoned from his organs, and sucked from his bones. In their place he felt the talent of his youth pouring back into him, his ability to sense water and to understand the essence of its mystery, his adoration for this bringer-of-life.

Dreaming, he smiled.

At dawn the sisters stood with Sarah on a gentle swell of earth looking down on the dowser as he strolled across the field to meet the farmers, his whalebone in his hand. His features shone with light as though he had been born again.

"Why not," Vannie murmured. "He dreamed well. Who in the world would choose to be a thief of power when faced with the chance to be a harbinger of joy?" She sighed happily. "When the mud caked hard and fell off him, he was like a new egg coming out of a shell. And not a bad-looking man, is he now, even without his rhinestones?"

Sarah stood mesmerized as the dowser shook Earl Taylor's hand, and then those of all the others, each in turn, every face shining with hope.

"From lead to gold, from dark to light . . ." The apprentice stopped. "Do I have it right?" She looked at Vannie out of eyes now growing tired.

"Yes, dear," Vannie answered. "That's the Great Work, passed down to us from the alchemists of ancient times, to transform the lead of negativity into the gold of beautiful character, first in ourselves, then allowing the light to shine on others. Just look at the radiance of that man!"

"I always did love a diviner," Alma sighed. "What better thing can a man bring to the Earth than water, for heaven's sake?" But her words were lost on Sarah. The child's mood had turned dark before their eyes like in the blackest hours of last night when the moon had been veiled by clouds. "Sarah?"

But it was too late. The eclipse was complete.

The sisters could sense the child's thoughts. Magic or no magic, her own problems seemed unsolvable. The people Sarah loved most were caught in hopelessness—mother, father, brothers, and sisters. It was beyond her power to help them, regardless of the assistance she might give to strangers.

She listlessly started back to the car.

The sisters took a while to watch the scene below them. A cheer went up as the flying shovels struck mud. Then not so very much later came pandemonium as the water spewed forth. It was a precious moment. So important to own it and give thanks.

They smiled at each other and celebrated the moment in a long embrace. Then they turned to walk back to the car and drive their little girl home.

23

The chattering of a hundred birds woke Sarah before dawn for the third day in a row, causing her to cover her head with her pillow to block out the noise. "Be quiet!" she croaked at them grumpily.

It had been another fitful night of dreaming often and waking up fretting, only to fall into more dreams, some of Momma looking thin and worn, others of herself running from monster forces that stormed down on her fleeing form. In others, Sarah struggled to solve the riddle put to her the night after she came to live in the sisters' house: *Who is the enemy?*

If the right answer was her father, she did not want to say so, even in a dream. Maybe saying the words would make them true; would solidify a world in which he would be a terrible man forever.

The damp, sweet air, which now carried the noisy birdsong out of the gray predawn and in through her window, smelled of green things. It had been a marvel to all of Willow Creek how soon the rains had come after that dowser man had struck water in field after field, assuring the citizens of a running creek and a plentiful source of underground water for cattle and crops. Right after he had been paid his full fees and gone his way, cheered on by a crowd of grateful farmers, the clouds had come, dark and heavy and ripe, to drop warm rain all over the county, steaming the countryside and inviting a return to life.

Many likened it to how often an infertile couple would give up waiting for their own child and adopt, only to have the wife come up pregnant within the year. "Them that has gits" became Willow Creek's own private joke.

"It's the gratitude," Vannie informed Sarah. "Swells peoples' hearts till the sky overflows in answer. Gratitude, trust, joy, exuberance. These energies create a resonance that will generate a world of wonder. They'll draw water out of a stone, if it's water you need."

"The music inside a person pulls life toward them," Alma put in. "The nature of that music determines the life events that condense and form their world. Most people think the right order of things is to wait till something good happens and *then* get grateful. That's backwards. The truth is if you can feel grateful you'll draw to you all sorts of things to justify the feeling."

Sarah rolled over and propped her weary body up on her elbows. It was time to try to be a better apprentice. If the sisters said that keeping your spirits up was a part of the magic, then it must be so. From now on she would try harder. She would force herself out of her bad mood. She knitted her brow in fierce determination.

The back door slammed. That would be Alma going out to feed and water the chickens. The sound of the pump handle and water splashing into a bucket told Sarah she was right. Tired as she was, she padded over to the window to peek out and saw Alma's form in the gray morning as she passed by the large oak tree with her bucket sloshing on the way to her hens.

The birds in the trees had quieted, and now it was easy to hear the barking of the gray squirrel mother sending her three babies back up the tree as Alma passed by. The babies were Sarah's favorite part of her new life. She had spotted them two days ago out by Alma's flowerbeds, eyes full of newborn innocence. They were smaller than most squirrel babies because of the drought, the sisters told her. In fact, they were smaller than any Sarah had ever seen. Little survivors, they were, like her. Their mother, skinny and brave, had made it through the drought by drinking water the sisters left in the hen house, scurrying in among the sharp beaks to steal it, and by sometimes snatching bits of chicken feed. She was still scrawny in spite of these last few weeks of easier pickings.

Brave mama squirrel. Sarah fought back a wave of loneliness for her own mother as Alma made her way back toward the house, empty bucket swinging easily. Sounds from downstairs of pots and pans banging around in the kitchen told her Vannie was preparing to cook.

The child took a deep breath. She'd be more cheerful today, she promised herself, even if it killed her. She skinned off her nightgown and went to her drawer for clean underwear. She was reaching for her work clothes when suddenly it began.

"ROW, ROW, ROW YOUR BOAT!" Singing. From the kitchen.

"GENTLY DOWN THE STREAM!" Vannie sang. Her song wafted up the stairs along with the sounds of utensils clattering against plates and coffee mugs and various skillets and pots banging their way onto the stovetop.

"ROW, ROW, ROW YOUR BOAT—" Now it was Alma, timing herself to come in late in Vannie's song so they overlapped each other in a round.

"GENTLY DOWN THE——————
——————MERRILY, LIFE IS BUT —A——
——————————LIFE IS BUT A———
ROW YOUR BOAT——
————————————ROW, ROW, ROW——
————————————————THE STREAM!——MERRILY——

MERRILY, MERRILY!———
———————LIFE IS BUT A—
————————————————LIFE IS BUT A DREAM!!!!!"

Sarah swallowed hard, feeling a desire to rush downstairs and see what the sisters were up to, to show them her new happy face, sing their song with them, and show them she was worthy of their dreams and expectations for her and of their belief in her talent at her apprenticeship. And yet, she was pulled in another direction, a deep, dark feeling tugging at her insides, a feeling that . . . what? That it wasn't right to be happy when people she loved were unhappy? That it was wrong to be fed when they were hungry?

"ROW, ROW, ROW—"

Sarah sank down on the edge of her bed. It seemed unfitting to go downstairs and sing with the sisters, disrespectful to her mother and the dangers she faced. Who were the sisters to suggest that she should laugh and sing and play in times like these? It was wrong of them to expect such behavior from her. Obviously, they didn't understand the harsher world around them.

"GENTLY DOWN THE—"

It was one thing to be cheerful, but to actually romp around and laugh and be silly? They were asking too much. And being a bit *pushy* about it, too! Hadn't she already made up her mind to put on a happy face for them? And here they were nudging her, bringing their noisy song right into her room before the sun was even up, for pity's sake, pushing, pushing, *pushing*, trying to get her to buck up. She knew that's what they were up to. How bossy of them! They had better stop that singing right now if they wanted any cooperation from her. But they didn't. Ridiculously, they kept right on, enjoying themselves, it seemed.

"——————————MERRILY, MERRILY! LIFE IS BUT A——
GENTLY DOWN THE STREAM!——
————————ROW YOUR BOAT——
——————————MERRILY, MERRILY, MERRILY, MERRILY,
————LIFE IS BUT A——
LIFE IS BUT A——

——————————LIFE IS BUT A DREAM!"

A dream. Like her dreams the night before. Again, the riddle crossed her mind. She hoped the sisters wouldn't bring it up this morning. Somehow, she felt they would. It was probably a test, maybe an important one, and she had no answer. None. Most likely, she thought guiltily, it was because she had avoided thinking about it as much as possible. Numbly, she started down the stairs.

"ROW, ROW, ROW——
————————MERRILY, MERRILY, MERRILY———"

"GOOD MORNING!!!!" she said loudly, coming into the kitchen and trying to make the singing stop.

It didn't.

Sarah crossly stumbled toward her place at the table, neither sister paying her any mind. Vannie was absorbed in stirring oatmeal into boiling water in a squat black pot with a wooden spoon, while Alma gingerly mixed eggs, milk, and flour into a batter. They sang and worked, worked and *SAAAAANG*.

"LIFE IS BUT A—"

Sarah had been sure when she woke up this morning that the sisters were tuned into her dreams, that they would be waiting to talk to her about them. Seeing them now, she was not so sure. It seemed that they had not a serious thought in their heads. They certainly showed no interest in whether or not she had an answer for their old riddle. Maybe they'd forgotten all about it. Still, they were tricky. Sarah eyed them warily.

"MERRILY, MERRILY—"

They danced as they worked. *Honestly. They could be so silly sometimes. So silly it made you dizzy to watch them.* The weariness born of her night of dreams washed over her. She felt weak and tired, sick of the singing. She longed for the sisters to stop bellowing and get quiet again.

"ROW YOUR BOAT!"

The sound echoed around the room, bounced off fireplace and walls, stove and pantry doors. It modulated now into other keys, their ear-splitting harmonies splintering into prisms of sheared tones. There was an odd beauty about it, but that made it somehow worse. It was all so unfamiliar. Scary, even.

The griddle was hot. Vannie covered her pot of oatmeal and slid it to a cooler spot, then reached over to take the mixing bowl from Alma. Soon she was spooning circles of smooth pancake batter onto the hot iron surface while Alma poured cream into a porcelain bowl and set to whipping it with a beater. The interlacing blades flashed. All this in rhythm with their incessant annoying song.

"ROW YOUR BOAT!"

Sarah noted that there were three boxes set near her place at the table, each wrapped in paper and tied with one of Vannie's satiny bows. One was black, one pink, and one green. *Presents? For who?* She tried to get the sisters' attention to ask, but getting an answer was out of the question. Vannie was flipping pancakes to Alma, who nimbly caught them with three big plates, one in her right hand, another in her left and the third balanced on her left forearm, alternating her catches according to whim, hurling her body this way and that, even turning to catch several hotcakes behind her back.

Soon there were three stacks, and Alma spooned them over with puffy cream. Something red and glistening waited in a glass bowl on the counter, a topping, no doubt, for the pancakes. *Probably strawberries,* Sarah thought absently. Sliced and all mushed up with sugar just the way she liked them.

"LIFE IS BUT A DREAM—"

Ugh. Double ugh. The thought of food made Sarah's head spin faster. All thoughts of putting on a happy face were gone. She hoped nobody expected her to eat any of that mountainous breakfast. There was a knot in her stomach the size of a fist. She closed her eyes for a second, and in that moment, she just gave up.

And then, amazingly . . . all was . . . quiet.

Silence, sweet silence, filled the room. Sarah almost sobbed with relief. Almost, but not quite. She swallowed hard, staring as Alma set three plates of pancakes on the table, all mounded with whipped cream. Alma ceremoniously reached for the glass bowl and held it out for Vannie to spoon. Shiny red dripped and drizzled its way over the blobs of cream on one stack after another until three red mountains glistened. Sarah leaned closer to a plate, her nose twitching. It wasn't strawberries. Instead it was . . . Before she could finish her thought the sisters solemnly bowed to her.

"Uh-one!" Alma exclaimed.

"Uh-two," Vannie answered, taking Alma's hand.

"And One, Two, Three, Four!"

The sisters began shuffling across the kitchen floor in an old soft shoe. *Flap-flap-flap, ball change, brush step, toe step, brush step, and slide!* Light on their feet and as graceful as Fred Astaire and Ginger Rogers in a movie the sisters had taken her to Louisville to see. *Flap-flap-flap, ball change, brush step, toe step, brush step, and glide!!!*

At the same time, they sang . . .

"LIFE IS JUST A BOWL OF CHERRIES
DON'T TAKE IT SERIOUS
IT'S TOO MYSTERIOUS."

They shook their heads from side to side, sounding now a lot like Jimmy Durante as they strutted on tiptoe, smiling into imaginary spotlights:

"YOU WORK, YOU SAVE, YOU WORRY SO
BUT YOU CAN'T TAKE YOUR DOUGH
WHEN YOU GO, GO, GO!"

Sarah gaped at the spectacle, all thought draining from her head. She felt herself shutting down inside, as if a succession of doors were closing, like slabs of marble sliding into place to seal every opening, locking her inside a vaulted chamber within the pyramid of her inner world.

Feelings of unreality and disconnectedness crept in as she watched the sisters cavorting about. It was as if she had blundered into another realm and found herself a stranger in a land where she didn't understand the customs and where she was essentially an alien. Or maybe it was the sisters who were alien.

Sarah reached out and fingered the bows on the packages in front of her, her sense of loneliness growing as the sisters strutted straight-legged on their toes across the floor, skirts swishing gaily back and forth. She felt horribly isolated, cut off, and the sisters sang on:

"SO KEEP REPEATING, 'IT'S THE BERRIES,'
THE STRONGEST OAK MUST FALL,"
Stride, Stride, Stride!
"THE SWEET THINGS IN LIFE, TO YOU WERE JUST LOANED
SO HOW CAN YOU LOSE WHAT YOU'VE NEVER OWNED?"

With every word she recoiled more. Why was she so out of sorts, on this day of all days when she had vowed to do better? She turned her eyes on the sisters as they finished their song with a flourish.

"OH! LIFE IS JUST A BOWL OF CHERRIES
SO LIIIIIIIIVE! AND LAUGH AT IT ALLLLL!"

They struck triumphant poses, arms stretched high in the air, waiting for applause.

Sarah blankly stared at them, not a thought or a feeling left in her. And then suddenly it was all too much. Something inside her snapped loudly like a tree splintering, then collapsed with a leaden thud. How could the sisters say, much less sing, such words? How could they even *think* that life wasn't serious? Couldn't they see? Didn't they have eyes? Not only was life serious, it was awful and terrible and sad.

Incredibly, they started humming the same tune all over again as they stood with arms still up in their finale positions, their eyes glued on her.

Sarah wondered if she was going to throw up. She reached out and shoved the presents away from her. If they were for her, she didn't want them. *They don't understand! They don't understand anything! Cherries. Oh. Oh.*

A pain shot through her mind and flooded her with brutal memories. She tried to run away, but found herself unable to even rise from the table. Another jolt of pain doubled her over.

At once the sisters were beside her, kneeling on each side of her chair. How they got to her so fast, she couldn't imagine. She felt their hands on her shoulders and arms and somehow knew they were back, the Vannie and Alma she'd come to feel so close to these months, not the strangers who'd been singing and dancing only moments ago. Their presence wrapped around her like flannel.

And *at last* the quiet was back.

Oh. Oh. Oh! Sarah's throat tightened, and she fought tears. She had not cried since leaving home. A low moan forced its way out of her. She heard it as though she were listening to another person, heard it rise to a scream. And at last here came the tears. A flood of them tore out of her. They wouldn't stop. They would never stop.

She gulped for air, still exploding her grief in all directions. "I . . . I don't know . . . what's happening."

Vannie folded a sturdy arm around the child's shoulders, supporting her as she wept. Tears dripped from her face and soaked her dress, jumped out of her eyes with such force that they splattered on the floor, bounced like raindrops, and puddled at her feet.

Alma produced a small porcelain washbasin from under the sink and brought it to Sarah, catching her tears as they fell. "I like these tears," she said quietly. "Such honest, pure tears, without a trace of self-pity in them,

LIFE IS JUST A BOWL OF CHERRIES
Home Sweet Home
PABLO FERRO

nothing but 100 percent beautiful sorrow. We'll save these in a crystal glass. Pink, I think, don't you, Sister?"

Gently, they ministered to their apprentice, Vannie wrapping a quilt around the girl's shoulders, while Alma fetched a warm rag for her face. Sarah slowly began to catch her breath, her sobs slowing to whimpers. Then stopped.

"What a storm," Alma said. "A regular little hurricane. You've done well, child, a very fine job with your homework."

"But . . . but I . . ." Sarah's confused red eyes met Alma's gaze. Nobody had mentioned homework, other than finding the answer to that stupid "how does a warrior princess make war" riddle. And well, maybe that part about finding her chalice and her shield. Just thinking about all that made her dizzy again.

"Sometimes homework gets done when we aren't even looking," Alma said. "In this case, your subconscious has done some real digging and brought you an important clue. You are much closer to answering the question 'who is the enemy?' Can you find the right words now to answer it?"

Sarah froze, memories of cruelty at the hands of father, uncles, and brothers resurfacing, but she pushed them away. Despite all the hurt, she still loved her daddy. In rare moments he had shown her a gentle side, and sometimes even a funny one. It was never there for long. Hard times turned him to whiskey, and the whiskey made him mean. But she knew a seed of goodness lay under all his frustration and rage. She did not want to call him an "enemy." She *would not*. Stubbornly, she set her jaw.

"Don't fret, child," Vannie murmured lovingly. "No person in the world is our true enemy. The enemy always lies within. Anything that keeps us from our truth is our enemy. And," she added pointedly, "our worst enemies are the ones hidden from our view. If we can't see them, we can't do anything about them, can we?"

Alma looked at the three packages, now strewn to the far side of the round oak kitchen table, and chose the one with the pink bow that sat teetering on the table's edge in a miracle of balance. "Open this one, Sarah.

Like you, it seems to be on the brink." She reached for Vannie's sewing scissors and handed them to the girl, handles first, along with the package.

One snip, and the ribbon fell away.

The apprentice gasped as she pulled out a luminous pink sphere, the color of cherries swirled with cream. She gazed into the rosy world and saw buttes and plateaus and canyons of silvery-white reflective matter in the stone's strata. It was a crystal ball. A *pink* crystal ball. Its magic spoke to her from across centuries and from other dimensions.

Seeing Sarah's delight, Vannie felt her own excitement rise. "There will be more to see of it when we take it outside into the sunlight. There's a secret the stone will share only in the sun's direct beams. For now, just warm it in your hands; help it to wake up and feel who you are. It is very much alive, dear. It can speak to you through the language of sensation."

Sarah busied herself warming the stone, holding it first in her hands, but soon she found herself rubbing it over her heart. The sisters saw that the healing properties of the sphere were touching the child, that she was sensing the stone's magnetics and subtle electricity. She calmed visibly, her breathing deepening.

"Your first enemy," Alma said, "is the one you have begun to face—buried sorrow. It has been blocking the flow of your emotion. Your 'E' motion. Energy in motion. It is a factor in personal power."

"But I thought . . ." Puzzled, Sarah looked up from her stone, still clinging to it, aware of how much safer she felt with it in her hands. "I thought I was supposed to be happy, like you said. And have gratitude," she finished weakly.

The sisters left her to think it through as they began straightening the kitchen, folding the flour back into its sack, placing the bottle of cream in the refrigerator, covering the hotcakes and putting them away, too. It would not be right for any of them to eat heavily this morning. The pancakes had given a more important service today, fed them in more ways than by providing physical nourishment. Later, they'd go to Babe Dawson for his pigs. The deva of cherries was silently thanked for her contribution, as well as that of the wheat and sugarcane. Appreciation was extended to the hens for their eggs and the cows for their cream, all this done as the kitchen was transformed back into its usual state of spotless hominess.

When they returned to the table, Alma took up answering Sarah's question, hoping to help her reconcile two seemingly opposite truths. One, that in order to generate positive realities, it is necessary to maintain a high emotional resonance. And two, that to be in our power, we need to feel the depth of all our emotions, exalted ones and painful ones alike.

"You've heard people tell you to keep things simple, Sarah. But when you do, life is harder. If you allow yourself to see things as complex, problems are solved more easily."

She pointed to the finished white dress with blue ribbons that Vannie had been sewing on the night of the spinning wheel. It hung on the door of the walk-in closet off the kitchen where iron and board were kept, hemmed now and finished with Alma's finest hand-embroidered lace.

"If Vannie were making a dress for you," Alma went on, "she wouldn't just cut out the material and start sewing, would she? That would be a simple approach, but it would lead to a terrible mess."

Sarah's eyes traveled over the dress, finding it unbelievable that a thing of such beauty was for her. She turned the stone over in her hands and let out a breath, feeling more receptive than ever before in her short life.

"Instead of just sewing away in a simplistic furor," Alma continued, "she first takes time to gather and pleat, then to pin her pieces in place. To measure and to carefully baste in her hems. And though her intricate process requires attention to detail, each step is simple in itself, able to be accomplished gracefully." She smiled at Sarah, seeing how the child's gaze still lingered on the dress. "Raising our resonance is not as simple as plastering smiles on our faces and deciding to buck up. Choice is a part of it, of course, but being happy is not an act of will power. We can't force ourselves to be joyful. We found that out the hard way this morning, didn't we?"

Sarah rolled the ball in her hands, allowing herself a glimmer of hope.

Alma put a hand over her solar plexus. "We raise our resonance by plunging into our true feelings and unlocking them. Once they are flowing, we can understand and release them. That is a way of loving ourselves, giving attention and care to how we feel. The love and the caring and the release lead to comfort, hope, and before you know it, perhaps even to trust and gratitude."

Vannie pulled her oatmeal from the back of the stove, stirred it, and placed it on a warm burner. The three of them would soon need something to eat. She put milk in a pitcher, brought butter and brown sugar to the table. Slipping the quilt from Sarah's shoulders, she spread it across the back of the child's chair, and took her own seat.

In a very low voice, Sarah said, "What I feel, Sisters . . . I don't know if I can do what you say . . . release it. How can I ever when . . .?"

"You remember how bad you and your mama felt when Sugar left?" Vannie murmured. "But still you both were happy for him. In fact, it gave you some hope, didn't it?"

"I thought he might come back and buy groceries for Mama. And a new dress."

"He gives your mama hope, too, Sarah. Not just because he may come back and take care of her, but because he's proof that life can get better. You do the same, child. As you let yourself rise, you affect the hopes of all in your family."

Vannie put her arm around her. "Child," she said, "don't think we don't know how challenging the task. To face such sorrow and to dare to transform it, you will need the courage of a warrior. To deal with your pain without falling into blame and self-indulgence, you will need the majesty of a princess. To allow yourself joy when those you love are still stuck in the mire will take every shred of power you can garner. Yet, it will be easier if you remember that you are a hope and a light for your family."

Sarah nodded slowly. "I think I understand."

"Are you beginning now to see how a warrior princess goes to war, without harming a hair on a head?"

A smile formed on Sarah's lips. "Yes ma'am." Tentative though the smile was, it was born of hope and based on the possibility of light at the end of her dark tunnel.

24

"We have *White Lightnin'* and *Hazel Eyes* and *Margie*," Sugar's new agent, Harve Cleveland, said, checking off his notes from his chair in the singer's shabby dressing room. "But I think *Lady Of Secrets* should be the album title."

Sugar choked on a deep swig of ice tea. Finally, he was able to strangle out, *"Album?"*

Harve grinned at him, marveling at the innocence of the best new talent he'd ever signed to a contract. "You thought you were going to be selling singles?"

"I . . ." Sugar shook his head. "I guess I didn't think anything at all about selling records. I kind of thought I'd just keep singing."

"Where? Here?"

"Well, I wanted to maybe work up to doing the Opry just one time in my life."

"Boy, you are a wonder. They're going to love you at the Opry, there's no doubt about it. In the meantime, we need another gear for you. You got something that will get 'em on their feet? You know, a barn-stomper?"

Sugar's unfocussed eyes still looked dazed. "Barn-stomper? Well, I've got *Country*. I use a harmonica and a guitar both to play it."

"Well, let's hear it!" Harve looked with bemused eyes at the kid who took a minute to spit-shine a spot on his old guitar. Then he carefully removed a homemade gizmo from the burlap sack that he always carried, stuffed with such things as the new cowboy hat he liked to sometimes perform in, a picture of his girlfriend back home, and rolls of music, some of it half-written as Harve had noticed on occasions when Sugar pulled out handfuls of the original sheets and sometimes jotted lyrics on to them in the middle of conversations.

"Okay, here comes *Country*," Sugar said, adjusting the harmonica.

In seconds the agent's feet were tapping, half from the music's exuberance and half from joy. With the harmonica blaring and Sugar's fingers flying on his strings, it was a wild romp.

"Outside I'm seeing how I like it to be
Birds flyin' high and miles of sky for you and me
Running for love, and feeling free
I ain't got much trouble, and that's alright with me.

"Oh, a problem ain't so bad, if tomorrow I confess
That I wanted it and needed it, but brother, what a test
And I barely got a dime, 'cause I paid up all them dues
And I swear that I can feel 'em, but I just can't play the blues.

"Two bits of nothing is a lot to take
Enough of enough is too much at stake
Laughter is raining and we all know the score
If you ain't got the picture, then just look at before.

"Oh, a problem ain't so bad, if tomorrow I confess
That I wanted it and needed it, but brother, what a test
And I barely got a dime, 'cause I paid up all them dues
And I swear that I can feel 'em, but I just can't play the blues."

At the last lick of his guitar, Sugar grinned, took his harmonica from around his neck, and sat to strum more quietly. As during other key moments in his Nashville existence, like the night he had found this shabby little cottage-like bar and grill where he now sang, he thought of the sisters and wondered if they could see him. Maybe they could. He had more than once found himself looking into Alma's eyes.

"Hey! Hazel Eyes
Shining from the Sky
Crossing sleepy sands
I see her ancient hands.

"She's reminding me
Of all I ought to be
My date with destiny
Inside my song.

"And God, it's strange to dream
And see her face again
A star above a missing love
Back home where I belong."

Sugar slowly put his guitar aside and turned to his dressing table mirror, not looking to put a comb through his dark hair or to dab on stage makeup. He didn't use the stuff and didn't care what he looked like. He only knew because of the women who chased him that he was considered a prize catch. He wasn't thinking of his fans either, or of himself, or even of Margie, who haunted so many of his dreams. He was thinking how low-down homesick he was, how miserable he was with longing to see the green swelling hills of Kentucky, and how strange it felt to be so close to his people and yet so far away. He thought of his mother and his siblings and his ornery pa, and finally of the two sisters, wondering once again if it was possible that they could actually see him through the mists.

"Someday," he said aloud, "I'll go home."

"Of course, you will, boy," Harve told him. "And when you do, you'll be a star."

Sugar grinned bleakly. "You think it's about being a star? Don't you know homesick when you're looking at it?"

"Yeah, boy, I do," his agent said more gently. "And I know pain and love and courage when I see it, too. It's all there in your music. But won't you feel proud when you go back to Kentucky?"

Sugar shook his head. "I'll just feel home."

25

With deepening twilight on that All Hallows Eve came a rippling wind that foretold of the shifting of the currents. The two sisters noticed it at once, opening the outside door of the Little Room and standing there breathing in the air. This night, they knew, would be like no other.

"Shadows over the town," Alma murmured. "Pretty soon we'll be smelling pumpkin steaming in the shell, candles lit and burning, spiced apple . . ."

Vannie moved through the open door and ran her fingers through the air as though testing material as to suitability for a garment she might fashion from it. Where her fingers stroked, an icy shine surfaced as though a silvery trim to a dark-gray vestment had revealed itself.

"Lovely," she breathed, both sisters standing perfectly still as a slow-moving car turned right off the old highway and made its way past the café and up the country road heading toward LaGrange. Its tires made a humming sound that fell soothingly on the senses.

Even as they stood there, twilight gave way to darkness. The sisters felt the parade beginning. Bands of ghosts and goblins and other assorted monsters were creeping from their houses, already on the prowl for candy and all sorts of other goodies that would certainly come their way on this free-for-all night. Parties of excited small fry, masked and rouged and tripping over their costumes, would be afoot, as well as roaming packs of teenage boys in ghoulish makeup. Of course, the sisters knew well that the teenagers would use the night as an excuse to go wild. They were even now armed with soap to smear on windows and toilet paper to string in trees.

With them came Shawn Prudence, leaving her house in her brisk schoolmarm's stride, checking the door behind her to see that it was securely fastened. She held a small pocketbook under one arm, a shopping bag in her other hand. *Of all nights,* she thought, *the sisters would ask for a favor.* She could not say no, but her lips tightened in annoyance at the timing of the whole thing, even as she pulled her trench coat into neater folds under its belt and brushed at an imaginary spot on her sleeve. Duty held reign. Had always held reign. The thought was with her as she headed to the garage for her tan Ford.

The sisters, watching her through the discreet vision of their minds, sighed under the weight that bore her toward them. Yet she was coming. She would be the part of the night that stayed with them long after the moon had set and the last of the goblins returned home. Homes that had seemed so dull at the beginning of the evening, yet would feel so warm and welcoming when they returned, chilled and burnt-out on ghouls and shrieks and horrific imaginings.

When the sisters finally returned to the warmth of the café, shutting the door softly behind them, it was to the first glints of a moon that promised to be huge and orange.

"Big old pumpkin in the sky, lit up for show," Alma said appreciatively. "And she's on the way, Sister."

"We're ready," Vannie said, not without a note of trepidation. All Hallows Eve was an unpredictable night to travel into realms of unconscious domain, yet it offered advantages. At no other night in the year were the veils between worlds so sheer, the world of *Other* so available to even the most insensitive. Allies of spirit—devas, elves, and other denizens of Faerie Realm—along with the spirits of the Earth, were all gathering even now, eager to join in this evening's great endeavor. As their numbers grew, magnetic energy heightened to a crackle, ready to surge. It moaned, straining against its bonds.

The few occupied tables and booths were full of older people who waited in comfort to see the event of Halloween unfolding before them. For, of course, there would not be a child—either young or teenaged—who would pass up a trip to the café. The interior was decked out in orange and black streamers, lights lowered, with shadows of black cats in the front windows and candles being lit even now on all the tables. An eerie light shone over the front door, and cobwebs glistened like nets of gossamer from the door to the candy counter. Rows of pumpkins were lit and glowing on both sides of the door, their faces in varying states of ghoulishness that would please bloodthirsty youth, several carved in opposing states of beauty to ease the senses of the few who looked for such things on Halloween night.

Beyond this, a strange apparition fell over the café. The silken mirage extended itself like a river of rippling water across the lower part of the restaurant, with ribbons flowing into the upper dining room. It spoke to the unconscious. Tonight, it said, our usual world, so locked in illusion, is rubbing shoulders with a realer world. If one only had the courage to take the first step, then tonight one might do anything. One might fly across the moon on a broomstick if the calling was a true one, founded on self-worth and buoyed by faith in transcendent miracles.

Shawn Prudence was the first to step into the magic of the sisters' candlelight. She came through the door in her usual efficient way, stepping past the spider webbing with no more appreciation than if someone had usurped space on the bulletin board in her high school English classroom and cluttered it with nonsense. She took no particular notice of the candles either, and ignored an inkling that something was brewing in the café, something as hot and rich as the sisters' coffee.

Her entrance served its usual function—to take the thrill out of the air and replace it with a dull sense of obligation, as if a scolding parent had stepped in to remind everyone that life is serious business not to be wasted in idleness. Guilt struck the clientele. After all, their own lives had no tragedies equal to those of Miss Prudence's family up in their big house with the white antebellum columns. The customers politely turned their eyes from her to eat the last of their deep-dish apple crisp and slurp down the end of their coffee, their talk returning to everyday practicalities, weather, the hay supply for the approaching winter, and the strange sickness that had befallen some of the milk cows. Still, floating in the recesses of their minds, were thoughts of old shouting matches and eerie screams. Some had heard them firsthand, but all had heard tales of the dreadful sounds coming from behind the thick walls of the old Prudence house, back when Shawn was just a girl. There had been so many rumors.

Only the sisters watched Miss Prudence. Along with the parrot, of course, who peered slyly from his cage, which had been adorned for the occasion in orange paper hair-like protrusions that the bird had been eating for almost an hour now. He stepped to the vibration he felt, slowly picking up one gnarled foot, then the other, bobbing his head like a scavenging bird alert on a carcass. His squawk was unintelligible, swimming in his throat like gravel.

Alma reached for Shawn Prudence's hand. "Thank you for coming, dear."

Vannie moved forward, her face as illuminated as that of any lit jack-o-lantern. "We appreciate your helping us tonight. You see, we've promised our young helper . . . Do you know Sarah? . . . that we would go out with her for a while and—"

"Go out with her? In the middle of the night?" Shawn Prudence raised her eyebrows.

"Halloween, you know," Vannie said. "Trick-or-treating."

"She's not here yet," Alma said. "Might I take your coat to the Little Room? What an attractive dress. I don't believe I've ever seen you wear russet."

Shawn's face was puzzled as she glanced downward at her dress. It was the exact color that picked up a bewitching prettiness of her dark eyes and her gypsy-like coloring that tended to muddy under the grays and browns that she wore most of the time. A trickle of moisture dripped through the back of her brain.

"Isn't that strange?" she murmured while Alma put her coat away and Vannie reached for her shopping bag. "I don't remember putting this dress on. I didn't even know I owned it . . . yet who would put a dress in my closet?"

"What's in your shopping bag, dear?" Vannie inquired as Alma reappeared with a glass of spiced apple cider and handed it to Shawn Prudence.

"Oh. I . . . I brought the children some treats. I thought I'd drop them into their bags along with yours."

"Of course, my dear, how thoughtful." Alma gestured toward a tray of wrapped candy corn and caramel apples. "The children will get one package of each of these." She made no mention of the protective charms that she and Vannie had secreted into the wrappings.

Glass in hand, Shawn Prudence stood in the middle of the lower dining room in the russet-colored dress, a tense smile glued to her lips, her dark hair neatly combed with bangs that fell in an odd arching curve down to her brow. On days when she washed her hair, she'd clip an empty toilet paper spool beneath those bangs and blithely run errands while they dried, fancying to herself that the spool was invisible to the eye. She would have melted in embarrassment had she known the jokes that had been made at her expense over years of using her "beauty secret."

"Have a taste of the cider, dear," Vannie invited her. "You've always liked cinnamon apples. This is similar."

"Cinnamon apples?" Shawn Prudence sipped reluctantly from the glass and then drank some more. It was delicious, but when had the sisters ever served her cinnamon apples? How could they know she had loved them as a child?

"Down the hatch," Alma instructed, as the schoolteacher stopped drinking and inspected the glass.

"But . . ." Against her own will, Shawn Prudence, who never drank all of anything, raised her glass and swallowed the warm cider in one gulp. It slid down her throat like an aphrodisiac. "Oh," she said in a stifled gasp, feeling her chakras light up. Even the ones in her lower torso. Flushing, she pulled the snug dress away from her slender, yet curvaceous body. She was no stranger to pleasure. It had long been an enemy, visiting her in pulsing dreams that tormented her in her cold bed. Waking her to a sterile reality of aloneness. Still in all her adult life, she had never worn a fitted dress like this one. Her skirts always swallowed her and hung down to mid-calf over unshaven legs in baggy nylon hose that bunched in wrinkles around her ankles. The effect served to camouflage every trace of her pretty body.

"Could I change, please?" Shawn asked hoarsely. "I brought a Halloween outfit in the shopping bag. I . . . I thought it would amuse the children." Unsteadily, she reached for the bag in Vannie's hand.

Though the thought of Shawn Prudence dressing in a Halloween costume seemed as farfetched as her wearing a bathing suit to the local swimming hole, Vannie handed over the bag without comment.

Watching Shawn weaving unevenly toward the ladies' room, Alma said softly, "Her heart has valor, Sister."

Not that Shawn was aware of it. Neither was she aware that every high school teenager sensed the desperation and humiliation beneath her odd quirks and buzzed about her. Especially when she read aloud in class and got so lost in the passions of "the Bard" that she blushed and wept, stifling sobs, and the students had to bite their tongues to keep from laughing. They also fought to keep straight faces when she sneaked behind her desk to roll her nylons over her garters a rung or two, thinking no one the wiser. And when she rose from her chair and strolled around with her back to the class, fishing under her waistband to pull up her slip, which always hung longer than her skirt. As a diversion, she'd snort sinus-clearing noises while she wiggled the slip up. Snorts or not, all eyes remained on her probing fingers and the slip, which would drop again at her next stroll around the room.

"Blind to so much," Vannie said softly. "But tonight she will see." Neither she nor Alma was pleased at the course that would run itself out this night. But it would be what it would be. And it had already begun.

Beside her, Alma murmured, weaving a protective barrier between all who would enter the café and the woman who had disappeared behind the door marked "Ladies."

The ambiance in the café grew thicker, like yeasted dough set in a covered bowl to rise. More unseen allies arrived, many of them from *Other*, the earthly realm that shared space with humanity, yet vibrated on a different frequency, indiscernible to most human senses. Tonight, the sisters would need the magic of this realm as they faced the hidden rage in Shawn Prudence. Sarah would have to face it with them.

"She's struggled so," Vannie muttered, her thoughts still on Shawn. "That old family name she's had to live up to."

"The worst of it," Alma said grimly, "is what she's had to live *down*."

There had been a dominating passion in Shawn's mother, Bess Prudence, to have her daughter maintain a life of propriety and excellence. If Shawn could attain this, perhaps a trace of dignity could be restored to the family name. Dignity. There had been so much of that in the years before Bess's own mother, Alicia Bolton, had driven her family into shame. Shawn's "Granny Alice" had been a towering woman who'd ruled the house and all who occupied it—husband, daughter, son-in-law, and grandchild. And most of all her son, just graduating from college and trying to carve a life for himself with a fiancée who had not met his mother's standards of breeding.

Inevitably, the worst had happened. In the ultimate act of rage, the son had taken his own life. No one but his mother ever saw the note he left addressed to her. But in reading it, Granny Alice had begun to scream and could not be comforted. In preparing for this evening, the sisters had spoken of that night and of what had taken place to leave the Bolton family a wreck of itself, like a grounded ocean liner left to rot on an alien shore.

Of course, the old lady had gone mad. It had been Shawn's parents, Bess Prudence and her husband, Jay, who had saved Alicia Bolton from the asylum. They brought home whatever part of her that still remained to grieve and rave and claw out her hair to live upstairs in the big house in the bedroom just above Shawn's crib, there to prowl the house in the midnight hours, an old spook creaking the floorboards and wailing out the window to the moon.

Underneath, Shawn had listened as the years passed and she grew from her crib to a bed, went from crawling to walking, and learned to understand the horror that raged on the floor above her. She had seemed the only normal family member as daily pressures rose to keep heads above rising water.

"Not easy being the only hope of those around you," Alma murmured, breaking off as the front door to the café opened. She gave a whistle of appreciation as a child passed the spider's web, stopping to enjoy the gossamer threads. Sarah was barely recognizable in the glamour of her pale green cotton gown with darker green velvet collar and trim, her waist belted in birch bark.

"And what have we here?" Vannie laughed, delighted with Sarah's regal poise. Though she had personally stitched the costume, she'd given the apprentice the assignment of defining her disguise: "I made it, you name it!" But Sarah had done more, surprising the sisters by gathering tufts of moss and hulls of seeds, weaving them through her long hair. Further, she had crowned herself with a circle of the same birch bark in which she had belted herself.

"I'm a faerie princess, Sister Vannie," Sarah said, blushing. "Not like in the school play. And not like Tinker Bell!" She adjusted her birch crown for emphasis. "A *real* one like you and Sister Alma talk about."

"More truth than fiction there," Alma said. She looked Sarah over, pleased at the blending of magic from Vannie's needle and the apprentice's enhancement of the design. Sarah's talents as a magician had ignited in creating her costume, art holding its origins in magic. And now here their apprentice magician stood, gowned like a wood nymph and self-proclaimed a princess, anticipating the night, but not yet knowing it rolled ahead of her like an ocean with dangerous riptides.

"I've met a few of your clansmen out in the forest down by the creek," Alma continued. "Quite a lively crew they are, too, the faeries."

"Are you teasing me?" Sarah's eyes sparkled with excitement. She struggled to keep her voice down as the several tables of elderly people peeked down at her, smiling in appreciation of her costume. "You've seen the faeries *for real*?"

Alma fingered a strand of the child's flowing hair. "Of course. Would you like to meet them?"

"Yes, please." Sarah's mouth suddenly went dry.

"Perhaps you shall," Alma said softly. "Perhaps you shall." Yet her eyes were thoughtful. Sarah was young to go to the faeries, younger than she or Vannie had been when they . . . Still, it would be safer to have Sarah hole up "over there" during the events of this night. It would not be the first time faerie folk had snatched a child from harm and hidden her away, then returned her to humankind after danger had passed. Jarred from her thoughts, she felt Vannie's hand on her sleeve and heard Sarah's gasp even as she turned to look at what had just walked out of the ladies' room.

There stood Shawn Prudence in cotton pajamas and a chenille bathrobe. Her daddy's ancient galoshes were on her feet, unbuckled and flapping around her skinny ankles. A fringed shawl from her mother's piano hung around her shoulders. In her right hand, she held a wood ax and in her left, the shopping bag.

The sight of their local schoolmarm standing there in her bathrobe and wielding an ax set more than one person to tittering. The laughter died when Shawn Prudence turned to glare up at them, her chalk-white skin shining like death. Out of the white shone one single black eyebrow, penciled on so darkly as to make the brightly rouged cheeks and the blood-red mouth below it seem even more bizarre.

"Oh, Lord," somebody whispered.

Shawn Prudence's attention swung to the table where the woman had spoken, the group of elderly citizens freezing into silence under her glare.

All eyes were on the heavy ax. It was, most likely, the one Shawn's grandmother had used on that Halloween night so many years ago. *If the rumors were true.* A moment later the teacher headed for the sisters and Sarah, her eyes under the dark single brow full of trouble. At the sight of Sarah, standing there in her costume, staring at her with awe, Shawn Prudence let out an ear-splitting scream and lunged at her.

Sarah jerked back, then feeling both sisters' hands holding her firmly by the shoulders, managed to stand her ground.

"Nice outfit, Miss Prudence," Vannie said calmly. "Very horrific. The children will love it."

"Nice acting, too," Sarah said in a small but determined voice. "And . . . and your hands. They're . . . good, too."

Miss Prudence looked down at her knuckles. They were bleeding. "Makeup," she said faintly, knowing full well that she had smashed her fists into the ladies' room wall. Where had all this come from? She looked down at herself, wearing the bathrobe and pajamas, holding the ax.

"Very effective," Alma said matter-of-factly. "Will you serve the treats to our first visitor of the night, Miss Prudence?"

The teacher's eyes regained focus. She set the shopping bag on the floor and lifted a bag of goodies from inside, putting the treats beside the sisters' corn candy and apples. Her bleeding hands reached for a wrapped fudge brownie from her own stock, then at Alma's nod she added a candied apple and a bag of corn candy from the sisters' tray and put the lot on the counter near Sarah.

"Eat, dear," Vannie whispered.

As Sarah's hand edged toward the bag of corn candy, Alma shook her head. "Not that one, Sarah. The brownie."

Sarah hesitated, and then reluctantly reached for it. The entire café seemed to stop breathing and time to halt as she slowly unwrapped the brownie and ate the first bite. Then the next, chewing deliberately and without enjoyment. Miss Prudence had never been an inspired cook. The high school children always laughed at the Valentine cookies she brought to class and distributed every year. There was no laughter now. Sarah felt terribly tense as she chewed, especially noticing the tear that sprang to Vannie's eye and the grimness of Alma's mouth as both sisters watched her gulp down another bite. Then another, and yet another. Even worse was the way Miss Prudence stared at her. Sarah hoped fervently that the wild-as-a-hurricane look in her eye was part of the Halloween spirit. Otherwise, she didn't understand. Just as she didn't understand the sick feeling that stole through her body. Her knees buckled; she started to crumple.

Vannie's arms closed around her, holding her up. "Breathe, Sarah. Center yourself."

"Pass out the treats, please, Miss Prudence," Alma murmured. "My sister and I will be back very soon." She moved around the counter and on into the kitchen, Vannie following with Sarah in tow, half-supporting the child.

Miss Prudence stood frozen alongside the treats as the front door swung open and a crowd of small ghouls and goblins sprang in, crying, "Trick or treat!"

Sarah stumbled along with the two sisters through the kitchen and gasped as she found herself in what should have been, but was no longer, the Little Room. Instead, she had entered a forest carpeted with fallen leaves, brown and crunchy and decaying into black mulch under a tangle of naked oak and maple branches. Overhead, unseen animals scurried in the trees.

"Breathe, Sarah," Vannie said again.

She breathed in scents of moss and damp-packed clay and stone, then perceived a sparkling creek meandering through the spot where the potbellied stove used to sit. She blinked several times, expecting somehow that on each quick opening of her eyes she would find herself safely back inside the small warm room that should have been here. But nothing changed.

Without a doubt she was in a woods on the bank of a trickling stream. No ordinary woods at that. As she gazed into the running water, it dawned on her that every rock and pebble, every decaying leaf and patch of mossy green, every root and stem in the woods, was awake with thought. Not human thought that jumped around all over the place, but constant, steady, deep thought. *Wordless* thought.

"Are the faeries here?" Sarah whispered. "Do they know about Miss Prudence?" The sickness receded, and her perceptions became more vivid. The moss on the rocks glowed iridescent, while the bark of the trees took on bizarre dimensions, like in the 3-D pictures shown through colored plastic lenses in the movie house. The woods were undeniably real. She tasted the bark on the trees just by looking at them and sniffed in the essence of every root and weed.

"The faeries are coming to you, Sarah," Alma said. "This is a rare privilege reserved for those who love the Earth and know her true essence, from which comes healing. For you, and perhaps also for Miss Prudence."

"Miss Prudence," Sarah echoed in alarm. "I feel her coming. She's walking through the forest. Swinging her ax. She—" Teeth chattering, she wheeled at the sound of steel battering against bark. Black energy shook the ground. From faraway shone the whiteness of a grotesque face, a single dark eyebrow, red cheeks, and a dripping red mouth.

"Where did you go?" the schoolteacher screamed. "What were you whispering to that child? Bad things! Bad things about me!! I'll not have talk behind my back!" Crash. "I'll find you!" Thump. Thump. Thump.

"Sisters, she's coming!" Sarah hissed.

"See that great tree down by the creek bed?" Alma pointed. "And the hollow in the trunk?"

"It looks big enough for me to climb into," Sarah whispered hopefully. "To hide."

"Would you be afraid of Miss Prudence if you were inside the tree trunk, Sarah?"

"Maybe . . . but . . ." She gulped. "Maybe not."

"Then we'd best go now!" Together, Alma and Vannie helped the trembling child scramble down the slope, plucking pieces of her costume from protruding tree limbs.

Alma spoke quickly as they went, straightening the child's faerie crown that had slipped lopsided. "This forest is an illusion, child, generated out of pure imagination."

"It doesn't feel like it." Sarah shivered. "It feels real."

"Oh, it's that, too."

"I thought you'd say that," Sarah said even more dismally.

"In the depth of imagination," Alma went on, ignoring the child's fearful glance toward the fast-approaching sounds of ax-crunching bark, "is a doorway that leads to all other worlds, those of this Earth and those beyond it. One of those worlds is Faerie."

"She's almost here!" Sarah gasped, hardly registering Alma's words.

"Slip into the hollow now," Vannie advised, "and close your eyes once you're inside. We'll show you the door and how to pass through it."

Sarah dropped to her knees and squirmed into the gnarled hole, finding a prepared nest of leaves inside and hastily curling into it. "I don't see any door," she breathed.

"It's inside you," Alma said. "The faerie world is a part of Earth's essence, but you cannot see it with ordinary eyes. You need to tune into it the way you dial a radio to tune in a station. Once you are within faerie frequency, you will be safe tonight. However, it is asked of you that you make a sacrifice for entry into their world. You must relinquish some piece of negativity."

Tightly curled into the nest, she looked up at them with fearful eyes. "Wh-what?"

"A piece of negativity," Alma repeated. "It's your entry fee to the Faerie Realm."

Even here with the sounds of the ax coming ever closer, Sarah's curiosity was aroused. She grew less afraid and more intrigued. "I could give up chocolate drops." She screwed up her mouth as these words passed her lips. If it were to be chocolate drops, she would miss them mightily.

"No, sweetheart. We are not talking of sacrificing pleasure, but rather of giving up something *un*-pleasant, something that stunts your growth and might block you from seeing the faeries. Try to think of a fitting sacrifice, honey, so you can help Miss Prudence. You will know it when you hit on it."

The child tried to concentrate, all the time hearing the slam of the ax and the rustle of weeds as Miss Prudence stalked through the foliage not faraway. "Is the sacrifice something that makes me sad?" Her face clouded, and she realized suddenly that she didn't want to give up that part of herself. Why, she wondered in this place of mystery and danger, did she cling to that sadness that at times filled her interior so completely? "I . . . I can't . . . stop . . . Why can't I stop feeling sad?" she asked, getting the point even here in the belly of fear.

"Hmmm, now why can't you?" Vannie murmured back. "Could it be that you feel guilty being happy outside your mother's home? If so, do you think you could release that guilt?"

Sarah shrank back into the hollow and closed her eyes, reluctant even in this frightening place to give up the guilt that she now realized she had clutched inside her since leaving her home that terrible night.

"It's a caring person who feels pain after escaping a prison that still holds the people she loves most," Vannie said gently. "But when caring turns to guilt, it loses its power for good. Perhaps you might let go of it just this one time? Will you try, sweetheart?"

Sighing mightily, Sarah tried to surrender her guilt-ridden sadness. *Just once. I can always get it back*. With the thought her heart suddenly beamed rays of light that spilled out of her hiding place and filled the forest with a second moon. Maybe it would only be for the night, but she had just given the faeries her payment of the moment. Her soft lips slowly curved into a smile, and her forehead relaxed.

"Alright then," Alma said. "Sacrifice made and accepted. Now open your eyes, and you will find the door. Take your time . . ."

"I found it!" Sarah gasped.

"Lovely! Climb through now, easy does it, and you will find yourself in the Realm of Faerie. Someone awaits you on the other side."

The sisters listened to the sounds of scrambling around, and then a total hush, followed by Sarah's awed voice drifting through the opening: "Oh, hello! *Hello!*"

Through a mist that covered each pair of eyes, the sisters smiled at each other. Sarah had made it through.

"I'm . . . I'm Sarah," they heard her gasp.

In the next second Miss Prudence burst into sight, eyes mad, ax raised over her head.

26

As Shawn Prudence lunged forward Vannie held up a commanding hand. "Not yet!" she ordered. "Just a moment!"

Miss Prudence froze, mouth agape, ax clutched in both hands and teetering over her head.

"Oh, Sarah?" Alma called into the hollow. "Please ask those with you now for help with Miss Prudence. She needs to take a journey that requires their attention. Do you hear me? Sarah?"

Inside the tree they heard a rustle in the leafy nest where the child had lain, then a *clunk*. Then a scurrying and what sounded like a rush of wind being sucked out of the tree through the far door.

In the next instant Shawn Prudence fell to the crunchy forest floor beside the tree and lay looking up at the sisters. "Where am I? Where is the child?" She squirmed under the sisters' quizzical gazes. "It's rude to stare, Sisters! What are you looking at?"

"At a woman in a costume," Alma said calmly.

"Some Halloween getup, huh, Sister?" Vannie hooted. "The boots and robe are silly enough, but the ax and the blood, oh, my! That outfit would set a vampire bat to screaming."

"Um, not that," Alma replied. "I meant her everyday façade. Quite detailed, isn't it? A complete and total disguise! And that witch's voice. Perfect!"

"Oh, you mean the schoolteacher disguise! Yes, it's a horror, alright!"

"Rude! Rude! Rude!" Shawn staggered to her feet. "Stop talking about me as if I were someplace else! I'm right here! Wherever in heaven or hell that is." The thought occurred to her that perhaps she had found her way into the mythical dark woods where one could get irrevocably lost. Shaken by the idea, she sank back against the hollow trunk.

"What is it, dear?" Alma asked gently.

"It's just . . . the little girl's dead, isn't she? Her little body's in there, isn't it? I've killed her like I've killed all of them." Tears leaked down her cheeks. "Oh, what will I do? What will I do?"

Instead of answering the sisters watched her, waiting for the words that had to come from Shawn Prudence and no other, even as the schoolteacher buried her head in her hands and sobbed. *"Please!"*

"Please what, dear?" Vannie asked. "I'm sorry to ask you to be more specific at such an emotional time, but you see, these things must be made clear. We wouldn't feel right being the ones to decide exactly what you had in mind, so we must ask—"

"Please help me!" Shawn sobbed in a frenzy, feeling she could bear no more.

The sisters smiled.

"Gladly," Alma said.

The teacher scraped her fingers across her scalp, loosening her tight bun and sending a cloud of silky hair cascading over her face, neck, and shoulders and swirling in the night air. "You did know, I suppose," she mumbled, lifting her tear-streaked face to the dark sky, "that insanity runs in my family. It's taken my grandmother; now it's taking me." Gobs of white makeup rolled down her face, blending with streams of red. "The absurd Miss Prudence, that walking joke, is falling apart at last. I knew it was only a matter of time." More tears streamed. She looked as if she had been crying forever, that tears had become an essential part of her.

Vannie produced a handkerchief from her apron pocket and handed it to her sister while she sat beside the schoolteacher. "Lie down, dear. Rest your head in my lap. You must ready yourself to journey, like Sarah has done. Though the portal she used is not available to you, she has provided another way, with some help from her new friends."

"To journey!" Shawn Prudence choked, throwing off Vannie's hand. "You mean to *die*, don't you, Sister? I've killed her, you know! Her and all the children of the town. What new friends? The angels? They've closed the gates to heaven and are dooming me to the fire!"

Alma dampened Vannie's handkerchief in the stream that flowed a few feet down the slope from the old tree and rinsed Shawn's face and hands. "Life has been hard, hasn't it, dear? Alone so long, after your parents died and left you to care for your grandmother. All that commuting up to the asylum to visit her, then she up and died on you, too."

"She was so old," Shawn said shakily, " that I thought she'd live forever. She got real sweet in the end, you know. She'd been docile for some time, so they let her out of that place and she came back home, then died right at Christmastime. I had no one left."

"No friends, darlin'?" Vannie murmured.

Shawn shook her head wearily. "We were so different from the other people in town. They talked about us behind our backs. I always felt ill at ease among them." She fell silent, surprised to find herself lying with her head in Vannie's lap while Alma still dabbed at her face with the damp handkerchief.

One of them lifted her hand and placed it inside the tree hollow. She clutched handfuls of small seeds and berries, touched a wreath of bark and leaves that sparked heat against her fingertips. She jerked her hand back. "It's hot . . . oh, no, I suppose I imagined it. It's the madness."

"No, just the faeries at work," Vannie murmured. "Sarah's left her seedpods and faerie crown as talismans for you. I suspect her faerie friends have left something there for you, as well."

"Faeries! Sisters, please do be sensible and listen to me."

"Not a chance, dear. Too much sensible thinking leads straight to the nuthouse. Be quiet and feel the lightheartedness flowing from the Realm of Faerie. Receive it from the child's belongings. Let yourself *be*, Miss Shawn!"

There was no help for it. On a long groan, Shawn finally just gave up and let go. *What a relief. I've been tight for so long.* But before she had time to linger in the peace, she was darting backward through time.

Teenage voices rang in her ears: *"HEY, MISS PRUDENCE! MISS PRUNE – ENCE!!!"* Traveling at lightning speed, she saw oversized stockings draped on her desk by snickering students. A cartoon delivered at her door of herself standing at the blackboard, a sea of nylon bunched around her ankles. Boys passing by her classroom, groping inside their pants to mimic her daily search for the frayed elastic that held up her baggy hand-me-down slip that showed everlastingly no matter how often she hitched it up.

Her own voice tortured her ears: "Watch your posture, boys and girls. Straighten up! And take that gum out of your mouth, young lady! The only difference between a girl chewing gum and a cow chewing her cud is the thoughtful expression on the face of the cow!"

There was Momma wrestling with Granny, trying to force her medicine down, and Granny cursing and spitting. Aunts and uncles whispering: *Such a shame about poor Shawn Ann . . . living in a place like this . . . such sights for young eyes! Shh! She'll hear you!*

Traveling farther into the mists in her mind, she saw her mama crying on the bathroom floor, Daddy sitting on the edge of the tub, his head in his hands. Herself in the middle of it all, a lonely girl who pictured herself a floating island in an alien sea. Then came the sound of the ax splintering Momma's fine dining table. Such a loss that was, but nothing compared to the loss in the next swing of that horrible weapon.

From the middle of her personal dark woods, Shawn Prudence screamed.

The sisters calmed her, stroked her cheeks, dabbed at her tears, and murmured gently, witnessing as Shawn Prudence fell to pieces.

"In our society, people call this sort of thing a breakdown," Vannie said. "In other cultures it would be honored as an opening of consciousness. Primitive cultures, most would call those, but actually some are more advanced than our own. In such places people who *don't* break down, who never face crisis head-on, are suspect. They are thought of as 'the people who don't make waves' and are watched most carefully. Isn't that so, Sister?"

"Most definitely." Alma reached into the tree trunk and fished around. "Aha!" She sat back, having retrieved the flat stone that had nestled inside Sarah's hidey-hole. "Wonderful! I had hoped to find something like this. It's a gift from our allies, the faeries. Don't be afraid of it," she reassured the trembling Shawn, who shrank from the cool stone as Alma placed it under her left hand. The heavy black rock was of uneven shape, rather flat, yet mounded in the center. An unearthly band of rainbows shone in concentric circles on its surface, dark prisms on a black pond in moonlight. Or so it seemed to Shawn who peeked at it through slitted eyelids.

"It will help you center," Vannie added encouragingly.

Shawn slowly lowered her palm onto the gentle mound of the polished surface, which molded to the shape of her hand. At her touch it gave off undulations, as though she had awakened it from slumber. Rings of dark rainbows rose from its core, the atmosphere thickening in a shadowy spectrum of hues that swirled around a powerful vortex at the stone's center.

Concentric rings of smoky color expanded in the night air. Shawn was swept into the center of them and hung suspended as they spun around her. She felt her stomach tighten as she began to slide down through loop after loop of shadowy rainbows, gathering momentum with each passing ring, then: *Crack!* She penetrated the black hole at the center of the stone and fell headlong into an intoxication more pleasurable than anything she had ever known.

I should resist. Exactly what, she was not sure. Yet all she wanted was to swim deeper into sensation, to answer its wild and reckless call. An intense throbbing played in her like music, its drums rising out of a dark jungle on a forgotten continent. Her fingers unconsciously undid her top button, then ran down her throat as the drums beat harder. She responded with a burst of heat in her deepest places.

"*Ahhh!*" She rose slightly, surrendering all resistance as her chakras opened and aligned themselves with the vortex of the stone, forming a funnel consisting of seven layers of whirling concentric circles of light. The drums built to a frenzy as she dived into feelings she had denied herself for years. Desires for love, joy, and freedom surged to the point of rapture. Then *pop*! She landed in another world, where at first she was *no . . . where*, surrounded by *no . . . thing*.

White light flashed and retreated so quickly into darkness that Shawn soon lost her memory of it. Silence replaced all recollection of sound, numbness overtook bodily sensations, and iciness crept through her heart and mind. She vaguely wondered if she were dead, yet she could feel solid ground beneath her feet.

A sense of circular motion continued in the barren landscape that emerged around her, and she struggled to make out objects in a night as black as pitch, as dead as charcoal.

A flash of blood-red light rose from the Earth below and bathed her in crimson, illuminating her surroundings briefly before fading once more to black. Yet in that moment of illumination, Shawn was stunned to glimpse giant standing stones ringing her in a circular field. She stood rooted as a gray dawn gradually brought the vast stones again into view. They towered over her, shapes hinting at past majesty, some of them broken, some erect, all part of an ancient ruined pattern that spoke to distant memory.

The sky pulsed streaks of light allowing her to find her way to the nearest stone. She rubbed her hands across its weathered surface. Under her fingers the stone seemed to breathe and to think deep, rich stony thoughts, heavy thoughts that made her stagger backward and gaze up to see if it had a face. There was none, and yet a low rumbling echoed within her, as if she herself had become a stone and now could perceive stone voices.

"*Walk the round,*" the stone said inside her.

Peering closer, she realized that inside the circle of stones was a floor of paved marble, slate, citrine, jasper, turquoise, and amethyst, carved in a concentric circular pattern, each ring a different hue of smooth polished rock. The seams between the rings were smooth and perfectly fitted, crafted with a level of artistry and mastery that sparked a sense of wonder within Shawn. The floor was so precisely carved as to seem capable of independent movement of all of its rings and had the effect of wheels within wheels of polished stone. In the center lay a circular slab of white fire opal.

"*WALK THE ROUND!*" The sound shook within her, no longer feeling like a mere suggestion. She gazed again at the giant stone and made the choice to obey.

Letting out a breath, she placed her foot on the smooth stone of the outer ring and tested her weight on it, then pulled up her other foot and stood. She let out a little cry, as vibration moved through her feet and traveled upward, waking her to memory of the recent past. Vivid awareness of the galoshes she wore, the bathrobe and smeared makeup, the foolishness of her appearance with the ax at the café flooded her. She looked down and saw that her hands were bleeding again.

"Blood on my hands! *Blood on my hands!*"

As if in response, the outer ring on which she stood began to move, turning on a central axis from the huge round floor and gaining speed. With speed came images in her head of herself as she'd baked brownies that very afternoon. She watched herself sift flour and sugar into the bowl, fold in eggs and butter and milk, then add the nuts. She gasped and swayed, trying to keep her balance, fighting off the memory of her hand reaching for the gray box with the skull and crossbones black against the label.

"*NO!*" Shawn closed her eyes to the sight and blindly leaped from the moving outside ring of pavement to the one just inside it, which was sitting quietly. She caught herself and looked about, suddenly aware that she was not alone on the floor of wheels within wheels. At various places around and among the several concentric rings of stone, symbols had been carved or inlaid into the floor, set in precious and semiprecious metals. Soft lights emanated from the symbols, and in the lights, strange creatures gained substance and gradually became discernable to her eyes. An echo of faerie drums throbbed in her veins as if in response to their presence.

Upon one symbol sat a giant spindle of a creature that reminded her of a daddy longlegs spider. It sat perched on its hind legs, whispery thin front appendages waving about its body, then dropping to almost touch the floor. A second creature across the way seemed almost to be a tree, with bushy hair of leaves, and skin as rough and woody as bark. Yet, the creature moved like an ape and gestured wildly with its long leafy arms. A small gnome covered in dust sat on a third symbol, his pear-shaped face thoughtful as he eyed her.

Shawn sensed other presences, yet could not see them. She hoped none of them had managed to read her mind and see her reach for the box of poison. She decided not to think about it again. Maybe if she avoided the whole episode, it would just go away.

"Oh!" Shawn staggered as the ring beneath her lurched, almost causing her to fall.

"Poison in brownies for children?" the gnome asked her as she moved past him. "How could you do such a thing? Explain, please."

"I couldn't help it!" Shawn shrieked, losing her balance as the ride speeded up. "I was powerless. It was a *compulsion*, okay? I couldn't stand against it! It was wretched, horrid! Please, can you slow this thing down? I'm frightened. Help me, please."

Yet, the stone spun on, only going faster. Her sole option lay in trying to leap inward to the next circular ring, which still sat quietly on the floor.

With sudden verve, Shawn jumped and sprawled hard on the smooth surface. The quiet was as stark as it was sudden. She instinctively checked for broken bones and bruises, marveling that she was uninjured from a jump that had seemed like a leap from a speeding train. She let out a relieved breath and stood, testing her legs.

Turning inward, she was shocked to find herself face-to-face with the daddy longlegs spindle creature. It eyed her furiously.

"This isn't fair!" Shawn blurted. "I'm outnumbered by y'all, and, as far as I can see, none of you is on my side! I really don't think I should have to suffer like this. None of this was my fault, you know."

The spindle creature was unmoved. Behind it, the gnome came to stand, flanked by a number of etheric presences. All proceeded to yawn.

She stamped her feet. "I inherited a bad gene! A very *bad gene*, I tell you!" Not a sign of empathy from any one of them.

Her fury grew. "How would *you* like it if *your* grandmother attacked your friends and you with an ax on Halloween night? *I was just a young teen, barely pubescent, with serious issues of self-esteem!*"

"Serious, were they?" The spindle creature laughed. It shook all over on its spindle legs and wobbled delicately in place, then bounced up and down as if on springs.

Shawn gaped at its spindle feet to see if they were equipped with pogo sticks, but the stone upon which she stood moved her away from the creature and his also-laughing entourage. She was soon whizzing so fast that it seemed she would melt. At every pass the tree creature whipped her with its foliage.

"I'm a good woman, you . . . you overgrown piece of shrubbery!" Shawn shouted at the tree person. Angry tears filled her eyes. "Nobody should have to put up with all I've had to face," she quavered. "The children don't obey me, and they talk in class, and . . . and they have downright *shoddy* study habits. It all falls to me, and *I bear this burden all alone*."

"Oh, piffle," the creature said.

The stone wheels speeded up again, though it was not clear to Shawn if they moved directly in response to her perfectly good excuses or by the magic wrought by the creatures standing on the glowing symbols.

"Stop this thing now!" she bellowed, struggling toward the middle circle, which somehow remained stationary, no matter how madly the rest of the floor might spin. As she gazed across the three remaining rings leading to the center, she worked to justify her position in her own mind.

With the first step, feelings of entitlement lit up inside her like firework explosions. Wasn't she owed a little slack after all her suffering? Why should she be judged by those who could never understand her sorrow? The stone lurched so suddenly as to almost break her ankle, and she sprang from it in the barest nick of time.

Throbs of intense self-pity flooded her as her foot touched down onto the new ring. "*Why me, why me?*" whined in her head. And greased the mechanism of the wheel. The circle spun out from under her, and she was forced to leap again, this time to the innermost ring bordering the central round slab of opal.

As her foot hit the stone, Shawn was jolted by sudden wrath, thundering with judgment and condemning her school children, *all* children, their parents, *her* parents, her grandmother.

But, most of all, herself.

Yet, she was catching onto this game of spinning wheels and felt the one beneath her lurch, ready to send her sprawling.

She gingerly made her move, arriving at the center stone against all odds—or at least, that was how it seemed to her—and collapsed, panting and dizzy, onto the motionless pavement.

Stomach churning, she sat up to rest, only to find herself shaking and crying on a floor that glowed in opal light. Gazing down through wet lashes, she saw flecks of gold and emerald green twinkling at her like shy stars in a misty heaven. As they winked and blinked, she clung tighter to her reasons for avoiding responsibility and tried with all her might to summon a belief in her rightness.

Memories of that other Halloween night so long ago surfaced and surrounded her, that one past event that had shaped all her futures. A single event that had ended her rebellion against her family's madness and defined her from that night on.

She and her best friend, Celie, had gone trick-or-treating together in the company of two boys, Jim and Pete, and had returned home to a nightmare. That nightmare had become her excuse for abandoning all she could have been and choosing instead a life of alienation and pain.

Trembling, Shawn gazed again into the opal slab beneath her, remembering Celie's excitement as she'd walked in with the boys at twilight, meaning to pick up Shawn. That Celie! How brazenly she had lied, saying her mother thought escorts would be important for safety on a wild Halloween night, and Shawn's mother could not say no, so impressed was she with Celie's parents and their prominent family.

No doubt about it, she and Celie had pulled off a teenage coup that night. Shawn almost smiled, thinking of it. It had been the first and last night out with a boy that she'd ever had, and it was with that dreamboat, Pete Tyler, best friend to Celie's boyfriend, Jim.

She allowed herself to be flooded with warmth, remembering how they'd sneaked off to the shores of the lake to kiss and touch in the moonlight in a time that seemed like a taste of forever. She had felt her body respond in ways she had never known before, and a flush of blood to her neck brought a joyous flash of emotion, which crashed as quickly as it rose to be replaced by tears. Shawn shook with them, remembering what had happened when they returned at the end of the evening.

Granny Alice had been waiting when Shawn said goodnight to the others and closed the door behind her. Granny screaming, "Evil children, dirty children!" rang as ugly in memory as it had on that night. The old lady must have overheard the girls plotting on the phone, because somehow she had known the secret of the evening. In some way it must have triggered the memory of Granny's own loss, the loss of a son to a young woman.

The old lady came at Shawn, ax swinging. Shawn fled into the dining room, Granny right after her.

In one mad blow, the old lady felled the dining table of polished oak. Oh, that horrible crash. The sound brought Celie and Jim and Pete racing in from outside. The second blow caught Pete's arm, slicing through a muscle. His blood gushed all over everything.

And still Granny kept swinging. The ax got stuck in the staircase, and the old lady was finally subdued, along with Shawn's image of herself and all hope for a normal future. She stopped seeing Pete, Celie, and Jim after that, and only returned to school after missing most of the year.

Shawn wailed. Flailed her hands against the glistening floor. Then jumped up, realizing that all the wheels within wheels surrounding the opal slab were again on the move. Sounds emitted from them, and music rose while they synchronized their turns and began stopping one by one.

As they did so, she saw that the symbols were lining up, pointing in the direction of a particular opening among the standing stones. The last wheel stopped, completing the pattern. In the sudden stillness, there could be no doubt. A path had been laid toward a prominent portal between two of the standing stones.

This way. The stones spoke into her head. *This way now you come.*

Shawn hesitated, sensing that this might be the only way she would ever leave this place. As if on cue, the creatures filed off the symbols, heading toward the portal. One by one, they stepped from the stone floor and disappeared through the opening in the massive standing stones before them.

Alone now and with few options, Shawn followed fearfully. At the edge of the paved floor, she stopped and gazed through the opening. She already knew what she would face if she passed though the giant stones.

It would be what she had avoided all her life: *herself.*

She stepped forward, and found herself suspended in a world between time and space, between being on the floor and being off it. Between being and not being at all.

Winds blew in a vacuous space around her, and chaos of mind, body, and heart exploded the circuits of her brain.

Who she was, or who she thought she was as a child, collided with who she was now and with the old woman she might one day be. Her nurturer clashed with her fighter. The accomplished schoolteacher with the lazy slacker. The winner with the quitter. Her intelligence with her ignorance. Her courage with her cowardice. Her kindness with her lack of it. And her hope with her despair.

All the faces of herself appeared at once in a blaze of stars against a dark sky and just as quickly fell away, leaving nothing but her core essence standing unadorned.

In this state she felt brave and strangely willing to be just who she was—no more, no less. Standing on that truth, Shawn straightened her spine, raised her head and arms, and felt her possibilities expand.

And then she felt the wind under her arms, and she was off the platform, past the *world of between*, flying through the portal into a paradise of enchanted faerie woods. She soared through them to land in a lush meadow, her body brought to rest in a soft place amid grasses and thousands of flowers. Over her was a weeping willow, and gathered around her was a fleece seemingly made of white dandelion seeds.

Shawn Prudence was so shocked at the all-encompassing beauty, that at first she didn't hear the faint, almost indistinguishable, footsteps nearby. Then she heard melodies played on unfamiliar instruments. Faeries. She had felt their drums pulsing in her veins before. Now she realized that she must be in their domain. An elegant grassy creature lifted a flower petal to her lips, sending drops of sweetness dripping down her throat, jolting and warming her.

Among the divergent creatures was a childlike figure, translucent as gossamer, a little girl. The girl smiled and reached down to hold her hand. She was the child from the café—Sarah!

"Drink this, Miss Shawn," she said, offering nectar from a scrolled bromeliad cup. "I had some, too. It was made 'specially by the faeries for children who have been hurt by . . ." The child swallowed hard. " . . . by the ones who were supposed to love us best. They put in some extra magic for you and me."

Dumbfounded and thrilled to see Sarah alive and well, Shawn sipped the nectar, keeping the child in sight as she danced among faerie shapes of all sizes and descriptions, clearly a princess in their midst. Sunbeams filtered through the canopy and went from the faeries into the child, and now she felt them coming into her, comforting and mending her, even as did the music and dancing. The circle of dancers parted slightly, and she stared uncomprehendingly at a bubbling cauldron in its midst.

"You put it in there," Sarah explained anxiously, seeing that she didn't understand.

"Put *what* in there?" Shawn drew back slightly.

"I . . . I don't know what yours is. It's supposed to be a sacrifice of something you're using to punish yourself. I put in my guilt at being happy when the rest of my family isn't." The child's smile wobbled. "I think if you come closer, you'll know what to put in."

Shawn considered running away as fast as she could. Instead, she took several steps closer to the cauldron and saw that while most of the faeries had distanced themselves, there were—she counted them—nine women in various array, gathered around the cauldron, stirring it and beckoning her forward.

"No," she whispered. "What if I *want* to be bitter? How about *that*?" She glared at the heavens, expecting to see her grandmother's berserk face up there, or the mother and father who were so stupid as to keep a crazy old lady in their house and bring ruin to them all.

The child looked up nervously, also obviously expecting to see them. "Oh, please," she whispered. "Couldn't you just try, Miss Shawn? If it would help, maybe I could put in one more thing. I guess I could put in my homesickness. Then I'd just have to call the whole world my home." She was shaky, but determined. "Let's do it together. Please."

"Let me get this straight," Shawn said. "I'm supposed to throw in my lack of forgiveness and then . . . *what*? Have a good life?"

"That's the ticket," a motherly Woman of the Cauldron said, looking over. She was round and extremely beautiful, her long copper-colored hair woven with maple leaves. She gazed at Shawn with soft gray eyes. "It's easy as pie," she whispered, beckoning Shawn toward the steaming caldron. "Please come to us. Give us all that bitterness, dear one."

Shawn still hung back, caught by how much she did not want to be healed. "And I'm supposed to let everyone off the hook? Do you realize that if I do, my family will never understand how much they hurt me? They'll believe that they . . ."

"Didn't ruin your life after all, didn't turn you into an eccentric, miserable person?" the same Woman of the Cauldron suggested.

"Well . . . yeah."

"That's a hell of a way to make them pay, dearie," a second Woman of the Cauldron chuckled, her dark eyes glinting. "Especially with them all dead and gone and not giving a hoot."

Shawn was both faintly scandalized and enchanted by the vivid tattoos that adorned the woman's glistening black skin and by her exotic headdress of shells, feathers, and braided ropes like those that adorned her full bodice and flowing skirt.

"Come on, Shawn," yet another of the women murmured. This one was a giant of a woman, yet graceful under the drape of her sari and with the most enchanting moon-like eyes that Shawn had ever seen. Muscles in her arms rippled as she stirred the pot.

The rest of the Cauldron Women nodded, intent on tending their brew that emanated essences that spoke. Of initiation. Inspiration. Dominion. Gracious love. Joy. Comfort. Challenge. Knowledge. And compassion.

Sarah was leading Shawn forward, and she could not resist. She was so deeply awed by what she felt coming both from the ethers and from this child that she found herself bowing to each beaming woman as she passed.

Then they were at the cauldron, feeling the bubbles fly up at them. Leaning over the pot, Shawn was surprised to find its steam pleasantly warm instead of scalding.

Sarah drew a long breath and stepped forward. "Here I go," she said determinedly. "Goodbye homesickness! Hello feeling at home wherever I am!" Yet, it wasn't easy for the child. She struggled for several moments. Then finally: "Got it!" she panted. Without more ado, she heaved the invisible mass directly into the bubbles.

Shawn caught a glimpse of something dirty gray and immeasurably depressing disappearing into the bubbling brew. It roiled, being sucked into the currents. Then . . .

"Look!" Sarah said delightedly, pointing. A cloud of glowing white light rose from the pot and poured over the smiling child.

Shawn saw pure happiness on the little girl's face. If the child had had this much courage, the least she could do was to follow suit. Yet, could she?

She at least had to try, even though she had no idea how to begin.

"Close your eyes, Miss Shawn," Sarah whispered anxiously. "Sometimes it's easier that way."

So she did. For the first time in her life, Shawn took instructions from a child and closed her eyes. In the darkness, breathing in steamy plumes from the cauldron, she reached inside herself and did her own grappling. Pulled out handfuls of grief and bitterness and hatred. Of sorrow and endless shame.

Somehow, she managed to direct the hideous mass into the cauldron. It made for a mighty and putrid flow. Looking at the floating garbage that had come out of her and that was already dissolving into the bubbles, she felt frighteningly empty. Drained and inhuman. Less than nothing.

Then came the Keepers' whispers: "Thank you, Shawn."

The Cauldron Women rose on all sides of her as they stirred the whole mess into the churning liquid. Without understanding why, Shawn Prudence felt lighter. Her spirits cautiously rose as colored bands of rainbow light flowed from the cauldron and into her.

But how could she feel better? How could anything really help her, when she had killed them all? Even Sarah, who didn't seem to realize she was dead yet.

No sooner had the thought formed than Shawn felt herself being drawn upward, spiraling through loops of the rainbow colors and hearing a familiar voice: "Come on! Atta girl! Journey's end!"

Pop! Her head fell into Vannie's lap in the Little Room of The Two Sisters' Café.

Jaw agape, Shawn watched translucent trees and mosses and rocks fade from view, and the faerie forest recede. Beside her, Sarah lay curled in a blanket with bits of seedpods tangled in her hair, her faerie crown in one hand. With the other she clutched Shawn's hand, her eyes still closed, her face oblivious as Alma finished wrapping a large black stone and slipped it into a velvet bag.

Looking at Sarah lying so still brought Shawn into a chilled sobriety. It had been a wonderful dream, but now she had to face reality. Shakily, she propped herself up on one elbow, her other hand still holding fast to the child's. "Oh, Sisters, I've done the most horrible thing." Her voice broke. "I didn't know what I was doing . . . I was so bitter . . . I wanted to – to . . ."

"Actually, you wanted to kill the world," Alma said matter-of-factly. "But instead . . ."

"Don't you understand?" Shawn interrupted, seeing that Vannie also looked much too unperturbed. "I've killed the children of the town. I . . . I put poison in their brownies and . . ." Startled, she quit talking as Alma chuckled.

"Nonsense," Vannie scoffed. "You never put in a thing in those brownies that wasn't supposed to be in there. Chocolate, milk, flour . . ."

"Weed killer," Shawn said in a choked voice, staring at the child who held her hand even in death. "Look at Sarah. She's dead, Sisters. I did that."

Vannie's brows rose. "Oh, no, you're mistaken. Believe me. Sarah's perfectly fine. We would never let anything happen to her, nor to any child in our town. And more to the point, Shawn, neither would you. If you would, dear, think back carefully."

Shawn's heart fell into her stomach. She saw herself standing in her kitchen, mixing the brownies. Then turning. To look. At the box of weed killer. Saw herself . . .

"Go ahead," Vannie murmured encouragingly.

Shawn gulped. Tears burned her eyes. Yes, there she was, picking up the bottle, then . . .

She hesitated, looking from one sister's face to the next. They were both trying not to laugh, even as she was suddenly stifling her own laughter. At that moment the child's eyes opened. She began to giggle softly as Shawn saw herself walk from the kitchen to the shed and put the weed killer on the top shelf. *Must take care of stuff like that,* she heard herself think. *Mustn't get it around the children's brownies.*

She sat up giddily, clutching her head in one hand as though expecting her mind to soar skyward like a kite. "I feel fluffy, Sisters," she said, laughing. "Can you imagine me feeling fluffy in this outfit?"

"What outfit is that, Shawn?" Alma studied her with mild curiosity.

"Why—this robe, pajamas, white clown makeup. The ax."

"What ax?"

Shawn Prudence stared down at the russet-colored dress that closely fitted her body as though tailor-made. Her matching pumps. She raised her hand and looked at perfectly manicured nails painted in rose-red. A shiver ran through her, followed by sheer delight as she gazed at Sarah, who smiled back at her, stroking the leaves and berries woven into her faerie crown.

"It's time to go now," Alma said. "The children are waiting for their treats."

"Shouldn't I wash my face first?" Shawn whispered, raising her hand to her lips. Her mouth and face felt soft, not stiff and damp from a combination of tears and nightmare makeup.

"Your face," Vannie began.

"Is just as lovely as ever, Shawn," Alma finished. "Just as your hair is as wild and free and so gorgeous as to be the envy of every woman in town."

Sarah peeked out at Shawn from her blanket. "I wish I had black beautiful hair like yours."

Shawn touched the child's shining head. "Yours is more beautiful, Sarah. I wish I had a little girl like you."

"But you do, Mrs. Shawn. Becky's a good friend of mine."

"Mrs—?" A shock wave of memory, a mixture of old and new, moved through Shawn as she looked at the sisters and the little girl. Shawn Tyler now. Not Prudence anymore. And she had a family. With wonder and reverence, she remembered it into being. *Becky,* she thought in a rush of exu-

berance. *My little girl. And the boys, Wally and Clement.* They looked like their father, the principal of the high school.

It all came to her in a flood of such intense feeling that tears clogged her throat. She had married the younger brother of her first boyfriend Pete. After he left for college and broke her heart by going steady with a girl he met there, she had turned around one day to find herself looking right into the eyes of his little brother, Don. She hadn't looked anywhere else since.

Her heart pounded. She was suddenly in a hurry, bounding quickly to feet that were already sidestepping in their eagerness.

"Let's go," she said, leading the way from the Little Room toward the lower dining area of the café. Don was there with their kids, along with Celie and her brood.

An acre of other children waited by the candy counter, all chanting: "Trick or Treat! Trick or Treat!"

"Hey! Where *is* everybody?" Don called, peering around the cash register.

Shawn Prudence Tyler glowed from lovely head to lovely toe and caught the two sisters in one last hug before she called back: "Coming!"

The sisters and Sarah watched her turn and run into the life she had just remembered. A life snatched from the ashes of an old reality she had left behind her forever.

Tonight, a gift of the Faerie Kingdom had turned into a double blessing—two princesses caught in starved and terrible childhoods had been saved by the faeries tonight. Each had witnessed the other's shame and sorrow, and in that witnessing, had healed her own.

"Thank you, Sisters," Sarah said, looking from Vannie's face to Alma's. "For the best All Hallows Eve in the whole world. Thank you for Mrs. Shawn and for the faeries. And for letting me help!"

"You're so welcome, Sarah," Alma said mischievously, "that you may take a special treat from the case for your candy sack."

Sarah grinned. She didn't even have to think what it would be. "Make it chocolate drops!"

Chasing after her, the two sisters went running to join in the fun.

27

Sarah gazed into the rosy depths of her crystal ball, her gift from the sisters on the morning of the cherry pancakes. In the bright blue morning, she turned it over and over in her hands, waiting for its other dimension to appear, the "secret" that Vannie had said would show itself only in direct sunlight. Although the child had observed this spectacular optical illusion many times since that morning, it never ceased to fill her with awe.

On this day, the first Saturday after Halloween, she was on a mission, a field trip more important than her usual activities at the big house or in the café. This was Sarah's first magician's assignment to be carried out all on her own, away from the presence of either of the sisters, that she might begin to utilize the resource of solitude and to strengthen her self-discipline.

"Follow instructions carefully," Vannie had told her. "For help, you may call on the spirit of your stone, or of the forest, or of the animal kingdom. Or you may invoke your inner council. But today, you may not turn to us for answers. Today, we will be silent. Pay special attention to the details of your task."

Focusing on the surface of her rose quartz sphere, Sarah observed the first streak of luminosity, reminiscent of a moonbeam bending around the stone. Leaning against the sunny side of the great oak tree between the General Store and the sisters' house, she turned the ball carefully, tracking the ray of light toward its source.

The squirrel babies had scurried up the trunk at her approach and stared down at her, almost invisible against the gray bark. Just knowing they were up there gave Sarah a warm feeling. Like her, those youngsters had beaten impossible odds. Maybe better times were coming for all of them. Hadn't Vannie told her that all bad things must come to an end? Today, this seemed truer than usual.

Careful to follow the moonbeam shining on its surface, she turned the crystal ball a quarter revolution. Yes, she could see the beam bent to encircle the entire sphere, beginning where it ended, ending where it had begun, bright as a halo around a Faerie Queen's heart.

Another slow quarter turn of the sphere showed that the beam intersected two other beams which also encircled the stone, but from different angles. Incredibly, all three halos intersected at a single point, forming a star with six arms. It blazed like Belle Taylor's star sapphire ring, only the arms on Sarah's star reached all the way around her pink ball to cross each other again on the opposite side, thus creating a second star that she saw when she turned the ball over, careful to keep proper alignment between the sun's rays and the sphere.

In their brightness, the stars appeared to be raised an inch or so off the surface of the ball, making the sphere look like a small planet enclosed in a cage of starlight. Sarah could position whichever star she chose upward and then by waggling it around in her palm could watch it shine an umbrella of light above the surface of the polished stone. She could even pass her fingers beneath its rays, wiggling them between the pink crystal and the star, and still it would hover there uninterrupted, its silent radiance hinting of other worlds. Its light was very like that of the Faerie Realm where she'd visited only days before and where she most desperately wished to return.

Not yet, she thought, biting her lower lip. The sisters had been firm about this. "Mustn't overdo visiting other worlds, Sarah," Alma had explained. "Too much diversion can keep us from mastering our work in this one. Beauty can be seductive and can cause that famous 'enchantment,' like that of the princess who woke to find the young man she loved had grown old and died while she was napping 'over there.' The poor girl was now a hundred years old and had never been kissed."

Sarah giggled, turning fiery red. "That could really happen?"

"Would I lie to you?" Alma winked solemnly. "If visiting other realms turns into an escape from daily life, it becomes an addiction instead of a resource. The Faerie Realm is especially seductive. That is why most apprentices wait till they have attained a level of mastery before going there. You have been an exception to the rule."

Still, the sisters had said she could go back from time to time. Provided she could find a portal. But how? And what kind of portal? As was often the case, the sisters had left her to ponder the possibilities on her own.

Sarah slipped her stone back into her pocket, picked up her thermos and sack of chocolate drops, and pushed on toward her spot down by the creek. She felt the gift-wrapped package—the long, slender green one given to her on the morning of the cherries—poking out of her left pocket. She pressed it deeper inside and felt around under it for the smaller package to make sure it was still there. Then saying a silent goodbye to the babes in the treetop, she set off.

A loud *Kreeeeeeeee* . . . sounded from the sky overhead, and she looked up to see the broad wingspan of a red-tailed hawk sailing on air. It slid before her, leading her through the gate in the backyard and across the fields where cattle grazed not far from the creek. To keep the hawk in sight, she was compelled to climb the far fence and dash after it past the tree line and on into the forest, shivering as a sensation of total isolation closed in on her. Overhead, brilliantly colored leaves swished against the sky, and trunks moaned as the trees swayed in a wailing wind.

"Hi," Sarah whispered, hearing creatures move around her. Seeing nothing, she moved more quickly, still following the distant hawk that led her deeper and deeper into the forest. Though sun fell through some of the less dense foliage, it was colder here, and she was glad to have worn the rose-colored, hand-knitted sweater that Vannie had given her only this morning. It warmed her, making her feel the sisters' presence even here in this seemingly distant and isolated place.

Her assignment had sounded simple enough. She was to find a clearing wide enough for sunlight to strike the forest floor from the time she arrived there until the end of the day. There she was to draw a circle, at least as big around as she was tall, and place her pink ball inside the circle, being sure to ignite the star in sunlight.

Make sure its rays shine bright, child. You may have need for such before day's end.

There sitting in the circle, she was to open her second present from the morning of the cherries. Her third gift from that morning, the smaller one wrapped in black, must be kept buried deep in her left pocket until she returned home. It was NOT to be opened today, though the sisters had assured her it would protect her wherever she went.

"Lessons and knowledge are gifts," Vannie had added as a last word before she left the café. "That's why we present many of your lessons with ribbons and bows. The package you will open today may lead to knowledge of the chalice, the third gift of the initiated magician."

As Sarah made her way farther into the forest, a feeling of safety crept into her bones, a kinship with these woods. Autumn crunched under her feet and blazed in the trees. She noticed the moss that grew on the north side of tree trunks and wondered if the moss knew it was a blanket for the trees. Did it choose on purpose to throw itself between them and winter's winds, rain, and cold? She trekked on, distracted by imagined conversations among ferns and grasses and falling leaves and was surprised to find herself on the bank of a running creek. The sisters had mentioned a creek, suggesting it might provide the proper setting.

Sure enough, her clearing showed itself to her on a slight rise over the creek bank. It opened to a wide stretch of sky, allowing the sun's rays to warm a patch of grass and an occasional seedling beneath. A tree stump near the center of the clearing seemed like a perfect place to display the pink crystal. She looked around for a stick so she could make her circle and get about her work. A fallen birch limb, a little taller than she was, turned out to be the right thing.

Standing against the stump, Sarah stretched the stick out in front of her and scratched the dirt with it, drawing the circle around her as she turned. Halfway around, she paused to survey the semicircle, then focused again as her stick moved on, finding its way through leaves and twigs, tattooing the arc around her. When she finished, the end of her line touched the spot where she had made her first mark, closing an exact ring around her. Sarah stared disbelievingly, wondering if the sisters were helping her, after all.

Pay attention to the details.

Heart racing, she reached into her pocket for her sphere and placed it on top of the stump, turning it this way and that to let the sun find the star. The six rays shot out in a pink-electric dance, and to Sarah's surprise, continued to grow, arching up and out to the rim of her circle like ribs of an umbrella.

Spellbound, she nestled in underneath the beams to sit next to the stump, then withdrew the long skinny package from her pocket. The elegant, pale green paper with a darker green bow pleased her, and she took a moment to admire the wrappings before setting about undoing them. She struggled for a moment with the well-taped layers of paper and tightly tied ribbon, then gave up on saving any of them and tore into the package with both hands, pulling its contents free.

Holy moly! It was the black wooden flute she had seen in the storage room in the sisters' house, the one that sat on the stool beside the oddly painted harp and across from the spinning wheel.

The child carefully turned the flute, noting that it appeared to be ancient, its wood from trees that perhaps no longer inhabited this planet, if ever they had at all, she thought dubiously. The sisters might have harvested and imported this wood from worlds far away. Its hardware was of old beaten silver. Most importantly, it was filled with un-played music. How she could hear it, she didn't know, but she did, just as she somehow knew how to produce the melodies in her head by directing her breath though the hollow chamber. If a master flute teacher had appeared before her in this moment, she would have stopped him before he could say a word.

I know how! I already know!

Thrilling to the music inside her, she put the flute to her mouth and blew a long breath into it, her fingers finding the stops without hesitation. The throbbing notes responded to her need for something childlike and carefree with almost chilling beauty that danced silvery on the air.

She stood and took a few tentative dancing steps, then danced in earnest, skipping around the stump, charming her own spirit as if it were a cobra rising from a straw basket, bobbing its hooded head above a coiled tail, somewhere on a faraway mountainside. She danced on and on until she felt drugged and depleted, exhausted and overwhelmed by beauty and ecstasy. Only then did she finally quit playing and lower herself to the ground, her head leaning drunkenly against the stump. The forest blurred before her closing eyes, and she slept under a parasol of light.

Sarah stared, blinked hard, then looked again, sure that something had changed while she napped. The sun seemed not to have moved very far in the sky; her ball still shone in an umbrella of light. The clearing was just as she remembered it.

Yet nothing seemed the same. The trees around her were the same trees. Or were they? Brighter golds, browns, reds, and oranges than she remembered leapt at her from more sharply contrasting shadows, lending an eerie sense of expectancy to the scene. Evergreens scattered among the taller broadleaf trees startled her with intense color. She tasted their green with her eyes and smelled reds, golds, browns, and other forest hues, even as her skin drank the scent of wildflowers. Under the rustlings of trees and the trickling creek water, there was a deafening hush.

Sarah's eyes sought out the nearby stand of sweet gum trees. Their branches reached down, their tips curled towards her. Gray-brown faces smiled, while others grimaced in the flowing black rivulets that patterned their bark. Butterfly wings rose in her stomach, and she realized that she had felt something like this before. Her journey on Halloween night replayed itself as the shapes around her took on new meaning. Remembering how she'd felt upon first stepping from the tree trunk into the faeries' domain, she was sure that she had stumbled yet again into the world of *Other*!

She touched the black package in her pocket, then, reassured, she looked around again, feeling her sensory apparatus shifting.

Other realms exist in the same space and time as ours, Alma had explained. *But they are in different dimensions, vibrating at different frequencies. To experience them, our senses must be realigned, tuned in the way you tune in a radio channel. This happens when we pass through a portal.*

A portal! She must have found one! There was no mistaking it. She felt dizzy as her senses fine-tuned their settings. Branches, leaves, twigs, and ferns zoomed into sharper relief. The air took on a golden tone. Rocks glistened silver among the mosses of the creek bank.

Sarah clutched the black flute in her hand, determined not to lose it, no matter what happened. She gradually perceived creatures appearing. They were like none she had seen on Earth, some tiny, some immense, and everything imaginable between the two extremes. Slender green nature spirits hid in the grasses, cleverly camouflaged as they huddled whispering, then spread among the stalks they tended, rubbing against them and infusing them with aliveness. Shape-shifters among the trees played hide-and-seek, taking on the appearance of bark or the tattered remains of a deserted nest. One went so far as to pretend he was a nut hanging on the limb of a beech tree, then had to perform some quick acrobatics to avoid a flying hairy lizard with three pairs of eyes.

Tiny gnomes resembling lumpy clumps of dirt waddled around on short muscular legs snatching life from the ethers, then dissolving into rocks, plants, and earth to deliver their load, then to pop back out looking much thinner. Faerie presences with legs like tree trunks and leaves or moss growing out of their heads loomed at her, some with tree fungus sprouting

PABLO
FERRO

on their shoulders and arms, others with stems of wild grasses poking from between their toes.

They climbed about directing traffic as the plants prepared for coming winter. Others looked more like humans, yet oddly different, more like the earth in their coloring and tones, and no two alike in size, shape, or apparel, as they blended into the forest and melted among the trees, appearing and disappearing at will.

Sarah found herself outside her circle, vaguely sensing that she had left her pink ball sitting on the tree trunk, spewing light as it tracked a golden sun across heaven. Her senses crackled, linking her telepathically to all the living things around her. She felt sap being withdrawn from leaves, branches, and trunks of trees into deep roots to wait out the winter and saw the ground move as insects furrowed in the dirt to hibernate. Flowers and plants spewed color as they lived their last days and prepared to exit the world. She heard all in the forest converse as it prepared for rest, the moss reassuring the trees that, of course, it knew to lay its blankets on their north sides!

Sarah saw that the forest was being stripped of its glory like a fairgrounds being dismantled, translucent air spirits ripping red and gold from the trees, breaking the colors apart and setting them to drift into thousands of small magic carpets zigzagging their way to the forest floor. Water sprites bounced like champagne bubbles on the surface of the flowing creek, giving the woods a sense of celebration.

Earth. Water. Air. An exhilarating mix. Yet a fourth element was missing. "*Where is Fire?*" she whispered, remembering that the sisters had said it worked with the other three. As soon as she said its name, fire's salamander spirit appeared to her, wriggling in a dance in her mind, awakening passion for being alive and happy, for learning and growing, and sparking compassion for every living thing.

Sarah's face burned red as she tuned into the fireworks in the forest. Inside every plant, every cell, a small furnace glowed. Some of the larger plants were burning out after their burst of growth in summer, but the show was far from over. Mosses and ferns, evergreens, and some grasses still stoked their furnaces, changing sunlight into chemical reaction to generate green bodies out of dirt and stone.

The fire spirit was helping some things to live and others to die, even assisting dead bodies that lay on the forest floor in a state of transition by hastening their return to the matrix for a new generation. She heard a kind of "snap, crackle, and pop" as dead cells collapsed back to the dust of their beginnings.

Swaying and entranced, she closed her eyes.

"Sarah?" The voice jolted her eyes open. "What are you doing, child?"

It was difficult to see where the voice had come from. In a mere blink of time, her senses had again shifted, calibrating now toward motion as her central perception. She sensed the forest moving, though usually no human could have possibly detected such a subtle flow. Even the trees, slowest of all the movers and shakers, had bark that flowed like rivers of neon or freeways of energy that were held together only by the tree blueprint supplied by the various tree devas.

With everything swirling, it took a moment to distinguish the form of a . . . woman? . . . though the luminous figure standing before her was nothing like any woman Sarah had ever seen before.

"Child?" the figure repeated.

Only seconds before, Sarah would have been content to do nothing but swim forever in the luscious flow of energy into matter and back to energy again, to bask in sensations of cells dividing, growing, and dying in the woods. Yet, the visage of this strange lady aroused her curiosity and gently pried her free of her trancelike state. Standing at least as tall as Sister Alma, who was of an impressive height, she was without doubt the most beautiful creature Sarah had ever seen.

Probably, Sarah thought, remembering Sister Vannie's nighttime stories, this must be an Ancient Faerie, or Faerie Queen, as some would call her. Her centuries-old complexion was as delicate as porcelain, allowing light to pass through it. Long flowing hair, which changed from silver to golden and back again, was woven with wildflowers and picked up the gray-blue of the faerie's eyes. Mosses clothed her; spidery silk laced her bodice and sleeves.

Mouth agape, Sarah stared up at her, feeling her power. Ancient or not, she was a creature to be reckoned with.

"Children from your world do not come here unattended, young lady." The faerie eyed her solemnly. "Even grown-ups do not enter this realm without guides and protectors. You are brave, if foolhardy. Still, it is with our permission that you are here. Would you like to know why?"

Awestruck, Sarah nodded.

"Because of two reasons. First of all, your visit with us on All Hallows Eve was granted for your safety. Your experience was somewhat restricted because we had no knowledge of how you would respond. For that reason, you dreamed through most of it. The sisters, as you call them, have alliances here, I among them. They know that even a single, fully conscious encounter with our world can give one a certain knowing. And with that knowing can come a permission to be all one can be. They wished us to help counter some difficulties you face in your world. The second reason we permit this somewhat unorthodox visit is because of your talent. Such power could not be held in check; neither could your spirit. We sense for you a destiny that demands that we share our knowledge with you. What have you come here to learn, child?"

Almost breathless, Sarah managed to croak, "I'm . . . I'm supposed to look for a chalice. Would—would you happen to know where I can find one?" She felt whorls of energy flowing from this faerie, one moment chaotic, the next morphing into form, her face shifting like patterns in a turning kaleidoscope.

"Hmm, a chalice." The faerie thoughtfully regarded her. "One of the gifts of the magician. Why, may I ask, do you search for this gift?"

"I'm an apprentice, and it's my homework," Sarah said, "but I don't know exactly why." She was a little embarrassed to admit it since she was supposed to be possessed of so much talent and yet didn't know the answer to this simple question.

Yet, the faerie did not seem perturbed. "Tell us what you have learned so far of the sword, wand, chalice, and shield."

"Well, I know that swords are for dis . . . er . . ." Sarah found herself sweating as she tried to remember exactly what Vannie and Alma had told her. "Discerning, that's it!" She let out a breath, hoping she had it right.

"That is correct, child. A sword cuts through confusion and readies the mind to perceive truth." In the faerie's face were all the ages she had been and would become, yet her eyes shone constant. "Its power," she went on, "slices away superstition and fear, frees one of negative beliefs, and can help end bad bargains holding back one's progress. Do you have such a sword in your keeping?"

"I don't *have* one," Sarah ventured timidly, "but I've seen two of them. A big one and a little one."

"Good." The faerie's silvery golden hair fanned softly around her head, occasionally flashing other times and seasons in its highlights, the blonds of her childhood, reddish browns of later years. "That will do for the sword then. To understand its workings even on an elementary level is an initiation in itself. Now please tell me what you have learned of wand."

"It's about pointing," Sarah said a little more confidently. "Pointing the imagination and the will. It's for focused intent."

"There is more to learn of wands, how to use them to direct healing energy, as well as to assist in manifesting dreams, but you will have many years to practice. And you say you've seen such a wand?"

"Just one. It was just an everyday wand. It was a . . . a sewing needle." She tried not to feel stupid. A needle still seemed to her a pretty sorry excuse for a magic wand.

"Actually, you have seen two. The needle is a wonderful example. Your black flute is another." The faerie nodded at the ancient flute that Sarah still clenched in her hand. "We congratulate you on your use of it. Vanessa and Alma are blessed to have such a talented apprentice."

Cheeks burning in pleasure, Sarah looked at her feet and struggled not to feel proud, barely able to make out her shoes amid the whirling energy that had become her world. She reminded herself that she knew almost nothing.

"You do not need to fear becoming arrogant, child," the faerie assured her. "Fear of arrogance is as limiting as arrogance itself and can block a healthy self-image. Protect yourself from your ego in this way: When you receive praise, hand that praise over to your Higher Self, your Soul, and your Spirit for safekeeping, out of ego's reach. They will see to it that such is used to build confidence and self-esteem. Now continue. What do you know about the chalice you seek?"

"Noth . . . nothing really." How could she have gone off on this quest without knowing what she was looking for? This was worse than a quiz at school when you hadn't read your lessons. Luckily, the Ancient One gave no sign of thinking less of her.

"Very well, then we will help you begin. What we will share with you will be only a starting point, a glimpse into the nature of what you seek. Listen closely, as there is no time now for lengthy explanation. The star on your crystal sphere still catches the sunlight in your world. Should that sun go behind the tree line beyond the creek, your star would go out, and with it your way of return. It would not do for you to spend the night here. One night in Faerie Realm could mean years in your world, child. You could return to find things not at all the same as you left them."

Sarah looked back in the direction from which she had come, or at least in the direction from which she *thought* she had come. The rivers of rippling color were rapidly settling, allowing her to perceive the forest in startling clarity. Through a corridor of trees, she could detect pink rays beaming from her world.

I must be getting used to things. Everything is slowing down.

Looking again at the Ancient Faerie, she saw that a large black cauldron had appeared between them, steamy vapors rising from its bubbling depths. A strange memory stirred in the back of her brain. She had seen this pot before, and yet the memory of when and where seemed veiled in the mist that drifted above the bubbling brew. Around her and the Ancient Faerie, other women, nine of them, also familiar, were gathering. They held faerie radiance, yet exuded earthy fertility and maternal grace. Autumn was woven into their very diverse clothing that mirrored images of cultures far beyond those of Willow Creek. Their skins ranged in tones that were not only white or black or brown, but also tinged with the autumnal colors of nature. Sarah caught glimpses of precious stones flashing in their attire and woven into their hair as the women glided forward, taking their places around the cauldron.

Yes, I know these women. Sarah felt a surge of love for them, not unlike the love she felt for her own mother.

The Ancient One greeted each in turn, then spoke to Sarah. "Come, child, come look into our pot."

As Sarah edged closer to the bubbling cauldron, the Faerie Queen raised her arms and the steam rose thicker, billowing wet and foggy clouds. The child watched them, thinking of Vannie's black iron pot bubbling on the sisters' stovetop. It seemed an exact replica of the one belonging to the Women of the Cauldron. The child wondered if the two pots were alike in more than just their looks.

Ah! Exactly so. The faerie was talking into her head now as her vision continued. *That cauldron, like this one, is used to transform one thing into another. Such is the nature of cauldrons. What else do you see? Don't bother telling us. Just envision it, and we will see it with you.*

Shivering a little, Sarah looked again into the mists and saw images of the woods veiled in fog, then flashes from the elements: fiery sparks, fizzy bubbles, and crystal dust filtering through funnels of twisting air and stirring memories again. But of what?

Of *me*, she thought suddenly. Me here in Faerie Realm, only a few nights ago! There I am, sipping elixir from the faeries on All Hallows Eve! There are Shawn Prudence and I together drinking ambrosia from a scrolled bromeliad cup. *Ummm.*

She tasted the elixir sliding down her throat, invoking awareness, and remembered her sacrifice. Now came flashes of other memories of that same All Hallows Night as she and the teacher, each in states of dream, had stood before the Women of the Cauldron. Each had placed sacrifices into the brew, things to which they had become attached. Hadn't the sisters often warned that it was as easy to become attached to sadness and bitterness as to happiness and love?

Strange, but true. Thus, it had not been effortless to throw their garbage away and see it engulfed in the steamy depths of the cauldron, gone forever. For just a second, Sarah had actually been homesick for homesickness. But, oh, the relief when it boiled away. She had stood there, radiant with happiness, catching glimpses of Miss Prudence standing in the steam, sacrificing her bitterness and her lack of forgiveness of others, her shame and blame, throwing strange symbols of all those into the cauldron: An empty toilet paper spool. A hatchet. And a box of weed killer.

How the brew had bubbled, stinking of rage, resentment, and unsolvable crimes of spirit. How Miss Prudence's eyes had squinted at the acrid fumes. Even now, the air was black with that remembered smoke and filled with the sounds of the wooden paddle splashing the brew, stirring its darkness.

Female voices had then spoken through smoke—voices of the Women of the Cauldron. "*Thank you, thank you, thank you.*"

Sarah frowned. *Miss* Prudence? But it was Mrs. Tyler, now. A new name, a new life. Exactly what had happened, anyhow? She remembered her lying on the ground, oblivious to the Cauldron Women whose breath caused the brew to bubble, their passions giving it warmth. And the way the cauldron's contents had absorbed all that both she and Mrs. Shawn threw in as the women stirred and whispered into the brew:

"From lead to gold, from dark to light
What is not denied can be made right.
What is not hidden can be healed

Let blackest secrets be unsealed."

The brew had grown more putrid as they stirred and tended it.

"Why did Mrs. Shawn fall asleep?" Sarah whispered to the Ancient One.

"She is not a magician, Sarah, and could only be allowed to remember as much as she might think a dream." The faerie smiled playfully. "Even you relinquished part of your memory that night as a gift to her."

But now Sarah was remembering more, especially the best part of all—the woman who had walked out of the forest, more beautiful than even the Ancient Faerie herself.

Dazzling light had poured from this radiant being, clearly of *divine essence*, who came forward to part the women and step to the edge of the great pot, which was emitting a horrid stench. Gracefully, she sat on its lip. Then turned and allowed her feet and legs to slide in, then lowered her whole body into the cauldron, drenching herself in the putrid swill. Tears had stung the child's eyes when the lady tilted her head back and dropped her lovely hair into the filth, then ducked her head to be totally submerged, suspended in the ugliness and pain of those who had placed their darkness into this vessel.

And then had come the miracle.

Sarah had been amazed to see the liquid change before her eyes into a clear, honey-colored, bubbling elixir, clean as an untouched mountain spring, fragrant as honeysuckle. All that had been putrid was now transformed into purity by divine innocence, changed by valor into ambrosia to be sipped out of faerie cups in a moment of crossing.

Sarah looked up now at the Ancient Faerie standing over the cauldron, the vapor receding and the other women smiling from behind her. As Sarah got her bearing, the old one spoke.

"Here is the answer you seek, child. You have seen the transforming work of cauldron magic. Now know this. The cauldron and the chalice are one with each other and also one with the grail. Vessels all, you see. Each is a symbol of the transforming power of love. When negativity is surrendered to love, whether in cauldron, chalice, or grail, something clean and pure emerges."

"But the lady . . ." Sarah knitted her brow. "She swam in the cauldron. She put her beautiful hair into it. Why didn't she get dirty? How did she make everything clean?" She remembered how the lady had walked back into the forest, more beautiful and pure than when she had first appeared.

"Ah, child. This is a mystery past all understanding. Love is a mystery, divine love the greatest mystery of all. Yet, know this: Any contact with the essence of innocence brings purification. What is positive and true is more powerful than what is not."

"But . . ."

"Do not question further, child. Our time is coming to a close." The faerie stood tall now, a sense of haste flowing from her. "Twilight approaches. You must return to your own world while your star still catches the sun. Do not pause to ponder these things. Put your flute to your mouth, and play your way home!"

Sarah found it hard to move, much less play her flute. Overwhelmed with images of chalice and cauldron, of elixirs and faeries and strange dreamlike creatures, she struggled to take in the faerie's words. A shock went through her as the wooden flute suddenly buzzed in her hands.

"Don't think, Sarah! Don't hesitate! Play!!!"

She numbly positioned both hands on the slender reed. Again, her fingers found the stops with certainty, as if she and the flute had been lifelong friends. Yet so many questions remained. She longed to linger with the faerie, to stay among the Cauldron Women and learn more from them, but something inside her was waking to the necessity of moving quickly, and she obeyed, raising the flute to her lips.

Then she was blowing into the ancient black wind instrument, exhaling a breath of passion she had not known was in her. The music turned urgent as she felt a building need to be back in her own world, her own woods, the sisters' house. Her own bed.

PABLO
FERRO

A thrill passed through her as she felt herself rising on the notes she played, levitating, drawn by a beam of light that reached through the twilight of Faerie Realm and beckoned her to her own world.

Dream yourself there, child! the Ancient One urged. *Dream it, with full intention.*

Sarah felt herself swept onto the highway of light bouncing off her pink sphere, zoomed along it at breakneck speed. There was a hum. And then a white nothingness.

She woke to find herself lying with her head on the tree stump in the center of her circle, her crystal ball mirroring the final rays of afternoon sun. The star shone, then suddenly was gone as the sun dipped behind the trees, burying its light in shadow.

Sarah sat up a little shakily, not altogether pleased to find herself alone in the forest in deepening twilight. It had been a very close call. She sensed the Ancient Faerie peering through the other realm and smiled back a bit dizzily.

"I made it!" she whispered. "Thank you. Thank you so much!"

Then with her flute in one pocket and sphere in the other, she picked up the rest of her things and hurried through the dimming forest, each step increasing her desire to be home. The Earth seemed foreign. Her legs felt rubbery, buckling as she made it past the last of the towering trees and headed across the shadowy field. Only her fear of catching her foot in a rut kept her from running. Finally, the gate loomed ahead of her. She emerged through it near the sisters' hen house.

What an adventure. Yet somehow, here she was, safe and home at last. For a moment, she hung on the fence reliving the time she had spent in the forest and feeling the regeneration of life all around, everything so much a part of the whole.

A deep breath, and then she willed herself to sprint toward the house. Her legs answered her with an explosion of energy, and in a burst of exuberance, she stretched her arms out to feel the wind beneath imagined wings. It seemed she might rise off the ground, sail up, and then land like a sorceress atop the hill.

A sound rose in her throat like the cry of the hawk she had heard and followed ages ago, this very morning.

Kreeeeeeeee! The shrill call sounded a declaration of her new sense of self, sounding out of her throat like a miniature of Alma's war cry on the night of the hailstorm. It was answered immediately:

Kreeeeeeeee . . . She heard wings overhead mirroring her imagined flight. Or was it she who mirrored the red-tailed hawk? It now led her home just as it had begun her journey. They two were part of each other, like the parts of nature gathered together in the forest. Suddenly, she intensely wanted to become one with the bird, to see the world through hawkish eyes. Become swift and wild. Fierce.

For an instant, the child tasted power known only to singular focus. Then she was again running up the hill, struggling to keep sight of the bird's wings, their majesty speaking to her of her own victory today traversing the boundaries between worlds.

The great hawk disappeared from the sky into the oak tree. It took a moment for her to realize what it was doing.

"No!" she screamed.

The mother squirrel barked. Sarah hurried closer with pounding heart, making out gray shapes against the bark and hearing the scratching sounds of scurrying on the tree trunk. Then giant wings spread, and the hawk took flight.

It rose to soar over the roof of the sisters' house and across the face of the moon, no longer full, yet fat and rising lopsided in the sky.

Clinging to its talons, or rather dangling helplessly from them, was a small struggling form. It was one of Sarah's baby squirrels.

28

Cleatis had known she was trouble the first time he saw her pull off the main road. Her rattletrap had bumped hard over the ruts in the deep backcountry woods, and he'd wondered then how she knew where to find him. Most women didn't buy their own whiskey. In fact, not a single Willow Creek woman had ever made it out to any of his distribution points in all the years he'd been selling; they left whiskey-buying to their men. Certainly, none had come alone. They wouldn't risk the danger, couldn't risk the talk.

And this one looked young, maybe eighteen. Maybe not. It hadn't taken him long to realize it wasn't just whiskey she was after.

Today, peering through the windshield and seeing her made-up face and long hair held back by a barrette on one side and carefully arranged to drape the other side of her face, her lips red and pouty, he knew it would be no different from the last time or the time before. He watched her car struggle in the ruts toward his old shed and thought about it again. Most likely, her father or an uncle had told her the way. Hers, or somebody else's. Strange to say, in their times together, not much information had passed between them.

Cleatis was pretty sure she got around. He told himself that most men would give her what she was looking for without thinking twice about it. Why shouldn't *he*?

And now she had parked again in the trees and was walking toward him swaying in her tight skirt. *Whew!* A hard grip in his stomach told him this would lead to no good. He'd felt that before with her, and if anything, the feeling was worse today. Just like his mood was blacker. A surge of heat in his groin said that whatever would be would just have to be.

She walked with her head high, but her slender shoulders gave her away, drooping down hard, like always. She clutched the cheap bag that hung on a strap under her arm until she reached him, then snapped it open to get out her money. After she paid him and took the bottle, she made her move, just the way she'd done it all the times before, slithering up against him like it was an accident.

Lucky the boys weren't around. Never seemed to be when she came calling. She seemed to know.

He grabbed her by the wrist and jerked her inside the shed. When he finished, she looked up at him and made a smart remark, like last time, daring him to hit her. She knew just what to say to make him mad. He gave her a good one with the back of his hand across her face. It would show. He'd left marks on her before, but none that she couldn't cover up with clothes. Now a red welt was coming up on her cheek, and her lip had blood on it, too. She smiled a little bit, triumphant, and for the first time, he felt a flash of fear.

"Git!" he barked at her. He stood there watching her sashay back to her car, laughing over her shoulder at him the whole way. She got in and slammed the door, still looking pretty damned happy with herself.

Damn, she made him nervous. He kept his eyes on her all the way back to the main road, had to hike a distance through the trees to do it, but he wanted to see her gone. Wanted to be sure she was fast on her way to as far away from him as she could get.

It wasn't until she pulled out that he noticed the other car. It had been off the road, backed in near a gate marked "Private, No Trespassing" that led to some pretty good woods that were posted against uninvited hunters. When she pulled off, the car followed.

Cleatis squinted against the sun. He hated what he saw. He didn't know the driver in that dusty Ford, but he thought he knew the man next to him. The girl was trouble, alright.

The second man in the car was Sheriff Jimmy.

29

The sisters' big house was as dark as the sky above it, except for the small porch lights that fought with the enormous black night. If there had been a moon, which there wasn't, no one would have seen it.

They slept now, in the darkened house, a dreamless sleep for Sarah and a busy sleep for Vanessa, who spent her lucid dreamtime weaving a veil around Sarah's intuition. Trouble with Cleatis was brewing, both she and Alma knew that much. Most likely, the block to their *sight* was of their own making; both dreaded knowledge that was sure to stun their apprentice when it came to light.

In the rear bedroom, Alma stirred in her big bed. She turned from her back to her side, hugged a pillow to her chest, and surrendered to unconsciousness. In the depths of sleep, the sky of her mind was as black as the sky above the house, and exhaustion overcame resistance to an image she had staved off for several months now, beating it back into darkness whenever it had threatened.

There would be no stopping it tonight.

The image ripped the fabric of her mind and exploded first as a bolt of lightening from a dream she had started long ago but had not finished.

Again, in the bright morning sky Sarah flew like a kite over Patterson's Funeral Home, and again was blown to smithereens, her beautiful young body turned to ash that rained from the heavens.

Alma stirred, fighting the dream, but it would not retreat. In the dark of her bedroom, she let out a cry, then surrendered once more.

The ash was now falling amid flaming bits of Sarah's clothing. Electric air crackled and debris drifted, and again, a pair of flames became a set of fiery eyes that remained in the sky, staring.

Half awake and still dreaming, Alma stared back into those eyes. Cleatis's eyes. Yet, what she saw in them at this moment was not his usual hatred or even his anger.

It was fear. Unadulterated terror mixed with all else that was Cleatis Curtis.

Alma bolted up in the bed and threw off the covers, overcome with sudden fury. Rage coursed through her, and she stalked about the room, fighting for calm.

Damn Cleatis. What kind of trouble was he in? And why did she hurt for him? Yet, the fact remained. Looking into those eyes and seeing his fear, she felt a fierce desire to protect him.

A noise in the house told her Vannie was awake, sensing her stress. She quietly slipped back into bed and pulled up the covers, determined to face the dream while it was still accessible. With some effort, she raised her eyes again to Cleatis's.

Gazing there, she saw events of previous months, visions of Cleatis with a young woman, not a local. A confused girl still bound by the emotions of past abuse. Alma saw her driving her old car, then bumping to a stop in front of an old shed, where Cleatis waited with a certain amount of edginess.

But he was a man, and none too advanced. He was no match for the girl. They went together into the shed.

Vertigo overcame Alma, and she gripped the side of the bed, groaning as the dream accelerated—the girl leaving with what she came for, a broken, bleeding face sure to enflame her father—which was what this was really all about.

And then Alma saw the car, an older man at the wheel, and Sheriff Jimmy in the passenger seat. Clearly, she heard the man's words to the sheriff. "We'll take care of this ourselves. It's family business. You see what's going on, so just keep out of our way, okay?"

The sheriff's eyes were noncommittal and thoughtful. Finally, he nodded. "But don't let it get out of hand."

Alma's eyes shot open and she pulled herself up against the headboard.

"Alma? Are you alright?" Vannie stood at the door in her nightgown.

"Vanessa. There's trouble . . ."

Vannie switched on the light and saw the bedclothes in disarray. Saw the wild look in her sister's eyes.

"It's alright, Alma," she said steadily. "You are dreaming in your special way." She watched Alma regain some focus in this world but did not speak again. Alma often dreamed for the two of them, with Vannie protecting her while she was in altered states and she herself receiving the dream through her *sister's intuition.*

She tiptoed to the door, whispering that she'd put on the teakettle.

"Thank you, Sister," Alma managed, watching her go.

Only then did she fully relax against the headboard, putting her fingers to her temples and emptying her mind. What she saw in the blankness sent fingers of ice fluttering down her spine.

Men gathering up crude weapons, a baseball bat, two-by-fours, iron pipes, and a hammer.

It was going to be a bludgeoning.

Without hesitation, Alma dived into the formless depths within herself, there to put out a call. It sounded in her unconscious and resonated in the unconscious of another, who immediately responded to the summons.

Quickly. Quickly.

Alma struggled to get up, but felt weak and sick. She reached out and steadied herself on the bedpost. At last, she was able to rise and put on her robe. As she reached the landing, Vannie came rushing up the stairs, having seen it all by *sister's intuition.*

They had work to do.

Vannie helped Alma down the stairs to the kitchen where a pot of tea in a cozy sat on a table near the hearth. Three chairs had been pulled up to the blazing fire. "We're ready," she said.

A rustle from Sarah's room brought their attention to their apprentice.

Both sisters put their minds toward cocooning her deeper in dreamless sleep, sealing her ears from earthly noises, which would soon be upon them. The house itself seemed to grow more alert, putting protection around the girl that felt like a thick wall of silence. The crackle of flames in the hearth seemed thunderous by contrast.

A tentative knocking at the front door sent Vannie bounding to open it.

"Jimmy," she said matter-of-factly, looking at the distracted man, who was still in uniform and seemed to have no clue as to how he had arrived at the sisters' home in the middle of the night. "Please come in."

Before the Sheriff knew what hit him, he was sitting before the fire, and Alma was pouring him a cup of tea.

"The one thing I'm a bit confused about," she murmured. "Just how long ago did this happen?"

He stared at her. "Did *what* happen?"

She stared steadily back. "You know."

Even as he shook his head, he felt the depths of his mind stirring, saw the images as she pulled them from him. Himself in the car with Inez's father. What he'd agreed to ignore. He had understood the man's feelings, had also known that it would be next to impossible to head off some kind of retaliation from the family. But the man had at least consulted the law, so when trouble came, Jimmy thought it would be kept inbounds.

Suddenly, he wasn't so sure.

"Sheriff," Alma said to him, "look into the fire."

Together, the three turned their eyes to the flames. So much dreaming on this night had opened channels into altered states, making it easier for all to enter. Alma, the dreamer, shared the dream state effortlessly. Images flashed rapidly in the dancing light.

The men were in an old pickup now. Three jammed into the cab, the rest in the truck bed, a couple with two-by-fours propped on their shoulders, all of them fingering weapons that made the Sheriff blanch, especially when an iron pipe hit a palm with intention, and the baseball bat struck a blow against the side of the truck.

"Oh, my God," Jimmy groaned, "how far are they from Cleatis's place?"

"No more than fifteen minutes, I'd say," Alma answered. "They crossed the county line twenty minutes ago."

Jimmy bolted from his chair and headed for the front door on a dead run. Just before he slammed it behind him, he looked over his shoulder and saw both sisters seated beside the fire, staring intently into the flames.

He headed straight for his police car that he'd left in the driveway. The motor was running, the light on top was lit and rotating, and his siren was already wailing. He had no time to be puzzled. He dove into the car and took off.

Inside the parlor, the sisters had not moved or uttered a word. Yet, as the minutes ticked by, things were fast developing inside their fire. The flames were now reflecting a scene of a man on his shabby front porch. He was a man they both recognized as he sat there, uneasily pulling at a three-day growth of beard.

"It's at his feet," Alma said tensely, pointing.

Vannie saw the shotgun lying there horizontal to Cleatis's chair. He'd had one of his hunches then. A strange thing about Cleatis Curtis was his power. For one who gave every appearance of living in an unawakened state, he possessed some pretty advanced instincts. And right now, he knew that trouble was heading his way.

They watched it unfold in blazing clarity as minutes continued to click away. Finally, the truck pulled off the road just half a mile from Cleatis's house where the brush was thick and the dark truck could be secreted in the shadows. The men collected their weapons and started moving up the road fast. With business like this, you didn't waste time. You just did what you came to do and got out of there.

"Come on," the girl's father said at the head of the pack. "Just remember, he's mine. If I need you, I'll tell you."

"Where's Jimmy?" Vannie asked, staring at the men as they walked toward the house.

"Still ten miles away," Alma said.

The men saw Cleatis on the porch, saw him pick up the shotgun, which only heated their blood. So, he knew they were coming, did he, the guilty son of a bitch? And by picking up that gun, he'd just given them all the license they needed to be as rough as they wanted.

"Don't take another step," Cleatis warned, raising his shotgun. "A man's got a right to defend what's his."

"We're of the same mind then," Inez's father said, stepping forward. "I'm here to defend what's mine, too. What kind of a man takes advantage of a girl young enough to be his daughter and then beats the hell out of her?" He kept coming.

Two of his cronies followed behind him, one with a baseball bat and the second with an iron pipe that he kept popping against his hand. The rest of the boys had spread out to surround the house. If Curtis tried to make a run for it, he wouldn't get far.

But Cleatis Curtis had no intention of running anywhere. He'd defended his stills often enough, and if need be, he was prepared to defend himself and his home. "Put down those weapons," he said, "or I'll blow you to kingdom come."

Inez's father stood his ground. "How about my men put down their weapons and you put down your gun? Then you and me fight each other, man-to-man."

The sisters saw the sweat running down Cleatis's throat as he tried to think. He had the gun, but as other men stepped from behind trees and closed in around the porch, he saw he was greatly outnumbered.

"You first!" Cleatis motioned with his gun. "When your boys put down their weapons, I'll put down my gun. And back 'em up, if it's gonna be me and you."

The uneasy pact was slow unwinding, but finally a few of the men threw down their weapons, then a few more, until Cleatis was convinced the entire lot had disarmed. With his shotgun, he motioned the men back.

"I want 'em off my property. Back up to the road."

Inez's father grinned and showed his empty hands. "Sure. No problem. Just me and you, like I said. Put down the gun and step out here."

"Not on your life." Cleatis stepped forward and took aim. "Now git! All a ya!" He had already made a mistake when he fooled with Inez. Now he had just made one with her father. Shadowy forms swooped at him from all directions. His gun went flying as strong hands seized his elbows and locked his arms behind him, opening his body for the first blow that came from Inez's father. And then the second one. Then a flurry of blows, too many to count.

From the sisters' fireside, they watched the escalating violence, one man reaching for the iron pipe he had laid on the ground, another picking up his bat. They heard the crunch of footsteps and the blow of a hammerhead smacking a tree trunk as the men closed in. The girl's father was pummeling Cleatis well below the belt. His lower lip bled from trying to bite back his howls of pain, but he could no longer suppress them. They rang in the sisters' ears.

"Sister, can we intervene?" Vannie asked tensely.

"This mess belongs to Cleatis, and a bit to Jimmy, too. But at least we can even up the odds a little. We owe that to Cleatis."

"Heat," Vannie said at once, her eyes focusing on several hot coals beneath the flames.

"Yes, nice and hot," Alma agreed. She held both hands toward the fire, welcoming the heat into her, then intoned: "Into the bones, under the skin, into the veins . . ."

"AND INTO THE PALMS OF THE HANDS!" both sisters

finished together.

The screaming from the men as they dropped their weapons from blistering hands was accompanied by the wail of an approaching siren. A moment later the squad car barreled into Cleatis's front yard.

Cursing and howling, the men ran for the road. Only Inez's father stood his ground. This time, his fists cut directly into Cleatis's face.

"This is for my girl," he grunted, between blows, making sure to split Cleatis's lip. "There, nice and pretty." Work done, he went running into the shadows after the others.

Even in the fire's glow, the sisters could see that Sheriff Jimmy had lost all of his color.

Without a word, he bent to pick up the groaning man, who could not stand, slipping from the sheriff's grip as he tried to lift him. Jimmy had to lean down again and was trying to get better leverage when the door of the gray house opened. The boy that ran out was Terry Joe.

The sheriff had had a few run-ins with him, but that didn't matter tonight. "Grab his other arm, Terry Joe, and let's get him inside."

Cleatis's left eye had closed up on him. The other one stared hostilely at Jimmy. "Nice of you to finally drop by, Sheriff," he grunted.

"I got here as fast as I could," Jimmy protested. "How was I to know?"

Cleatis gritted his teeth as they pulled him up the steps. The sheriff and Terry Joe walked him past a white-faced Nadine, who held the door open.

Bobby Dean came out then, shoved Jimmy away, and took his daddy's other arm. "We don't need no sheriff here."

The boys half-dragged him inside, but Cleatis's battered face kept turning back to the sheriff. "What happened?" he managed through a mouthful of blood. "You lose your invite to the party?"

Before Jimmy could protest, Cleatis took the last words: "I know what you did. I saw you in the car with him."

The door slammed in the sheriff's face. He stood there looking at the unpainted wood and felt the poverty all around him, a poverty that went deeper than just being without the necessities of life. This kind of poverty depleted the spirit of a man.

A man that Jimmy had not looked after tonight. He shook his head slowly. Like most people, he had been wrong at times in his life, but never before had he known what it was like to be *this* wrong.

"A good thing for a law man to know," Alma murmured. "May he never forget."

"Amen, Sister," Vannie agreed.

Then the sisters closed their eyes, allowing the dying embers to warm them before stumbling off to bed and the cold comfort of a sleep without dreams.

30

A bitterness in the early cold that settled in the nights and lasted into icy mornings set many in Willow Creek and the surrounding counties to complaining of stiffness in joints and aches in muscles and bones. For the most part, the complaining was habit, a tip of the hat to discomfort that had been around for so long it was almost an old friend. Remarks about the "arthur-itis" and the "burrr-situs" got chuckling responses, wry shakes of the head, and mock frowns as people met and greeted each other running the errands of daily life.

For Cleatis, the cold was nothing to laugh about and neither was the effect it had on his deep bruises, broken skin, and aching bones. He couldn't sneer off this hurt like a bad hangover or make it a big joke to share with the guys at the still. Since he didn't want any of them seeing him broken up the way he was, he had been holing up in the shed at the hideout back in the woods, the very one where Inez had come to see him.

He looked out through a crack between the boards of the flimsy shed and watched his brother Harley gunning the truck over the ruts on his way back up to the main road. He'd dropped a sack of food outside today and every day since the beating, but he didn't stay once he was satisfied his brother wasn't dying.

Cleatis didn't make a move to retrieve the sack. Right now, he didn't care if the raccoons and possums got it. His jaw hurt in a way that made him wonder if it was broken. He could move it, but when he did, pain went through every bone in his skull and then shot down his spine like it was fired from a gun. And that shot was the only thing that put a momentary stop on the hurt in his ribs, his legs, and his groin, where one of the bastards had kneed him. He grabbed for the whisky jar. White lightning was his friend now. Maybe it was the only friend he'd ever had.

As the whiskey slid down his throat and into his gut, he was caught off-guard by feelings he didn't like naming and suddenly lost his balance, grabbed for his chair, then fell as it slid from under him, causing him a wrenching jolt that made him scream and curse.

How could he have let this happen, this torment that had no end? The town would be talking about this; everyone would know this new shame on his head. Black despair stole the breath from him, and he fought it with a spew of rage and frustration, adding a blinding headache to his woes. Over and over, he asked himself where he'd gone wrong. When had he lost control? Used to, nobody had paid much attention to him. Now the eyes of the whole town were on his house. His kids. His business.

Everything had changed after those two women got hold of his oldest boy and ran him off and then took his girl to live with them. They made all that commotion coming to get her on the very night his stills got busted up. Was it the commotion that brought the law, or did *they* bring the law with them?

He could get his breath now, energized by the sensation of anger surging up through his body. He pulled himself up and tested his walking skills, clenched and unclenched his hands to see if they could hold a steering wheel. It wouldn't be fun, but he knew he could do it.

He sipped the whiskey slower now and made his way to the food sack on the other side of the door. It was time to get his strength back. He knew where the trouble in his life was coming from and had an idea what he could do about it.

31

Deep in the night, Sarah stirred under her warm blankets. Caught between sleep and the intuition of her magic, she rubbed her arm across her eyes and slowly pushed herself up in bed. Her beautiful room lay in quiet shadows around her, and, listen hard as she could, she could hear no sounds in the house other than the usual settling of its boards and wind moaning through the chimney. Her gaze wandered uneasily toward the window, beyond which she could hear that same dismal wind sawing the bony limbs of the trees.

There was nothing else, yet something drew her from the comfort of her bed and into the reading nook in the far recess of the room. She walked barefoot, shivering a little, and crawled up on the loveseat, balancing on her knees, her hands on the curved back, as she stared through the window behind the seat.

The night was black as death, without a sign of a moon. She could barely see the slant of lawn, yet far in the distance she detected a glint of creamy white. The café, she had always thought, had a light all its own that could shine through utter darkness, like on this night.

Keeping her eyes fixed to that glimpse of white, she could make out nothing else. Probably she had imagined the bending of a shadow, something moving slowly across the face of the cottage-style café.

For several moments she didn't move, hardly breathed, so intent was she on something she sensed rather than saw. Finally she shook her head, convinced that her too fanciful imaginings had deceived her. It wouldn't be the first time. She had awoken one night and had a very sensible conversation with her rocking chair before falling soundly asleep once again.

Slipping back across the room, she plowed into her feather mattress and pulled the covers snugly around her before once again laying her head on her pillow. She composed herself for sleep, but her usual alignment with the calming energies that flowed so easily through this room was absent. Instead, she felt worried for no good reason.

Out of synch with the universal flow.

A kernel of fear formed in her chest. Whatever was happening, she didn't like it. Heart pounding, she called on her unseen council—the ancients, the weavers of destiny and dreams, the sublime beings who always listened when called in the spirit of caring, compassion, and obedience to the highest law: with harm to none.

Yet instead of the calm that always followed this summoning, Sarah felt only urgency.

Flooded in panic, she got back out of bed, this time swiftly, her feet scrambling around on the floor, feeling for her bedroom slippers, only to immediately take them back off and run first to turn on the light and then to the closet for a warm coat and shoes. Still in the icy grip of fear, she nevertheless remembered her flashlight from her bedside table, and almost ran from her room and to the stairs.

She thought of the sisters halfway down. They probably would wish her to wake them, but they needed their sleep after the long hours they both worked. Besides, how silly would she feel if she woke them for nothing?

Biting her lip, she continued on down the stairs with new resolve. The sisters had vested her with their trust. They had taught her so much, took her on as an apprentice, and initiated her into magic. She owed them everything. In the unlikelihood there was danger, she would not let them down. She would put up her shields and disarm any wrongful action.

Walking from the stair landing, she passed into the front room and then into the dining room and living room, tiptoeing past the big bedroom where Vannie slept. She quietly opened the front door and stepped out into the dense blackness.

The cold stabbed her like a thousand ice picks. She gagged on frigid wind and for a moment was unable to breathe. Then finally she grasped the frozen railing of the porch and stepped carefully down the iced-over steps leading down from the stoop.

Avoiding the slippery walkway, she walked carefully across the lawn, feeling the winter grass crunch under her feet. Now that she was in the darkness, she could see more than from her window—the bare limbs of the trees, the dormant weeping willow that separated the lawn from the gravel parking lot.

Something stopped her from turning on her flashlight. Better, she thought, to be invisible. Even the sound of her heels grinding into the gravel below the lawn made her jump. She wanted to not only be invisible in the shadows but also as silent as air. Walking up the little hill, she soon found herself on the narrow island of grass looking across the road to the white-adobe café.

What she saw caused her to freeze. Trembling so hard she could hardly stand, she turned on her flashlight and stood wagging it with both hands, shining it in all directions. The windows of the café had been smashed. Chards of glass lay over the frozen ground, mixed with a stream of liquid. The front door had been opened from the inside, and a dark figure could be seen splashing something from a can over tables, counters, walls . . . everything in sight.

Rooted to the spot, she could not make a sound, yet she felt mesmerized by the grunting, thrashing noises that came through the front door. A long moan issued forth, like that of a wounded beast caught between rage and despair.

Then a line of fire exploded down the middle of the café. A loud explosion followed, drowning out all but the bare echo of a scream from inside. Billowing smoke rolled through windows and the front door.

By now Sarah was crying. She had recognized that man struggling about with the big can, splashing kerosene on the counter, interior doors, and walls. But she was still unable to move, even when she saw his darkened figure lunge through the door. Billowing with smoke, he staggered out and ducked for cover just as The Two Sisters' Café exploded into flames from top to bottom.

In shock, Sarah felt the roar of heat in her face, registered the panic and hurt inside her, barely noticing that her hands were raised and that she had begun to chant. As if by guidance, she called on the most powerful energies first, those of divine love, then of grace and majesty of spirit, invoking protection, light. She stumbled on the words asking for forgiveness, then somehow carried on, remembering that the sisters said it was second in power only to love and essential for all change.

On she chanted, forcing back desperation and despair, summoning the members of her inner council and calling on the Ancient Ones for Protection of the Ancestry and the Cauldron Women to bring healing and comfort and magic. And still the café burned. Face streaked in tears, Sarah kept saying the words, yet heard an explosive *BOOM* as ceilings collapsed and walls fell in. A deafening roar told her that the gas tanks had exploded and the fire raged to new intensity, and still she held her arms high, even as her knees buckled and she dropped to the ground.

She felt she had been here for hours, years even, watching the end of a world she had come to love like no other. She had failed the sisters, and it was her own *father*, her very own father, who had splashed the kerosene and struck the match. She watched him now, scurrying back toward his truck, dragging a foot behind him and holding one arm at a funny angle.

Lost in a storm of hopeless tears, she buried her face in her hands. And cried, and cried, and cried.

At first she didn't feel the hands on her shoulders or hear the soft voices calling to her through the roar.

"Sarah?"

"Dear one?"

Instead of comforting her, the voices caused another outburst from her depths that collapsed her, like the ruined building. But the hands held on, steadied her as she turned to look up into the sisters' concerned eyes.

"I . . . I'm sorry, Sisters. I tried so hard to stop him. Daddy. I thought I could, but . . . but my magic . . ." Her tears choked her until she had to spit out the words. "My magic wasn't strong enough. I didn't do it good enough! I tried. I really did try. I'm sorry." There were no more words; she was overcome with grief.

The world suddenly went silent. Bewildered, Sarah studied the two gentle faces above her. There was no sound of her father's truck or of roaring flames. It was so still she could hear her own heart beating.

"Darling," Alma said gently, bending to dry her face. "You are wonderful."

Sarah bitterly shook her head. "I tried to stop him. With my magic. But . . . but . . . it's all gone. Everything's gone!"

Vannie crouched in front of her and smiled comfortingly. "Sometimes a magician doesn't even realize her own power."

"But . . ." She fought their hands that patiently turned her toward the café, but felt herself revolving until she faced the charred remains of the . . .

She blinked and looked again.

The café stood before her, its walls pristine, unmarked by fire or smoke. There was not a trace that anything had happened except for a kerosene can in front of the building.

Her heart thundered. "Did I *imagine* it burned?"

"Ah, child," Vannie murmured. "That is a more profound question than you realize. Our reality is only an interpretation of what is real. It is filtered through our beliefs and expectations. What we experience is always a product of imagination, a blend of what is real and how we perceive it. Did the café burn? Yes it did, and now, thanks to you, no, it didn't. You have worked exceptional magic tonight. Reality is fluid until the moment it is observed, then it becomes set in stone. Only the very few can change an event once it has been observed into reality, but this you have done tonight.

"Can you sustain this level of choice? *That* will be the question and your challenge. What will you imagine to be real in coming days, and how strong will be your focus? These are the more important questions."

Even now Sarah quaked with shame, remembering her father, deformed in his rage and negativity, performing the atrocity against the café.

"You are a powerful magician, Sarah," Vannie said with authority. "Stand tall and appreciate the fact that you changed an outcome, stopped your father's intended action and sent it back to the hell from which it came, moving it out of this world back into his demented dreams. He may try again, but for now you have prevented a nightmare reality from occurring. Take heart in the courage of your mother, which is part of you."

Sarah's spirits lifted at mention of her mother, but still she was afraid of her father. Afraid of all that had happened. Maybe she had just gotten lucky this time. Maybe next time . . .

She shivered and vowed never again to let down her guard.

32

Through November, the rumor dug its feet into the land and became fact. When you read the ad in *The Hole In The Wall*, your own local newspaper, you had to believe it. The circus was coming to town, would open at the LaGrange Fairgrounds on the first Thursday in December and play through three weekends. Rumor had it that a couple of local men had found jobs mucking out the elephants' quarters.

"I might take on helping with the tight-wire act," commented Donnie Marble, who was known to walk a wicked straight line with two pints of whiskey sloshing around inside him, "but damned if I'm gonna shovel shit."

"Dung," Carolyn Houseman corrected him.

"Call it what you want," Donnie said, "but I ain't shoveling it."

Excitement ran high, even if it was privately admitted that this little circus had a "Big Top" less than half the size of the Shriner's Auditorium in Louisville, where the "real" circus performed every year.

Still, this smaller, less prestigious circus that had never come through these parts in anyone's memory had a unique charm. There was something raw about it, something that danced along the nerves of children and grown-ups alike.

The Patagonian Circus Of Stars arrived on schedule, held a parade through LaGrange led by a woman in spangles sitting on top of an elephant, and opened for business on the first Friday evening in December.

Alma and Vannie decided to wait for the last weekend, close early on that Sunday afternoon, and take Sarah to the final performance.

"The last show is always the best one," Alma assured Sarah Friday night as they carried sandwiches to the crowd just back from the first show.

Sarah turned clouded blue eyes to Alma's face. "Why don't you and Sister Vannie go? I could look after things," she finished vaguely.

"What things, darlin'?"

"Just . . . things."

Alma didn't press any further. She and Vannie were all too aware that Sarah had remained on guard since her father's attempt to destroy the café. Since that night, the child had never really relaxed. The sisters were apt to peek into her room at any hour and find her on her knees staring over the back of the loveseat, her sleepy eyes straining to see through the window and across the road to where the café stood shrouded in shadows.

To no avail, they tried to remind her that she had used her magician's powers with excellence and that her focused intent would hold to protect the café, whether she was there or not. Elevated resonance, they told her, was more powerful than standing on guard. Yet, they full well understood her dread and her reluctance to leave her post.

The weekend passed and the following week as well, with more and more excited descriptions of the circus performances, and the final weekend loomed ahead with Sarah even more steadfast in her decision to remain behind. The sisters must go without her, she declared over and over.

Still, Vannie and Alma noticed her wistful face when the Taylors described the Flying Maldoni family and their fearsome somersaulting in midair from trapeze to trapeze. And her excitement when customers came in wearing circus hats, carrying colorful programs showing clowns with big red noses and the amazing Tumbling Turners and beautiful ladies in sparkling silver costumes that some of the women called scandalous.

The café was quiet on Saturday night with so many off at the circus. When the sparse dinner crowd thinned, Alma slipped into the kitchen and made cotton candy. The jukebox was going, and the upstairs dining room was half full of the last of the diners when she came out of the kitchen into the counter area with a tray. It was loaded with rolled-up newspaper cones that were filled with clouds of spun candy in a sugary myriad of colors.

After one quick glance at the spun candy, Sarah turned away and busied herself examining coins from the cash register, looking through her magnifying glass at the dates on pennies, dimes, and nickels and comparing them to the sisters' list of valuable coins. She would find out one day that these coins had been tucked away to help send her to college.

"Here's a silver dime." Sarah put the dime beside several copper pennies that were lying in a separate pile. "I 'spect I've found ten of these this week alone."

"Good practice for you," Alma said. "Finding real metal amongst the fake sharpens the eye of a young alchemist." She set the tray of cotton candy by the cash register and bent over Sarah's small stash, noting that the child's gaze was irresistibly drawn toward the confection as she continued silently with her work. A moment later the screened door between café and gas station opened, and Vannie came in from pumping gas into a traveling salesman's car. Andy Poole was on a late dinner break, and his two cronies, left to watch over things, had fallen asleep in their rockers. Even the salesman's tires running over the cord and triggering the customer bell hadn't roused the lazy coots.

"What a tale that salesman can weave," Vannie said, pleased at finding a fellow storyteller of the first water. "Would you believe the motel room he slept in last night had a snake along its beams that must've been forty feet long with a mouth the size of two manholes? That poor man's getting tired now but still jumpy as a cat. He asked me if our rooms had any snakes, and I said, 'No more than usual,' but he drove on . . . Oh, what's this?" She peered at the tray of cotton candy.

"Fresh off the stove," Alma said, watching Sarah frown as Vannie reached over the tray, her hand hesitating over the pink-and-blue swirled cone.

"Now I wonder," Vannie said, "if I'd fancy this one or the red-and-white. Hmmm. I think, after all, I'll take the red. Though the pink one is very tempting, isn't it now?" Her hand swayed for a second, just before Sarah lost her self-control and grabbed the pink-and-blue cone.

"Since you want the red," the apprentice said, "I guess I'll go ahead and take the pink-and-blue."

"Good idea." Vannie extracted the red cone from the tray.

"Go ahead, Sarah," Alma urged. "Take a big bite."

But the fastidious little tongue was already in delicate motion, always after the taste before taking the big bite. A real scientist of life—that was Sarah. She frowned as the wisp of cotton candy dissolved on her tongue, then tried again. Once more, the candy evaporated.

"What kind of dumb stuff is this?" she asked, trying again. Once again, the candy disappeared, leaving behind an unappealing, gritty sweetness.

"They'll be selling it at the circus when we go tomorrow," Vannie said, poking her tongue into a cloud of red and white.

It seemed to the apprentice that Vannie had somehow gotten a real taste of the candy. She saw a wisp of red lying on the sister's tongue for an instant before she swallowed it down.

A dreamy quality descended on the café, and Cathy's Clown came on the jukebox. Upstairs, a couple of teenagers rose to dance slowly across the oak floor.

"Reality," Alma said, "is as real as you're willing to make it. It can vanish in a *poof*, or it can be as hard to chew as a piece of leather. When you're a child, it's difficult to fathom that you are creating your own reality, spinning it like a web around yourself. Most young minds can't grasp this, and so to them, events appear to just *happen*. But as one gains perspective, it is possible to start creating reality consciously.

"We do this by facing obstacles along the way, many of which we chose ourselves, between lifetimes, in the space between worlds."

Sarah's eyes marveled. "You mean in empty space?"

"My, no, it's full of soul and spirit, of guidance and alliance. Universal Force joined with Divine Creation. From that space, we spin out realities that are just as solid as . . ."

" . . . cotton candy," Vannie finished and bent to take another mouthful.

Sarah stared at the candy that didn't evaporate at all, but stayed on Vannie's tongue, clouds of red and white, as colorful as a clown's painted face.

"Take a bite, come on, try again, Sarah," Alma urged. "You will see that reality can change, if you let it."

Sarah's first instinct was to disobey. But instead, she obligingly raised the paper cone and stuck her tongue forcefully into a pile of pink-and-blue confection. Startled, she began to nibble at the candy that lay like froth on her tongue.

"Nice, isn't it?" Vannie smiled. "You can have more at the circus tomorrow night. And other kinds of things just as magical. Alright?"

Sarah searched for the stubbornness to refuse. She needed to stay here, on guard, watching the café every minute.

But magic was in the air, and she was first and foremost an apprentice to its art, an initiate. She could feel it bouncing off the ceilings at her, sending chills along her arm and into her hand where she still held the cone of spun candy, and could no more resist its pull than drawing her next breath.

"Alright," she said, smiling up from her cone in spite of herself.

The next afternoon at the café, people talked of circuses, and children came back from the early show loaded with balloons and souvenirs that made Sarah's eyes goggle. Her reluctance had been replaced with almost too much excitement to bear and was building every moment. She who had never even been to a county fair was going to a real circus, complete with clowns and . . . maybe much more. Or so she intuited.

The time finally came to close the café and head toward the fairgrounds. Sarah sat in the backseat of the Buick, for a while looking back toward the café to reinforce her spell of protection, then turning forward and shrieking as the distant lights of the Big Top splashed the blackening countryside with glitter.

The Buick wound its way into the fairgrounds, inching forward in a long line of cars that pulled through the gates, where Vannie paid a dollar to park in the meadow adjoining the main tent.

"Come on!" Sarah called excitedly, nudging the sisters into a stream of friends and neighbors, all heading toward the Big Top. Belle and Earl Taylor were in line in front of them. Belle's star sapphire ring caught Sarah's eye, tempting her with thoughts of faeries and portals to other worlds, but she soon looked away from it and back up at the taut canvas tent tops held in place by thick ropes. Her eyes followed the ropes down to where they were tied to stakes pounded into the earth.

Outside the main tent were program and drink peddlers, as well as booths selling lion tamer kits with whips and toy guns, spangles, glitter hats, postcards, toy animals, and other paraphernalia, along with food booths featuring lemonade and soda, cotton candy in paper cones, ice cream, hot dogs, sausages, and fried potatoes and onions.

Sarah stopped at the largest booth, positioned directly in front of the center doors leading inside to the main event, *THE SPECTACLE OF STARS*! The display consisted of a large colorful board, covering about five square feet, with tiny posts attached to it, many of which were affixed to harnessed chameleons and to the small vials of enriched water that kept them alive.

"Triceratops," Sarah breathed, pointing to one of the small creatures, frozen on a pattern of green forestry. "Look, Sisters! Doesn't it look like a little dinosaur?"

The chameleon had strange eyes, independently moving in their sockets and seeing in two directions at once. One of them rolled toward Sarah. The tiny creature panted, its small, forked tongue moving in and out. Its V-shaped feet clung to a serration of the board, its tail in a tight spiral.

Vannie leaned in closer to look at the creature's gaping mouth. "The little guy's too hot," she murmured to the fast-talking man in charge of the display, a wad of money wrapped around his fingers.

The salesman looked past her, swiftly unclipping a chameleon from the board and putting it on the sweater of a small girl, who beamed as her mother pinned it in place. The child skipped on, her excited squeals peppering the air, her mother and older brother laughing as they hastened to keep up with her.

"Now then, little lady," the salesman said, turning to Sarah. "Have you picked out the one you want?"

Alma, who had been silent, jabbed her thumb at the booth's proprietor. "How about *him* on a leash, Sarah? With a vial of water pinned to *his* leg, of course."

The man chortled. "Them things don't know they're alive, don't waste a thought on 'em." Plucking one off the board to give Sarah a closer look, he turned back to find Alma in his face. He stood frozen—hit full force by the image he saw in her eyes—himself pinned to a mountainous board and a giant-sized child pointing to him.

I'll take that one!

Seeing his terror, Alma murmured, "I apologize. Sometimes I get carried away."

All the while Sarah's eyes had never left the tiny creatures pinned to the board.

The man, recovering himself, said somewhat uneasily, "Course, they make great pets. Pretty and unique. You can invite all your friends over and show 'em what a swell souvenir you got for yourself."

"Whichever one she picks out," Vannie said, "will die before the sun comes up."

"If it does die," the man said, "then you can use the body to rid yourself of curses. That's the legend."

Tears sprang into Sarah's eyes at the thought of the tiny dinosaurs dying sad and lonely deaths. Especially the one that had first called to her and was still staring at her from the upper corner of the board. More than anything, she wanted to touch it. To let it sit on her blouse and feel her heartbeat and know it was safe with her. Maybe her love could keep it alive. Maybe she could find it something to eat.

She gulped back a sob. The sisters must have heard it, because Alma gave the man some money, pointed out the chameleon Sarah had been staring at, and knelt down to pin it to her collar.

"Hi, Little Joe," the apprentice said solemnly, seeing that he was looking into her eyes. The name had come instantly; she had no need to question it. "Don't worry anymore. I'll take care of you." She fanned Joe to cool him off with her program as the sisters ushered her through the open doors.

"Bottom tier, to your left, second row in the box seat section," the ticket taker said with that edge of respect reserved for those who had spent the most money.

It was all so overwhelming to Sarah. Huge. Alien. She couldn't take it all in. The odor of wild animals poured up her nose, different from any smell she'd ever known. It seemed too acrid, too rank, for civilized people. It reeked of breeding, territory marking, and species identification. Of urine, of animal sweat. Sarah instinctively reached into her pocket to touch her black stone, her third present from the morning of the cherries. As usual, it was an anchor, giving her something to hold onto when her excitement was rising so fast that she felt she might come out of her shoes and lift into the sky.

With the sisters' permission, she had torn open her black package on the night she returned from Faerie Realm. Somehow, she had known it would be a stone. Also, that it would be as black as the wrappings around it. What she had not expected was the feeling she got when touching it or gazing at the odd, white markings etched onto its face. She felt sure they were ancient writings.

Sitting now under the Big Top with Little Joe on her collar, she rubbed the stone between fingers and thumb and surveyed the crowd around her. The tent was almost full with late arrivals hurrying to their seats. She saw Elmer Bailey proudly guiding Edith toward a well-situated box nearby. The sisters nodded to him as he helped his wife get settled in the better of their two seats, closest to the center with a clear view of the whole arena.

A hush fell over the crowd as a brassy *Ta-dah!* of music sounded. Sarah clasped her stone as the lights dimmed, and a spotlight landed on a cordoned-off part of the bleachers over to the left where tiers of musicians were stationed, sustaining a musical note that trembled over the crowd. The band was dazzling in white uniforms decorated with gold ropes and epaulets and matching military hats with gold plumes. As the bandleader sharply lowered his white baton, the musicians struck up a marching song. Trombones slurred their metal slides; brassy trumpets marked the pace, while clarinets, flutes, and piccolos trilled high notes. Snare drums scratched and *tap-tapped*, while a bass drum drove the cadence smartly and cymbals smashed. Tubas snapped from side to side, snorting melodies of their own, and a pretty young girl about Sarah's age struck a metal triangle, raining silver stars over all.

The march came to an end, and the dark room fell silent. Sarah felt her heart pick up speed. The circus was about to begin.

Sure enough, the bandleader pointed his stick and drums rolled. Spotlights fell on the center area of the far side of the tent.

In a crash of cymbals, tent flaps opened and a Ringmaster strode into the spotlights, letting the flaps close behind him. He lifted his top hat, flashed a blazing smile, bowed this way and that in his tight white britches and dashing black, long-tailed coat, and then brought his microphone to his mouth.

"LADIES AND GENTLEMEN, BOYS AND GIRLS!!! CHILDREN OF ALL AGES!!!" he boomed over the crowd. "THE PATAGONIAN CIRCUS OF STARS PRESENTS FOR YOUR ENJOYMENT, A ONCE-IN-A-LIFETIME SPECTACLE OF SPECTACLES!!!"

Lights came up under the Big Top to reveal three great circles laid side by side in the arena, defined by low, curved wooden markers. Enclosing the three circles was an oval sawdust track, passing in front of the bleachers all the way around.

"The circles are the playing areas, Sarah," Vannie murmured. "They're called rings, and there will be different acts going on in all of them. Keep an eye on all three, so you don't miss anything."

Alma chuckled, her eyes on the Ringmaster, who had moved to the middle of the center ring. He leapt up on a low wooden platform and boomed:

"SO WITHOUT FURTHER ADO, YOUR PARADE OF STARS!!!"

The tent flaps behind him flew open again and stuck there, as if by magic, and the band began to play.

And here came the Patagonian Circus of Stars, marching to the music and parading around the track. First came the tumblers, doing cartwheels, handsprings, and flips. Then young women, dazzling in pastel-colored tights and net skirts with glittering bodices, leapt onto the shoulders of muscled young men and posed there, followed by clowns balancing plates on tall sticks and men juggling wooden clubs. Next came the show horses, tails plaited, adorned with spangles. Sarah's jaw dropped open at seeing the circus riders balanced straight-legged on the horses' bare backs, smiles as big as moons.

It was all so . . . like cotton candy that melted on your tongue before you could actually swallow it.

She blinked. Something had flashed in her periphery, disappearing before she could focus. It may have been the clown throwing small prizes to squealing children. Or perhaps it was one of the trapeze artists, or the lady scrambling along with the barking dog act. It dissolved in a blur, as Sarah's vision fixed beyond them on several elephants coming through the flaps. The first one was a giant, obviously queen of the herd, swaying to the music as she regally lumbered along, lifting her trunk in greeting to the cheering children.

Sarah watched the young girl in the light-blue leotard who rode on the queen's neck, bare legs tucked behind the huge floppy ears, and thought she must be the happiest girl on Earth.

The next two elephants were slightly smaller and wore suede harnesses cut with stars and crescent moons. They shambled along less enthusiastically than their queen and were followed by a still smaller calf perhaps just a few years old.

"There they go," Sarah said regretfully as the beasts plodded by, each holding the tail of the one in front with its trunk, forming a royal daisy chain following the big matriarch around the track.

CRAAACK!

The crowd gasped. Sarah turned just in time to see a lion tamer rewinding his long black whip into loops. Then he slashed it again. Behind him, three cages, each painted with circus scenes, rolled along. In the first, a huge tiger paced darkly, eyeing the crowd and tasting the air through its open mouth. In the next, a big yellow lion sat on his haunches and snarled, sending shivers up Sarah's spine. An even larger lion occupied the third cage. He shook his black mane and raced at the bars, his roars filling the air and inciting shrieks from the crowd.

By now, a tent flap had opened across the way and the performers at the head of the parade were disappearing through the dim opening, others peeling off and heading toward the three horizontal rings.

A small circus boy, about Sarah's age and height, brought up the rear of the parade, walking behind the last cat cage. His turban sported a blue ostrich plume, and he wore harem pants, girded with a sash. A wooden saber hung at his side. The boy's gaze was fierce as he strode along with his hand on his sword hilt, his black eyes glued to the crowd, daring them to exhibit any disrespect as he took long strides to keep up with the cages.

Not disrespect to him, Sarah realized suddenly, *but to the cats.* He was guarding them. How strange to see a boy so small protecting beasts so large and ferocious. The audience chuckled at his giant steps as he went sternly on, but Sarah sensed that he was not performing for their entertainment. This was no joke to him, not at all.

The next moment she saw proof that she was right.

A teenager in a front row seat suddenly hurled a bag of peanuts at the tiger cage, his shrill voice ringing out in derision. "*Dumb ole cats!*"

Before the word "cats" left the teenager's mouth, the circus boy was running. He sprang in the air, snatched the nuts, and flung them back into the crowd so hard that he fell, sprawling on his haunches in the sawdust. Some of the crowd laughed, but the boy's face showed fury as he scrambled up and raced hotly toward the teenager who had thrown the nuts.

Sarah could hear his thoughts: *You leave them cats be! They're better'n any one a' ya!!!* She felt his emotions pounding in her own chest and wondered how she could bond so closely and so quickly with a total stranger. She could have known him for years. Longer even than the span of her life.

By now the teenager was sliding down in his seat. Disgustedly, the circus boy turned and hurried after the wagons. Much of the parade had already exited through the tent flaps, but the cat cages were only halfway round the track and still within view of the sisters' box.

Midway to catching them, he stopped short, pulled out his wooden sword, and slowly turned around. Then he thrust his sword upward, letting out an eerie, high-pitched *Yi-yi-yi-yi-yi-yi yiiiiiiiiiii*!

The sound rose out of him as feral as anything Sarah had ever heard. At the sight of him stretching toward the sky, head back, his cry rising in pitch, a strange sensation washed over her. She knew this boy, recognized him somehow, and she strained for distant memory. Something called from beyond the limits of her brain. Fragments of fleeting images: A desert youth dressed in flying linens raced a horse across the sand, the same high-pitched cry tearing from his throat. A boy in a leather thong danced under a scorpion sun, his tan face splashed with paint. A girl, with a face like Sarah's own, brought the boy water from an earthen jar.

Yi-yi-yi-yi-yi-yi yiiiiiiiiiii! The sound rose from their throats, warning others of approaching riders. Together, they fled through canyons of dry red rock. Flashes of other times and places, too quick to be captured, collided and receded so rapidly that Sarah almost swooned. Yet, that sound echoed within each image. In answer, a single word rose in her mind that repeated again and again: *Home. Home. Home.*

The word generated a new scene, and she found herself standing among slender trees at the edge of a forest. Across a wide clearing she saw the boy, a dark feather hanging in his long straight hair. On his left forearm was a leather band, and perched on the band was a bird of prey. The boy and the bird both stared at her through time. The boy raised his arm to wave a greeting, even as the great bird spread its wings and started to fly.

Straight at Sarah.

It glided toward her on wings as silent as death. She saw herself in the bird's golden eyes as its talons reached for *her* eyes, which fortunately, she had squeezed shut, protecting them behind her forearms.

Sarah opened her eyes and looked for the great hawk. It was gone. She sat there shaking with a thundering heart, and gradually the sounds of the circus returned. She sensed the sisters on both sides of her and remembered her current life in Willow Creek.

All that other stuff had been just a kind of dream.

She let out a breath and clasped her stone, looking across the Big Top. The last cat cage was stalled at the dark hole between the tent flaps. The turbaned boy strode out and pushed it through the gap, following it into the darkness beyond, even as the Ringmaster leapt back onto the low platform in center ring.

Sarah was surprised how very sad she felt to see the boy go.

Then cymbals crashed, startling her, and once again the Ringmaster boomed:

"AND NOW!!! LADIES AND GENTLEMEN!!! WHAT YOU'VE ALL BEEN WAITING FOR!!! THE PATAGONIAN CIRCUS OF STARS IS PLEASED TO PRESENT IN THE NEAR RING, ON THE HIGH WIRE, MISS MIMI AND HER AMAZING TROUPE, THE MERLINDAS!!! TIGHTROPE WALKERS BEYOND COMPARE!"

Vaguely, Sarah heard him go on about Miss Mimi, *the greatest tightrope artist on Earth*, and other acts in the other rings. But she was still too shaky to register it all. The band played more softly, a haunting tune she had never before heard. Alma seemed to know it and began humming along.

Beside her, Vannie absently held out her bag of peanuts to share. Above them, in center ring, trapeze artists were shimmying up ropes toward platforms near the tent top. They would occasionally stop climbing and strike poses, holding to the ropes by one arm and one leg, turning slowly in the lights. Suddenly, the music swelled.

"Some enchanted evening," Alma sang along with the orchestra. *"You may see a stranger . . ."*

A loud boom drew all eyes to the left ring, where a clown had been shot from a cannon and was landing on a big trampoline held by other clowns who used it to fling him skyward again. Soon the clown, who was obviously a master acrobat, was doing flips and twists, bouncing higher and higher and higher.

A second cannon boom brought Sarah out of her seat.

Whoosh! She was catapulted upward as if she herself had been bounced off a trampoline, but instead of falling back to Earth, she found she now hovered in midair. She could feel her bare toes in her cotton socks as she kicked at nothing and realized she must have flown straight up out of her shoes.

"Sisters," she croaked, aware that no one could possibly hear the muffled sound that rose from her tight throat. "Up here!" She was now about twenty feet high and hung over the track, facing the sisters' box. Looking down, she saw them gazing up at her.

"What's happening?" she shouted. It felt ridiculous to be dangling there in front of the whole audience, though no one seemed to notice her other than the sisters.

Wait a minute! WAIT A MINUTE!

She squinted harder and saw herself still sitting down there on the seat between Vannie and Alma. She watched the other Sarah take a peanut from Vannie's bag.

"You may see a stranger . . ."

"Sensory overload," Vannie said. "Opens up the sight, don't you know? Puts you at the brink of . . . Well, that will be for you to discover, should you choose to go on through."

"Go on through *where*?" Sarah looked around curiously but could see nothing to go through.

"Why, the portal, of course. After all, it's you that's got it open!"

"Across a crowded room . . ." Alma sang.

A light wind in the tent drifted into an undulating dance, like show horses with bobbing plumes cantering around the track, while Alma began humming a different melody from the one played by the band, a counter song that fit between the notes of the other. The two melodies wove together in an odd, grinding braid, spawning a dissonant *thrum* like bagpipes on a far-off shore.

The arena tilted and spun, sending showers of light spilling across the tent. Dazzled, Sarah thought of cotton candy spinning into a cone, colors swirling together. From a distance, she heard Vannie call: "Child! You know of chalice, sword, and wand. You have need of a shield! Look for one!"

With that, Sarah spiraled upward through the helix of cotton candy lights that shimmered like the tresses of an Ancient Faerie Queen, rising higher and higher, soaring toward the ceiling of the Big Top.

Bobbing there like a balloon escaped from the fingers of a young child, she felt her head bumping gently against the sloping canvas ceiling and wondered if she could ever get down again.

"Hello there, Sarah."

Her head whipped around, images of lion tamers and whips, boys with feathers in their hair, and tigers and elephants flying through her head.

A portal. Vannie had asked if she wanted to go through. She couldn't remember saying yes, but she must have. Inside the circus tent, the colors had taken on unearthly tones, and the sounds had been altered by soft echoes and the feeling that they came from afar.

"Hello, child." Butterflies flew in Sarah's stomach as she recognized the voice of her Ancient Faerie friend. She would have known her anywhere. The faerie's delicate form was only inches from her, perched on the trapeze artists' highest platform, overlooking the center ring. Centuries were honored in the soft creases on her face, yet eternal youth shone from her eyes. Not even the lilies in Alma's garden could approach her beauty. The old one reached out a translucent hand and pulled Sarah to sit beside her.

"Looks like we meet in all the best places." The faerie's clothing was laced with tiny stars in keeping with the circus. Glitter sparkled in her yards of silvery hair. She smoothed her gown and made more room for the child on the narrow seat beside her. "No portal like a circus, is there, child? Such a place! Illusion upon illusion! Where better for an apprentice sorceress to cross through the veils!" She turned from the spectacle to Sarah. "So, tell us, dear. To what do we owe this visit? Why have you come to us?"

Sarah opened her mouth and then closed it again. She didn't have an answer since finding the portal had been largely an accident, as far as she could tell.

"An accident!" The faerie smiled, seeing Sarah's eyes go wide at having her mind so easily read. "Well, that shows aptitude. We see you brought the whole circus with you. We're all most grateful." She gestured with a delicate hand, and for the first time, Sarah saw that the Big Top was packed with beings from the world of *Other*.

"Don't be surprised, dear. After all, a portal works both ways, don't you know?"

Sarah was beyond speech, transfixed on gnomes, faeries, and elves tumbling among the circus performers. Some had shaped themselves like coiled whips or trapeze bars, insect-type legs and arms sticking out of them. Water sprites teased the youngest elephant, spraying her with cool moisture as she danced on a stool beside her elders in the right ring.

The Ancient One cleared her throat. "You say your coming here was an accident, dear. But are you sure you're not running from something in your world?"

"Who, me?" Sarah asked, wide-eyed. "I'm not . . . oh, look!" Below her, she spotted the sisters sitting with the other Sarah. A gnome disguised as a clump of sawdust had climbed into Vannie's lap and was stealing peanuts from her bag.

"Very clever, isn't he? But you were saying?"

Sarah could feel the faerie's eyes studying her as she started to squirm. "It's just that bad things happen sometimes, and I don't know how to fix them."

"Why do you think it's your job to fix them?"

"Well, I . . . I'm learning magic. Magicians are supposed to be good at fixing things, aren't they? But when something bad happens, I don't always know how to . . ."

How could she make the faerie understand? There wasn't enough magic in the *world* to save her mama and brothers and sisters from Daddy or stop hawks from stealing baby squirrels. She had saved the café once, but her whole body had been stiff ever since from worry that she might not save it the next time.

"It's too big," she finished quietly.

"Such a trap the ego lays, Sarah! It whispers that since you've learned a little magic, you're supposed to solve all the problems. You aren't the first apprentice to fall into *that* hole."

"But I want to save the café," Sarah whispered. "More than anything. The sisters have been so good to me. And I want to help Mama. She gets so sad. And so do Lillie and Annabelle and Terry Joe and . . . everybody. And I can't do anything about it."

"Patience, girl. We can only give what we're ready to give and what others are ready to receive. Sometimes, that means we do nothing. Good for the humility, don't you know?"

Seeing the child's wrinkled brow, the faerie laughed. "Of course, there will be times when your magic surges and all your wishes come true immediately. This is the joy of the magician's life. Your challenge is to be patient when the magic wanes."

"It doesn't wane for you or the sisters!"

"Not so." The faerie pulled the child close to her surprisingly sturdy frame. "All magicians have times of feeling powerless, Sarah. This is not a sign of weakness. After all, we are but pinpoints of consciousness inside an Infinite Oneness."

"But what if I don't have enough talent?"

The faerie looked tenderly into the apprentice's solemn face. "It is never a question of how much talent we have been given, child. A spark of divine creativity has been placed within each of us. The few who answer the call to develop it fully are magicians, plain and simple, whether they would call themselves such or not. Have courage, dear. Be slow to abandon the light within you. It speaks to you of destiny."

She laid a hand on Sarah's shoulder. "When you feel separated and lost and absent of your power, do what the great magicians do: Feel love, even the tiniest spark of it. Then hold to that love until the light returns."

Hold to your love till light returns.

The phrase repeated in her like a metronome. The trapeze artists below flew to the sound of it.

Swish. Hold to your love. *Swoosh*. Till light returns.

Swish, tumble, catch.

There was so much to love. The sisters at the counter, a doll before them, making magic out of flour paste and locks of hair. Vannie telling stories by the hearth of Camelot magic, of Lemurian mists, of Atlantis reached through portals of fire. Alma teaching dream magic, showing how to dream other dreamers awake.

Sarah smiled, picturing Mama holding out her arms to her.

Swish. Hold to your love.

Two trapeze artists swung below her now: a young woman, pretty and quick, on the swing just below, and a muscled man on a trapeze across the way who hung by his legs to catch her as she somersaulted to him. A flip, and back she'd go, just in time to catch her own trapeze as it returned to her, each time adding an extra revolution to her spin.

Swish, double tumble, catch.

Sometimes when Sarah was with the sisters, she felt time stop. Then she'd touch a love that was forever. Why did the bad times make her forget the great ones? Because she'd thought that good magicians had all the answers and never had bad times?

Swoosh, triple tumble, fly!

But it wasn't so! The Ancient Faerie had just told her that all magicians had dark moments.

Swish. Swoosh. Hold to your love.

Other artists lined up on the platform below, adding more performers as the act progressed, swinging out to meet the catcher. One, two—now a third, this one another catcher, who delivered tumbling bodies to and fro and then onto the platforms.

Swish. Swoosh. Swish. Swoosh.

The rhythm moved into her. It was like jumping rope at school. You had to watch the dance of the ropes and feel when to jump in. Swinging on trapezes was the same. For two cents, Sarah thought boldly, she'd prove it.

What a silly idea.

"Go ahead, child," the faerie whispered into her ear. "You have made an important shift in awareness. Sear it in your memory with an act of celebration."

Sarah looked at her to be sure she understood correctly. And, at the faerie's nod . . .

. . . She jumped!

She didn't think at all, just turned and dropped and reached for the trapeze that was swinging toward her and caught it easily.

Just like on the playground!

She felt a smile spread across her face. Heard a little shriek of joy, then realized it was coming from her own throat. She pumped higher and higher, seeing the strong arms of the catcher on the other swing reaching out for her.

Free.

Up, up, up. And somehow, she knew just when to let go. She was flying. *Flying!* In cartwheels, back and forth, caught in strong hands and passed to the second catcher, the whole troupe now getting into the act. Taking care of her like a little sister. Making her safe. She careened like a flying porpoise through the lights of the Big Top.

She spun higher and faster, her pinafore flapping in ruffles around her. She soared. Sailed. Again, she was a fledgling sorceress flying up the hill to land in the sisters' backyard, her mind at one with the soaring hawk's, a lopsided moon in her face.

And again, a mother squirrel barked in distress as the hawk stole her baby.

It was that thought that spoiled her timing. Jarred her into self-consciousness for the split second that it took to make her fingers slip beyond the catcher's grasp. Her stomach turned inside out; her fingers clawed the air. Below her, sawdust rose fast to meet her. She braced for the crash.

Instead, her cheek found something soft. She felt herself cushioned against something warm, something smelling of lilacs. Something with a heartbeat.

"Gotcha!"

The Ancient Faerie had plucked her out of the air and now carried her effortlessly back up to their perch near the tent top.

Sarah did not know there were tears in her eyes till the faerie reached over and brushed one away.

"Is your stone still safe in your pocket, child?"

The question sent her to digging into the cotton folds of her dress. Probing, she felt the rock twisted in the deep pocket amid Vannie's reinforced stitching and brought it out to look at the carvings etched by nature's hand. She wondered for the hundredth time why it was the wings of a hawk she saw among the writings there.

"Ah, yes, Hawk," the faerie murmured, peering down. "The messenger! He screams to look with keener vision, listen with sharper hearing. But to you, Hawk means even more. Every magician has one animal that is their special ally, Sarah. The spirit of this animal enhances the magician's power. Do you understand what spirit is?"

Sarah blurted, "Is it wind and fire?" She was astonished by her own words.

The faerie smiled. "You knew that, did you? It is that, yes. It is the breath that fills us with aliveness, the wind that sets us free, the fires of will and passion and individuality and decisiveness! Hawk's spirit is strong and swift. He is your power animal, child. Your companion in magic."

Sarah found herself trembling. "But . . . but he kills things."

"Is this not the way of your world? He challenges you to look at death and loss. How better to gain power over fear? Hawk, the messenger, brings your fears to light. He screams of power locked up behind those fears. Power that can be yours again, should you care to take it back. Next time he comes to you, do not run. Let him take you beyond fear. We promise, you will not go alone."

Sarah's gaze shifted toward the other Sarah down in the bleachers. Her time with the faerie was coming to a close. She could feel herself being drawn back. Even now, she was aware that she and the faerie were floating lower, down past the trapeze artists in center ring.

In the left ring, Miss Mimi and her troupe tiptoed along the high wire, umbrellas over their heads for balance, then exited by sliding down a sloping wire. Raised arms. Smile. Bow. And out.

The Ancient Faerie mischievously eyed the vacant wire. "How about you and I have a bit of fun, 'ey, Sarah? Before we take you home?"

Holy moly! Sarah found herself teetering alongside the faerie on the high wire. A long pole appeared in her hands, its length horizontal across her body as she tested her balance.

"I think I'm about to fall, Mrs. Faerie."

"If that's what you think, it's likely you will. Belief shapes our world and sets every boundary. Choose new beliefs, and you choose new destinies." Sarah watched as the faerie pitched forward and, without further ado, sailed across the wire on one foot, as steady as a schooner in a breeze, startling Sarah to bolt upright on the wire.

"Come on, Sarah!" As Sarah inched cautiously forward, the faerie continued, "When you feel fearful, choose a different belief, one that sets you free." She grinned. "What would you like to believe at this moment?"

Sarah gulped. "I would like to believe I can stay up here on this wire."

"Then believe it."

The wire immediately became charged under Sarah's feet. As she straightened more confidently, her toes locked into the current that flowed along the wire. She felt it surge up through her legs and rise through her body. Tiny sparks of electricity spewed from her pores. Or was it just the lights of the Big Top reflecting off her skin in a blaze of golden white?

Before she knew it, she and the faerie were frolicking on the wire doing eye-popping feats of balance and agility. Sarah giggled, thinking how funny they must appear. An Ancient Faerie with silvery hair and a little girl in stocking feet, both scooting at top speed along the high wire. Hopping, skipping. She blinked as the faerie did a series of back flips.

It seemed the perfect ending. Sarah felt satisfied. It was time to go home now. She set her pole down, balancing it expertly on the wire.

"Thank you, Mrs. Faerie." She smiled up into the beautiful old face. "I'm ready now."

"Yes, dear, we know."

Looking up from the faerie's eyes, Sarah saw a flurry of motion. Golden lights revealed giant wings overhead that drenched her in feathery shadows. Sarah felt the air grow cool. Felt herself jerked upward. Something strong and hard had her by the back of her neck now. It had been such a sudden blow that it didn't hurt at all.

Hawk. The merciful killer. The old one spoke into her mind. So. Sarah's worst fears had come to pass. The hawk had finally gotten her.

I must be dreaming, Sarah thought hopefully, feeling herself being drawn up through the opening in the tent top. She imagined how she must look, a limp shadow trailing from the bird's long claws.

Not a dream, Sarah, a vision. Give yourself to it. Let Hawk take you to the end of your sight and beyond.

Hawk flew higher, soaring across the full face of the moon, then swooped down closer to the earth. Under them was an expanse of rolling fields. Sarah saw their moon-shadow black against the glowing landscape.

Sarah? What are you doing now?

Flying! I'm flying! She had become part of the night and the sky. Part of the great bird that carried her.

An updraft of air caught the Hawk's wide wings. She sensed the softness of the under feathers, somehow knew what it was to be a chick nestled in their fluff. She would have liked to run her fingers along the hard scaly legs and feel the power flowing through them. But her arms hung limply, unable to do her bidding.

A sudden rise, then they dropped to land on a pile of twigs in a treetop. Stars appeared overhead as the bird folded its wings. Sarah heard a flurry around her, and found herself among the hawk chicks, all babies with spiky quills and open mouths. Her mouth opened with the others, waiting to be fed.

Then she was no longer a hawk chick, nor Sarah either. She was her baby squirrel, wrapped in bands of golden talons. Held down and bound. She looked into the golden eyes, the sharp beak so swift she didn't see it coming.

Sarah?

She couldn't answer. She was being pulled apart in all directions, torn and shredded between great beak and talons. She was poked this way and that, melting warm inside the bodies of the little chicks.

Sarah?

The feeling of melting was delicious beyond anything she'd ever known. She felt too peaceful and happy to even bother a response.

Sarah? Speak to us, child!

The faerie's voice became an irresistible call. Finally, Sarah found the will and the voice to answer.

I'm here, Mrs. Faerie. And I'm not scared anymore.

And with that, Sarah put down her burden. Under the starry night sky, she saw Hawk perched on the highest branch. The chicks below, nestled together, new life melting into them. There was no Sarah to be found.

Mrs. Faerie? It's all over. I'm all gone!

Ah. Then who's talking?

A thousand colored lights exploded in her head. Music from the big top made its way into her senses. *Pop.* She was back in her shoes again, toes against leather, her body slumped between Alma and Vannie. Little Joe looked at her with a lazy eye from his place on her collar. The song from the band was just ending, and with it, Alma's haunting counter melody. The *thrum* slowly died in its wake.

"Some enchanted evening, indeed." Alma smiled at her. "Nothing in the world as good as a circus, is there?"

Sarah blinked and looked up, thinking that she saw a hint of silver light around the highest platform, just above the trapezes. Hard to believe she'd been gone for only the length of a song.

The elephant act had just ended. Watching the elephant matriarch lumber her way from the right ring, moving toward the tent flap opening, Sarah began to regain her equilibrium. The Queen raised her head, gazing toward the sisters' box, then flipped up her trunk, and turned to walk into the dark opening.

A sound accompanied her walk: *Clink. Clink. Clink.* Something of heavy metal. The Queen wore chains.

"That's not right!" Sarah whispered to Little Joe, who seemed to be daydreaming at the moment, held fast in his little collar that had once seemed so cute. He shouldn't be tied up. It wasn't fair.

"May I go outside, please?" She was ready to explain about freeing the little one, but saw from Vannie's face that there was no need.

"Go out the front, turn right. Then right again, and go straight on. You'll find just the right spot." Vanessa moved her feet back so the apprentice could pass.

The air outside was chilly, and she hurried down the row of booths, quiet now that the show was going on. Inside the big tent, lions roared and a whip cracked. She was missing the tamer act, but that wasn't what bothered her. She was worried that Little Joe wouldn't do well out in the cold.

Turn right. Then right again and go straight on. She'd done that. Where was the perfect place she was supposed to find?

Up ahead were the three rolling cat cages, empty now with the cats off doing their show. The smell of them was exciting and wild as she peeked into one cage, then the next. A stir in the back corner of the tiger cage made her jump.

Even as she stared, a mound of black shadow moved from behind the cage. A voice said, "Don't pay no attention to him!"

Sarah froze.

"Just a circus boy in there," the voice continued. "He helps look after the cats."

Turning slowly to stare at the man, she already knew who it was. She'd known that voice her entire life. Sure enough, she found herself face-to-face with her father. Unable to move or speak, Sarah stared up at Cleatis, confused to see a shovel in his hand. It looked dirty, caked with dung. He was flecked with the stuff, too.

"You . . ." Sarah gasped, trying to find voice. The old, familiar, learned panic knocked in her stomach; her pulse pounded. She'd been afraid of this man for so long that she didn't know another way of meeting him. "You work for the circus?" she managed to gasp, wishing someone would appear so that they needn't be alone.

Even in the dark, she could see dark bruises, which he tried to conceal by tilting the brim of his hat. He didn't reply, but she suddenly remembered hearing that a couple of local men had found work shoveling animal dung. So the whisky business wasn't good these days.

As she faced him, something fluttered in her. Something strong with tough feathers and sinewy legs that ended in claws. The golden eyes looked through her own. So strongly did the Hawk rise in her that she realized the animal had always been with her, her animal spirit, the strong and fearless fighter in her that had waited all this time for her to take notice.

Cleatis moved uneasily, watching his daughter draw herself up. The look on her face was at once noble and fierce. It was nothing he had ever seen on a human face in his life, much less his own daughter's. She hadn't even worn that look the night he thought that he'd burned down the café, only to find he had dreamed it. Yet, even in the dream, he had felt her power.

Trembling, he looked away from her and inched backward as she glanced once again at the cat cage where a small body was curled up in the straw.

"Why is he in there?" she asked, tilting her head toward the cage, no longer cowed by being alone with her father in the dark.

"Takin' a nap," Cleatis grunted. "Circus is leavin' tonight." He supported himself on the shovel he used to scoop elephant dung. "That's prob'ly all the sleep anybody around here'll get for a while." His tongue flicked nervously at his dry lips.

Sarah looked back at him, studied the nervous sweat that ran down his face.

He realized she had probably never seen him work before, save for selling moonshine. "Yeah. I'll be helping to break down the booths and the tents and all. Decent pay." He straightened a little.

"Good," she murmured. She watched him, waiting for the semblance of their old relationship to return. But just as quickly, she knew that no matter what he did, he could not rob her of her newfound sense of self. That was hers, and hers alone, and he could not take it. She looked him in the eye and held her ground.

He was the first to look away.

"Well," he began, and then stopped.

"Yessir?"

"Come see us, when you have a mind to. Your momma misses you."

She nodded. "I'll come by."

"Take care of yourself then."

"Yessir," she said, watching him limp off into the shadows back of the tents. He was gone.

She should have been weak with relief. Instead, she felt calm as she turned slowly back to the cat cage, straining to see the sleeping boy. He lay wrapped in a black cloak with only his eyes visible. As she watched him, they opened.

"Whatcha' doin' out here?" he asked, not moving.

"I came to let my lizard go free, but it's too cold, and I can't."

"Let me see." He scooted over near the bars. Sarah saw he had changed clothes. He was wearing plain brown pants and a white shirt too big in the collar. She unpinned the chameleon and handed it to him through the bars.

"His name is Little Joe." It felt easy talking to him. Like she'd known him for all of her life. Longer. "If I keep him, he's liable to die, since I don't know how to feed him and he's really hungry. But I can't leave him here in the cold. He's too weak. He'd die."

The boy looked closely at the chameleon, letting him perch on the edge of his hand. "Right. We're headin' off for Car'lina tonight. Florida after that. It's warm down there. I could take him for you, if you want me to. There's bugs he can eat here, some in the cat cages and in the elephant hay, too. He'll just need a longer string so he can hunt 'em; then when we get to good weather, I'll let 'im go."

"Promise?"

"Promise." He smiled at her. He would be good as his word, she could tell.

"That would be good." But suddenly, she didn't like the idea that the boy was leaving and going so far away that she'd probably never see him again. They stared at each other, neither knowing what to say.

"Well, see ya," she said.

"See ya," he echoed, his eyes not letting her go.

She turned and ran then, not sure why she was running; it seemed the only thing to do. As she hurried back toward the tent entrance, she wondered if the hurt she felt in her heart was for Little Joe or for the boy. She'd only spoken to him for a moment, but she realized she was going to miss him fiercely.

At the tent entrance, she stopped to look up at the night sky. What was it that the faerie had said? *Choose new beliefs, and you choose new destinies.* Looking at the stars, she wished to choose something, even though she didn't know exactly how.

The Dog Star in the southern sky brightened at her gaze, flooding her with warmth. *This world is cotton candy,* she thought. *I can keep spinning the same troubles around me, or I can dream good dreams and make them come true.*

The star winked at her. She was sure of it. She closed her eyes and made a wish with no words. Only feelings and colors. The colors of a blue ostrich feather and a pair of black, black eyes. The boy's face flashed in her mind like heat lightning in a summer sky, then was buried in forgetful shadows, along with a distant future that had for an instant prickled her spine.

In the shadows, there was calm. A sense that from this moment on, everything would be different.

Bumping along in the car, Sarah raised her head off the backseat and pulled on Vanessa's sleeve. "Sister Vannie? You said to find a shield. I forgot. I didn't look for one."

Vannie leaned back to tuck the coat over the child. She smoothed her hair, then gave her a gentle push so that she'd lie down again. "Ah, but you found one, Sarah."

And then she slept, dreaming of Hawk. Bumping along the dirt road, then onto the highway and a smoother ride.

33

Winter came again to Willow Creek, and the townspeople hunkered down and grew closer together. The sense of community that existed all year long was even more pronounced when snow drifted from the sky and silence settled deep in the countryside. In these cold, quiet months, folks gathered often at The Two Sisters' Café to drink hot coffee and enjoy each other's company and the fire that always roared in the huge grate.

"My field is so quiet, damned if I can't hear my trees thinking," Earl Taylor said to the upper dining room at large. "Anybody else ever hear a tree think?"

"If I did, I wouldn't tell it," Donnie Marble said over the rim of his coffee cup to roars of laughter.

Usually, the jukebox was playing, and most often of late, it was Sugar Curtis's hit single called *Lady Of Secrets* from his album of the same name. Alma could often be seen standing in front of the fire dancing slowly to Sugar's song, her fingers moving dreamily in midair. Sometimes, Sarah danced with her, or spun joyfully around her too excited to be contained. She had heard and been comforted by her brother's singing throughout the year, and was thrilled that the song he had sung to her, sometimes on her own private player and sometimes through the radio in the sisters' car, was now on the regular jukebox for all to hear.

At the end of December, exciting news came. Now that Sugar could afford a wife, he was coming home in mid-January to marry his old sweetheart, Margie Roberts, and take her back to Nashville with him! As if that wasn't exciting enough, the sisters were throwing a quilting in Margie's honor.

With no time to lose, colors and sample designs were soon displayed in the Little Room, along with quilts hung on rungs of an old-fashioned drying rack and boxes of pre-washed pretty fabrics, quilting frames, fabric pencils, templates, and all sorts of pins, needles, and scissors stacked on all sides. The quilt would be assembled at the party for Margie, but there was much to do ahead of time, especially deciding on the all-important individual squares that would have historical or family significance and depict memories of friendship, enhanced by symbols meant to bring comfort, good luck, and fertility.

As the women worked at lightning speed, the men decided that Darryl Houseman, Ed and Carolyn's son, would host Sugar's bachelor party on January 15, the eve of the wedding and the same night that the quilting would be held for Margie. His wife, Maybelle, would bake the cake "just to make sure no girl popped out of it," and offers of food came from all over Willow Creek. There was hardly a man in town, young or old, who didn't plan to attend.

No one knew exactly when Sugar was expected home, except probably Margie, and she wasn't telling. Then on Tuesday night, the 10th of January, Sugar walked in the front door of the café with Margie on one arm and carrying his guitar under the other one.

The whole place froze and then exploded. Margie stepped away, making room for Sarah, who flew into her brother's arms, with most of the town crowded close around them. The sisters stood in the background, smiling and saying nothing. It was not their time. This time belonged to Sugar. Yet, with his arms folded close around Sarah, his eyes found theirs over the top of the crowd.

Tears were in his as they saw his lips form words: *How'd I do, Sisters?*

"You were a bit of alright," Vannie whispered back, looking at the young face, already bearing the indefinable stamp of manhood. Handsome as ever, he was, and just as defiantly rough around the edges. Yet somehow, you had only to look at Sugar Curtis to know that he had found a large chunk of himself since last they had met.

With the jukebox braying out *Lady Of Secrets* at its highest volume and Vannie bawling with happiness, Alma shook her head. "There are times a man can amaze," she confessed.

The next night at the café belonged to Margie, what with Sugar safely disposed of, along with the entire male population of Willow Creek. All was in readiness. The café tables were covered by good quality cloth with favors at every place setting, the largest table spilling over with flowers and presents for the bride.

Ribbons hung from balloons and ample refreshments were arranged on three separate serving tables put together as one long covered board. Along with the beautiful frosted cake with salutations to the bride edged in icing were finger sandwiches, salads, plates of thinly cut meats and cheeses, and rows of hot casseroles, courtesy of most of the Willow Creek women. There was also a cauldron of vegetable soup, a full coffeepot, and a cut-glass punch bowl offering frothy, pink punch.

Since some of the women objected to Banshee's swearing, the parrot had been banished to the Little Room, from where an occasional ill-tempered *squawk* could be heard blistering the atmosphere.

As was traditional, tables had been moved back from the fire to allow space for comfortable chairs that had been pulled close together, both for companionship and to accommodate the women who, by eight-thirty that evening, were just finishing with the multicolored, diamond-patterned patchwork quilt. It was a beauty, they all agreed, one of their best. Though they always got around to saying this, it was always true. Every quilt was in a class by itself.

Yet, not only did this quilt rise above any in recent memory, the night itself shone like a polished jewel. "A right-around miracle kind of night," Carolyn Houseman pronounced it as she sewed in a Town Council square, decorated in tiny cakes and pies.

What bigger miracle than Nadine Curtis showing up, part of the town's sisterhood at last, if only for this night? But if the assembled women had anything to say about it, they would never let her go again. She would be asked to council meetings, taken to church outings, and included in bake sales.

Of course, Nadine was silent as usual, looking self-conscious and awkward, rather than glamorous, in her finery, the likes of which had never before graced a Curtis clothes rack. The three daughters she had brought along with her were in spanking new clothes, too. All through the bounty of Sugar, naturally, not that anybody asked. Annabelle was in pink and white checks, Lillie in sky blue, and sweet baby Ellie toddled all over the room in a fuzzy yellow outfit while Sarah chased after her, enjoying her sisters with every fiber of her heart and soul, so much so that Alma whispered to her that she didn't have to do it all on one evening; there would be plenty of time. Which made Sarah suddenly burst into tears of happiness and that made more than a few ladies cry, too.

Including Nadine. She wiped away her tears with her raw knuckles, and her worn face took on a haggard beauty.

"A kind of *radiance*," Belle Taylor whispered to Martha Burden, thinking she must remember to tell Earl. He loved that kind of thing. And he no doubt would find a lot of significance in the square that Nadine had brought to sew into the quilt—an old simple pattern of a rising sun. "A symbol," he was sure to say solemnly, "of a new day."

Margie was thrilled that her future mother-in-law had come to be with her on this special evening. She had hoped she would come, of course, but hadn't let herself believe it would really happen. After all, Nadine didn't go anywhere. But she had come here tonight for her.

Imagine that. Margie's eyes lingered on the worn figure bent over the quilt, ever so carefully stitching in her square, and she had to snuff back the tears. It was her night, and she was determined to stay beautiful for it, and that included not having mascara running down her face.

She found herself more interested in the proceedings than she'd expected, and laughed more frequently than she could have thought possible. Though she had attended many quiltings for other women, traditionally on the same night that the bachelor's party was held by the men, she had not particularly looked forward to her own special night at The Two Sisters', nor had she expected to feel any great attachment to the quilt that was a gift from the entire female population of Willow Creek. Now she was surprised at her delight, her anticipation at showing it to Sugar and using it for cold nights on their bed in Nashville. It would bring *home* so much closer.

At the thought of Sugar, whom she had loved long before the night they had danced together in her basement, she gave herself a little pinch, just to make sure she wasn't dreaming. Sugar, who had taken Nashville by storm, had not forgotten her, after all, as she had been so sure he would. She'd heard from him often in letters, and she would never forget the Sunday afternoon that he had secretly driven all the way from Nashville and knocked on her door. The minute her father opened it and she had stood rooted, looking at him disbelievingly with her mouth hanging open, Sugar had dropped to one knee and proposed to her right on the spot with her daddy watching. Within two breathless wonderful hours, her parents had given their permission, the wedding date had been set, and Sugar was back on the road. He had to perform that night.

Mascara or not, tears of happiness suddenly filled her eyes as she glanced around the quilting circle and saw her own pleasure reflected in the faces of every woman and young girl present. Thelma Blaney, who would seem too old for quilting (yet somehow, she had contributed a finely made square featuring a cluster of dark-purple Concord grapes), began to speak of her memories of early quiltings when she was a girl in Willow Creek.

A respectful silence settled over the room, and women strained to hear Thelma's every word, with only the youngest faces attesting to boredom, for she was by far the eldest senior citizen in the county, and as such, was honored for her wisdom.

"When I was a girl," Thelma murmured, "every young lady had a quilting. But then, don't you know, the tradition up and died on us. Must have been about ten years ago that the sisters resurrected it after the old dog here taught them a few tricks," she added with a wink. There was no trace now of the crusty old woman she once had been. She leaned closer to Margie and covered her hand with her own.

"Now let me explain, dearie, just what it takes to organize one of these quiltings. First off, you have to pick your background color. And then . . ."

While Thelma went on talking, Loretta Smith took a picture for the paper—Margie perched on her white bridal bench, her eyes rapt on the older woman who sat beside her in the easy chair that the sisters had placed for her in front of the fire. Every woman in the room would study that picture over and over, remembering Thelma explaining in her wavering voice to the young bride-to-be how each of them had brought a square to the sisters, who had done the initial work on the quilt, positioning the squares and then basting them in. They had also kept records of each woman's contribution, thus avoiding repetitions. Some of the squares had been re-worked over and over until they met the highest quilting standards.

"Every one of these squares was the product of patient hands, loving intent, town history, and family significance," Vannie said. "This quilt reflects not only your life, but that of every woman who lives, or for that matter, *ever has* lived in our town." Her fingers flew now as she attached one of her last squares.

Farther along the expanse of the quilt, Alma and other women worked at attaching their own last squares, not without a bit of squabbling about whose squares had ended up in key positions.

"The spirits and traditions of the women in Willow Creek," Vannie continued, "are all here in this quilt. We hope you will keep it on your bed on cold winter nights and perhaps use it to cover your children in the years to come. May it remind you that you are loved during the hard times that cause you to falter and feel alone. We offer it to you in love and friendship to remind you of this time when you sat with us on the eve of relinquishing your girlhood and declaring your womanhood, which brings you to a full-fledged membership into the sisterhood of our town.

"As you may know, this great event does not always come by way of marriage. Other women, who never marry at all, arrive at this moment through other singular events that bring them to maturity. At those times they, too, are honored by the presentation of these quilts. You have, of course, waited through a very challenging time over this past year to come to this special night. You are a young woman who knew her destiny and had the courage to wait for it."

Margie found herself quite moved by the rather formal speech. Now Alma and several other women rose to display the finished product, picking out key women to help in the presentation. In the end, the picture Loretta Smith took was of Margie's mother and youngest sister holding fast to the far edge of the quilt, and Nadine and her daughters holding on to the other side. Even little Ellie, in Nadine's arms, had a piece of quilt clutched in her tiny fingers.

"*Ta-dah!*" Alma exclaimed. "Our masterpiece!"

Margie's spine tingled when the room erupted into applause as the quilt was officially presented to her. Some of the women dabbed their eyes. It was as though Margie had been surrounded all these years by a great mystery of sisterhood, of which until now she had been only partly aware. How strange that she would feel this connection to her own gender the eve before the ceremony that would join her with the man she had chosen to be her husband.

"This is your moment, Margie," Alma said gently. "Speak to us from your heart, thanking us only for what you are truly grateful."

Margie looked around, uncomfortably aware that every eye in the room was now trained on her. She stood and slowly turned to face them as so many before her had done, recalling snippets of phrases that she had heard other women say on these occasions. Their speeches suddenly seemed too brilliant to follow. If only, she thought miserably, she had prepared something to say in advance. Yet the sisters had made her promise not to. It was important, they had told her, to speak only what came into her heart at the moment she was presented the quilt. To trust that the right words would come to her.

As Alma rose to place a fold of the quilt in the bride's hands and then sat again to listen, Margie saw her mother bend forward with a glowing face and eyes that were full of something she had never seen there before.

"Why, Mama," she said before she thought. "I never thought your love for me could *grow*!"

"Not my love, honey," Christine Roberts said. "It's *you* who have grown. I'm so proud of you. I've been a mother for a long time now. Just not the mother of a grown woman, I guess. And grown so early, too. How did you ever do it?"

"I watched you, Mama."

The eyes of the room were still on her, but she was no longer threatened by them. Instead, they empowered her and brought her strength.

She stared down at the quilt in her hand, and the first thing she saw was a square of swimming goldfish. "I know who this square is from." She looked at her first cousin, Charlotte. "I remember the old goldfish pond. We threw pennies in there and hoped our wishes would come true. This square is your wish for my happiness."

As Charlotte dried her eyes, Margie moved on to the next square. "It's a picture of my old teddy bear. This square's from Grandma." The older woman nodded. She had made the bear herself for her first grandchild, and now passed its beloved memory along in the patchwork square.

Margie now looked at a field full of wildflowers and leaned over to hug her best friend, Dixie. "We walked through that field after school and planned out our lives together. I'd recognize it anywhere."

She went on from square to square, knowing who made most of them with a certainty that brought its own exhilaration. The train was from Belle Taylor, whose daddy used to be a train engineer. A dowsing tool was in the next square. Who could forget that night? There was a friend's pony she had once loved to ride. A simple sprig of rosemary that made her repeat the old phrase: "Rosemary, that's for remembrance," and she knew that Aunt Sally meant her to remember Uncle Joe, who used to say that phrase a lot when he was living.

Even Loretta Smith had contributed a square, featuring *The Hole In The Wall* newspaper. The square with the tornado puzzled her for a moment, but Edith Bailey put up her hand, and she remembered that people were apt to say that Elmer Bailey had never been the same since the day when all the tornadoes had formed in Willow Creek's skies. The Halloween mask . . . well, that was an easy one, when you remembered who loved that holiday more than any other. Her mother's square was five small people representing her family. One of her sisters had managed a close replica of their old dog, and the youngest one had stitched together ABC because Margie had helped her to learn the alphabet. There were pictures of a red barn, the town church, the café, the parrot, a bicycle, and a family of ducks.

Then she looked at Nadine. "I can never tell you what it means to have you here with me tonight. I'll love the sun you put into our quilt forever." There wasn't any answer, of course, nor had she expected one. But all she needed was in the glowing eyes that Sugar's mother raised to her.

Finally, almost in wonder, Margie realized she had come to the very last square. It was a rainbow. A double rainbow, in fact. Well, why not? There were, after all, two sisters.

"Thank you all so much," she said softly, her eyes going from woman to woman and lingering on every face. "I think, even more than the squares, I value the threads that can't be seen, because you've done it all so skillfully and beautifully—those threads that connect one square to another. I know that every one of you sewed in threads tonight, along with those of the sisters' that were already there, connecting your square to all the others that touched it. For the first time in my life, I can clearly see and feel those threads that connect my life with all the other lives in this town. Of course, I've felt it for my whole life, but until this moment, I've never completely realized it.

"I want you to know that I will do as you've asked me this evening. I will reach for this quilt when I need to remember I have friends. I will cover my children with it. I will tell my husband the significance of it so that he will honor my relationships with other women. I will look at this quilt and realize that, for as long as I live, my life will touch other lives, and I will try to keep my own connecting threads neat and skillful and sew them with the same love you have sewn for me tonight. I will start my own traditions. I will remember that life is a continuation, and someday, I hope to pass this quilt along to a daughter or a son and . . ." She paused mid-thought. There was nothing more, really, to say.

Already, arms were reaching for her, young and old. She went willingly, working her way down the line, feeling at that special place where tears and laughter become one. Last of all came the sisters.

"Well done," Vannie said in one ear.

"Magnificent, darlin'," Alma whispered in the other.

Margie had never felt more honored. She might live away from Willow Creek for many years, or even for the rest of her life, but it would be her home forever, hers and Sugar's. And someday, perhaps, she would bring her daughter here to have her own quilting at The Two Sisters' Café.

EPILOGUE

The new dreams were coming almost nightly now.

In them, she'd find herself floating on her back down a river, tall canyons for banks, curving wide around a bend under the sun. She'd squint at light bouncing white off the ripples on the surface of the water.

A flare up ahead, a blinding flash, the water around it a whirlpool, drawing her into its spiral. The spiral would tighten to a spin, and at the center of the spin, the light would take her.

She'd travel in the light, meeting others along the way, some that she knew and some she did not. They'd chat excitedly among themselves until they arrived on a shore where two suns rose in a lavender dawn.

The Shining Ones would gather them all into a circle, there on the coral beach, her and her fellow initiates.

"Prepare yourselves," they would say. "It begins."

Author's Notes

In writing this story of magic and fellowship, I leaned on one of the great fathers, Dr. Bob Yates, who plowed through acres of nostalgia to unearth memories of the White Cottage and the people who made it ring with laughter and joy, in particular Virginia ("Ginny") Winburn and Ethel Batts who served so well and with so much love, and to the Staples family who leased the gas station and were like family. My thanks go to the following people as well:

My mother, Claudine Morgan Yates, who is hopefully shedding her light on us from afar and feeling my gratitude for her magic and love. My sisters, Jackie West and Jill Dunlap, who were the other little girls of the White Cottage. Louise Allgeier, who shared her great memories of the old days. ET "Hammer" Smith from the Henry County Historical Society for sharing information about historical Henry County. Alice, Jared, and Eric Noble, who gave us an inside view of the solar plexus. My good chums and cheerleaders, Dixie Hughes-Britton, Linda Radcliffe, Marilyn Montgomery, Courtney Lorenz, Barbary Azrialy, Helen DePrima, Michael Shimkin, and Mike and Dianne McCune.

Love and thanks go to my son, Ken Eulo, Jr., who lights up my life. Also to my father-in-law, Vincent Valva, Sr., who advised and encouraged, and to my incomparable husband, Vince Valva, who helped in every imaginable way and treated me with love and patience in the homestretch.

Special kudos go to our mighty team, John Raatz and David Langer of The Visioneering Group; to Benjamin Cziller for his remarkable cover and website design; to Chongyang Luo for his technical skills; to CJ Schepers for her expertise and spirit; and to the wonderful father-and-son team, the Ferros: Pablo Ferro whose delightful illustrations breathed such whimsical life into our characters and Allen Ferro who executed graphics with such creativity and artistry. And to Bill Macy, who has gifted me over many years with his humor, his friendship, and now with his belief in our magical café.

~ Elena Yates Eulo

Author's Notes

I gratefully acknowledge the community of artists, healers, metaphysicians, teachers, and spiritual sojourners who contributed to our efforts to include elements of Western Magic—both ancient and New Age—in this book. A special tribute goes to the late Ann Davies, who initiated aspirants into the once-secret teachings of the Cabala, another to Eckhart Tolle for *The Power Of Now* and *A New Earth,* most particularly for revelations about the pain body and how it functions; and yet another, along with my heartfelt thanks, to Jach Pursel and Concept Synergy for the Lazaris material. I owe a debt of love and gratitude to the late Buddy Hackett for a conversation that inspired the character of the little circus boy, and one to my brother, Peter Harper, for supplying the lyrics for two of Sugar's songs.

Thank you to those who read and reread the evolving manuscript, giving invaluable feedback: Mary Dorn, Jackie LoGiudice, Miriam Saia,Veronica Thompson, Sal Griffis, Judy Kerr, and Mike Shimkin. Hats off also to friends who have added their visions, dreams, and support to this project, among them Grif Griffis, Tara Guber, Daphne Russom, Cindy Futter, Tawny Moyer, Topaz Jan Abbott and Pablo Ferro, who also provided the enchanting illustrations within the book, adding elements of genius and fun to our efforts, and to his son, Allen Ferro, who executed exquisite graphics and also directed and edited my audio recording of an excerpt of the book for our website.

I echo Elena's thanks to our team at Visioneering, including John Raatz, David Langer, and their associates, especially CJ Schepers, and to the designer of our book, its cover, and our website, Benjamin Cziller, along with our computer programmer Chongyang Luo, creative magicians all. Finally, my deepest appreciation goes to my husband, Bill Macy, whose passionate support has enhanced this project, as it has every facet of my life.

~ Samantha Harper Macy